with lot
love

A YEAR OF MR MAYBES

JUDY LEIGH

B
Boldwood

First published in Great Britain in 2022 by Boldwood Books Ltd.

Cover Design by Debbie Clement Design

Cover Photography: Shutterstock

A CIP catalogue record for this book is available from the British Library.

Paperback ISBN 978-1-80162-344-5

Large Print ISBN 978-1-80162-345-2

Harback ISBN 978-1-80162-343-8

Ebook ISBN 978-1-80162-346-9

Kindle ISBN 978-1-80162-347-6

Audio CD ISBN 978-1-80162-338-4

MP3 CD ISBN 978-1-80162-339-1

Digital audio download ISBN 978-1-80162-341-4

Boldwood Books Ltd
23 Bowerdean Street
London SW6 3TN
www.boldwoodbooks.com

To Loveday Moons, everywhere...

PROLOGUE
LAST CHRISTMAS

The smell of sizzling turkey and roasting potatoes wafted from the kitchen, drifting on the air. The dining-room table was set for two, gleaming china, silver cutlery, a linen cover, crystal glasses and two gold crackers embellished with the words 'Merry Christmas'. A bottle of Chilean red wine was open; the smart speaker was playing all the Christmas favourites and currently Bing Crosby was warbling 'White Christmas'.

Outside it was raining, an incessant lattice of drizzle, grey and cold from sky to tarmac. Val wasn't surprised: it was typical winter weather in Merrynporth, a quiet inland town in the north of Cornwall. What mattered today was that Christmas dinner would be perfect. She glanced at the clock; it was ten minutes to two. Ray had promised to be home at two on the dot. She had time to baste the bird, check the Yorkshire puddings and stir the gravy. She glanced at the tree; the twinkling lights were off. She touched a switch and the little bulbs flickered, then the pine branches became dancing red berries.

Brenda Lee began to sing 'Rockin' Around the Christmas Tree' and Val hummed along, slightly out of tune. Even though it was just the two of them – Tom was living in Canada now – the idea of Christmas with Ray filled her with contentment. They'd spend quality time, a late Christmas lunch, then exchange presents in front of the television. Val had bought Ray a Fire Cube; she had no idea what a Fire Cube was, but he'd said he wanted one, so she had secretly wrapped it in pretty cream paper covered in smiling snowmen and placed it beneath the tree.

It was almost two. Val hadn't minded when Ray had suggested he might pop out for a swift drink with the boys from the bowling club. He'd said he'd only be an hour or so; she'd kissed his cheek and joked that he shouldn't drink too much or it would ruin his appetite. He'd have a pint and make it last; he didn't want to spoil the wonderful lunch.

Chris Rea's gravelly voice came through the speaker, singing 'Driving Home for Christmas'. Ray would be home at any moment. Val scuttled into the kitchen and opened the oven. Steam surrounded her face, rising like a magic spell; the turkey was golden brown, the potatoes mouth-watering. It was perfect. She closed the oven door and hurried back into the dining room to check the table. There was a smudge on one of the crystal glasses; Val picked up a napkin and wiped it. She checked her reflection in the mirror; her hair was neat, freshly coloured. Her cheeks were glowing a little from the heat of the oven but it gave her a healthy sheen. She adjusted her Christmas jumper, emblazoned with a robin wearing a red pom-pom hat. For a woman in her early seventies, she looked fine.

Val glanced at the clock on the wall; it was ten past two. She checked her phone in case he'd left her a message. Nothing, just the text from Tom that arrived an hour ago.

Happy Christmas Mum and Dad!

She gazed around the room. The tree was bright with clusters of flashing berries; the table was pristine; there was nothing left to do. Mariah Carey was singing 'All I Want for Christmas Is You', trilling the high notes. Val hummed along: Ray was late.

She peered through the curtains. The drizzle was persistent, the slanting downpour that soaked quickly into clothes. An idea popped into her head. The Salmon and Sprat was a fifteen-minute walk away, but only a five-minute drive. Ray was probably on his way back, but she'd pick him up in the car, he'd be home and dry and lunch would still be perfect. Val grabbed her jacket and the car keys to the Duster. Ray would be glad to have a smiling chauffeur to bring him home; he'd peck her cheek, happily installed inside the warm, dry car. She glanced over her shoulder, silently going through a checklist: food, wine, tree, music. Everything was fine, ready for when they arrived back home. It was all Happy-Christmas-Perfect.

Val parked outside The Sprat and wished she'd brought a hat. The rain was torrential now and her hair was completely wet. She rushed into the bar and glanced around. Festive lights flashed from every corner; the smell of hops hung heavily. Voices chattered, some loud, laughing, others low, a chuckle from a joke, a steady drone: someone was telling a yarn. She stood still, glancing around for Ray, for his white curls just visible below a fisherman's cap, his navy-blue jacket. There were several older men in groups seated at tables, seventy-somethings clutching pints and chatting. She assumed they must be the bowling club. She couldn't see Ray amongst them.

She sidled through the bar, past the throng of people waiting to be served, and stood in the doorway that led to the almost-empty snug. Ray was in there, sitting down; she spotted him straight away. His hat was off, his jacket too; he was sporting the Christmas jumper that proclaimed the words 'Bah, Humbug!' She'd bought it for him a week ago. He was cradling a glass of beer.

Val stared harder and realised that it was difficult to breathe. She had forgotten to exhale. She was holding air in her lungs as she watched her husband, his arm around a woman; they were talking together as if it was the most natural thing. Val scrutinised the woman; she was in her late fifties, younger than Ray, younger than Val. Val took in the tinsel she wore like a crown, the flaxen hair, short skirt; she wasn't at all like Val. Ray whispered something into her ear and she squealed as if she'd been pinched.

Ray put a hand to her face, gently removing something, glitter, a hair, a crumb. Val noticed the tenderness of his fingers, the intimate way he brushed the woman's cheek, their mutual trust. There was a practised familiarity between them. He hadn't just met this woman; they had known each other for some time – it was an established affair. The woman pressed her lips against his and laughed again. Val stared, not knowing what to do. She was filled with a sharp new realisation that made her take in every vivid detail. Then the woman glanced up and caught Val's eye, a moment's recognition that this must be the wife. In that instant, they both knew. The woman turned to Ray, alarmed. Val gasped, stepping backwards, stung, then her feet were carrying her through the bar, out into the pelting rain and back to the Duster.

She started the engine, listening to the soothing rumble and then, like any other woman driving a car on Christmas Day, she pulled calmly out of the car park and drove home. She deposited the car in the drive and walked into the welcoming warmth of the hall. The rich aroma of the roast filled her nostrils, the promise of Christmas cheer. Before she entered the dining room, Val could hear The Jackson 5 singing 'I Saw Mommy Kissing Santa Claus'. She closed her eyes. She'd left home over twenty minutes ago; now she was back, everything she'd known as normal had changed forever in an instant, forty-seven years of marriage gone in a blink. She took a deep breath. She wouldn't cry; she wouldn't be angry. She wouldn't let what she had seen in the pub spoil her Christmas.

She locked the front door, bolting it firmly. Then rushed to the back door and turned the key. She drew the curtains in the dining room with a swish and spoke to the smart speaker. 'Louder. Louder again.' Elvis Presley was crooning 'Blue Christmas', his voice sorrowful, mourning. Val hurried into the kitchen, returning to the table with dishes of steaming roast potatoes, vegetables, hot gravy, Yorkshires. She rushed back to the oven, hauling out the huge turkey, easing it onto a serving dish with a flourish.

Val sat at the table, her crystal glass brimming with Chilean wine, her plate piled with a steaming lunch, her fork held high. Then, shattering the chirpy song from the speaker, 'Santa Claus Is Comin' to Town', there was the clatter at the door she'd been expecting, keys being turned. Seconds later there was a rattling, the door being pushed against a heavy bolt, then an abrupt banging of a fist against wood and a man's plaintive voice. 'Val. Val. Let me in.'

Val began to eat. She sipped wine. 'Winter Wonderland' drifted smoothly from the speaker. She helped herself to more gravy, the brown liquid splashing across the plate.

'Val, open the door, please...'

She stabbed a Brussels sprout, coated it in gravy, held it up on her fork to examine it and then pushed it whole into her mouth.

'Val – if this is about what you saw in the pub – if it's about Monica, I can explain. Val – please.'

She sliced a piece of turkey in half with her knife, then sliced it again. She pierced it with her fork.

'Val...'

Val gulped wine, hacked a Yorkshire pudding in half. She hummed aloud to the music. Lunch was delicious. Lunch for one with Ray outside, soaking wet and cold, harsh though it was, was the most satisfying thing in the world right now.

'Val...' Ray pleaded. He waited a moment, then his tone changed to one of irritation. 'Val, I'm freezing out here.'

She helped herself to more wine, more turkey, more of everything. That was what she'd do now: she'd help herself to whatever she wanted without thinking about anyone else, without thinking about Ray.

'Val, let me in.' He sounded pitiful, but she wouldn't relent, not now, not ever. Ray's voice was a tight whine. 'Val, please... I'm getting really cold.'

Frank Sinatra started to croon from the speaker, 'Let It Snow, Let It Snow, Let It Snow!'

Val took a deep breath and turned the volume up in the hope that Ray would hear every word, and went back to her Christmas lunch for one.

1

THIS CHRISTMAS…

Lowenstowe was a jewel on the coast of north Cornwall, sparkling like a sapphire in the white winter sun. The small seaside town was five miles from Merrynporth, from The Salmon and Sprat inn, five miles from Ray and Monica. It was the perfect place for Val to find refuge, to start again, to allow the winds from the west to blow painful memories away, to watch waves ebb and flow, and to heal.

And on this Christmas Day the breeze-blown beach was almost empty: a jogger loped along the shoreline and a man in a brown coat strode in the other direction alongside a bear-like dog. Down by the water's edge, a woman in a beret and aviator sunglasses stooped to pick up empty bottles. The tide was rolling in, splashing surf over smooth sand, tugging away again. Overhead, a seagull swooped down with a throaty caw to snatch a fast-food carton from the ground. Beyond the beach, small fishing boats clustered in a little harbour, bobbing gently, knotted safely to sturdy poles. The sun dipped behind a cloud as the wind rippled the water.

Not far from the beach there was a row of three traditional fisherman's cottages, each with a square patch of garden in front, a privet hedge, a larger rectangle to the rear. The street was deserted. Sand swirled by the kerb, grains lifted and dropped in a sudden gust of wind. A flame-throated robin settled on a rickety gatepost, its beady eye searching for grubs. On the walls of one of the end cottages, colourful lights flashed and twinkled.

Inside the middle cottage Val was busy arranging photographs, plumping cushions, positioning books on shelves. She stood back and surveyed the living room; it didn't feel like home, not yet. Val pushed a strand of hair behind her ear, a thick pale tendril that had escaped from the scrunchie. One of the straps of her dungarees had worked its way down her arm and she hauled it over her shoulder. She glanced around the lounge; the fire blazed in the wood-burning stove; gold lights winked from the tiny tree in the corner. This was her new home. It still felt strange, not quite hers yet. The Merrynporth house had finally sold; she'd moved to Lowenstowe two days ago. She'd been desperate to be in her new house by Christmas Day, and she'd just made it. She hadn't unpacked everything yet, but she was determined that her first Christmas alone would be about new beginnings, a chance to indulge in everything she'd enjoy, especially after last year's fiasco. She needed a new start; she needed to move forward. She needed time to settle.

But, of course, it wasn't her first Christmas alone. She closed her eyes and recalled the lunch last year, Ray banging at the front door for almost half an hour, his face shining and wet with rain. She remembered his whining tone, his initial lies and excuses and then, eventually, the truth about the affair. By that evening, Ray had moved in somewhere with Monica and Val stayed put for the next eleven months, stuck inside the house that contained so many memories, until it was finally sold.

The divorce had been lengthy. She had bought the three-bedroomed terraced cottage near the seafront; she had a car, a second-hand black Mini Cooper, parked outside – Ray had taken the Duster – but it was little consolation, after so many years. With a pension from almost forty years of teaching in a primary school, the last ten as Deputy Head, she was independent now. But it wasn't going to be easy. Losing Ray was like losing an arm; she still woke up thinking he was there next to her, his head on the pillow. There were many bad days, and Val wondered if this Christmas Day might be another. Feelings were still raw, memories still hurt.

Val flopped down on the sofa, picking up a pile of Christmas cards. One was from her younger sister in Manchester just inscribed to Val, no mention of Ray now, signed from Trisha and Bob. One was from her son in Canada with love from Tom and Lottie, his girlfriend since last March. Another card, a glittery picture with a jolly robin on the front, conveyed best wishes from Ray and Monica. Another difficult moment and all couples. Val sighed. She couldn't remember how many cards she'd posted this year.

Val wondered what she would cook for Christmas lunch. Not turkey, never again: the thought of it made her stomach lurch. An omelette maybe, with a glass of red. Chilean, of course. Or just an apple, a bar of chocolate. She could do as she liked now.

She glanced at the little television set; she wouldn't turn it on today. She preferred the radio, a friendly voice, or the smart speaker, a few random Christmas songs or the lilt and swell of an orchestra. Ray had kept their flat-screen TV and she recalled how he would always have the television blaring loudly from the moment he woke up: there would be the constant rattle of football, golf, snooker, news, soaps, quizzes. He'd watch everything while Val curled up quietly with a book. He'd wanted to keep the set; he was probably watching it now with Monica. The familiar painful feelings of inadequacy and rejection welled up again and Val gritted her teeth, determined to be strong.

She had loved Ray, of course. If she was being honest, she still loved him. He'd been her every day, her normality. He was sweet and handsome, a doting father, a generous husband: there had always been little gifts, compliments. Life had been steady. He'd been a civil engineer before he'd retired; they'd holidayed abroad every August. Then, after Tom had finished his degree in environmental science and settled in Bristol, Val and Ray had visited him regularly until the split with Sophie, which had sent him off to work in Montréal two years ago. He'd been back twice; he loved Canada and now he had a girlfriend there. Val thought she might visit him in the new year and meet Lottie. She sighed. Tom had barely mentioned the split from Ray. He'd just asked if she was all right, and each time she'd answered with a stoic yes, he'd proceeded to tell her about how wonderful Montréal was. Val picked up Tom's card again and studied the photo: snow drifts, pine trees, the sky bright blue. What wasn't to like?

Her fingers moved to the card with the glittery robin, Ray and Monica's. Inside was a folded note; it was one of those 'what we did together this year' photocopies that they'd have sent to everyone who knew them. Val could see the corner of a photo: Ray's chin, a tuft of flaxen hair against his cheek. She wouldn't read it. She supposed that the card was an apology of sorts; he was probably still fond of her. At moments like this, she was overcome with sadness all over again.

There was a soft knock at the door and Val glanced up, surprised at the interruption to her quiet Christmas. She lugged the strap of her dungarees back over her shoulder and padded softly into the hall, dragging back the heavy curtain that kept out draughts. She opened the front door and gazed at a striking woman standing on the path. She was around Val's own age, early seventies, with light hair cut to frame a pleasant smiling face and twinkling eyes. She held out a hand. 'Hello. I'm your neighbour.'

'Val Maxwell.' Val took the hand, strangely conscious of using her maiden name; it had been Watson for so long.

'Cornelia Randall – but call me Connie. I just popped over to introduce myself. I won't stay. It's Christmas Day, you've probably got a house full of family.'

Val listened hard to the woman's voice. She had a pleasant accent, probably not English. She was holding something in her hand wrapped in paper. Val said, 'Oh, do come in, Connie. It's freezing out here – what am I thinking? Happy Christmas.'

She ushered Connie into the warmth of the house, closing the door firmly, leading the way into the small square lounge. Connie gazed around, taking in the pale walls, the colourful cushions, the blazing fire, the tiny tree, the coffee table. She rubbed her hands together. 'You've made it so lovely in here. Are you sure I'm not interrupting…?'

'No, not at all.' Val felt a little awkward as her visitor moved towards the hearth to examine a photo of Tom, his graduation, years ago. She gave a little cough. 'Can I get you a drink? Tea? Coffee?' As an afterthought she added, 'Sherry?'

'Oh, tea, please – anything herbal,' Connie said hopefully.

'Please – sit down,' Val offered and Connie dropped to her knees next to the fire, nestling on the rug like a happy cat.

'It's so cosy…' Connie sighed.

Val hurried to the kitchen and returned carrying a tray, two steaming mugs, and a packet of chocolate biscuits, making a mental note to herself to stock up on herbal teas in case her neighbour called again. She offered a tentative smile. 'Blackcurrant all right?'

'Perfect,' Connie replied. 'It's good of you to make tea. I just called round to introduce myself. I saw you arrive two days ago and I've been meaning to pop over to say hello. I wanted to say Happy Christmas.'

'And to you.' Val lifted her mug. 'Which house is yours, Connie?'

'The one directly opposite – Honeysuckle House.' Connie glanced up. 'The Simpsons who lived in this house before you were lovely, but I don't think I've been in here more than half a dozen times. They were from London – this place was a holiday cottage. But then you probably know that. They had two teenagers – I don't remember it being as homely and comfortable as this.'

'I'm going to love living here.' Val cupped her mug in both hands. 'So – what are you up to for Christmas?'

'Nothing much,' Connie said, gazing into the fire. 'I was going to have a quiet day. I really didn't intend to interrupt yours – you must have plans.'

'I haven't. Why don't you stay for lunch?' Val decided that Christmas was a time for sharing, and it might be nice to get to know her new neighbour.

'Oh, no, I'd be intruding. I feel so awful, barging in on Christmas Day.'

'Not at all,' Val said cheerfully. 'I'd enjoy the company.'

'Then I'd love to...' Connie's eyes shone with gratitude. 'I brought this by way of a gift.' She handed Val the package folded in tissue paper. 'It's just a small thing. I popped over to say welcome.'

The tissue paper unwrapped itself in Val's hand revealing a pretty lilac tea light, the holder carved from teak. Val sniffed the candle and exhaled slowly.

'Lavender,' Connie explained. 'Very relaxing.'

'It's lovely. Thank you.' Val offered the biscuits and Connie shook her head, sipping from her mug.

Val coughed politely. 'So... how long have you lived across the road?'

'Almost two years,' Connie replied. The light from the fire illuminated one side of her face, glowing orange. 'I had an antique shop over in Penashberry for a long time. It was well past the time for me to retire, so I sold it. I wanted to live near the sea, so I came here. I live a quiet life.'

'And is there a Mr...?' Val tried to remember her surname. 'A Mr Randall?'

Connie shook her head again. 'Mike died twenty years ago. Since then, it's been just me.'

'Oh, I'm sorry...'

'I just worked and worked. The antiques gave me something to focus on.' Connie waved away Val's embarrassment with one hand. 'And is there a Mr Maxwell?'

'No.' Val's voice was emphatic. She squeezed her mug as if trying to throttle it; feelings of rejection were flooding back. 'Divorced. I'm moving on.'

'Then we're both single women,' Connie said.

Val thought about the accent. 'You're not English – originally, I mean?'

'I'm from Leiden, in Holland. I've been living here for...' Connie counted on her fingers. 'I met Mike when I was twenty-five and I'm now seventy-four, so close to fifty years. Can you still hear the accent?'

'A little.'

Connie indicated the photo on the mantelpiece of Tom skiing. 'Is that handsome young man your son?'

'Tom, yes – he's working in Canada.'

Connie shook her head sadly. 'Our children don't stay close, do they?' She gazed into the flames. 'My son lives in New Zealand. I'm hoping he'll visit next year. It would be nice to see him.'

Val agreed. 'Maybe we need to go to them and stay for a month or two?' She had almost finished her tea. 'New Zealand looks lovely in photos. I've never been to Canada. I need to travel more now – now I'm on my own.'

'I'm with you all the way on that, Val,' Connie said. 'It's so nice to have a new neighbour. I tend to be a bit reclusive, living by myself – it will be good to have someone to talk to.' She put out a hand and touched Val's arm, suddenly apologetic. 'Oh, I didn't mean I'd be pestering you all the time.'

'Not at all,' Val replied. 'So, tell me about the other neighbours. I haven't met them yet.'

Connie's face shone in the firelight. 'On one side, there's Kevin and Alice Holmes. They are lovely. On the other side is Ben Berry, he's a fisherman, in his seventies. He's usually out on his boat. Sometimes I go weeks without seeing him, but he's very nice, an interesting man with a busy life.' She sighed briefly. 'It's very quiet round here but the sea is only a few minutes' walk away – just beyond the harbour there's Breakstone beach.'

'I love being outdoors,' Val said. The glow of the fire and the twinkling tree lights suddenly lifted her mood, reminding her that it was Christmas Day. 'So, you're staying for lunch.' Val pressed Connie's arm. 'It'll be the perfect opportunity for you to tell me all about the town.' She was thoughtful for a moment. 'I'll need a social life...'

'Can I help you to cook?' Connie's eyes shone. 'It's such a treat to be in someone else's kitchen.'

'Be my guest.' Val struggled to her feet, picking up the tray and the unopened biscuits. 'We can eat whatever we like. Afterwards it'll be a nice glass of something delicious – port or Irish cream.'

'I haven't had port in years,' Connie exclaimed. 'And I've never had Irish cream. I might try both.'

'Great.' Val's smile widened. 'What would you like for lunch?'

Connie shrugged. 'A sandwich would be fine.'

'We can do better than that today.' Val waved a hand towards the kitchen. 'How does salmon with lemon and parsley sound?'

'It sounds heavenly.' Connie closed her eyes, her face dreamy.

'Come on, then – let's do Christmas.' Val launched herself

towards the kitchen, Connie one step behind her. She suddenly recalled her previous Christmas lunch, the fiasco: Ray outside, soaked to the skin, yelling, the rain beating against the window as she sat in the dining room at the pristine table. This Christmas couldn't be more different, and it already felt much more enjoyable.

2

_____

Val woke up early, dressed and rushed down to the kitchen. She was going to make some gooey chocolate brownies for the neighbours. Christmas Day with Connie had been pleasant; they had sipped Irish cream and talked into the evening. Connie seemed quite a reserved person and she said that the neighbours mostly kept themselves to themselves, but Lowenstowe was Val's home now; she wanted to integrate, and the best place to start was with the people who lived close by. She no longer had any contacts back in Merrynporth. She and Ray had often spent time with other couples, Paul and Helen, James and Kathy, but now she was no longer married, they'd lost touch.

Val sighed. The men were all members of the bowling club; the women were simply their wives. Val shook flour into a sieve. She had firm feelings about that: she'd never really enjoyed those social events, and now she wasn't going to be _just_ a wife any more, being friends with her husband's friends' wives for the sake of convenience. Ray had never noticed her uneasiness as he'd played bowls with the men. But Val wasn't an appendage now. She'd make new friends, and they wouldn't be women with nothing in common who gathered while the men were enjoying themselves to talk about their grown children, reality television and how much better life was now the menopause was over.

She placed the brownies in the oven. Yesterday had been a wet Boxing Day and she'd spent the day unpacking. But today was bright, the pale winter sun high in the sky; she was determined to be sociable, and the best way was to offer the neighbours fudgy chocolatey brownies.

When the brownies were baked and cooled, Val placed four wrapped portions in a basket, tugged on a coat and stepped outside. Across the street was Connie's home, Honeysuckle House, with a green door beyond a little gate. There was a brass knocker shaped like a horseshoe: Val rapped, waited, then she knocked again. No sound came from inside so Val presumed that Connie must be out or still in bed. It wasn't yet ten o'clock, so either was possible. Val placed a wrapped portion of four brownies on the step and hoped Connie wouldn't squash them if she arrived home in darkness.

She turned back to gaze at the block of three cottages, her own little house, Teasel Cottage, nestling in the middle. Cloud Cottage, to the left, was very tidy, with leaded light windows and a smart black door. Any available space on the outside had been crammed with twinkling fairy lights. A glittering Santa held up his thumb and winked with an LED light as he clambered towards the roof on a ladder that flashed red and gold. To the right, the walls of the other cottage were overrun with clambering ivy and there was no light inside. The rickety gate at the front had been tied with rope. Val decided she'd try the dark house first, then deliver the last brownies to the bright house where people were almost certainly at home. She was looking forward to meeting them.

She unhooked the rope and approached the front door. A faded sign, Crab Claw Cottage, painted on a piece of driftwood, hung on a single jutting nail. Val knocked at the door. Old paint was flaking.

She knocked again, but there was no answer, so she placed the foil-wrapped brownies on the step and backed away, closing the gate firmly behind her.

Music came from Cloud Cottage, the blaring of a television that flashed from inside. A huge glittering reindeer head, the mouth gaping, was stuck to the window with little suction pads. Val knocked and the door was opened almost immediately. A woman wearing a long dress, her hair a mass of curls, waved a hand. 'Hello. Are you our new neighbour? Pleased to meet you. I didn't call round before – I didn't want to bother you straight away as you'd only just arrived but...' The woman took a breath. 'Come in. You're welcome.'

She led Val into a warm hall, then into an even warmer lounge with a leather sofa, a tall Christmas tree and a huge television screen, which was being watched by a large man in a colourful T-shirt and jogging bottoms. A modern gas fire was belting out dry heat. The man twisted round, his face shining. 'Hello. Who's this, then?'

'Kev, this is our new neighbour; she – oh, I'm so sorry, I didn't get your name. I'm Alice – and this is Kevin.'

'Val Maxwell.' Val held out the brownies in tinfoil. 'I brought you these. Happy Christmas.'

'Oh, lovely.' Alice unwrapped the brownies, crumbs falling onto the floor, and handed them to Kevin who took one and crammed half of it into his mouth.

'Lovely,' he repeated, chocolate on his lips.

'Cup of coffee?' Alice was already on her way to the kitchen to make it.

Kevin gazed up, his brow wrinkled. 'So how are you settling down in Teasel Cottage, Val? Just you, on your own, is it? The Simpsons were nice enough people. From London. They only came here four times a year so it's good to have someone next door all the time.' He laughed. 'It was mayhem here on Christmas Day, the whole family round the table for lunch. I'm glad of a bit of peace and quiet today.' He stretched out his legs. 'But that's how I like it, just me and Alice now the kids have grown and flown.'

Val listened to the television rattling and distant clattering sounds coming from the kitchen. Alice dropped something, muttered, 'Bugger!' then shouted, 'Kev – Dolly's out.'

Val had no idea what Alice meant but Kevin was already on his feet, staggering towards Val as a bullet-headed dog rushed into the lounge, leaping up at the furniture, at Val, at Kevin, circling in a frenzy and then hurling itself at Alice as she tottered in with a tray. Kevin grasped the dog by the collar and stroked her with his free hand. 'Dolly. Dolly, calm down. You'll soon get to know Val from next door. Calm down.'

The dog licked his hand and leaped onto the leather sofa, turning round twice before curling up and resting her head on her paws. Kevin sat next to the dog and indicated it affectionately with a nod of his head. 'This is Dolly.'

'She's a Staffordshire bull terrier,' Alice said by way of explanation. 'Kev loves her to bits. She's called Dolly after Dolly Parton.'

Kevin cradled the dog's hard head between his hands, placing a kiss between beady eyes. Alice proffered a cup of coffee to Val. 'Shall we have one of those delicious brownies each? Come and sit down and you can tell us all about yourself. I love being next to the fire – I hate the winter, it's too cold.'

Val plonked herself on the sofa next to Kevin and an already-snoozing Dolly. She brought the mug to her lips and sipped, taking in Alice's friendly smile and Kevin's arm wrapped tightly around the dog. Val instinctively liked them both, their welcoming, generous natures, but she was less sure about the boisterous dog.

Alice reached over and patted her knee. 'Lowenstowe is one of the nicest towns in Cornwall. You'll soon settle here. Before long, you'll know just about everyone. Where did you move from?'

'Merrynporth,' Val replied.

'Oh, it's nice there.' Kevin was still staring at the television. 'I have a few regular customers in Merrynporth. Some good pubs there too.'

Val nodded, although she didn't want to mention The Sprat – the memories of last year would start to tumble again.

'It's better here in Lowenstowe though,' Alice chirruped. 'We're a friendly lot. You won't need to worry about anything at all, Val. Anything you need, just ask. Kev's always on hand too, if you need a bit of DIY.'

'I'd be glad to help,' Kevin said.

'And the brownies... Best I've ever had. You'll have to give me the recipe,' Alice gushed.

Val found herself relaxing into the softness of the sofa. Kevin winked conspiratorially as Alice continued to explain the delights of Lowenstowe and how Val would soon be part of the furniture. Val smiled happily; they were both generous, kind-hearted people and she already felt welcome. The heat and the soft lilt of Alice's voice made her eyelids droop. She hoped she wouldn't drift off to sleep.

* * *

An hour later, Val felt the brisk tingle of cold, bracing winter air against her face as she strolled to Breakstone beach past the harbour wall and onto the sand, the breeze tugging long strands from the scrunchie. The coastline stretched into the distance as far as the eye could see, rugged cliffs rising like jagged teeth to the left, the tide frothing to the right. She smiled. Cornwall was locked in her heart; being outdoors made her feel happy. Lowenstowe was a breathtaking place with its dramatic shores, pounding surf, craggy rocks, little fishing harbours and beyond, the pretty town with its slow pace of life and warm-hearted people. Val knew that it would come alive with a buzz in the summer, which brought in visiting families, bronzed tangle-haired surfers, so many bright camper vans. But the winter had its own desolate beauty, when the beaches were bare and the weather fickle. Val always felt at home on the beach, inhaling clean air, the brightness of the vast sky making her blink. She was hugged in the arms of the wind, buoyed along by the constant surge of the sea, wide awake now, the wind so forceful and cold it seemed to press hard against her eyeballs and make her eyes water. The waves whispered in her ears, the sand extending for miles ahead, and the cold air stung her cheeks. She felt full of energy.

She was glad she'd chosen to move to Lowenstowe. Alice and Kevin were welcoming; the neighbour on the other side was solitary and mysterious – Val was looking forward to meeting him – and Connie was delightful. Val decided she'd call in to Honeysuckle House later to check that Connie had found the brownies on the doorstep. Her feet picked up a rhythm as a song repeated in her head, 'Three Little Birds' by Bob Marley. Three seagulls soared overhead, swooping down onto the beach to peck at a discarded food wrapper, standing together in the sand, so still as if made of wood. Val's footsteps matched the song's beat and the lyrics repeated in her mind. She felt happy. She had moved house and now she was on the way to reclaiming her life.

The sea rushed forward and sucked back again, crinkled as tinfoil. Behind the water was a silvery sky, the sun high and pale. Her boots sank slightly into the softness of the sand, and she strode forward, filled with optimism. A new year would begin soon, full of opportunity; this last year had been busy and fraught with change but she was determined to heal. It still hurt to remember, but Ray had become someone she didn't know any more. He was Monica's partner; he was someone else. The thought filled her with sadness, but Val pushed it from her mind.

Further down the beach, a man and two small boys were throwing a stick towards a leaping black and white shaggy dog. Val wondered if it might be nice to own a pet. She recalled Dolly, Kevin's boisterous Staffy, with a fond smile and decided a cat might be easier, purring gently, sleeping in front of the log fire on a rug. A man was jogging close to the shoreline, a beanie on his head. He was no youngster, probably her own age: Val wondered if he felt the cold. His arms were tanned, sinewy; he seemed fit, certainly. She wondered if she might take up jogging on the beach in the new year. She might manage a mile each day. No, walking was much easier on the ankle joints nowadays.

On the horizon a little fishing boat nodded steadily on waves that sparkled in sunlight. The coming year loomed in the distance like a boat on the ocean with gleaming white sails. Val could navigate wherever she wanted to go and the journey would be an exciting one; she was at the helm, ready to discover uncharted waters. Each morning she could take bracing walks and in the evening, she'd stroll in the sunset. She could lounge by the lapping waves in the summer, sit in a beach-side café sipping tea in winter. Life would be perfect.

Val turned round and headed towards the harbour, her little cottage less than half a mile away. She'd go back to her new home, unpack a few more items, make some warming soup and contemplate what she'd do in the coming year. Perhaps she'd make a list. She pushed her hands deep in her pockets and smiled.

3

Val was in the kitchen surrounded by trays of pastries, the aroma of baking in the air. The smart speaker was playing cheerful pop songs and she was humming along tunelessly. She had just returned from the beach; it was the last day of the year, the sun high in a perfectly blue sky. The sand glittered, diamond hard, and the wind had lifted her cares and blown them away. She wasn't superstitious but if she had been, the omens were good.

Now that Christmas was over and almost everything was unpacked and in its place, she felt more settled in her new home. She'd noticed a few days ago that the package of brownies in silver foil she'd left at Crab Claw Cottage had disappeared. Then yesterday Alice and Kevin had turned up with mince pies and mulled wine; Connie had called round with soup she'd made from home-grown vegetables. And this evening, New Year's Eve, was going to be a delightful celebration. Connie would come round at seven for supper, then Alice and Kevin would arrive just before midnight to celebrate the arrival of the new year. The neighbours were welcoming her into their lives and Val intended to be equally hospitable; she'd make cheese straws, mini quiches and some more of her famous brownies.

On impulse Val wiped her hands, pulled her scrunchie from her hair and set off for next door. She still hadn't glimpsed the mysterious inhabitant of Crab Claw Cottage, but it was time to introduce herself and invite him round for some New Year festivities.

As Val stepped outside an icy wind cut through the thin layers of her clothes, making her shiver. The breeze blew in from the ocean, slicing the air. She lifted the coil of rope that held the gate closed. The garden was unkempt, a few weeds growing through clumps of flat grass, the hedge spiky and overgrown. There were no lights on inside. She imagined the scene: the front door would creak open and a short man wearing a fisherman's cap would peer out. He'd have a white beard and snowy hair; he'd be stocky, wearing a stripy jumper, a yellow oilskin jacket. He'd have bright eyes beneath bushy white brows; at first he'd seem anxious, then she'd say she was his new neighbour and his face would relax, he'd thank her for the brownies and invite her in to his modest home.

She knocked again but there was still no response. Val shivered. It was too cold to wait any longer so she hurried back to the warmth of Teasel Cottage, to the kitchen that smelled of savoury onions and sweet baking.

Several hours later, she was arranging nibbles on the coffee table. Everything was festive, the fire blazing, tree lights twinkling, paper napkins stacked on gleaming plates. Val's thoughts moved to Ray and she felt sad. He'd be with Monica in The Sprat tonight, counting down the seconds to midnight, kissing her unashamedly under the mistletoe. A sharp pang of regret cut through her. She pushed it away and concentrated on the preparations: she'd make some mulled wine next.

Her phone buzzed and she pulled the mobile from her pocket. A cheery voice exploded in her ear.

'Hi, Mum.'

'Tom! Great to hear from you. Happy New Year.'

'Thanks, and to you too. It's snowing here. You'd really love it in Canada – it's so... Christmassy.'

'Well, it *is* Christmas.' She realised she was smiling, although there was no one to see it. 'How's Lottie?'

'Ah, fine.' Tom's voice was hesitant. 'Er, Mum... I need to talk to you...'

Val frowned. Tom was about to share some news. She wondered if he and Lottie had broken up; it would be exactly as it had been with his last partner, Sophie. He'd been distraught; the split had affected him and therefore Val badly; there had been nothing she could do to make him happy. She couldn't kiss the hurt better. Ray had said as much to her at the time, that Tom was a man now – breaking up with his girlfriend wasn't like grazing a knee.

'Tom, are you all right?' Val realised she was clutching the phone in her fist.

'Mum – I wanted to tell you first...'

She held her breath. Lottie had definitely dumped him. Val's mind searched for the words she'd say to make him feel better. Tom was miles away – she couldn't hug him.

'Mum, Lottie and I...'

'Tom?'

'We're getting married...'

Val felt delight mixed with relief. Ray's rejection had left her always expecting the worst. She was suddenly full of enthusiasm. 'Oh, that's great news. I can't wait to meet her.'

'The wedding's in December next year. I want you to come – we're getting married on Christmas Eve.'

'Oh, how lovely...' Val was imagining herself in Canada in a house made of wood surrounded by mountains, a log fire burning inside; then bunched in a happy throng outside a snow-topped church, standing with Tom and his smiling bride as bells pealed. 'Tom, that's wonderful.'

'We'll send proper invitations out soon, but I wanted to talk to you first...'

'That's great news. I'm so pleased for you both.'

'Mum, I want to invite Dad.'

'Of course.'

Tom's voice was suddenly quiet. 'And he'll want to bring Monica.'

'Ah.' Val exhaled. 'Well, yes, of course.' She felt her heart lurch.

'Would you be okay with that?'

Val put a hand to her head. She didn't want to see Ray at all. Being alone was the best way to stop painful feelings from flooding back. She forced a smile. 'Why wouldn't I be?' Val's voice was excessively cheery. She tried again. 'Tom, it's your wedding and I'll have a lovely time. Of course, your father will want to come and he'll want to bring his – his – Monica. That's fine.'

Tom paused. 'Are you sure? I mean, Lottie and I thought we could say just parents and no partners, since you're on your own...'

'No, no, not at all.' Val's voice was soaring. 'I'm just thrilled. What brilliant news. A wedding – oh, that's so wonderful.'

'Thanks.' Tom sounded relieved. 'I'm so glad you understand. Well, – I'd better ring Dad now so – Happy New Year.'

'And to you too.'

'Mum...'

'Tom?'

He sounded concerned, so far away on the other end of the phone. 'I hope this year's going to be better than the last one was – it must have been tough, what with the split with Dad, and I'm sorry I wasn't around to—'

'Not at all. I'm fine. Totally. In fact, I'm loving life here and...' Val said. 'You really don't need to worry. This year will be wonderful. And you're getting married – I'm so excited!'

'Thanks, Mum. You're the best. We'll talk later.'

Tom was gone and Val stared at the phone. Her thirty-nine-year-old son was getting married and she was going to Canada. It would be perfect, except... She felt an uncomfortable sensation in the pit of her stomach, a feeling that was spoiling the joy. She knew what it was, of course. She'd be at the wedding, and Ray would be there with Monica, and she'd have to pretend the whole time that she didn't mind when, in fact, she minded very much.

Val wished she didn't care: Ray was free to lead his own life now. Besides, the wedding was a year away – hopefully, by next December, seeing him with Monica wouldn't hurt so badly. But in her heart, she had to admit it made her feel miserable.

She wondered if she'd find herself in the same hotel as Ray and Monica; they might even be on the same long-haul flight. Val exhaled slowly, pushing the sadness away. She'd concentrate on bringing in a new year, full of hope and positivity. She'd pour some wine into a saucepan, add some cinnamon and sugar, and make mulled wine for this evening. She rushed into the kitchen determinedly and grabbed a pan in one hand and red wine in the other, squeezing the neck of the bottle as if she were about to throttle it.

Val sipped spiced wine and stared into her glass. 'It was what Tom said to me, Connie. He said that he and Lottie could just invite parents and no partners since I'm on my own. As if I was some sort of lonely old woman who needed to have allowances made because I was all by myself. He was being kind, of course, but it's ridiculous. It doesn't matter that Ray is with Monica; I can still go alone.'

'Of course.' Connie stared into the firelight. 'You must be looking forward to a wedding in Canada.'

'Oh, I am.' Val closed her eyes for a moment. 'I can just see myself outside the church, mother of the groom in a new hat, Tom and Lottie so happy together.'

'You'll have a wonderful time.'

'I hope so, Connie.' Val studied Connie's face; her expression was one of sadness.

'When Will got married, I didn't go – he was in New Zealand and I really should have been there but – you know, Mike died the year before and Will's fiancée's family were all together, one big happy throng, and...'

'And what?'

Connie sighed. 'Honestly, I would have felt so lonely by myself. I regret it now – I should have forced myself to go. I just couldn't seem to make myself move.' She gazed at the flames, lost in thought, then she turned to Val quickly. 'Oh, I'm sorry, Val – this isn't about me... You'll have a wonderful time – you'll really enjoy seeing Tom and Lottie...' She paused, tears gleaming in her eyes.

Val breathed out slowly. 'You must miss Mike very much.'

'I do, every day.' Connie dabbed her eyes with a tissue.

'It was a long time ago.'

Connie agreed. 'It seems like a lifetime. Twenty years. Mike was completely healthy – I mean, he was so active, full of life, never stressed...' She threw out a hand to emphasise the ridiculous situation. 'He enjoyed cycling, running, we'd go hiking, camping, and then, at fifty-six, he had a heart attack.'

'It's not fair,' Val said.

'It's not.'

'There has been no one since?'

'Oh, no,' Connie replied. 'I don't think I could...'

Val filled up Connie's glass. 'I'm sorry.'

'We were happy.' Connie's eyes brimmed with tears again. 'Being alone can be so difficult. Like this wedding – your ex will be there with his new woman and... just imagine the photos afterwards, the lack of balance – you on one side and him and his girlfriend on the other.' She put a hand to her mouth. 'Oh, that was so insensitive of me. My emotions are all over the place, talking about Mike and weddings. After all these years, I still feel... sad. I was just wondering – how do you manage being by yourself?'

'I won't let it bother me,' Val said grimly. Connie hadn't meant to upset her, but the sudden image of Ray and Monica together at Tom's wedding filled her with fresh anxiety. Val waved a hand, dismissing the emotions that were already swelling. 'I'll be fine.'

Connie lifted her glass to her lips. 'I'm sure you will – you seem so strong, Val.'

'So do you, Connie.' Val sipped mulled wine, swallowing hard. She took a deep breath and spoke her thoughts aloud. 'Nothing is going to spoil Tom's wedding.' She considered her words for a moment and was surprised at the strength of the surfacing emotion. 'But you're right – those wedding pictures will last forever and there will be Ray and his new partner on one side and me on the other. I can just hear the grandchildren of the future...' Val imagined two little versions of Tom, a boy and a girl, and the injustice overwhelmed her. 'They'll ask why Granny was all on her own and Grandad was with Monica. Oh, damn!'

Connie glanced up, alarmed. 'Val?'

The words burst from her lips. 'It's just so unfair. I mean – Ray at the wedding without a care, and me feeling like a spare part.'

'That won't be true though, that's just the slant that society puts on single women, that they arrive at a certain age and are suddenly unwanted.'

'It makes my blood boil.'

Connie reached out a hand. 'But you could still find someone.'

Val shook her head. 'I don't think I could be bothered. What would be the point?'

'Maybe just for the wedding?' Connie said. 'How about taking a stand-in – you know, not a real partner, just a temporary plus-one?'

Val hooted, glad of the opportunity to push aside the overwhelming sense of betrayal, to share a joke. 'A handsome guest. Well, that would make everyone sit up and take notice.'

'Imagine the wedding photos.' Connie laughed. 'Ray and his partner, and then you, holding hands with a dreamy man. That would show Ray that you were over him.'

Val's brows knitted together. 'Yes, that would be a photo for the grandchildren.'

'It most certainly would...' Connie said. 'Val, you're not seriously thinking...?'

'Why not?' Val swigged mulled wine, an orange segment in her mouth. She swallowed it, the juice sharp as it burst on her tongue, sharp as the new idea that was suddenly forming. It would help her to cope with the feelings of being abandoned and unloved. 'Yes, I have a whole year. I'll find somebody who's just picture-perfect.'

'A partner?'

'No.' Val's eyes widened. 'Not in the sense of a permanent relationship. I mean someone who will be my – date – just for the wedding. I'll show anybody who thinks older women are past it that I can shine from that wedding photograph forever.'

'Exactly. People think that it's all right for a man in his seventies to find a new girlfriend, but not a woman of the same age.' Connie leaned forwards. 'This is what we'll do. We'll start in January and audition contenders and by December we'll have found you the perfect guest. You never know, you might even find Mr Right.'

Val shook her head. 'I'm not looking for Mr Right, Connie. I'm looking for Mr December.'

'What if you find him too early? What if you find him in June?' Connie asked.

Val smiled. 'Then I'll just have to string him along for a few months...'

'Oh, this is fun,' Connie said. 'I'm looking forward to this new year so much now.' She met Val's eyes. 'To new beginnings.'

'And auditioning new men.' Val's enthusiasm was building. 'A whole year of them – until I find the perfect plus-one.'

'Absolutely.'

'I'm not being the lonely old woman standing all by herself with everyone feeling sorry for me.' Val thought for a moment, and then the right words came. 'To equality, Connie. And to revenge.'

'To revenge.' Connie clinked her glass against Val's.

There was a sharp knock at the door and both women sat upright, listening, then Val glanced at the clock. It was half past eleven. The knock came again and then Kevin's excited voice rumbled from behind the door. 'There's champagne on ice out here – it's bloody freezing. Let us in, Val.'

'Just coming.' Val winked and raised her glass again. 'To a wonderful year, Connie – this is going to be the best.'

MR JANUARY

4

The next morning, the first of January, Val slipped through the front door into a biting wind, rushing towards Crab Claw Cottage. She left a plastic box with a mince pie, a slice of quiche and two sausage rolls on the step, with a small card that simply said, 'Happy New Year, Ben'. No sound came from inside. She hurried back towards her house and was met at the gate by Connie, snug in a warm jacket, a laptop under her arm. Val pointed towards Cloud Cottage; the Christmas decorations were switched off and the curtains were drawn. 'Alice and Kevin are still asleep.'

Connie raised an eyebrow. 'They both enjoyed themselves last night.'

'Happy New Year.' Val hugged her neighbour. 'It was a lovely celebration.'

'I was shattered by one o'clock. But I haven't enjoyed bringing in the new year for such a long time. It's a good job we all live next door.' Connie clutched the laptop. 'I'm so excited about our plan, though.'

'Oh, yes – our plan.' Val's teeth were chattering.

Connie said. 'Grab your coat.'

Val glanced down at the dungarees. 'Do I need to get changed?'

'Not at all,' Connie replied. 'We're going down to The Boat House.'

'Where's that?' Val had the front door open and was reaching for a warm coat on a peg.

'It's our local inn, ten minutes away, down by the harbour.' Connie winked.

Val laughed. 'Oh, do you go to the pub often?'

Connie shook her head. 'I don't get out much, but Dave and Jackie, who run the place, are really nice and they put events on sometimes. I went with Alice to the Christmas singalong.'

'It sounds lovely,' Val said.

'It is,' Connie agreed with a smile. 'The perfect location for a meeting.'

At the bar, Val asked the landlord for two orange juices. He guffawed. 'No hair of the dog for you today then?'

'No, just juice please.' Val looked around. 'It's quiet in here.'

The landlord scratched his beard. 'It's only just past twelve. The lunchtime boozers will start filing in at one.' He raised heavy eyebrows. 'I haven't seen you in here before, have I?'

'I've just recently moved to Teasel Cottage.'

'Ah.' The landlord nodded. 'John and Carole Simpson's house, the emmets from London. I'm glad they've sold to someone who'll live there all the time. It's the cottage next to Ben Berry.'

'Does he come in here much?' Val handed the barman a ten-pound note.

'From time to time – he'll have the odd glass of Bodger's Cider,' the landlord said. 'He's a good bloke; he ploughs his own furrow, does Ben. Nice to have you living here.' He handed her a handful of coins. 'I'm Dave, by the way.'

'Val.' She picked up the drinks and headed towards the snug. Connie was sitting in an old armchair in the corner by the open fire, the laptop open on her knee. Val plonked herself opposite, placing the drinks on a low table. She gazed around the room; the walls were pale brick, pictures of boats and fish on the walls, a few Christmas lights twinkling over the door. It was quiet; the snug was empty; music drifted from the bar.

'Right,' said Connie. 'Let's do this.'

'What exactly are we doing?' Val asked, watching coils of smoke drift up the chimney from the hearth.

Connie gazed up. 'Getting organised. I've learned from running an antiques shop – things need to be sorted out.'

'Okay.' Val was determined. 'I'm up for this.'

'Oh, it's so nice to be busy. So, first question – what sort of relationship are we talking about here? Love? No strings attached?' Connie raised an eyebrow. 'Platonic?'

'I hadn't really thought...' The warmth from the fire was making Val's cheeks glow. 'Let's start with platonic, shall we?'

'A good place to start.'

Val was thoughtful. 'The thing is, I'm not really looking for a proper relationship...'

'What's your type?'

'My type? Connie, I have absolutely no idea.'

'Butcher, baker, millionaire?' Connie typed something. 'We need to find out. Right. So – we consider each man on his merit.'

Val took a gulp of orange juice. 'You make it sound like it's a marathon. I only need one.'

'But we could focus on one each month, just while we sift through what's available, and analyse your type.'

'A calendar of men?' Val found it funny. 'That's brilliant.'

'Contenders. We can learn something from each one. Even if they aren't Mr Right, it will help us decide who we're looking for.'

'Of course. It's – research. Mr Maybes.'

'So, each month we'll suggest a Mr January, a Mr February, and so on, until we find the one that's right.'

'Mr December.' Val suppressed a laugh.

'We'll nominate someone each month...'

'Nothing serious, though...'

Connie agreed. 'You're in the driving seat, Val.' Connie's fingers tapped on the keyboard. 'But shall we not rule the millionaire out?'

Val smiled. 'If you say so.' Then she was thoughtful. 'I just need to like him enough to go to Canada with him.'

'And he has to look good on the photographs. That's the whole point.' Connie's fingers rattled the keys again. 'So: single, attractive.' A thought came to her and she glanced up. 'Do you want someone your age? Younger?'

'I suppose I'd pick someone about the same age as I am...'

'Not sixty or eighty?'

'Honestly, I don't really care...' Val shrugged. 'Mental and physical fitness are a bonus, I suppose.'

'But it's about that photograph. I'll put down a septuagenarian hunk and we'll see what happens.' Connie laughed.

'All right...' Val leaned back in the armchair, amused.

'So...' Connie asked. 'Where are you going to meet these men?'

'Locally? Connie, I'm so out of practice. I haven't dated for fifty years.' Val put a hand to her head, realising that she might actually have to meet a real person. 'You know, I really don't mind going to the wedding by myself.'

'You could. But why be next to Ray and Monica alone, when you could be standing next to a gorgeous man?' Connie put her laptop on the table and met Val's eyes with a direct stare. 'Right, let's think. People mostly meet their future partners – where?'

'At work?' Val suggested. 'I don't work any more and when I did, there were no suitable men at the primary school.'

'On the Internet?'

'No.' Val was firm. 'I'm not doing online dating. I'd end up swiping right or left or whichever way you swipe, hoping to meet someone drop-dead gorgeous, and when he turns up he'll have used a photo from the nineteen sixties and be over a hundred years old and toothless.'

Connie grinned mischievously. 'So, teeth are important?'

Val nodded. 'They'd be a definite bonus.'

Connie's eyes sparkled. 'Now we're getting somewhere, Val. Does this man need to have hair?'

'Bald men are attractive.'

'Beard? Moustache? Clean-shaven?' Connie asked. 'Slim? Muscle-bound?'

'I really don't mind.' Val pressed her lips together, trying unsuccessfully to be serious, then she said, 'Anything in trousers, really.'

'Would a short man be acceptable, though? No, not shorter than you on the photographs – it wouldn't look right. He must be photogenic, with teeth. I'm getting it all down.' Connie typed frantically. Val smiled; they were both enjoying themselves far too much.

'So...' Connie pulled herself together. 'We can meet these men – how?'

'We?' Val raised an eyebrow.

'I'll make a list of all the eligible men we already know.'

'I don't know any, not now.'

'I must know someone from the antique shop days.'

'Okay.'

'We might meet someone socially – here in the pub, quiz nights, karaoke...'

'I can't sing.' Val imagined herself in costume, mic in hand. An idea came to her. 'Perhaps we could double-date, Connie?'

'I don't think I could.' Connie paused for a moment. 'But I'll help in every other way.'

'Right,' Val said. 'What about clubs – you know, painting, reading groups?'

Connie sighed. 'I used to sing with a group on Tuesday evenings. There were six of us, all women, not a baritone in sight. It lasted for a year, then the group just fizzled out – I used to love it. It was the only thing I was involved in. Since then, I've hardly been out at all.' Her face brightened. 'This project is really giving me something to focus on.'

Val offered a sympathetic gaze. 'There's volunteering, rambling – we could join a gym...'

'Yes, I ought to be more sociable.' Connie's fingers tapped again. 'And you just have to put yourself out there.'

Val squealed with laughter. 'I'm not that sort of woman, Connie.'

Connie grinned. 'Do you think you could make the first move though, talk to someone you don't know?'

'Oh, definitely – I'll talk to anyone,' Val said. 'After all, faint heart never won fair man...'

Connie gazed up, her eyes full of admiration. 'Oh, Val, you are so confident and positive – we are going to have fun finding this wedding guest. And who knows what might come out of it?'

Val agreed. 'And you're the perfect dating coach.' She finished her juice: Connie hadn't started hers.

'In the summer there will be more people in town, holidaymakers, tourists.' Connie paused. 'But we don't want a fair-weather holiday romance.'

'What do we do now, in January?' Val asked.

'I'll go through all my old contacts from the antique shop.'

'Great.' Val clapped her hands. 'Right, meeting over. Shall I get us another drink?'

'It's my turn,' Connie protested, closing her laptop.

Then a deep voice came from the doorway. 'Hello, there. I don't see you in here very often, Connie.' An unsteady figure lurched into the room. 'If you want a drink, you only have to ask me.'

Val glanced up to see a broad man with a tired face filling the space in the doorway; his stomach pushed through an expensive coat. He was carrying a pint of ale in one hand and a glass of whisky in the other. He staggered forwards, lowering himself in the seat next to them, stretching out his feet towards the fire. A deep sigh escaped from wet lips as he placed his drinks heavily on the table, spilling froth from the beer. He leaned towards Connie. 'I have to say – I thought you sang very well at the Christmas singalong. You have a lovely voice.'

The man's speech was slurred; he had beads of sweat on his brow. Connie turned to him calmly, her face full of compassion. 'Thanks, Dennis. Happy New Year to you.'

'Ah, it won't be a happy one. It will be as bad as last year, I'm sure.' He raised a paw like a wounded bear. 'Let me buy you something...' He turned to Val. 'And your friend.' He held out a broad hand. 'Welcome to The Boat House. I'm – a friend of Connie's...'

Connie offered him a warm smile as Dennis leaned precariously towards the table, his face fixed in a troubled expression. Val could smell aftershave, a pungent odour of spice. 'Have a drink with me, Connie. There's nobody at the bar yet. I can't drown my sorrows alone.'

Connie said, 'I'm sorry, Dennis. Val and I were just leaving. I could ask Dave to call you a taxi?'

The man's face drooped with disappointment. 'I'd love to tell you more about my wife...'

Connie shook her head. 'You should get yourself home. Maybe I can buy you a small glass of something next time.' She turned to Val. 'We probably ought to go, I think...'

Dennis attempted to turn around in his seat, almost losing his balance. 'Stay, just for a chat. I need a friendly face.'

'Another time perhaps. I hope things will work out for you this year.' Connie stood swiftly and was on her way out of the pub, her laptop under her arm.

Val glanced at the unfortunate man wedged in his seat clutching a half-empty glass, and said, 'Goodbye, Dennis – it was nice to meet you.'

He lifted a hand to wave, almost spilling his beer, and slumped down in his chair, his expression morose. Val gave him one last look of sympathy and followed her friend out into the fresh air.

5

It was bitterly cold; the wind had ice in its breath and a promise of frost but Val was desperate to be outside. The January chill cleared her mind and helped her to think. She was wrapped in a huge coat, fur-lined boots and a hat that covered her ears but even so, her cheeks were tingling. The salty tang of the sea blew the invisible cobwebs inside her head away and she was surprised how quickly fresh thoughts came. The coming year stretched before her like a winding path, ending with Tom's wedding in Canada.

The beach was deserted. The low winter sky was stuffed with thick clouds merging with the metallic sea, a uniform grey line of an artist's soft pencil. Val strolled along, recalling the man in the pub, Dennis Cargill, who had clearly been drinking heavily. Connie had explained that he was a local businessman, well known in Lowenstowe, but he spent a lot of time in The Boat House since his wife left him. Val felt sorry for him – it was so easy to let things slip. Ray had deserted her; her self-esteem had plummeted too. But thankfully she had a new project, new friends, a new home; she would emerge into the new year with new self-respect. She had been Ray's wife. Now she was going to be Val and she was determined to enjoy every moment.

She saw the familiar jogger a distance away, wearing a beanie. Val pushed her hands into pockets and resumed her thoughts. Connie had made progress on the search for Mr December: she'd found a few phone numbers from the antique shop, and was already calling old contacts.

Val was very fond of Connie. She was becoming fond of her other neighbours too; the Holmeses were welcoming people. Several days ago, Kevin had called in to fit a curtain pole in the second bedroom and Alice had turned up at the door with a bag of sticky buns, asking for contributions for the charity shop where she volunteered. Val still hadn't met Ben Berry, the inhabitant of Crab Claw Cottage. She had popped round yesterday to ask if he needed anything as she'd been going into town to do some shopping, but it had been quiet inside the cottage and she'd left without seeing him.

It had been her first foray into Lowenstowe, which was a pretty town but desolate, quiet in the winter, as if it were holding its breath. Val thought Connie had been holding her breath too since retiring. She seemed so glad of a new friend and a new project.

Val tried to imagine what Mr December might look like. It was difficult, because the image of Ray kept appearing. She tried again, picturing someone tall, his large hand holding her smaller one. In her imagination it was a bright summer's day on Breakstone beach; Val was barefoot and her hair was a little longer. The man was wearing shorts, but she couldn't imagine his face. It didn't bode well that she had no idea what sort of man she'd choose. Perhaps she was open-minded. Or perhaps she wasn't interested enough. The thought jolted her. Perhaps she had no intention of falling in love in case her heart was broken again.

Breakstone beach was slowly coming alive. Val gazed at the seagulls whirling overhead, their feathers smooth against the wind.

Beyond them, the sun slid from behind a cloud; the sky brightened, a blinding white, blank as a sheet of paper. The tide was coming in, breakers rolling, surf frothing then rushing back leaving the sand darkly damp. In the distance a teenage couple strolled by the sea wall, their heads together, stopping to kiss. Val couldn't remember ever being carried away by the overpowering swell of romance. Her relationship with Ray had been affectionate but practical. There had been adolescent crushes before that; she'd had several liaisons that had lasted a few months, but no one had really swept her off her feet. Val wondered if she was simply too sensible.

Then she saw him walking towards her, the perfect man with the perfect dog. Val caught her breath, momentarily stunned. The dog was a rich brown colour, big, fluffy, a breed that seemed a cross between a bear and a lion, with a huge tail that curled round on itself. Its tongue hung out, blue-black, as if it were carrying a single spare sock in its mouth. The dog was arrestingly beautiful. Its owner was arrestingly beautiful too. He was around her age; he wore a thick woollen coat in matching brown, a pale cream scarf, a woollen hat covering his hair. Val gazed at his smooth dark skin, a frosting of grey in his neat beard, broad shoulders swaying and long legs moving with ease. He was exactly the man she could imagine herself with. For the first time in many years her pulse was racing.

Val watched the man lope away, his strides matched by the swift trot of his dog. She wished she had spoken to him, said something, anything, just to hear his voice. She was sure it would be a deep sexy rumble. Val was suddenly filled with excitement; she wanted to message Connie. She delved deep into her pocket and dragged out her phone, texting with one cold finger.

can you believe ive just seen the perfect mr january on the beach

Val made her way towards the steps leading to the harbour wall, full of new energy. Her heart thumped and it was a pleasant sensation, one she wasn't used to. Then, in a moment, she was seized with anxiety: if she fell in love with a man like Mr January, what then? She'd risk being hurt all over again, and she couldn't allow that. Val breathed out slowly; she needed to be inside her new home with a cup of hot tea. Philosophical thoughts about love would have to wait.

As she approached the group of little terraced houses, Val saw a figure emerge from the end cottage. She recognised the woman in a duffle coat being dragged forwards, the dog straining on a leash. Alice lifted a hand and Val waved back. They drew level and Dolly leaped up at Val, bashing her knee. Alice muttered, 'Dolly, get down,' through gritted teeth. Dolly ignored her, pulling the lead so tight that her tongue hung out and she began to wheeze. Alice shrugged apologetically.

'It's my turn to take Dolly out. She's been stuck indoors for hours, bless her. I've been in the shop today.'

'Oh?' Val put out a hand to stop Dolly's claws raking her thighs. 'Have you been to the sales?'

'No,' Alice replied as the wind swept a cloud of curls across her face. She scraped them back with cold fingers. 'I volunteer on Fridays – the PDSA in Fore Street – but I promised to cover today. The woman who runs it is always busy with other projects.'

'Oh, that's a great thing to do.' Val was impressed. She pushed Dolly's nose away gently and rubbed her ears.

Alice tugged at the lead. 'Kev's gone to sort out an emergency, a blocked sink. I'll walk Dolly and then start cooking tea. I'm freezing in this wind.' She rolled her eyes. 'It's all go – no peace for the wicked.'

'Pop in for a cuppa on your way back,' Val offered, then she imagined Dolly racing around in her small lounge, cannoning into the furniture.

'I'd love to, Val – but I'm so busy. Maybe next week, when I've got less to do. Soon though. And I'll make some brownies from your recipe – Kev keeps asking for them.'

'I look forward to it,' Val called as Dolly hauled Alice away. The wind took her words upwards and she wasn't sure if Alice had heard.

Val shoved open the gate to Teasel Cottage, delving into her pockets for keys. Something on the doorstep caught her eye. It was her Tupperware container, the one she had left at Crab Claw Cottage a week ago. She picked it up. It was clean and empty. She shoved the door hard – the wood had expanded, making it difficult to open – then she stepped inside, feeling the immediate swell of welcoming heat from the radiator.

She was pouring steaming water onto a fruit teabag when she heard a rap at the front door. Val tugged it wide to find Connie standing outside, her arms folded tightly against the cold wind, smiling broadly. 'Val – I need to hear all about him.'

Connie followed Val into the kitchen, where they cradled hot drinks. Val muttered, 'It was icy cold on the beach today.'

'I'm not here to talk about the weather.' Connie's eyes were bright with excitement. 'Tell me about Mr January.'

Val smiled. 'He was very, very good-looking.' She grinned mischievously 'And so was his dog.'

'Tell me more.'

'That's it, really.'

'Well, describe him.'

'Handsome, fluffy, curly tail, huge blue tongue.'

Connie spluttered. 'The man?'

'The dog.'

'Tell me about the *man*,' Connie said.

Val rolled her eyes. 'He was gorgeous...'

'How gorgeous?'

'Very gorgeous.'

'What type of gorgeous?' Connie persisted. 'George Clooney gorgeous?'

'More Idris Elba gorgeous.'

Connie was thrilled. 'The man in the big coat in the detective series?'

'He had a big coat, yes.'

'And did you speak to him?'

'No,' Val said. 'I was too busy staring.'

'You should have spoken to him.'

'I was tongue-tied...' Val suddenly realised. 'Oh, I should have said, "What a lovely dog." I've just missed a massive opportunity.'

Connie agreed. 'Then he'd have invited you for coffee...'

'I'm fifty years out of practice,' Val admitted. 'Connie, this is ridiculous. I'm behaving like a teenager. I see one handsome man and... whoosh.'

'We have to meet him again – we'll need a smart plan.' Connie smoothed her windswept hair. 'For example, you drop a handkerchief or even better, a wallet. It'd be empty, of course, apart from a stunning photo of you and a scrap of paper with your address, then he'd have to call round to return it.'

'He might just keep it...'

'We'll keep an eye out for him. Meanwhile...' Connie sipped tea gratefully '... I have some news too.'

'Another contender?'

'Sort of. I rang a contact from the antique shop days in Penashberry, a woman I used to know quite well, Boo Fraser. I sold her some lovely pieces over the years.'

'And?'

'I just rang to say Happy New Year.' Connie was pleased with herself. 'She invited me to a Burns Night party. I asked if you could come too and she was delighted – apparently they are short of females to make up the numbers.'

'Oh?' Val was interested. 'So, you think there might be a plus-one or two going spare?'

'We need a backup plan in case your handsome stranger doesn't reappear.'

'Okay,' Val agreed. 'And when is Burns Night?'

'On 25 January, a Tuesday.' Connie's expression was smug. 'And the dress code's full tartan. So, we have eighteen days to plan what to wear and how to bag the perfect wedding guest.'

'Only eighteen days?' Val raised an eyebrow. 'Hell, Connie, we'd better get a move on.'

6

Val rapped at the door of Cloud Cottage. The fairy lights had been taken down and the outside walls were white in the sharp sunlight. The echo of rowdy barking came from inside the house, then Alice opened the door holding Dolly by the collar.

Val held up two bulging recyclable bags. 'Here are the things I promised you – stuff I don't wear now.'

'For the charity shop. Oh, that's great.' Alice's brow puckered. 'Can you just chuck the bags in the hall, out of Dolly's reach? She'd probably eat them.'

Val plonked the bags on the carpet, glad to be rid of clothes she'd worn when she'd been with Ray. It was another steady step forward.

'Thanks.' Alice manoeuvred the dog towards her. 'I'm late for everything today. I have to take Dolly out, and I'm due at the charity shop at two – it's past one already. Kev's at the builders' merchants, buying radiators – he has a job on next week at an old house in Bude, renovating the plumbing throughout.' She gasped. 'Dolly's always restless when he's not here – she's been driving me bonkers all morning.'

'How about I take her, since you're so pushed for time?' Val asked. She was shocked by her sudden generosity. She had just offered to take Dolly for a walk and the idea filled her with fear: the dog was a muscle machine.

Relief spread across Alice's face. 'Oh, would you? That's just amazing.'

'Any excuse to be outside.' A new thought leaped in Val's mind. There was a brilliant ulterior motive: dog owners always talked to each other, didn't they? It would be a great opportunity to meet Mr January. She felt a familiar fluttering heartbeat and she laughed inwardly at her own silliness. She grinned. 'Dolly will love the fresh air.'

'You're just the best neighbour in the world,' Alice said and Val felt a sudden pang of guilt. Alice rummaged in her pockets and brought out a handful of small plastic bags. 'Here – you'd better take these.'

'All right...' Val wasn't sure what the bags were for.

Alice made a face. 'She'll probably need to stop on the beach. You know...'

'Stop?' Val didn't know at all.

'Kev spoils her rotten.'

'Does he?'

'He feeds her crisps, toast, all sorts of rubbish she shouldn't eat. Then, as soon as she's outdoors... boom!' Alice gestured with her hands to indicate an explosion.

'Oh, dear.' The penny dropped and Val took the bags, pushing them deep into her pocket.

'She always needs a loo stop. But you're an angel for offering to take her – thanks so much. I'll make it up to you.' Alice pushed the lead into Val's hand. Dolly was already charging out of the door. Val shortened the lead and the Staffy stayed stubbornly where she was.

Alice stepped outside, struggling into her coat, Val's bags of clothes in one hand and her handbag in the other. 'You're a star, Val.'

'It'll only take an hour...' Val called, wondering what she'd do with Dolly for the rest of the afternoon.

'Don't worry.' Alice was already opening the door to her small red car. 'Kev will be back home soon.'

Val set off cheerfully towards Breakstone beach, Dolly scurrying at her side. As they walked past the harbour wall Dolly began to tug, her little feet tapping on the ground. Val spoke gently. 'Now stop rushing, Dolly. You and I are out for a gentle stroll.' Dolly's pace increased to a fast trot; as the collar tightened, she strained and wheezed. Val walked faster, pleading, 'Please be a good girl, Dolly. No hurrying – and perhaps we can still get you back to Kevin before you need the loo.'

Dolly forged mindlessly ahead, grunting, refusing to slow down. Val increased her pace until she was almost running; she'd need to be as brawny as Kevin to cope with this determined dog. She panted as she jogged along the beach, hauled on the end of a lead, doubting her skills as a dog walker. She'd hoped to impress Mr January by sauntering seductively with her obedient dog, but here she was being dragged along furiously.

She'd researched Mr January's dog on the Internet and discovered it was a Chow Chow. Apparently, they were loyal but not very sociable animals, sometimes inclined to be possessive. Val gazed down at Dolly surging forward for all she was worth and imagined her leaping energetically towards the Chow to make friends, the huge brown beast baring its teeth, and handsome Mr January baring his teeth too, coolly demanding that Val keep her unruly dog under control. Perhaps stopping to talk would be a mistake. Val would simply sashay past looking mysterious, a faithful pooch trotting by her side, leaving Mr January wondering who the glamorous woman with the obedient Staffy was. The idea filled her with cheerful optimism but Dolly hurtled onwards with no intention of impressing anyone.

Val's boots sank into the soft sand and she felt her heart soar. The vast openness that led to the rushing ocean, the expanse of pale sky, gave her an immediate feeling of freedom and happiness. The sun was a halo of silver and the sea's soft breath was soothing. Val glanced around the beach. A few children played with a football; a collie dog ran free next to an athletic young man in shorts. A fishing boat was bobbing on the ocean, red and blue against the grey swirl of foam. She scoured the distance, hoping for a glimpse of a tall man in a brown coat striding alongside his thick-furred dog.

Down by the sea, a solitary figure wearing a blue anorak was crouching, strands of hair waving like antennae in the breeze. The woman was doubled over; Val wondered if she was in pain, clutching her stomach, so she manoeuvred Dolly to change direction. Then she noticed that the woman gripped a sack in one hand and was collecting something. Val called out softly. 'Hello.'

The woman glanced up; she wore aviator sunglasses, a beret over one ear. Her white hair was wound around her head in two thin plaits and her brow was creased in concentration. Val assumed she was at least eighty years old, but the woman's gloved hands were nimble as she shoved something inside a coarse cloth bag. The woman muttered, 'The emmets have been in their holiday homes over Christmas, leaving their rubbish about. Some of them are all right, they respect the place, but others don't care – it's not their town. Those people don't think about the damage it does to wildlife. They just chuck it about anywhere.'

'Emmets? Oh, you mean holidaymakers?' Val said. She could see now that the sack was brimming with cans, cardboard and empty bottles from fizzy drinks.

The woman went back to her work. 'Some locals are as bad. Look at this – bits of old fishing nets, too – you wouldn't believe the rubbish I pick up when I'm down here.'

'Are you collecting litter?' Val was impressed. 'That's great.'

'It needs doing, so I do it,' the woman said matter-of-factly. 'I tell our councillor, the one that's responsible for the welfare of Lowenstowe, but he's not very helpful, is he?'

Val shrugged. 'I don't know.' Dolly leaped forward to stuff her nose in the sack, then turned around, scraped sharp paws in the sand, squatted and sat very still. It took Val several seconds to work out that she was doing her doggy business.

'Oh, no,' Val exclaimed.

The woman folded her arms and frowned, unimpressed. 'I hope you're going to clear that up.'

Dolly sniffed the sand then tugged away, dragging the lead tight. Val reached in her pocket and brought out a handful of clear plastic bags, bending over to retrieve the unmentionable mess, when she heard the woman snort loudly.

'Plastic bags?'

Val was nonplussed. 'It's not my dog – I was just...'

'Did you know that dog poo sits encased in plastic in some landfill site somewhere for all of eternity?' The woman put her hands on her hips.

'I'm sorry.' Val couldn't think of anything else to say. 'It was the best I could do – the poo bag, I mean, not the actual poo – that was the dog, not me...'

The woman huffed. 'You need a bit of newspaper, right? Bring a bit of old paper. It's bio-degradable.'

'I'm genuinely sorry,' Val repeated. 'Yes – newspaper is such a brilliant idea. I'll bring some next time.'

The woman stood up and heaved the coarse sack onto her

shoulder. She met Val's eyes, a smile flickering across her lips. Her expression softened. 'Ah, don't mind me. I don't mean to be so cross. It just gets my goat, the way people don't care enough about this beautiful place we live in. We get it all here, car fumes, overfishing, food coming in from miles away. I've been cleaning this beach up for over ten years. And it's not just Lowenstowe, it's everywhere. It makes me mad, it really does.'

'I understand,' Val said. 'You're doing good work.'

'I do my best.' The woman gazed up and down the beach. 'I just wish there were more of us to make a difference. Well, it's nice to meet you. I'd best be off home now. My John will be waiting for me. It's gone half past three.'

'Ah, well, it's nice to have met you too,' Val agreed.

'And don't forget – bring a bit of newspaper next time your dog needs to go. What's she called?'

'Dolly,' Val said awkwardly. 'After Dolly Parton.'

'Sweet dog. She looks like a happy little girl, very lively, full of bounce. Well, you have a nice day. It's a lovely one for a walk. But then, you can't beat a Cornish beach, can you, on a day like this? Best place in the world, Cornwall. Like I say, you take care now.'

The woman lifted a hand in final greeting and marched away. Val glanced down at Dolly, who was shoving her nose into the sand, sniffing something. Val scanned the beach, hoping for a glimpse of Mr January, but there were few people left, just the lone runner and the older lady in a blue anorak striding towards the wall. Val sighed, shrugging away a sharp pang of disappointment, hoping instead that Kevin would be back from the builders' merchants, that she could hand his beloved Staffy over, complete with the plastic bag, and suggest that he replaced it with an old piece of newspaper in the future.

She retraced her steps, Dolly trotting along obediently, happy now. Val fancied there was a curved grin on the Staffy's face as she scuttled contentedly towards home. They'd be back well before it became dark and Val could light the fire, sit on the rug and read a few chapters of her book. She'd definitely have earned a cup of hot chocolate and a small fudge brownie by the time she arrived back at Teasel Cottage.

7

Val opened the bedroom curtains to a damp day. She ate a hurried breakfast, grabbed her keys and bag and rushed outside. Incessant rain soaked through her coat, darkening the pavements, spreading into puddles on the ground. She spent an hour in Finest Choice, the local supermarket, stocking up on provisions. Then she drove home and made a batch of Scottish tablet, a creamy fudge that she had to stir for thirty minutes until it was sticky, then beat hard for another fifteen minutes to thicken it. After waiting half an hour for it to cool, Val cut her fudge carefully into squares. It looked wonderful; she planned to give the sweets to her neighbours to celebrate Burns Night.

She searched in her little back garden, collecting several small smooth stones. Then she pored over each one, painting them in acrylic in various colourful designs: delicately petalled flowers, bright yellow suns, a vivid rainbow, a crimson heart. Then, when the pebbles were dry, she varnished them so that they gleamed. She'd always loved painting, and she enjoyed the calming process, completing each detail meticulously.

Val had decided to give some traditional fudge to the hosts, Boo and Douglas Fraser, to thank them for their invitation. She also secretly intended to hand out a favour box or two to any interesting single men. She carefully placed the pebbles in boxes, inserting a pretty card that said *Handmade by Val* and her email address. Then she finished each favour box with a thin strip of tartan ribbon.

Val was pleased with her handiwork: the favour boxes were quite professional. She wondered if any of the recipients would assume that she painted pebbles for a living and email her with a bulk order. She hoped not. She'd place six boxes in her handbag to give away. Val wondered with a smile if there would be as many as six men at the party that she'd find interesting. But first she'd deliver some fudge to Connie, to Alice and Kevin, although she could imagine Dolly eating it all, and to the mysterious neighbour, Ben the fisherman.

The Burns Night favour boxes and the name tag with the email address had of course been a romantic ruse devised by Connie to find Mr February. Connie was convinced that if Val slipped a favour box into the hand of a handsome reveller, he would contact her for a date. She hadn't seen Mr January since the initial crossing of their paths on the beach. She was still hopeful. It had been a long time since any man had made her heart beat faster, and the feeling was oddly pleasant. There might be more good-looking strangers at the Burns Night celebration. The thought made her feel cheerful, masking the painful memories that were constantly lurking.

Val felt buoyed by optimism as she tugged on a warm jacket, picking up two batches of fudge to deliver to her neighbours. She stepped out into the downpour and made a rush for Cloud Cottage. There was no sound inside, no lights on, no television, although it was approaching four o'clock. Val assumed that Kevin was at work and had taken Dolly with him, and that Alice was at the charity shop or in town. She pushed the tartan-ribboned gift through the letter box.

There were no lights on at Crab Claw Cottage either and the curtains were drawn, although the downstairs windows were clean and someone had hacked back the hedge and tidied the garden. She rapped on the door and listened. As expected, there were no lights, no approaching footsteps. Val gazed up at the heavy rain; her hair was soaked and her face wet. She dropped the fudge through the letter box and rushed back to her cosy cottage. She'd have a long soak in the bath, then it would be time to meet up with Connie for the evening's entertainment. Val had never been to a Burns Night celebration before – she was looking forward to it.

* * *

By seven o'clock, Val and Connie were ready, Connie in a black dress, a tartan sash fixed with an ornate pin. Val had found some tartan trousers and a white frilly blouse in her wardrobe, and a tartan beret that someone had given her years ago – this was its first outing. Connie was nervous, clutching bottles of wine and lemonade, proclaiming that she was driving and wouldn't drink but Val could have one to calm her nerves. Val didn't feel at all nervous, but she was looking forward to the dancing far more than meeting male guests.

They drove slowly in Connie's Fiesta through slanting rain to Penashberry, the route taking them through dark lanes across the countryside, past muddy farmland. Connie peered through the windscreen in her driving glasses, wipers sloshing, and eventually they arrived at an ornate set of double gates, lit yellow in the downpour by soft round lights. The car rolled slowly to the end of the drive outside a vast brick house with tall rectangular windows. As they eased themselves from the car, Val and Connie heard thumping music, bagpipes and drums booming from the house. The wooden door was ajar and Connie led the way in through a wide stone hall lit with tea lights in jars. At the end of the passage was a broad-shouldered man in a kilt with his hands on his hips who boomed, 'Connie. Welcome. And your friend too. Come in. Come and see what Boo's done with all your antiques.'

Val assumed this was Douglas Fraser. His voice was all rounded English vowels as he shook Val's hand heartily. 'Glad to meet you – Val, am I right? I'm Dougie.' He pronounced it Doo-gee. 'Come on in and have a glass of something.'

'Thanks.' Val delved into her capacious bag crammed with favours boxes and held out a box of Scottish tablet. 'This is for you. Happy Burns Night.'

Dougie took the box with enthusiasm, digging his hand in and pushing a square of fudge into his mouth. Val and Connie followed him into an enormous room where people were dancing, mostly in couples, jigging and skipping in response to the instructions of a man at a microphone. Val had always liked ceilidh and Scottish reels, lively music that made you want to join in immediately, and she started to tap her feet. She gazed around, hoping to dance with lots of partners: this was the perfect opportunity to meet Mr February.

Connie was talking to a tall confident woman in full Scottish regalia: plaid dress, tam-o'-shanter, sash, her hair a mass of red curls. She grabbed Val's hand. 'Delighted to meet you, Val – I'm so glad you and Connie could come.' She had the same cultured tones as Dougie. 'I'm Boo – short for Brenda but no one calls me that – no one would dare to.' She barked a laugh. 'Get yourselves a drink. And you must see what we have done with the Georgian sideboard. And the Baroque mirror you found for me has pride of place. Just come and see...' Boo beamed in Val's direction and tugged a protesting Connie away.

Val moved her head in time to the music, watching the dancers twirl. Couples bowed and parted, stepped with one pointed toe then with another, then clasped hands and jogged a few paces together in time, faces shining.

Val felt someone press her arm and Dougie was next to her, holding out a drink. She gazed up at him, his swept-back hair, broad chest and shining buttons, and took the glass from his hand. He smiled and his face became handsome.

'Punch,' he explained. 'Apples, honey, cinnamon and a dash of whisky.'

'You're not Scots, are you, Dougie?' She noticed again the pure English voice, his confident boom.

'My grandfather was from Edinburgh – he was a Douglas too,' he replied. 'I'm from Hampshire. How's the drink?'

'Lovely.' Val had only taken the smallest of sips.

'Then shall we dance?' he asked.

'Lovely,' Val repeated as he grasped her waist and flung her into the jigging throng.

Val and Dougie tapped their toes, advanced, retired, swung to the left and to the right, and whizzed round in a circle twice. Then, as the music swelled, Val panted, 'Doesn't Boo like dancing?'

'Oh, she's incredible at everything.' Dougie gave a deep laugh. 'But she's busy...' before he hurled her into a charge, his arm around her, almost cannoning into another couple.

Dougie and Val danced The Gay Gordons, The Dashing White Sergeant and Strip the Willow. They paused for breath and were about to launch into St Bernard's Waltz when a man in a red tartan kilt tapped Dougie on the shoulder and said, 'I wonder – may I cut in?' Dougie raised his eyebrows and stepped back as the new dancer took Val's hand, his arm on her waist in a less insistent manner.

'I believe Dougie intended to keep you to himself all night. I thought it was time to intervene.'

Val scrutinised her new partner's face as they waltzed sedately.

His hair was brushed smartly and his face was pleasant; his chin was a little soft. He noticed her gaze and said, 'I'm Nigel Carrow. And you are...?'

'Val Maxwell.' She had her breath back. 'I've come with a friend to make up the dance numbers.'

'And I'm so glad you did. I was hoping to find myself an attractive partner to dance with...' Nigel replied, moving her expertly into a space between two other couples.

Val wondered how he'd look in a wedding photo. He was well dressed, from what she could see from the vantage point of being stuck in his arms in a waltz, and his bearing was quite distinguished. He was certainly unlike Ray, who probably wouldn't be at all comfortable in a suit. Nigel, however, appeared as if he'd been born in one; the word cultured could have been invented for him.

The music came to an end and the caller announced in a soft Scottish brogue, 'You are all invited to attend the dining room, where the feast is prepared and your hosts await. And remember the old saying, *a hungirie man suin sniffs out meat.*'

Nigel offered an arm and a gallant smile. 'Shall we partake?'

Val had no idea where the dining room was, but everyone else in the room was scurrying towards the door. She and Nigel followed them across the hall into a large room with a heavy crystal chandelier hanging over a long table piled with food. A waiter in a kilt was rushing round with a tray, handing each guest a glass of something bubbly. Val took one and was tempted to drink it straight away, she was so thirsty. Instead, she watched as vast pots full of steaming vegetables, stews, potatoes, salads and a whole salmon were brought in. Loud chatter came from each corner, rumbling laughter, friendly banter. Connie was on the other side of the room next to Boo. She waved, gazed at Nigel and offered a discreet thumbs-up. Val, in return, shrugged slightly, implying that he'd do. He was quite handsome, he was male – at least he met some of the criteria on her list.

Dougie lifted a finger and everyone was suddenly quiet. Then a piper began to play from outside the room, a low drone, as a man entered with a silver salver, carrying it high. Nigel caught Val's eye and whispered, 'It's the hallowed haggis – we're in for a feast.'

Dougie coughed, paused for attention and began to recite in an exaggerated Scottish accent. Val recognised the poem by Robert Burns in appreciation of the haggis. Then, ceremonial knife raised theatrically, he sliced the haggis and everyone applauded. Boo was by his side, raising a glass, and Dougie lifted his goblet high, speaking in his mock-Scottish accent. 'To ye all. Gentlemen, will you please join me in a toast? To the lassies.'

Val raised her glass and realised that only the men in the room had raised theirs so she lowered it quickly. Then Boo lifted her glass, smiled in the direction of Val and Nigel and called, 'To ye all – a toast to the laddies.' Val brought the cool bubbles gratefully to her lips. She muttered 'To the laddies,' gave Nigel a sidelong glance and wondered what February might bring.

8

'I didn't drag you away too early, did I?' Connie was peering over the top of the steering wheel as she drove down a narrow lane, the headlights illuminating rain sloshing against the windscreen. 'It's just that I was worried about the journey home.' She gave Val a sideways glance. 'You seemed to be enjoying yourself though.'

'It was good fun.' Val yawned. She was tired; the energetic dancing had really taken it out of her. She snuggled down in the softness of the seat and closed her eyes.

Connie was excited. 'So, tell me about the charming man you spent the entire evening with.'

'He's called Nigel Carrow, he's seventy-two, he lives outside Lowenstowe, he used to be a financial analyst, and he's just recently met Dougie Fraser.'

'And did you like him?'

'He seemed nice,' Val suggested. 'It was hard to tell – we only danced the ceilidh and talked a bit during the buffet.'

'Did you get his phone number?'

Val shook her head. 'Just as we were getting our coats, I rummaged in my bag and gave him a favour box. I still have all

the others – I was hoping to change partners more often but
Dougie hung on to me, and then Nigel did the same.' She
shrugged. 'My email address is inside so you never know, he
might get in touch...'

'An ingenious plan, though I say it myself.' Connie peered
through her driving glasses and negotiated a corner slowly. The
wheels slid through mud. 'So, is he a contender for Mr February?'

'He might be...' Val stretched out throbbing legs. 'Right now, all
I want to do is sleep. Finding Mr December is proving to be hard
work.'

'You'll be feeling more optimistic tomorrow after a good night's
rest.'

'I'm sure I will.' Val closed her eyes again. By the time they
arrived back in Lowenstowe, she had fallen asleep.

* * *

The next morning, Val was eating porridge, remembering the five
favour boxes tied with tartan ribbon still stuffed inside her bag. She
wondered what to do with them and decided to leave them there:
after all, it was only January. Beyond the window, Lowenstowe was
considerably brighter; the sky was pale, the sun hidden behind a
wedge of cloud. Val's legs ached from last night – the dancing had
left her feeling lethargic and a stroll would probably do her good.
She was pulled from her thoughts by a sharp rap at the door.
Connie was outside, smiling and holding up an envelope. 'Hi, Val –
I found this on your step.'

Val opened the envelope, taking out a small card with a pretty
picture of a Cornish cove on the front, sunlight glinting on
turquoise waves. 'It's from Ben next door.'

'Oh?'

'Yes – it's a thank you card for the fudge. He's put, "Thank you

kindly for the sweets, they were very tasty. Best wishes, Ben Berry."
His handwriting is beautiful.'

'How lovely,' Connie exclaimed.

'He left the empty box on my step that I filled with goodies on
New Year's Eve too.'

'Have you met him yet?'

Val shook her head. 'I wouldn't know him from Adam.'

'He's nice – I saw him a few days ago, early in the morning. He
was going fishing, he had oilskins on. He always says hello and
comments about the weather. Sometimes, I think he wants to stop
for a chat, but I never really know how to reply.' Connie followed
her inside the house. 'The Burns Night was quite a success. How are
you feeling this morning?'

'Shattered,' Val said. 'The dancing was great fun though.'

'We just have to wait for Nigel to email you now.'

'He might. I don't mind either way.' Val thought of handsome
Mr January with his dog. 'To be honest, Connie, Nigel didn't set my
pulse racing.'

'How do you know until you see him again? Can I ask – was Ray
your type straight away?' Connie asked.

'I suppose so,' Val said sadly. 'I thought so once.'

Connie offered a sympathetic grin. 'We'll find someone suitable
by December.'

Val agreed. 'A nice person I can take to Canada, who will be
good company for a few days...'

'It's lovely outside,' Connie said. 'Let's take a walk.'

* * *

Val strolled next to Connie, the wind making her eyes water. She
felt exhilarated, the salty air filling her lungs. The tide was out,
the beach empty except for a woman with two Labradors who

sprinted around her ankles and chased a ball as she flung it towards the waves. Even the feisty woman scooping litter into a sack at the water's edge was nowhere to be seen, and there were no fishing boats bobbing on the ocean. Val watched the sun sparkle on the waves, making ripples sharp as diamonds, then she dragged her thoughts back to Connie, who was still chattering.

'... if Nigel is Mr February, but I think the evening at The Boat House might be a really good idea.'

'Sorry – I missed the first bit.' Val was puzzled. 'What are we going to do at The Boat House?'

'There's a Valentine's Night karaoke in the pub. We dress up and do a song,' Connie said. 'I've signed us both up with Dave, the landlord.'

'Connie, I sing like a frog.' Val recalled how her terrible singing had always been a standing joke between her and Ray. He'd always loved to serenade her at any opportunity, his voice sweet and melodious, and then Val would join in badly and they would collapse laughing together. It seemed such a long time ago now.

Connie shrugged. 'I can help you practise. I love singing. I've said I'll do the Elvis song, "Can't Help Falling in Love".'

'You'll be brilliant.' Val's voice was warm with encouragement. 'Can't I just come on stage with you and bang a tambourine?'

'It was our song, mine and Mike's.' Connie's eyes were misty for a moment, then she gazed at Val. 'No, you need to be noticed. Do a song and dance like – Beyoncé or someone.'

Val laughed. 'You want me to twerk?'

'If that's what it takes.' Connie was serious. 'There will be lots of people there – The Boat House is inviting other local pubs – so it's really important that we get you noticed.'

'I sing like Bob Dylan, Connie, I'm croaky...'

'Maybe we should practise one of his songs – a romantic one?'

Val roared a line, her voice a tuneless groan. '"Just Like a Woman"?'

'"I Shall Be Released"?' Connie sang, her voice sweet and melodic.

'"Every Grain of Sand"?' Val droned, whirling round.

'"Blowin' in the Wind"?' Connie trilled.

'"Like a Rolling Stone",' Val bellowed.

'"The Times, They Are A-Changin'",' Connie crooned back.

Val glanced up at the sky and bawled, '"A Hard Rain's A-Gonna Fall".'

They sang at the top of their voices and fell about laughing. They hadn't noticed a man walking by, a fluffy dog at his side, who commented, 'Oh, big Bob Dylan fans, eh? Very nice.'

Val stopped, listening to the low rumble of his voice. Then she reached for Connie's arm as they watched the man in the brown coat stroll past, a thick-furred Chow Chow on the end of a lead. Val observed his broad back, his easy stride. 'Connie... That was him.'

Connie knew straight away. 'Goodness me, Mr January! Oh, Val, you weren't wrong – he'd look gorgeous in a wedding photo. He's devastatingly handsome.'

'He is,' Val said. 'And he's just heard me singing karaoke – I've no chance now.'

'No... think positively,' Connie said. 'Maybe he'll come to The Boat House. He'll know you'll be there... He... he...' She grinned excitedly. 'He'll turn up and sing "Wonderful Tonight", just for you.'

Val's eyes twinkled. 'Oh, just imagine that... I'd be in heaven!' She watched, hanging on to Connie's arm as the brown coat and the brown dog became smaller in the distance. Their laughter was therapy: Val felt her spirits soar.

'He's very nice, isn't he?' Connie agreed. 'So, we have Mr January – and Mr February, Nigel – so we're getting closer to working out your type. And the Valentine's karaoke will be a huge

opportunity – the place will be heaving.' She faced Val determinedly. 'And if that doesn't work, we'll have to spread our net
further...'

'Further?' Val smiled wickedly. 'You don't mean... Devon?'

'I mean Alice and Kevin.'

'I'll have to walk Dolly?'

'No, Kevin is a plumber. He'll have customers.' Connie folded
her arms.

'Ah, well.' Val's expression was full of mock-resignation. 'I'd
better start practising for the karaoke...'

* * *

Val spent the next few days rehearsing to an invisible audience,
strutting her stuff. She sang her heart out to Beyoncé's 'Single
Ladies (Put a Ring on It)', Joan Jett's 'Bad Reputation' and Pink's 'Get
the Party Started'. She shook her booty and twerked, determined to
perform something feisty. She wasn't going to sing 'Cry Me a River'
or 'The Tears of a Clown'. But her voice was a tuneless growl. It
wouldn't matter how hard she practised or how enthusiastically she
danced, gorgeous Mr January wouldn't succumb to her singing like
the sirens who lured sailors to their Greek island with their
hypnotic voices. The thought made Val laugh; he'd row the
other way.

On Sunday evening, the thirtieth, Val sat in front of the fire, her
laptop on her knee, replying to a message from Tom. He'd sent
some photos of St George's, the church he had booked for the
wedding on 24 December, an old building in Montréal that was so
beautiful it made Val catch her breath. She was beginning to realise
that the wedding was really happening and her heart sank at the
thought of seeing Ray again. The image of a wedding photo
appeared in her imagination: the happy couple, Ray and Monica,

Val and Mr January. Balance would be restored. She felt a rush of gratitude for Connie's help.

Val's email was full of excitement: the church was perfect; she was thrilled about the wedding and couldn't wait to see Tom and to meet Lottie. She wouldn't mention a plus-one yet, or anything to do with Ray and Monica. She signed off, *Love from Mum xxx* and immediately launched into the chorus of 'Stand by Your Man', which was being played on the radio, purely to try out the high notes. Her voice squeaked, the sound of nails scraping down a board. Val grinned. She certainly wouldn't be singing that song – no one would want to stand anywhere near her at the karaoke. Just then, another email arrived. Val was initially puzzled by the sender, NigeCar@hotmail, then she caught her breath. It was from Nigel Carrow.

She read his brief email saying that he'd been delighted to discover her email address in the favour box, that he'd immensely enjoyed dancing with her and he hoped she'd had a marvellous time. He had two tickets for *The Magic Flute* in Plymouth on Saturday 5 February and would she like to accompany him, and maybe have dinner beforehand?

Val considered his invitation carefully. It would take an hour and twenty minutes to drive to Plymouth, which she wasn't keen to do by herself. But she hadn't been to an opera in years – Ray hadn't been a fan. He'd preferred ballads and pop while Val loved the strong passionate voices. She recalled how she'd enjoyed visiting art galleries too. Ray had been bored after half an hour. It would be interesting to share an evening of culture. Then she wondered if she ought to say no, thank you – she wasn't sure that she was attracted to Nigel Carrow and she had no idea what to talk about during dinner. But it would be an opportunity to practise her dating skills, which were very rusty.

Val reread the email. It was courteous, friendly, a one-off invitation from a pleasant man, nothing more. The opera was next Saturday, so she had plenty of time to make up her mind.

She stared at the screen and, for a moment, she imagined how much nicer it might be to go with Mr January instead. He'd look wonderful in a dinner jacket and she'd heard the sexy rumble of his voice. Val had to admit she'd feel much more excited about a meeting with him than spending the evening with Nigel.

But she had to start somewhere, and she reminded herself that it was all purely research, a single date, just friends, no strings. She'd enjoy it; she'd make the most of what would be a pleasant evening. Yes, she would go. She picked up her phone to tell Connie the news.

MR FEBRUARY

9

Val gazed out of the window of the passenger seat watching cars whizz by, while Connie peered over the steering wheel, driving glasses on the end of her nose, trying to find somewhere to park in Plymouth Hoe. They passed a parade of colourful shops and cafés, arriving at the famous red and white striped lighthouse surrounded by perfectly cut grass overlooking the turquoise curve of the sea. Connie muttered, 'I hoped we'd find a side street to park in, but it's so busy this afternoon.'

'I'm sure I saw a multistorey – just turn round and go back,' Val said. 'It's lovely here in Plymouth – the sun's out.'

'I'm gasping for that cup of tea.' Connie followed a blue sign with the letter P. 'Then we can discuss tonight.'

'I thought it was decided – we'd do a bit of shopping and have a cuppa somewhere; you drop me at The Duke of... whoever, and go on to the spa. Then you pick me up at ten thirty and we drive home.'

'We need to discuss the finer points, Val.'

'What finer points?'

'The obvious ones...' Connie winked. She turned into the multistorey car park, driving steadily up a ramp, finding a space for the Fiesta. 'Right, here we go. We'll park for two hours – that should give us enough time.'

Val glanced around. 'Let's hit the shops.'

'Yes, let's.' Connie reached for her handbag. 'I'm so looking forward to an afternoon out, I might forget about your date with Mr February.'

'Yes, I'd almost forgotten too.' Val was beginning to feel distinctly nervous about a date with a man she hardly knew.

'Grab the bag with your posh dress and the heels,' Connie reminded her. 'You can get changed in the loos in the tea shop.'

'It's just like being seventeen again.' Val was encouraged by her friend's excitement. 'Okay, let's go.'

Just after four o'clock, Val and Connie were perched in the window seat of an old-fashioned café sipping Earl Grey, watching the shoppers stroll by. There were bags of shopping by their feet: Val had bought a Himalayan salt lamp for her living room and Connie had haggled for twenty minutes before buying a beautiful china bowl in an antique shop. Val gazed through the window, wondering if a facial might be more therapeutic than the opera.

Connie read her thoughts. 'Are you looking forward to tonight?'

'A bit.' Val reached for the teapot and refilled their cups.

'We need to talk about Nigel,' Connie said seriously.

'Isn't that a book – and a film?' Val joked.

'That's Kevin, isn't it?' Connie grinned. 'No – we need to be organised. What if he tries to kiss you?'

'In the back seat of the opera?'

'It's wise to be prepared.'

Val was astonished. 'It's just a date, as friends.'

'So that you can work out what your type is.'

'I'll do my best.'

'And we have the karaoke to fall back on.'

'I've been practising,' Val admitted. 'But I still can't carry a note in a bucket...'

'You'll be wonderful.' Connie glanced at the clock on the white brick wall. 'We should pop to the loo, get changed for the big date. I'm dropping you off for dinner at the hotel at six, right?'

'Right – and you'll have a swim, grab something to eat back at the hotel and collect me at the theatre at ten thirty.'

'Which gives you time to peck his cheek, say thank you for a wonderful evening and disappear into the night like Cinderella,' Connie said firmly.

'Sounds simple.' Val gave a single laugh. 'I'm starting to feel nervous.'

Connie's eyes sparkled. 'Tonight is strictly research.'

'I almost wish I was coming to the spa with you.' Val sighed.

Connie reached over and grabbed Val's hand. 'Seriously, I'm so grateful that you've included me in this adventure. Shopping, tea, a spa session, dinner and being your date coach – I don't think I've had this much fun in ages...' Connie paused, her eyes suddenly filling with tears. 'Do you know, Will asked me to move to Auckland after I sold the shop? I seriously thought about it.'

'Why didn't you?'

Connie took a breath. 'Promise you won't think I'm silly?'

Val offered an encouraging nod.

'Mike is here in Cornwall – his grave is here. I didn't want to leave.'

'I understand,' Val said sympathetically.

'But sometimes I wish I'd gone to New Zealand. I could have spent time with the grandchildren. I hardly know them. I've been so alone.' Connie turned grateful eyes towards Val. 'Since you came to Lowenstowe, I've had more fun than I've had in years.'

'You should go and see Will,' Val said softly.

'I should. I've been too afraid. I miss my son so much but then –

I've vegetated, stuck. You've no idea how much I needed to get out. And now here I am, off to a spa...'

'Fun's what it's all about.' Val smiled. 'Right, let's get my dating face on and we'll see what tonight brings.' She winked. 'I still wish I was coming with you.'

* * *

'Val, I have to say, you look simply wonderful.'

Nigel was waiting on the steps outside the Duke of Cornwall, a grand nineteenth-century Victorian building, all grey brick and arched windows that glimmered gold inside. He was wearing an expensive overcoat; his eyes shone as Val approached. He held out a hand graciously. 'I'd forgotten how stunning you are.'

Val smiled, but only because she was bewildered. Nigel was not quite as she remembered him – he seemed a little plumper and his chin a little softer beneath a new jaunty moustache. She took his arm.

In the vast restaurant with glittering chandeliers, they were shown to a table set with white linen and gleaming cutlery. The waiter took their order and then their eyes connected. Val wasn't at all sure what to say.

Nigel raised an eyebrow. 'Well, it was nice of you to see me again.'

'It was nice of you to ask me.'

'I have two tickets.' Nigel patted his pocket. 'I need a guest.'

'I haven't been to the opera in ages,' Val said. 'Or an art gallery...'

'Your ex wasn't a fan, I assume?' Nigel asked.

Val didn't recall mentioning an ex; she had no intention of discussing Ray, so she launched into conversation. 'The last opera I saw was *The Marriage of Figaro* in the seventies. It was an amateur production – a work colleague of mine was playing Susanna.'

'What an exciting life you must have led,' Nigel replied. Val wasn't sure if he was being sarcastic. He puffed out his chest. 'You'll like *The Magic Flute*. It's an amusing little story. I was Papageno the bird catcher in a production at university – very me. I really enjoyed the role, as you can imagine. I find a rousing opera always gets me in the mood...'

Val offered her most inquisitive expression. 'So, you're a singer, then?' She was thinking of Ray again, his soft romantic voice. She'd always told him he sounded like Cat Stevens, whom she'd loved as a teenager.

'Baritone.' Nigel's smile was smug. 'I enjoyed treading the boards – theatre, especially, at Cambridge. I was Valmont in *Liaisons Dangereuses* and Petruchio in *The Taming of the Shrew*. I was always cast as the ladies' man, the seducer, the one they could never quite resist.'

He leaned forward suavely and squeezed her knee. Val almost spluttered into her wine, then she blurted, 'I played a horse's bottom in panto once, *Jack and the Beanstalk*.'

'Oh?' Nigel raised an eyebrow.

'My son, Tom, was twelve – he was playing Simple Simon and someone dropped out of the horse, so I – dropped in.'

He gave a short laugh. 'Very entertaining.' The soup had arrived and Nigel began to eat, talking between mouthfuls. 'Of course, I miss being on stage. I find it most satisfying, amateur dramatics. My wife, as Mary was then, had no spark of creativity – she didn't encourage me, but there were plenty of leading ladies who did.' He glanced at the waiter, who was pouring red wine, and lifted his glass. 'And now here we are, you and I together. To you, Val, and to an evening of new discoveries.'

Val was puzzled. 'So where is Mary now?'

'Who knows?' Nigel sipped wine and slurped soup. 'We're happier apart.' He turned his gaze fully on Val. 'So, let's talk about you. I want to know everything. You live in Lowenstowe, don't you, all by yourself?'

'Yes... in a little terrace surrounded by neighbours.' Val felt panic rise. 'It was my neighbour who gave me a lift here today.'

'I'd have gladly brought you in the Audi.' Nigel reached over, leaving his palm resting on her fingers. 'I'd have liked that. You only had to ask.'

'Ah.' Val stared at his hand on hers. She had no idea what to talk about.

Nigel took over, his eyes sweeping over her. 'I've been looking forward to our date. I must say, I do like you in the dress you're wearing. Very fetching. I prefer a woman in a dress, something clinging, feminine. I can't abide women who wear shapeless clothes. Imagine the sort of woman who'd wear dungarees. Hideous. A woman should always look like a woman, and dress to please the eye.'

Val slid her hand away as subtly as she could and grabbed her spoon. 'So, are you still a financial... analyst?'

'Retired – but I dabble. Dougie Fraser, you know, from Burns Night, asked me for some shrewd advice. That's why I was there. Nice man. Very nice wife too.' Nigel was thoughtful for a moment, his eyes glazed, then he said, 'And what about you, Val? What do you do for pleasure?'

'I walk on the beach.' Val immediately regretted her words – Nigel would know where to seek her out – so she added, 'I cook... I paint a little...'

'The pretty flower you painted on the pebble...' Nigel's eyes twinkled. 'With your email address inside the box. That was such a clever ruse to get my attention. And it worked so well, and now here we are.'

'Oh, I don't usually go round handing out favour boxes,' Val protested, putting her spoon down. Her appetite had disappeared, but Nigel's bowl was empty and his eyes were appraising her again.

'Well, I'm delighted you offered your favours to me.' Nigel arched an eyebrow. 'I do enjoy the company of attractive women. I'm glad you agreed to dinner this evening, and then, afterwards, Plymouth is our oyster.'

Val felt clearly out of practice at dating. Nigel was pleasant and attentive but she was fairly sure that, beneath the charm, Mr February was exhibiting all the signs of someone who believed he was the perfect seducer of women. She studied him as he spoke effortlessly to the waiter, winking in her direction, saying that he had an appetite this evening, demanding his steak was cooked medium rare before he turned back to her with a charming smile, his brow arched in question. 'Now, where were we, Val? Oh yes – dinner, a naughty dessert to get us in the mood, the opera, and then... Who knows what lies ahead? The night is still young.'

Val breathed out slowly: Nigel might be sophisticated, cultured, but he was definitely never going to be Mr December.

* * *

The Magic Flute was superb. Val enjoyed it immensely and the performance had flown by. Now she stood on the steps of the theatre facing an attentive Nigel and muttered, 'Thanks for this evening.'

'I do hope you had a good time, Val.'

'Oh, I did.'

She walked across paving slabs and past a bronze statue towards the road, then Nigel placed a heavy arm around her shoulders. 'The Mozart was very enjoyable, a rousing performance.'

'Indeed.' Val shivered, glancing around, hoping to see a white

Fiesta. It was at least ten twenty-five – Connie would arrive at any moment.

'I must say...' Nigel grumbled '... it's a shame you have to be whisked off so soon, back to Lowenstowe.'

Val said, 'It's a long drive home.'

'But there are some good hotels locally. We could still make a weekend of it.'

'A weekend?' Val gasped.

'Oh, there's so much to do; we could get to know one another better.' He arched an eyebrow again – it seemed to be his signature gesture, saying one thing while suggesting another. 'What if you don't go just yet, Val? What if we find a nice room in a plush hotel? I know a very sumptuous place...'

'Oh, well, I promised...' Val glanced over her shoulder at the passing cars, hoping to see Connie.

'We could have a nightcap in a little bistro somewhere. Or we might simply choose to stay in our room and get acquainted over champagne...'

Val inhaled sharply. 'My friend should be here any minute.' She held her breath as he wrapped the other arm around her, stepping closer.

'You could pack her off home and stay here?'

Val took a step back. 'I really ought...'

'Val, it's been a most wonderful evening.' Nigel's voice had become a low murmur and his lips were approaching, his eyes closed in anticipation. She felt the soft connection, his mouth squashing hers, and her body tensed. Then, from behind her, there was the sound of wheels against tarmac and the single hoot of a horn. Val pulled back, grateful.

'Oh, there's my lift now. I – I'd better go – she can't really stop here... yellow lines...'

'Of course.'

'Thanks again...' Val was already on her way towards the white Fiesta, tugging the passenger door open. 'Goodnight, Nigel.'

She breathed out a sigh of relief as Connie eased the car into traffic, twisting to glimpse Nigel on the steps, outside the theatre. He was already walking away. Connie's voice was low. 'Well? Did you have a good time?'

'The opera was great.'

'And Nigel?' Connie raised an eyebrow. 'Was he great too?'

'Very charming, but I'm not so sure if we're suited.' Val pushed his suggestion of a night in a hotel to the back of her mind. She turned cheerily to Connie. 'How was the spa? Dinner?'

'Heavenly.' Connie approached a road island, selecting a lane, overtaking another driver cautiously. 'So, is a second date on the horizon?'

'I don't think so, no.' Val thought for a moment. 'I think he's looking for someone who – isn't me.'

Val smiled. It didn't matter that Nigel wasn't her type – she had managed to get through the date in one piece; she'd practised the art of conversation and successfully negotiated the obvious pitfalls of a man who believed he was an irresistible love god. She'd taken the first step on the road to recovery. That was a result, as far as she was concerned.

Connie hummed to herself, then she murmured, 'Ah, so we'd better concentrate on the karaoke, then?'

'Yes, I'd better start practising,' Val said.

She imagined Nigel slobbering in a hotel suite, then she imagined bawling 'I Will Survive' in a spotlight while the audience ignored her and slurped into their pints. Moving past Ray was always going to come at a price.

10

Val knocked at the door of Cloud Cottage and heard energetic barking coming from the hall. She could hear Alice shrieking, 'Dolly, get down.' The door was pushed ajar and Alice's smiling face appeared in the gap as she struggled to hold Dolly back with her thigh. 'Val. Hi. Do you want to come in for coffee?'

Dolly pushed a flat nose out and Alice made a desperate grasp for her collar. Val grinned. 'I just wondered if you had anything I can borrow to wear for the karaoke? I've got to find a fancy dress.'

Alice leaned forward. 'What are you singing?'

'Connie's got me doing "It's Raining Men".' Val was unimpressed. 'I'm going to be carrying an open umbrella. Unlucky for everyone. I'm not looking forward to it at all.'

Alice and Dolly wrestled in the doorway. 'What about a leopard-print pants suit?'

'Oh?' Val was suddenly interested. 'Do you have one of those?'

'No, but – down, Dolly! So, yesterday I put this outfit in the PDSA window. It's grotesque, a silky thing; it's about a fiver, not much more. Why don't you pop in and get it? It would make a fun costume.'

'Is the shop open?'

'Someone will be there until four so – yep, you've got an hour.'

Dolly lurched towards Val, who put a hand out and rubbed the protruding nose. 'The PDSA is Fore Street, isn't it?'

'That's right.' Alice held Dolly by the collar, muttering, 'Calm down – Daddy will be home soon.' She winked at Val. 'Dolly thinks Kev should be here by now – she misses him, bless her. We both do. I always watch the clock when he's away. He's not back until after six today.'

'Bless.' Val patted the dog again, fondling soft ears. 'Okay – well, I'd better get myself down to the PDSA and buy the latest look in leopard.'

'Come for a cuppa soon.' Alice almost fell over as Dolly bolted for the opening in the door. 'If not, we'll catch up at the karaoke.' She crouched next to the Staffy, who licked her hand. 'We're Elton John and Kiki Dee, singing "Don't Go Breaking My Heart". We wanted to be Sonny and Cher but someone's taken that one already.'

'Great choice.' Val was full of enthusiasm. 'It'll be an interesting night – I sing like a grizzly bear.'

'So does Kev,' Alice replied. 'I'm just making his tea.' She lowered her voice, almost mouthing the words. 'It's sausages, but I can't say that too loudly in front of Dolly. They're her favourites...'

The dog barked once and Val said, 'Okay, I'll be off now. I hope nobody's bought the silky leopard – it has my name written on it. Right – enjoy the sausages. Oh – sorry!'

Dolly yapped loudly and leapt up frantically, tongue hanging out. Alice hoisted her back, closing the door with a snap. Val tugged her car keys from her pocket. She was off to buy a costume.

* * *

There were a few shoppers shuffling around Lowenstowe but the town was almost deserted. Two main streets intersected, a chilly sea breeze funnelling down High Street and Fore Street, a majestic Victorian hotel perched on the corner next to busy traffic lights. There was an assortment of old and new buildings: an eighteenth-century workhouse was now a trendy pub; a brick-built bank had become a pizzeria, and there were half a dozen charity shops. A new square-shaped building set back from the road behind the hotel housed several offices for local businesses, a vet, an accountant, a trendy barber's shop. Several other shops were empty, To Let signs in the whitewashed windows. In the town centre, a bench outside the fish and chip shop, The Tasty Plaice, marked the spot where residents loitered for a chat and a man in a heavy coat sold *The Big Issue.*

The PDSA charity shop was easy to spot in Fore Street, with its bright slogans and a huge banner asking for donations. Val peered in the window and saw the leopard-print pants suit. It was a zipped-up onesie in yellow and brown, worn by a headless mannequin. The price was marked as ten pounds but the garment was perfect and the money was for charity: Val was delighted. She stepped inside, weaving past racks of clothing and rows of plates, cups and teapots, approaching the counter where a woman was standing next to the till, her head down.

Val said, 'Good afternoon...'

The woman replied immediately without raising her eyes. 'I'm doing sums. I'll be with you dreckly...'

Val waited, watching the woman, whose shoulders and neck were bent forwards as she pressed a pen into paper, writing down a number. Her white hair was wound around her head in two thin plaits, loose strands escaping at the back of her neck. She stared at Val. 'I always add up on paper. I can't be dealing with bleddy calculators. Every time I press the buttons, the wrong thing always comes up.'

Val tried again. 'Can I see the leopard-print pants suit in the window?'

The woman frowned, a deep indentation in her brow. 'What on earth do you want with that?'

'It's for karaoke...' Val began, then she smiled broadly. 'I recognise you. You were down at the beach picking up litter.'

The woman put her pencil down. 'That's right, that would be me.' She scrutinised Val. 'I don't recall meeting you.'

'I was walking a dog.' Val shrugged apologetically. 'You advised me to bring newspaper...'

The woman gave a wide smile of recognition 'Oh, yes – I remember.'

Val held out a hand. 'I'm Val. I'm Alice's new neighbour.'

The woman didn't move. 'Alice?'

'Alice Holmes. She volunteers here on a Friday.'

'Oh, that Alice.' The woman nodded, as if she knew many Alices. Then she said, 'Loveday Moon.'

'Pardon?' Val was confused.

'I'm Loveday Moon.' The woman arranged her face in an expression that might have been a smile. 'I manage this place, in between picking up all the litter on the beach and lobbying our town councillor. Pleased to meet you again. Are you new to the area?'

'Yes, I arrived at Christmas time.' Val remembered the leopard pants suit and tried again. 'So, Loveday, I wonder if I could buy...'

'We need all sorts of donations for this place – quality stuff that will sell. Anything that is in good condition and can find a new home where it can be loved...'

'So, the leopard—'

'We sell most things here. We need more coats, toys and bric-a-brac at the moment. You could volunteer to help out too; we always need someone on the till – this place gets very busy most days.' Loveday eyed Val inquiringly. 'You wouldn't believe how hard it is to drum up any support. Cornwall is such a beautiful place, but it's neglected and there's so much that needs changing. I write to my councillor about the rubbish on the beaches and our MP about the big stuff, you know, overfishing, global warming, but I wish more people would get on board.' She folded her arms. 'To tell the truth, I'm properly grateful for any help at all.' She paused for breath and then patted Val's arm, a gesture of warmth. 'What did you come in for?'

Val was sheepish. 'The leopard-print pants suit.'

'Oh, yes, you said...' Loveday smiled broadly. 'I don't know why anyone would want to buy that floozy costume. Anyway, it's all for charity. Wait there – I'll just go and get it.'

* * *

Val was wearing the leopard pants onesie beneath a raincoat, carrying a folded umbrella that she intended to put up and hide behind during her performance. Connie wore a fringed dress, a warm jacket on top, already practising, trilling lines from Elvis's 'Can't Help Falling in Love' as they stood together, arm in arm, in the function room of The Boat House inn. The pub was already crowded, music blaring from huge speakers. Val stared at the microphone on its tall stand in the centre of the empty stage, ominously ready for each act. Above was a banner that proclaimed The Boat House Valentine Karaoke surrounded by red hearts, and the stage glittered with twinkling lights. Val groaned inwardly. Connie was staring around at the crowd. 'I don't think he's here,' she said.

'Who?'

'Mr January.'

Val wasn't sure if she wanted him there to hear her sing. 'Maybe his dog wasn't allowed in...'

Connie grinned. 'Oh, there's Alice.'

Alice pushed through the throng of drinkers. She was dressed in pink dungarees and a brown wig. She hugged Connie and Val. 'Kev's at the bar, getting the drinks. Dutch courage. We're on first.'

'How's the rehearsal going?' Val asked.

'Badly. Kev's rubbish at remembering the words and he keeps doing my bit by mistake. I was hoping this would be something fun to do together – we don't go out enough. Kev likes to sit on the sofa and relax after work, but I hoped he'd enjoy coming out with me.' Alice pulled a resigned face. 'It'll be okay – it will give the audience a good laugh.'

Kevin arrived wearing a checked jacket and oversized glasses, but that was where the resemblance to Elton John ended. Globules of sweat studded his forehead. He swigged from a pint of lager before handing a glass of wine to Alice. He was visibly nervous. 'Here, Kiki, get your laughing gear around this – Dave says we're on in a minute.'

'Oh, right.' Alice reached for the glass, gulping a mouthful.

'Well, good luck,' Val said amiably. 'We'd better get drinks and then we'll give you some moral support.'

'Oh – we'll be terrible.' Alice grimaced.

'We've only practised twice. Dolly joined in,' Kevin grumbled. 'She sings better than I do.'

Val and Connie left them rehearsing lines and pushed their way to the bar. Dave, the landlord, was dressed in an orange and black striped shirt; he and another young man who wore denims and a wig, long sideburns glued to his cheeks, were busy serving customers. Dave raised an eyebrow, indicating that he'd be with her in a moment, and Val turned to Connie, speaking loudly over the noise. 'Shall we have fruit juice?'

'Oh, yes,' Connie agreed. 'I need to be sober to sing.'

'And I won't be any better with the benefit of alcohol,' Val said ruefully. 'I might *think* I'm better, but there's no point fooling myself.'

'You'll be fine.' Connie met her eyes. 'Remember there may be someone special watching.'

Val spluttered. 'I can't see myself winning any admirers.'

'What about Mr February?'

'What about him?'

'Have you agreed to another date?'

Val shook her head. 'He hasn't emailed me. I didn't pass the first-date test.'

Then Dave was calling from across the bar. 'Val, Connie, I'll be with you dreckly.' He scratched his head. 'We're packed out tonight. We invited a lot of other local pubs to join in – The Bear from Curmouth, The Salmon and Sprat and The Globe from Merrynporth, The Prince William from town, and I've got a fill-in barman helping, but he's off to do Shakin' Stevens in a minute. Jackie isn't well. We were going to duet.'

'Sorry to hear she's unwell,' Connie offered.

'We were going to sing "Wild Thing", The Troggs.' Dave came across to serve them. 'The only wild thing about poor Jackie is the state of her tummy. She's stuck in the bathroom with awful—'

'Oh, poor Jackie,' Val said quickly. She noticed Dave staring at her costume.

'That's leopard print, isn't it?'

'Oh, this? It isn't mine.' Val indicated the pants suit beneath her raincoat. 'I mean, I got it in a charity shop.'

'It's perfect.' Dave's face had lit up.

'Perfect?' Val wasn't sure if Dave wanted to borrow it.

He put on his most pleading expression. 'Val – do "Wild Thing" with me. It's a great duet. We'd be hot stuff.' He indicated his orange shirt in a tiger print, then he tugged on a long wig and raised his hands, bending his fingers as claws. 'Grrrrrrr!'

'Instead of "It's Raining Men"?' Val was inspired. She had already made her mind up. 'You're on. That will be much more fun – and I can just shout the words.'

'Won't you need to rehearse? Jackie always needs lots of practice.' Dave was concerned.

'Oh, no – I'll just throw myself in at the deep end. I'll be fine.'

Val's bravado seemed to cheer Dave up. 'Right, Val, Connie – drinks on the house.'

'Just orange juice, please,' Connie said. '"Wild Thing" will be great, Val – it's such a sexy song.'

'I'll wing it.' Val grinned.

'I love the chance to get up on stage and show off,' Dave agreed, already pouring juice into glasses.

Then a voice came from behind Connie. 'Why not put a gin in those glasses, Dave? On me.'

Val recognised Dennis Cargill from in the snug on New Year's Day. She took in his expensive overcoat, the beads of perspiration on his face. Dave's eyes flickered towards Val, waiting for her reply.

'Thanks,' Val said politely. 'We're just drinking fruit juice.'

Dennis patted Connie's arm. 'Then may I buy those?'

'Oh, please don't worry,' Connie replied.

Dennis asked, 'Are you karaoke-ing this evening, my dear?'

'I am,' Connie said.

Val leaned forward. 'Are you singing, Dennis?'

His eyes rested on Val for a moment. 'Oh, I thought about doing "I Will Always Love You". That was our favourite song.' Dennis's mouth turned down sadly. 'I've been meaning to say – last time we met, I was a little the worse for wear.' He gave a little cough. 'I was worried that I might have offended you.'

'Oh, please don't think that,' Connie said anxiously.

He ran a hand over his hair. 'I do apologise, Connie.'

Dave leaned over to her. 'I'll catch up with you soon, Val – we're not on yet.'

'Scotch for me, Dave,' Dennis said smoothly, before turning his attention back to Connie. 'Please – let me buy you something? Two more orange juices, Dave. I – I need some friendly company more than ever this evening.'

Dennis took the whisky glass that Dave was offering and held out a twenty-pound note. Dave brought two more bottles of juice, filling their glasses to the brim.

'Thanks – that's really kind, but we're going to support our neighbours in the karaoke,' Val explained. 'Maybe we'll catch up later?'

'I hope so,' Dennis muttered sadly. 'I always find women are such good listeners. My friends at the bar just want to laugh and joke...'

Val and Connie moved through the crowds back towards the stage. Alice and Kevin had just taken their places in front of the microphone. She whispered to Connie, 'He has a broken heart.'

'I feel so sorry for him,' Connie said.

'And he looks to you for sympathy,' Val agreed. The opening bars of 'Don't Go Breaking My Heart' blared loudly; she squeezed Connie's arm. 'Come on – let's enjoy ourselves. You can sing your favourite song and I can show off on stage with Dave – it will be brilliant fun.'

'You're right. Alice is on now – let's go and give her some support.'

Alice and Kevin had thrown themselves into the song, arms around each other, knees wiggling, channelling their best Elton

and Kiki. Kevin had already made several mistakes, bawling out
Alice's lines, forgetting his own. Alice was laughing uncontrollably
as the background music boomed, Kevin jumping up and down,
missing his cue. Somehow, they managed to reach the end of the
song, Alice wiping away tears of amusement. They clambered down
from the stage, Kevin grunting into the microphone, 'I'm going to
the bar now, Alice. I need a bloody drink after that embarrassment.'

Alice arrived, her face flushed. 'Thank goodness that's over.' She
was breathless. 'Well, do you think we've set the standard for the
evening?'

'Definitely.' Val hugged her warmly.

'We should have sung Sonny and Cher. The next couple on are
doing it.'

Val glanced towards the stage. A woman wearing a furry gilet
top, boots and a long black wig had taken her place next to the
microphone. A man had joined her, wearing hippy fashions from
the sixties, a wig with a long fringe and sunglasses obscuring his
face.

The couple held hands and began to sway as the opening notes
boomed and they launched into the song, their eyes glued on each
other, completely besotted.

Alice pointed. 'Their costumes are perfect. And he's got a really
good voice. They'll make us look rubbish, Kev.'

Kevin shrugged. 'We should've stayed at home.'

Val watched as the couple gazed rapturously at each other,
crooning 'I Got You Babe'. Sonny wrapped his arm around Cher,
who batted her long eyelashes and snuggled closer. Val was frozen
to the spot watching, her heart thumping, listening to Sonny's sweet
voice. He sounded exactly like Cat Stevens. Dave had said he'd
invited singers from local pubs; he'd distinctly mentioned The
Sprat in Merrynporth. Despite the wig and sunglasses and hippy
costume, she would have recognised Sonny anywhere: she had

been married to him for forty-seven years. She knew the voice almost as well as she knew her own. It was Ray, who'd always sing at any opportunity, and now he was singing his heart out to Monica. Tears brimmed in her eyes. She couldn't believe Ray and Monica were here in Lowenstowe, let alone together on stage in front of her, proclaiming their love to the world.

11

For the next hour Val smiled so much that her cheeks ached. She chatted animatedly to Connie, gabbled to Kevin and Alice hoping that Ray wouldn't notice her or, if he did, she'd appear to be enjoying herself and not shrivelling up inside. She was unsure if Ray would come over to talk to her, especially with Monica in tow, so she just needed to keep up the act until the end of the evening. Connie took her turn to sing, standing quietly in a spotlight, whispering in a tiny voice, 'This song is for Mike.' Modest and unassuming, she performed such an emotional version of 'Can't Help Falling in Love' that Val's eyes gleamed with tears. She noticed Dennis watching from the bar, a glass in his hand.

But Ray was nowhere to be seen. Sonny and Cher were easy to recognise. Val hoped they'd gone home. Connie rushed back excitedly just as Dave arrived in the wig and the tiger shirt, handing them more glasses of orange juice.

He grinned broadly. 'These are from me to whet your whistles, with thanks from Jackie. She's so glad I have someone to sing with. She'd just come out of the loo again, bless her.'

'I hope she'll feel much better soon.' Connie took the glass.

'We're on in a minute.' Dave met Val's eyes; he was suddenly hyperactive.

'We'll be great.' She patted his arm in a calming gesture. 'It's a good audience – the place is packed.'

Dave said nervously, 'That's what I'm worried about.'

Connie hugged Val. 'Go on, enjoy yourself. You look a million dollars in that crazy leopard suit – you'll knock 'em all dead.' She leaned closer and whispered, 'I can't see Mr January though.'

Val marched forward, tugging Dave's arm, staring around, hoping she wouldn't bump into Ray and Monica, but they had disappeared. She clambered on stage, knowing that all eyes were turned in her direction. She ruffled her hair so that it was messy then she struck a pose, a wild animal with unsheathed claws, Dave leaning towards her, his paws raised. The first raunchy guitar notes rang out and Val imagined Ray in the audience, his eyes on her. She was immediately filled with new energy, sass; she would perform as if she didn't care less that he was there. Her nose in the air, Val threw herself into the song.

The audience cheered and applauded as she pranced around, arms above her head, turning to bawl the words at Dave, leaning towards him defiantly and then strutting away as he followed her on his knees. The tinny guitar rattled as Val purred into the microphone, then raised her voice to a howl as she sashayed away. Dave crawled after her on all fours, relishing his rampant animal character far too much.

Val was hamming up the role of a wild thing as Dave threw himself across the stage, growling and gurning. Then the song finished and Val held a final pose in the spotlight, an arm around Dave, nose to nose. The crowd clapped and hooted as Val stepped towards the edge of the stage, ready to climb down. It was then that she saw Ray. He was still wearing the wig and the hippy clothes but he had taken off the sunglasses and he was staring at her. Monica was oblivious, a drink in her hand, chattering to him, but Ray simply stood watching her. Val's heart thumped again. Dave took her hand, helping her down from the stage, and wiped a hand across his brow. 'Phew. I enjoyed that.' He was clearly pleased with himself. 'I think we were pretty good, Val.'

Val caught her breath, turning her back to Ray. 'We were astonishing.'

He beamed. 'How about a glass of bubbly for you and Connie, to say thanks? I've got some Prosecco on ice.'

Val was delighted. 'Just one glass would be great. I'm dying of thirst.'

'I'll just pop behind the bar...'

Then Dave was gone and Val looked around for Ray again. Monica had reclaimed his attention and they were talking, then he caught her eye and she quickly glanced away.

Connie was by her side. 'You were amazing, Val. And you did all that without rehearsing.'

'I've always been a bit of a show-off, so it came naturally,' Val said, wondering if Ray was still watching her. 'Dave's bringing Prosecco. I think he enjoyed himself.'

'He was in his element,' Connie agreed. 'Alice and Kevin have gone home – they want to get back for Dolly. It's past ten already.'

Val was keen to leave. 'We should go too, when we've had Dave's drink.'

'Mr January didn't come to watch. He'd have definitely fallen in love with you after seeing you perform.' Connie seemed disappointed.

Val exhaled. Ray and Monica were here in The Boat House, in her safe space, invading her thoughts. She suddenly made up her mind. 'I might find a new person to date in March, Connie. And I haven't given up on the gorgeous Mr January.'

Connie was delighted. 'This is going to be such a good year.'

Val needed distraction from the image of the loved-up Sonny and Cher; she hoped desperately that Connie's project would help her to recover. Then there was a voice at her elbow. 'I've brought your Prosecco, ladies.'

Dennis held up a bottle, twisting the cork, filling glasses. Val looked around. 'That's kind of you, Dennis. Where's Dave?'

'There was a rush at the bar, people congratulating him on his performance, so I offered to bring the bubbly. I'm not having the best of evenings. One or two of the songs have got to me a bit.' He handed her a glass and then pushed one into Connie's hand. 'I thought you sang the Elvis song beautifully, Connie.'

Connie sipped bubbles. 'Thank you.'

'A song can break your heart into a thousand pieces.' Dennis had tears in his eyes. 'Yes, I need cheering up now. I shouldn't have come to the karaoke. I think I'll have a drink with you and go home.'

Connie patted his arm. 'I'm sure there's someone out there for you.'

'There was, once. And now there isn't. She's moved on. That's the problem.' Dennis sniffed sadly, lifting the bottle to his lips and taking a deep swig.

'I'm sorry to hear that,' Val said sympathetically. She glanced over his shoulder and saw Ray turn in her direction. He raised his eyebrows in a gesture of recognition as if he might come over to speak to her and Val's knees buckled. It was time to leave. She took a final gulp of her Prosecco and whispered, 'Shall we go?'

Connie nodded cheerfully and they shuffled towards the door. Val called back over her shoulder. 'Thanks for the drink, Dennis. Take care.'

'You too... 'til next time,' Dennis said sadly. He raised the bottle and guzzled again, then he ambled away.

Val steered Connie towards the exit, and they stepped out into the cold air. Connie exhaled. 'Well, that was an interesting night.'

'It was,' Val agreed, but she was still thinking about Ray, shivering with shock and cold. 'Come on, Connie, it's chilly. Let's go home, shall we?'

'Yes, let's. You didn't want more Prosecco?'

'No...' Val was feeling relieved that Ray didn't have the chance to speak to her.

Connie sighed. 'Poor Dennis, all alone and sad. I often feel like that when I'm by myself.' She turned to Val. 'How do you cope with the loneliness?'

'I have you as my friend,' Val replied with a determined smile.

Connie's eyes shone. 'My life's so much better now you're here. I can't begin to tell you.'

Val and Connie strode briskly away from the bright lights of The Boat House inn, towards the shadows, past cottages in darkness, and an empty holiday cottage with an overgrown garden. The wind blew in from the sea and the moon hung low in a starless sky. They walked on, arms linked, through the streets, not saying a word, lost in their own thoughts until they reached their own little row of cottages. Val hugged Connie and they whispered a brief goodnight, promising to catch up for a chat soon. Then they parted and moved to opposite sides of the road, unlocking their doors and disappearing into the warmth of their own homes.

* * *

Above, the living-room curtains of Crab Claw Cottage twitched, although there was only a dim light inside. A man peered out as the women spoke in the street and he listened until he heard two doors shut with a crisp clunk. Then he let the curtain fall from his weathered hand and disappeared back into shadows, a smile on his face. Ben Berry hovered next to the radio, listening to the shipping forecast for a moment, then he turned it off and picked up his empty plate and mug from the table. He walked softly into the kitchen, washing the crockery beneath running water, glancing at the clock. His neighbours had been out for the evening and they were safely home; he could go to bed now. He was tired. It had been a long day.

* * *

Val opened her eyes to gaze into darkness. Rain was hammering against the window panes. It was 4:15; she ought to roll over and try to sleep but her mind was a beehive of thoughts. She was suddenly back in the function room of The Boat House inn dressed in the leopard pants suit. She recalled the exact moment when Ray turned from the chattering Monica and their eyes met, how it felt like an electric shock to the heart.

She swung out of bed and pushed her feet into slippers, reaching for a dressing gown. Padding down the stairs into the kitchen, she filled the kettle and flipped a switch, listening to the comforting hum of water boiling, pouring steaming water onto a teabag, taking the cup to the kitchen table. She sat down to think.

Val wanted to believe she was over Ray. He'd made his choice; he wasn't the same man she'd fallen in love with. She told herself she didn't care about Sonny and Cher crooning to each other but her eyes filled with tears at the memory. She sipped her tea, breathing deeply. Surely Ray hadn't planned the evening knowing he'd see her in The Boat House. Surely he hadn't come to gloat. Val doubted it. He'd just responded to an opportunity to sing. Dave had told her that several local pubs had been invited, including The Sprat. It had been a coincidence. Ray might have said once that Monica was originally from Lowenstowe; he knew Val lived there. Cornwall was a hive of close communities. It was always likely that their paths would cross at some point.

But the same thought kept buzzing: Val should have been able to stroll over to Ray, kiss his cheek lightly and purr, 'Ray, Monica, how are you? You sang so well...' After almost fifty years of familiarity, she should have been able to talk to him. But she couldn't even mention his presence to Connie, whom she trusted. Val had felt uncomfortable during the entire evening. The thought made her shiver; she was still in love with him.

Val sipped tea to calm herself. Ray was Tom's father, that would never change but she had a new life now, a new home, new friends. The Sonny and Cher incident was a mere setback. She breathed steam from the cup and felt slightly better. She'd go back to bed, snuggle into the warmth and sleep for a few more hours. She wouldn't let the events of one single evening worry her. Then the image of Tom's wedding photos came back to her, Tom and Lottie smiling, Ray and Monica on one side, their arms around each other, and on the other side Val, alone in stiff new clothes, glaring at the camera. The sensation of loneliness took her breath away.

The dregs at the bottom of her cup were cold and she sat up, suddenly alert. Val's mind was made up now. She'd be proud to go to the wedding, Tom's mother, Lottie's mother-in-law, cheerfully alone. She didn't need a partner to balance the picture. She'd do it by herself.

Val rinsed the cup under running water. The feeling of hurt was still very much with her, but tomorrow she'd tell Connie that the search for Mr December was over. It had just been a bit of fun, a moment's silliness, nothing more.

Val raised her hands above her head in a long stretch, then she flicked off the kitchen light and made for the stairs. As she reached her bedroom, she was humming a tune. 'Wild Thing'. She was determined to be strong; in all honesty, she wasn't over Ray yet but, in time, things would improve. She could be whoever she wanted to be now.

MR MARCH

12

Val returned from her morning walk. It had been wild outside, the sea rough as broken glass. There was no one around, just whirling seagulls bent against the breeze and desolate stretches of pale sand. She stepped gratefully into the warmth of her cottage, pushing the front door closed against buffeting gusts that swirled dust into the hall. Val threw a log in the wood-burning stove and stood back, watching the flames flicker. She was about to warm some soup for lunch when she heard a crisp knock on the door. Connie was outside, smiling and shivering, holding out a package wrapped in brown paper. 'I made sourdough bread, Val. I brought you some.'

'Come in.' Val held the door wide. 'It will go with the soup I just made. Stay for lunch?'

Connie's cheeks glowed. 'I'd love to.'

Val led the way to the kitchen, heating the soup, waiting for Connie to start talking about happier days. It had become a regular part of their lunches, Val listening while Connie shared stories about Mike, about her son, how the weekly Zoom calls often left her feeling empty. Val was still unable to reminisce about Ray but she knew the reason too well. The feelings were still raw, scars unhealed.

Val filled two bowls with soup, cut bread into chunks and they sat down at the kitchen table. They ate in silence for a few minutes, then Connie murmured, 'Did you go to the beach this morning?'

Val nodded, her mouth full.

'Any sign of Mr January?'

'No,' Val said sadly. 'Not since the last time when we were singing Bob Dylan.'

Connie was thoughtful. 'It's a shame. He was nice.'

'Connie...' Val took a breath. 'I've made up my mind. I'm fine by myself. I don't need a date for Tom's wedding.'

'Are you sure?'

Val exhaled. 'I think so, yes.'

'It was such fun, planning, dreaming...' Connie said apologetically. 'I loved how we had a project together.'

'There's still lots we can do.' Val was full of enthusiasm. 'We can go out for day trips. And I've thought I might volunteer at the PDSA, just one day a week. I'm sure they need people. Loveday Moon is quite a character.'

'Who?' Connie asked.

'The woman who runs the shop, the one who cleans up the beach.'

'Oh...' Connie was thoughtful. 'Perhaps you'll meet someone in the shop.'

Val rolled her eyes good-humouredly. 'Maybe I will – who knows?'

'What about Mr February?'

Val picked at a piece of bread. 'I haven't heard from him.'

'That's such a shame.'

'Oh, not at all. I enjoyed the opera, and the date was a one-off experience...' Val said, remembering.

Connie was staring out of the window into the small garden. The sky had darkened to a deep shade of indigo, low brooding clouds overhead. 'I think it might rain.'

Val stood up, pushing back her chair. 'Right, I'll make a cup of tea, we'll take it into the lounge and you can tell me all about Will and his kids and I'll update you about Tom's wedding plans. He rang yesterday. It's all getting very exciting.'

Connie met her gaze. 'But you'll have no guest…'

'I'll have me, Connie. That's all I need.' She glanced over her shoulder as she filled the kettle. 'Peppermint or blackcurrant?'

'Oh, blackcurrant, please,' Connie said. 'That would be lovely. And you can tell me what you're going to wear in the icy Canadian winter for Tom's wedding.' She met Val's eyes sadly. 'After all, you can wear what you like now – you won't have to worry about matching someone else…'

* * *

Later that afternoon, Val called into the PDSA shop. It was fairly quiet, just one lone shopper, a woman in a thin coat trying on a pair of heavy boots. Loveday Moon sat behind a screen, bending over the counter. As Val approached her, she spoke without looking up. 'I'm sorting out prices. I'll be with you dreckly.'

'I thought I might volunteer…'

'Hang on a sec.' Loveday wrote the number five down slowly and a pound sign, then gazed up. 'Oh, I know you. You've been in here before.' Her eyes sparkled with recognition as she mumbled, 'Leopard-print floozy suit.'

'That's me.' Val grinned.

'Great to see you again.' Loveday resumed her pricing. 'Thursdays, ten 'til three.'

'Pardon?' Val wasn't sure if Loveday was still pricing items.

Then she smiled. 'You can do Thursdays with me. I'm on my own: you can start at ten. Don't be late.'

'Oh, right.' Val was quite pleased with the outcome. 'I'll see you then.'

'Indeed. It'll be lovely to see you. You're all right, you are, Valerie. You're not bad at all.' Loveday wrote down more prices on tags. 'Yes, I think you're all right.'

* * *

Val knew every corner of the stockroom at the back of the charity shop. For the last three weeks, she had sorted, folded and priced previously loved clothes, shoes and bric-a-brac. It was ten minutes to two as Val carried two steaming mugs of tea out to Loveday, who was in her usual position at the till. Loveday met her eyes. 'They'd better be proper leaves.'

Val nodded. 'Of course. I don't always use teabags.'

'I like tea leaves and a good sturdy pot,' Loveday said. She took the mug from Val and sipped gratefully. 'Ah, that's nice. Can't beat a cuppa. You can go on the till next week if you like.'

'Oh, that would be great.' Val meant it. 'Well, what can I do for the last ten minutes? Do you have anything that needs sorting?'

'You can keep me company. I've got biscuits in my bag – we'll have one or two of those.' Loveday raised her eyebrows. 'We can get to know each other.'

Val agreed. 'That would be nice.'

Loveday leaned back on her stool, gazing around. There were no customers in the shop. Val sat on the edge of the counter to rest her legs. 'It's quiet in here today.'

Val eased herself upright. Loveday coughed. 'So, you live by yourself, you said?'

'I do,' Val admitted.

'No husband, then?' Loveday delved into her bag behind the counter and offered a Hobnob from an open packet.

'Divorced,' Val said as she took a biscuit and then, noticing the intensely inquisitive stare, she added, 'He left me – he found someone else.'

'Oh, that must be hard for you.' Loveday moved her head as if calculating some difficult numbers. 'Lonely life, living alone, I suppose.'

'Not at all.' Val's voice was deliberately breezy. 'I love it.' She thought about her words for a moment. 'I do just as I please. There's no one else to think about but myself.'

'Selfish,' Loveday said, and Val wondered if she wasn't being a little harsh, then Loveday continued, biscuit in hand. 'It must be nice to be a bit selfish, not having to think of someone else all the time. Your ex-husband wasn't a great catch, I'm guessing? You're probably glad to be shot of him.'

'Ah, well.' Val's sigh was one of acceptance. She recalled the Christmas meal, the food on the table, the fiasco. 'I think we started off all right at the beginning when we were young, but after my son grew up and moved to Canada, we focused on all the wrong things. You know, we had a nice house, car... dinner service,' she added, reflecting on the Christmas table laid for two as the old painful feelings flooded back. 'But we'd forgotten about each other, I suppose.'

'Conversation, that's what really matters,' Loveday said. 'Sharing. Respect. Listening.'

'You're so right.' Val was surprised that she'd started to open up about her past. 'Are you married, Loveday?'

'My John can't get out much now. He was in the police force for years. He has a pension, thank goodness, or I don't know how we'd manage. I used to worry about him all the time, out on the beat, especially when Morwenna was little.' Loveday closed her eyes and when she opened them, her gaze was softer. 'But every evening now we spend time together, talking, listening, being in each other's company. That's love.' She sighed softly. 'That's what I'd miss most if I was alone...'

'Doesn't he mind you being here in the daytime?' Val asked.

'John and I met when we were youngsters. He knows everything about me, how I feel about what's happening to the planet, how I have to do everything I can to change what's wrong with it all while I'm still here.' She met Val's eyes. 'My John respects that.'

'It sounds like you have the perfect relationship,' Val said.

'We do.' Loveday's face crumpled into a frown. 'Those were the best days, when we were young and we could get outside, go down to the beach together, walking and talking and planning a future. Oh, I have wonderful memories. John and I were engaged before we were twenty. We had Morwenna, and we were such a happy little family. We'd go everywhere, the three of us – picnics, Morwenna playing in the sand, John laughing and joking and holding my hand. And even in those days we brought our rubbish home with us. You know, Valerie, John was such a big man, strong and powerful. But lately, he's not been so good. That's why I clean up the beach every week. For John. And for future generations, so that the kiddies will enjoy what we had.'

'I understand that,' Val said. 'Breakstone beach makes me feel happy.'

'You could still find someone. You're not past it yet.'

Val grinned in amusement. 'You sound just like Connie.'

'Who?'

'My neighbour, she's a good friend. She has tried to get me to go on a few dates.' Val smiled. 'She wants me to find a partner for my son's wedding in December. Ray, my ex, will be there with his. But I'll be okay alone.'

'You're a nice woman, Valerie.' Loveday was serious. 'I bet some chap would properly enjoy going to that wedding with you. Just imagine all those speeches, you sitting there by yourself and having no one to whisper comments about it all to.' Loveday rubbed her hands together. 'Get yourself a bloke.'

'Oh, there's no one out there for me now.'

'You're seeing it from the wrong bleddy angle. It's easy to get selfish when you're by yourself.' Loveday leaned forward. 'It's not just about what someone can give you. It's about what you can give back to someone else, someone who's lonely, who'd like a bit of what you could offer. You've got lots to give to someone.'

Val thought about Loveday's words and shook her head slowly, hoping tears wouldn't come.

Loveday laid a firm hand on her arm. 'Right. It's sorted.'

'What is?' Val said anxiously.

'Tomorrow, you turn up here at lunchtime, twelve thirty. I'll have someone ready to meet you.'

'A date?' Val was surprised. 'No, I don't think—'

'You don't need to think.' Loveday's eyes danced with mischief. 'Twelve thirty, my girl, and not a moment too late. It'll just be time well spent with someone who'll talk some sense into you. After all, there's more to meeting someone than thinking about whether it suits you or not.'

'But—'

'Twelve thirty.' Loveday's mind was made up; she was delighted with herself. 'Outside the shop. And don't you be late, mind. This chap is special.'

* * *

It was an icy cold day, the windows at Teasel Cottage stuck with frozen shards that glistened in the pale sunlight, when Connie knocked excitedly at the door. Val invited her to step into the warmth. Connie was all smiles. 'So, you have a date today?'

Val nodded. 'Loveday's arranging it. I've no idea who I'm meeting.'

Connie rubbed cold hands together. 'Are you going somewhere local? I wonder what Mr March will be like.'

'I've no idea,' Val said. 'That's the worst thing. It might be a lunchtime session playing bingo with a widower who wins a bucketful of cash and takes me out to all the pubs in Lowenstowe on a bender.' She laughed. 'Come to think of it, that might not be so bad...'

Connie took her arm. 'You clearly need your date coach to help you prepare.' She smiled, a moment of triumph. 'Right, let's decide what you're going to wear.'

By twelve thirty, Val was standing outside the charity shop in heels, hugging her best coat, her teeth chattering. She was a little nervous. She gazed through the shop window. Alice was inside on the till, talking to Loveday, and she met Val's eyes and waved an arm in greeting. Then Loveday glanced up, suddenly delighted; she marched over to the shop door. Val greeted her with a breezy smile.

'Hi, Loveday. I'm bang on time. But it really doesn't matter if—'

Loveday held up a finger. 'Ollie will be here any second.'

'Ollie?' Val was puzzled. 'Is he a friend of yours?'

'He's my grandson, my daughter Morwenna's boy,' Loveday said. 'He's taking you for some proper Cornish fish and chips.'

'Oh...'

'And make sure you're nice to him. He's a bit apprehensive about meeting you.' Loveday pressed Val's arm through the coat. 'He's a lovely young man. I've told him to give you the benefit of his wisdom. He's very clever.'

'I'm sure—'

'So I've told him to talk some sense into you. Ah, here's Ollie now.' Loveday waved towards the young man who was approaching, wearing a dark green parka jacket and new jeans. He was tall, lean and muscular, with cropped dark hair and a troubled expression on his face. Loveday beamed.

'Ollie, this is Valerie. She's meeting you for lunch.'

'Thanks, Grannie Loveday.' Ollie met Val's eyes and glanced down quickly, then he held out a hand. 'I'm very pleased to meet you. We're having fish and chips.'

Val looked towards Loveday for support, but she was on her way back inside the shop. She turned to Ollie, who was already on his way, so she rushed to keep in step.

Ollie chatted as he walked. 'We're off to The Tasty Plaice. Grannie Loveday gave me some money. She says it's important to be nice to you because you need cheering up. I'm quite reasonable at cheering people up. She says I should try to talk some sense into you because you don't always understand sense.' He pushed his hands deep into pockets. His face shone. 'I'm twenty-five, but Grannie Loveday says I'm wise for my years. She says there are older people with no common sense whatsoever but she likes you, and if she likes you then you must be all right. We'll have lots of interesting things to talk about. I've made a list.'

Val walked quickly. 'I'm looking forward to it.'

'That's good,' Ollie said. 'I'm not shy or nervous, although first meetings can be traumatic. My last girlfriend was called Lauren. She worked at Finest Choice. I have Asperger's syndrome, although it's called ASD now. That means that I have unusual social skills and obsessive interests. Lauren liked me but she moved away. I drew her portrait. It looked exactly like her, she said. I like drawing and painting. My favourite artist is Van Gogh. I like the colourful self-portraits he did. One day I'll be an artist, but for now I work in Finest Choice, in the office collating the money. I never make mistakes. I'm very good at maths.'

'I like painting too, and visiting galleries,' Val agreed. 'I especially like making brownies. My favourites are chocolate ones.'

Ollie licked his lips as they passed a parade of shops. 'Chocolate is my favourite too. I live with my mum. Sometimes she gets depressed because she's a bit lonely. I'm not usually depressed although when things get a bit much for me I have a meltdown, and that usually sorts me out. I make my mum a cup of tea and a biscuit and we have a chat when she's sad. I'm good at cheering people up. I read a lot and I never forget what I read so I'm quite good at conversation too, but being a listener is just as important. Well, we're nearly there now. Grannie Loveday said we have got to have a nice time.'

'And we certainly will.' As Val and Ollie crossed the road, she inhaled the rich aroma of frying. 'Right, Ollie – I'm starving.'

MR APRIL

13

It was perfect thinking weather and Val had a lot to reflect on after lunch with Mr March. Loveday had been right: Val had been seeing the possibility of meeting someone from the viewpoint of what she wanted, not what she could offer to someone else, and spending time with Ollie had helped her realise that friendship and shared laughter were what mattered most.

It was a blustery Saturday morning, the sky packed with rumpled clouds that were constantly buffeted along, shredding and reforming into new clusters. Beyond the beach, the sea was the colour of iron. The breeze cleared her head, pushing her forwards. Val had enjoyed lunch with Ollie, who had told her between mouthfuls how drawing and painting took every moment of his spare time and that his greatest ambition was to get married, buy a house and own a car. Val had done all that – she'd even confided in Ollie about Ray and Monica and the Christmas fiasco – and he'd told her philosophically that her ex was not a very compatible man and that she should make a list of her ambitions in life and tick them off, one by one.

As they'd left the café, Val had promised that she'd buy the chips next time. Ollie had held himself stiff as she'd hugged him and explained that even though she'd got the first husband wrong, she could still get it right the second time. Mistakes, he had told her wisely, were the path to learning and future success. After all, he had liked Lauren a lot, but he wasn't nervous about trying someone else, someone who'd be just perfect. Val wanted to tell him more about Ray, how she still felt rejected, even now. He'd have understood; he'd have said something wise and comforting. She was smiling as she walked along the beach. The brisk wind tousled her thoughts and she felt happy.

Her phone buzzed in her coat pocket. Val pulled it out and held it to her ear. 'Connie?'

'Are you on Breakstone beach?'

'Yes. It's lovely down here.'

'Can I come and join you?'

'Of course.' Val wished she'd called at Connie's house and invited her along. 'Are you all right?'

'Yes, I'm just a bit...' Val could hear Connie choosing the right word. 'I've spent too much time by myself indoors. I spoke to Will yesterday and I miss him.' Connie sighed. 'I could use some company to cheer me up.'

'Me too,' Val assured her. 'I've been a bit self-absorbed. Come down.'

'I'll see you in fifteen minutes.' Connie sounded happier already.

Val pushed her phone deep in her coat pocket. Loveday was right: she shouldn't lose sight of what she could offer to others. She scanned the beach, wondering if Loveday was somewhere in the distance picking up litter and if she could help. It occurred to Val that it might be a way to put something back, to show her appreciation for Cornwall, the county she called home. The beach was almost empty except for several joggers and a couple walking arm in arm. It was bitterly cold. Val assumed Loveday would be at home now, cooking dinner with John. She imagined them in a warm farmhouse-style kitchen, Loveday with her sleeves rolled to her elbows, peeling potatoes or skinning a rabbit, John in wellington boots pouring home-brewed beer into a heavy glass. Val was becoming fond of her. Loveday was a one-off, a real character; despite her brusque nature, her heart was in the right place.

Then she gazed into the distance and felt her heart lurch: it was definitely *him*. She recognised the brown coat, the brown fluffy dog by his side. Val caught her breath. She'd decided not to take a Mr December to Tom's wedding but it would do no harm to speak to Mr January. After all, they knew each other, almost: he had commented on the Bob Dylan songs. She took a deep breath as he strode towards her.

Val changed direction a little, moving closer to the sea so that their paths would cross. She imagined his eyes meeting hers, warm with recognition. He'd linger for a chat. Perhaps he would comment on how cold it was and invite her for a coffee, to a great little place not far from the beach that was dog-friendly and made the best lattes.

He was a few metres away, the Chow Chow trotting obediently on the end of a lead. Her heart bumped, despite her thinking that these new sensations were ridiculous. As they drew level he was gazing ahead, so she waved a hand and said, 'Hello. That's such a gorgeous dog you have there...'

He had no idea who she was. He half-smiled a 'Thank you,' and continued strolling. Then he was gone. The moment had passed; he hadn't remembered her. Val watched him walk away, feeling brushed aside, thinking gloomily that she should be used to being rebuffed by now. Mr January was the only contender for Tom's wedding. Daydreaming of him as a plus-one was nothing more than therapy; it somehow took away the sadness of Ray's rejection and his good looks made her feel sixteen again. His almost-smile was gorgeous and Val wondered if there could have been a moment of recognition, attraction even. She knew she was trying too hard to convince herself. But she wouldn't rule him out, not yet.

She sighed, a moment of resignation, then she gazed to her right and saw Connie rushing towards her over the soft sand. A tall man was behind her, burly in a thick coat. Val could see his mouth moving, then, in seconds, Connie was next to Val as Dennis Cargill caught up with her panting, his brow damp with perspiration. He muttered, 'Hello, Val,' then he turned his attention to Connie. 'I have been looking for you since the karaoke in The Boat House.'

'Nice to see you, Dennis.' Connie smiled. 'It's lovely out here in the fresh air.'

'Too fresh for me,' Dennis said. 'But I wanted to invite you to lunch. I need a guest for the annual business meal I'm attending.'

'I don't know...' Connie shrugged awkwardly. 'I don't do dates since I lost my husband.'

'And I lost my wife.' Dennis's expression was desperate. 'Please, don't say no.' He glanced briefly at Val. 'It will be a wonderful lunch. Everyone's going – even the man you were just talking to. He'll be there too.'

Val frowned. 'Who?'

'Timothy Keita. The man with the big dog. He's a client of mine.' He patted Connie's shoulder. 'Timothy is a local writer. I manage his accounts.' He screwed his eyes small against the wind. 'He lives in Lowenstowe. He'll certainly be at the dinner. Please say you'll be my guest, Connie. It would mean so much...'

'I'm not sure I can...' Connie gazed at Val for support.

'I can't be alone again this year,' Dennis said. 'Please, I need to take someone.'

'But...' Connie was searching for an excuse.

'I'll go,' Val said quickly. 'That's if you don't mind, Dennis.'

'Well...' Dennis seemed to notice Val properly. 'If Connie can't come then I'd be glad for you to be my guest.' He seemed happier. 'It's at The Unicorn Hotel, one o'clock on Saturday the sixteenth in the White Room.' He moistened his lips. 'They always do a good menu there. And it's a free bar.'

'Ah, Dennis... there's one thing.' Val took a breath, a little nervous. 'I'm pleased to be your plus-one – ah, it's not my business, I know but – can we do lunch and maybe have just one glass of wine? I mean, if there's a free bar, I'd rather you didn't... Oh, I'm sorry – is that rude of me?'

Dennis was suddenly self-conscious. 'I do understand. But a drink takes the memories away. Since my wife left, it's been so difficult...' He turned to Connie. 'We all have our crosses to bear, our broken hearts.'

'Just a nice lunch, a drink or two?' Val said. 'I'd really enjoy that.'

'Of course, yes, why not? Thanks, Val.' Dennis tried to smile. 'I'll look forward to it.' He turned away, his back to the sea, and slogged sadly towards the wall.

'That was kind of you.' Connie watched him. 'Poor man. Do you think I should have accepted?'

Val frowned. 'Not at all. I don't mind going. I know you don't want to.'

'Not after Mike. It wouldn't be right.' Connie's face crumpled. 'It was so sweet to say you'd go instead of me.'

'Meeting Dennis is a different sort of date. Maybe I'll learn something new, practise a different type of conversation.'

'Oh, Val!' A thought had occurred to Connie and she gasped with delight. 'What an opportunity. It's your big chance to talk to *him*.'

Val shook her head. 'I don't understand.'

'Not Dennis – to Mr January. He'll be there. Go to the lunch and meet the handsome man with the dog.' Connie was delighted.

Val was unsure. 'I can't do that. Dennis is lonely. I'm his guest. I'd hate to hurt his feelings. It wouldn't be fair to use him in order to talk to someone else.'

'You could sit in between them during lunch, cheer Dennis up, be your usual sparkly self and impress Mr January at the same time. I know you can do it.'

'But all the dating is off now. I don't need to find anyone for Tom's wedding.'

'It *was* off. But Timothy Keita though... he's gorgeous and he's an author. I wonder what he writes. Detective thrillers, mysteries, I bet.' Connie rolled her eyes. 'Did you speak to him? What did he say to you?'

Val shrugged. 'I told him that his dog was nice.' It was the truth; Val decided to omit the fact that he hadn't recognised her.

Connie was full of enthusiasm. 'So, think of the lunch on the sixteenth as a chance to take things to the next level. And Dennis has you as a lunch date. It will make him much happier.'

'Okay, why not?' Val said. 'I have to admit, Timothy is the first man I've found attractive in years. It's therapy: I'll give it a shot. But after the sixteenth we go back to no more dates, promise?'

'I promise,' Connie agreed, her cheeks glowing in the pummelling wind. She closed her eyes for a moment. 'I'm just imagining you and Timothy Keita in the wedding photo together, smiling ecstatically, he's holding your hand.'

Val laughed. 'I wouldn't say no.'

The two women turned to walk back home. Connie pushed her arm through Val's in an attempt to warm them both. She lowered her head against the powerful gusts that whipped sand into the air. 'Do you want to come in for a cup of tea?' Connie's eyes shone with delight. 'I have some new photos of my grandchildren.'

'Great. I'd love to see them,' Val replied. They turned the corner and the little row of cottages was in sight. Val could see Alice outside Cloud Cottage; Dolly was on the end of a lead, leaping energetically up at Alice's legs. Alice waved energetically and, as Val and Connie approached, she rushed towards them. 'I just knocked on your door, Val.'

'Why? Is everything all right?' Val put a hand out to pat Dolly.

'I've just come from the supermarket. I went to get a few things, milk, bread, sausages. Down, Dolly!'

Dolly barked excitedly. Val knelt next to the Staffy and rubbed her ears, making a soothing clucking sound.

'So, as I left Finest Choice, guess who was outside, shouting at Lowenstowe's council representative?'

'Loveday?' Val guessed.

'Carrying a placard that said "There is no Planet B".'

'She was by herself?' Connie asked anxiously.

'Shouting slogans and demanding action,' Alice said. 'She's drawn a crowd. There's a security man at Finest Choice. What if he rings the police?'

'We'd better get down there,' Val suggested. 'Shall we take my car? It'll be quicker than walking.'

'I'll come with you,' Connie agreed.

'Dolly and I will sit in the back.' Alice followed Val as she tugged keys from her pocket and the three women and Dolly leaped inside the Mini Cooper. The engine rumbled and the car moved off.

* * *

The door to Crab Claw Cottage opened and a lean man stood still, watching the car pull away. He held a package wrapped in foil, blinking against the strong wind that found the tiny holes in his jumper. He didn't seem to notice as he closed the door softly behind him and walked on silent feet towards Val's cottage. He had intended to introduce himself, to offer her a piece of freshly caught fish, but he'd missed her again. It didn't matter – she'd find the pollock on her step when she returned.

14

A crowd had gathered outside the supermarket, close to the entrance. Val could see a placard being held high with the words *No Planet B!* written in a large inky scrawl. She recognised the high Cornish voice before she saw Loveday, who was shouting, 'We need proper policies for Lowenstowe that address the needs of local Cornish people. We have to take a stand for our town.'

A male voice could be heard, deliberately low and level. 'This is not the best place to discuss environmental issues, Mrs Moon. I only popped out for a packet of biscuits. I'd rather you made an appointment to visit me in my office at the town hall.'

Val wriggled through the crowd, Connie just behind her, Alice and Dolly bringing up the rear. She saw Loveday, chin thrust out, the placard gripped in one hand like a weapon, talking to the man in a smart suit. 'I know you come here around this time. I have several things to say to you, Mr Scott. A few more litter bins would be useful, but there's a list as long as my arm of local concerns and it's your job to represent our community.' Loveday noticed Val and her eyes widened. 'Ah, reinforcements.' Loveday tucked her placard under her arm like a lance and sniffed. 'Valerie, we'll explain to Henry Scott what we want him to do.'

'We?' Val repeated.

The security guard from the supermarket rushed through the revolving doors followed by a smart woman wearing a navy suit. The woman walked up to Loveday briskly, facing her square-on.

'Are you the person who has been standing outside here shouting for the last half an hour?'

'I am. Loveday Moon, that's me.' Loveday met her gaze boldly. 'Who are you?'

'I'm Mrs Diane King. I'm manager here at Finest Choice.'

'Pleased to meet you,' Loveday said brusquely.

Mrs King turned to Henry Scott. He was soft-bodied beneath his suit as if he had no muscles. He extended a hand to the supermarket manager. 'Henry Scott, Lowenstowe's councillor. Have you come to ask this lady to leave?'

Val positioned herself next to Loveday, ready to shepherd her away from confrontation.

Mrs King shook her head. 'No, I've come to have a quick word with you, Mr Scott. Here at Finest Choice, we do our best for the environment. We're not a big chain supermarket; we don't get a lot of options about our suppliers. It's tough in Cornwall, so far away from major UK producers. We do our best to get organic and local food, but it's often quite expensive for customers. Like Mrs Moon, we worry about air miles and plastic. We try to source our fish as locally as possible, but the seas around here are overfished—'

'Hear, hear,' Loveday cooed.

Mrs King continued, 'We're very proud of our Cornish heritage and Finest Choice does its best, but we need to know you'll represent our concerns.'

'This supermarket has recycling and food bank collection

points, and Lowenstowe needs you to be on board with the push, Henry,' Loveday persisted. 'Too many children here suffer from food poverty, there's a lot of unemployment, incomes are low and there's not enough housing...'

'Mrs Moon is right: we need you to represent our concerns, take them to a higher level, be an ambassador for Lowenstowe,' Mrs King said with a smile.

Henry Scott seemed momentarily flustered, his hands moving to his head. Then his voice was smooth as melted butter. 'I understand all your worries. They are mine too. So, please, Mrs Moon, do make an appointment with my secretary to come and see me at the town hall. I'd love a chance to talk to you and maybe then we could discuss the issues calmly—'

'Let's discuss them now in front of all these people.' Loveday waved a hand towards the crowd. 'I'm sure they all agree with me.'

A cheer went up from a group of youngsters. Val moved closer to Loveday and whispered in her ear. 'We should take him up on his offer, go and talk to him. We can write down exactly what we want and hand it to him.'

'I'll type everything up,' Connie offered.

Val addressed Henry, a smile on her face. 'Thanks, Mr Scott. We'll come and see you at the earliest opportunity.'

Henry looked relieved. 'That's good. Ah... I'll look forward to it.'

'That will give us a chance to tell him what we want him to do,' Val murmured and Loveday smiled. 'And we can do it together, as a team.'

'All right. I'm glad you're helping me – strength in numbers.' Loveday folded her arms. 'Yes, we'll make an appointment.'

Mrs King put a hand on Loveday's shoulder. 'Mrs Moon, why don't you come in to Finest Choice and have a cup of tea in our café – it's Fair Trade, and the milk is organic – on the house, as a gesture of support for what you're doing for the community? I'll throw in some nice Cornish fairing biscuits too.'

'Oh, that's handsum...' Loveday said. 'And can my friends come with me?'

Mrs King looked from Val to Connie and then to Alice. 'Of course, but I'm afraid the dog can't come in.'

Alice was suddenly awkward. 'Oh, I'll wait outside with Dolly.'

'Doesn't Ollie work here in the office?' Val asked. 'Would it be okay to ask him to take Dolly for a walk, just while we all have a cup of tea?'

Loveday was delighted. 'Oh, he'd love that.'

'No problem at all.' Mrs King waved an arm towards the supermarket. 'We can manage without him, just for a short while.'

Minutes later, the four women were hunched over hot tea in the café. Loveday gripped her cup tightly and said to Val, 'I'm properly glad you were here to help me deal with that councillor. But why did you agree to a meeting? I was on a roll.'

'It's probably the most reasonable way to get things done,' Val soothed. 'You're a brave woman taking action like you did today, but we ought to plan a strategy in order to get our way.'

'Our way?' Loveday smiled slowly. 'You'll join me?'

'Most definitely,' Val said. 'I'd really like to support what you're doing.'

'Me too. It's so important,' Connie agreed.

'Kev and I'd be glad to help too. Lowenstowe's our home,' Alice said before gazing through the glass windows, anxious about her dog. Then she caught sight of Ollie walking towards the car park with a determined Dolly tugging on her lead.

'The councillor doesn't want to be confronted in public,' Val suggested tactfully. 'It's quite reasonable for us to meet him in the town hall.' She moved closer to Loveday. 'We'll go together, and we'll be as professional and organised as possible.'

'There will be no more shouting and hot air, you mean?' Loveday blurted.

'You've done so well,' Val soothed. 'We can organise a list of what we want him to support, write to the newspapers. We'd be a proper local group. Cornwall has the most beautiful coastline – we could do with more help from the likes of Henry Scott to stop it being spoiled. If we can get the issues resolved, it will be even more beautiful. Imagine, Loveday, the holidaymakers have more bins for their litter; we have a strategy for proper recycling. The supermarket is already on side with sourcing local food.'

Loveday's eyes filled with tears. 'I can't believe it. I thought I was all on my own.'

'Not at all,' Connie said kindly.

'We'll help,' Alice agreed.

'Then it's sorted. We'll make a list of demands and pay Mr Scott a visit.' Val raised her cup. 'To a greener and happier Lowenstowe.'

Loveday patted Val's arm affectionately, her gaze soft with admiration. 'Like I said, Valerie, you're a nice woman. I'm beginning to like you a lot.' She turned to Connie with an expression of triumph. 'She'll make some bloke a very happy man.'

'Oh, no,' Val protested. 'I'm perfectly happy as I am...'

* * *

As Val drove the Mini Cooper out of the supermarket car park Loveday, who was sitting next to her, the placard on her knee, cackled triumphantly. 'We showed Henry Scott, my luvvers. Now we can tell him what we want done.'

Connie was squashed in the back seat, Dolly attempting to lick her face. She rubbed the dog's head nervously and added, 'Val had another word with the manager as we left. Mrs King wants to be a pioneer; she's getting rid of excessive wrappings, prioritising local produce even more and she wants to develop the food banks. She's a good sort.'

'It's so exciting, being part of something this important. It's nicer than sitting at home watching TV. I wonder if I could get Kev to join us.' Alice tugged Dolly's lead gently; the Staffy was attempting to climb onto Connie's knee. Dolly scrabbled onto Alice's lap instead and she hugged her neck tightly.

Val checked the driver's mirror and turned a corner. 'You live in Pennywell Road, Loveday? It is this way, isn't it?'

'Just a few minutes from here now, in one of the old fishermen's cottages.' Loveday turned and the placard swung in front of Val's vision for a moment, then she pointed to the road. 'Just down here aways. As the crow flies, I'm not too far from you at all – if you were to walk down the beach the other way for half a mile... Ah, here we are. Stop, right here by this white door.'

Val pulled in next to an old cottage nestled between two smartly renovated ones. Either side, the houses were freshly painted cream with new doors. Loveday's home was dilapidated, the plaster crumbling, the old wooden window frames rotten. Behind the downstairs window hung yellowing net curtains and several china ornaments were clustered together. Val smiled.

'So, here we are...'

'Oh, yes, here we are. Home sweet home. I won't ask you in, though.' Loveday grasped the handle next to the passenger seat and pushed the door ajar. 'My John isn't really up to having visitors. I'll get the kettle on and get the fire going.' She met Val's eyes, pushing a strand of hair from her eyes. 'Well, Valerie, Connie. I'll see you dreckly, and you too, Alice, next week in the shop. Thanks for the lift.'

The three women watched Loveday wriggle from the car, dragging her placard, and pause on her front step, searching deep in her pockets for keys. She pushed the front door open with effort, stepped inside into darkness and let it slam without looking back.

'I thought we might get a cuppa,' Val said, disappointed.

'Oh, no,' Alice called from the back. 'No one ever gets an invite into Loveday's house.'

'Is it to do with her husband being so unwell?' Connie asked, her voice full of concern.

'I expect so. He never goes out – I've never ever seen him,' Alice explained. 'For all anyone knows, he doesn't even exist. Loveday told me once that she has to do everything, cooking, shopping, fixing broken tiles, unblocking the toilet.'

'Oh, dear.' Connie sighed.

'Perhaps Kev could pop round and help?' Alice suggested. 'I'll ask him.'

Connie moved to sit in the front seat to give Alice and Dolly more space. Val started the engine. 'Right. Have you all got time to come back to my place for a cuppa?' She manoeuvred the car onto the main road. 'I made a batch of brownies earlier for when I see Ollie again. He says they are his favourites.'

'Kev's too,' Alice added. 'He asked me the other day why I couldn't cook like you do.'

Connie winked. 'Loveday said she'd be a great catch for any man, our Val.'

'Oh, not any man,' Val said quickly. 'Not any man at all, in fact.'

'But there's the dinner date with Dennis.' Connie grinned. 'And you might talk to someone special.'

'Dennis Cargill?' Alice gasped. 'He does Kev's accounts. Kev says his wife left him. He's really...' Alice searched for the word '... heart-broken. He used to be slim and cheerful, and now he just drinks and mopes. I feel proper sorry for him.'

'I'll do my best to cheer him up.' Val had arrived at the little row of cottages as Dolly barked, excited to be home. She slithered from the driver's seat and stood on the path, staring at something on her front doorstep. 'Whatever's that?'

Connie was next to her. 'It's a package wrapped in tinfoil.' She frowned. 'Perhaps it's just rubbish someone has abandoned?'

Alice tugged Dolly's lead as the three women gazed at the foil package on the step. Val picked up the tinfoil, sniffing it. 'I think it's fish.' She opened it tentatively, revealing a whole white fish. She glanced at Connie and Alice for help. 'It *is* a fish.'

'It's a cod,' Connie suggested.

Alice took the silver wrapper and examined the contents. 'It's a pollock – someone's given you a pollock, Val.'

Val was thrilled. 'Pan fried, with lemon juice and capers tonight, I think. Anyone for pollock?'

'I've got sausages in for Kev,' Alice said and Dolly yelped excitedly, leaping frantically.

'Connie, come for dinner – I can't eat all this by myself.'

'I'd be delighted to, Val. But where did the fish come from?' Connie wondered.

'Well, I can guess.' Val smiled. 'There can only be one local fisherman who's kind enough to leave a pollock on my step.'

The three women gazed up towards Crab Claw Cottage. No lights were on inside and there was no one to be seen.

Val held the fish up and called out, just in case he was within earshot. 'Thanks so much for the lovely pollock, Ben.'

Val and Connie hugged Alice goodbye, and rushed into Teasel Cottage as Alice tugged Dolly towards her home next door.

* * *

Behind the curtains of the upstairs bedroom in Crab Claw Cottage, a man was watching thoughtfully. He lifted a hand in a wave but Val didn't see him. He hoped his neighbour would enjoy the fresh fish he'd caught only that morning. He was pleased to be able to repay her kindness. He would cook his own piece of pollock, have an early night and be up early tomorrow; the fishing would be good again. He turned away with a smile and walked back into the shadows.

15

Val clutched the brownies wrapped in reusable wax paper and made her way to Crab Claw Cottage. It was a bright April Monday; a seagull sat on the roof of Honeysuckle House, still as stone, its round eye on a carton by the side of the road. It swooped down on elegant wings, landing on the gravel, and snatched at the scraps with a stabbing motion. Val strode briskly up the path, gazing at the windows to see if there was any sign of movement inside but there was none. She rapped at the door, waited then rapped again. Ben was probably out at sea, fishing for more pollock. She deposited the brownies on his doorstep with a little card thanking him for the fish and turned away.

Val drove into the centre of Lowenstowe, another package of brownies in her bag and parked a few moments' walk from The Tasty Plaice. She passed an empty shop, once selling expensive gifts, now closed down, and followed the smell of fried fish into the café. Ollie was already seated in the corner wearing his green parka, drinking something fizzy. Val ordered their meal at the counter and went to join him. Ollie greeted her cheerfully.

'Hello. How are you doing, Val?'

Val smiled. 'Hello, Mr March.'

'No, I'm Mr Moon,' Ollie explained. 'My mum's Miss Morwenna Moon because she isn't married. My dad was a gate bleddy tuss – Grannie Loveday calls him that.' He noticed Val's frown. 'That means he was a foolish man. I don't really know if he was or not. I never met him.' Ollie took a gulp from a glass containing bright orange liquid and wiped his mouth on his hand. He stared as Val placed the wax wrapper on the table. 'What's that?'

'Chocolate brownies.'

'For me?' Ollie had already unwrapped the package. He rearranged the brownies in neat rows before taking a bite. 'That's handsum. I brought something for you too.' He handed Val a large envelope. She opened it, pulled out a thick sheet of paper and gazed at a perfect likeness of herself rendered in charcoal. 'I did that from memory.'

Val gasped. 'That's wonderful.'

'I like to draw with conté sticks. They are compressed powdered graphite or charcoal mixed with a clay base.'

'I'll display this on my fridge. Thanks, Ollie.'

A waiter in an apron put two plates piled with fish, chips and peas on the table and Ollie rubbed his hands together, using his fork to make a space between the fish, the chips and the peas. 'Proper handsum.'

They began to eat before Val asked, 'How's life, then?'

'Same old.' Ollie was munching. 'I like working at Finest Choice. I enjoy the mental challenge of adding up money and recording the information, although I prefer the creative freedom of drawing and painting.' He waved his fork in the air. 'I wish I had a hobby where I could meet an interesting girlfriend though.'

'Don't you know anyone?'

'There was Lauren: she was my girlfriend for eight weeks and four days, but we split up when she moved back to live with her mum in Padstow.'

Val chewed thoughtfully. 'What sort of girlfriend would you like, Ollie? If you could choose.'

'One who's compatible. She'd ask me to draw her picture and it would make her heart full of joy.' He didn't hesitate. 'She'd be someone who'd read lots of books and likes museums and art galleries and TV programmes about nature.' His smile broadened. 'She'd be someone kind-hearted, who'd want to be with me more than anything else in the world.'

Val was impressed. 'That's so wise.'

'And what about you, Val?'

She picked up a chip. 'What about me?'

'What sort of boyfriend would you choose?'

Val shrugged. 'I don't know.'

'Perhaps you should make up your bleddy mind.' Ollie's voice was the perfect imitation of his grandmother's.

'Well, it wouldn't be the man I have a date with soon. He's not my type.'

Ollie was puzzled. 'So why are you going on a date with him if he's not compatible?'

'It's complicated.'

'No, it's really easy.' Ollie chewed thoughtfully. 'You should only go out with someone you love who'll love you back.' He considered the options. 'Unless it's me going out to lunch with an older person like you to talk some sense into you, but we've become good friends now.'

'We have.' Val watched as Ollie finished his lunch. She pushed her plate away.

'Aren't you going to eat those, Val? I'll have them. I have a fast metabolism.' Ollie's eyes were round as he pushed his fork into Val's chips.

She leaned forward. 'Ollie, what sort of man do you think I should look for?'

'I don't know. If I were you, I'd make a list of qualities you think are important.' Ollie shrugged. 'I would say a rich one with a nice car, but Grannie Loveday says you're already rich and you have a nice car so I don't suppose you need someone like that.' He thought for a moment as he selected the last chip. 'I think you should pick someone who would be interested in the same things that you are, who deserves someone as nice as you and who'd have intelligent conversation and make you smile.'

'You're right,' Val said. 'I should listen to what you tell me. You talk so much sense.' She pressed her lips together. 'Can I ask your advice about something else?'

'Of course you can.' Ollie was still chewing.

'I know this man – well, I know him a little. I see him on the beach sometimes. He's very handsome. He has a handsome dog. I might want to go out with him but I don't know him very well. Do you think I should try to get to know him better so that he'll ask me out?'

'What's his name?'

'Mr January.'

'Does he smile a lot?'

'I've seen him smile once...'

Ollie shook his head. 'I wouldn't pick a girlfriend who didn't smile. That's not very compatible.' He tried a joke. 'I think you should just go out with his dog instead.'

'Maybe you're right,' Val said as she watched Ollie stack the brownies one on top of the other, his eyes shining. 'You're a very wise young man. I'll have to take you out for fish and chips again and get more advice on dating.'

'And you can give me more advice about finding a girlfriend.' Ollie sighed. 'A nice compatible girlfriend, that's what I want more than anything in the world – even more than your brownies.'

* * *

On the morning of 16 April, Val and Connie stood in Val's bedroom sorting through her wardrobe. Val groaned. 'Best jeans and a jacket, Connie. It's just lunch.'

'But you can do so much better than jeans,' Connie said. 'You need to look stunning.'

Val shook her head. 'I'm going to cheer Dennis up – he won't care what I wear.'

'You're dressing to impress Timothy Keita.'

'I'm not sure...' Val was a little embarrassed by the idea of meeting Mr January for the first time. 'If he likes me, it'll be for who I am.' She recalled Ollie's wise words.

Connie tried again. 'What's wrong with a little black dress?'

Val pulled a dress from the wardrobe. 'There's this old thing – it hasn't had an outing in ages. 'She took a deep breath, determined to put her most confident foot forward. 'Yes, you're right. Dennis was kind enough to invite me, and the lovely Mr January will be there. I need to make the effort.' Val held the dress up in front of her and did a little shimmy. 'Connie, I've got this. I'm off to The Unicorn, to enjoy a wonderful lunch, seated between two lovely men. One I'll cheer up with my wit and repartee and the other, I'll dazzle with my smile and my posh frock. Bring it on.'

* * *

At exactly ten minutes to one Val approached The Unicorn Hotel, a five-storey Victorian building towering on the corner of High Street. Traffic rumbled by as the lights turned green, and Val wobbled on high heels, shivering inside the black dress. She was feeling jittery, more from nerves than from the chilly wind, as she gazed up at the embellished Unicorn sign, the white facade, the huge double doors framed by tall pillars, wide windows, polished glass gleaming in the sunlight. Dennis wasn't outside waiting for her so Val put on her most confident expression and sauntered through the doors.

She paused in the plush red-carpeted foyer with a heavy chandelier in the centre. A woman at the reception desk was helping two customers. Val took three paces forward and stopped. She recognised the man who was talking to the receptionist, his hand resting against the back of a tall slender woman, her red hair swept in a coil. It was Nigel, Mr February.

Val's immediate reaction was to rush over and say hello. But there was something about his stance, the tension in his body beneath the dark suit, that made her think again. He spoke to the receptionist, taking something from her, a key probably, before he shepherded the tall woman towards the lift. He glanced over his shoulder and his eyes met Val's, hesitating a moment too long. She moved her fingers in a little wave and he twisted away quickly, hastening his lady friend towards the lift, rushing inside as the sliding doors swallowed them. Val frowned: he had ignored her. She had no idea why. Perhaps it was because they had only dated once. Perhaps he'd been in a hurry. Her eyes fell on a sign pointing to a flight of marble steps, indicating the White Room, and she made her way upstairs.

She pushed through the double glass doors to the White Room and stepped in, wandering through groups of smartly dressed people, mostly couples talking together. Val gazed at the high ceilings, the white walls embellished with gilt mirrors and soft yellow lights. At the far end of the room was a bronze bar. She ambled towards another set of double glass doors and peered inside. A long table was set for lunch, white linen, bright lights reflecting from a chandelier, rainbow colours dazzling, making glasses and cutlery gleam. She glanced around for Dennis. Val walked back through groups of guests and her nose was immediately assailed by various types of perfume, strong floral notes, musky scents and sharp aftershave. It was then she spotted him, the broad expanse of his back in a navy suit, leaning against the bar. She walked over, tapping him gently on the shoulder.

'Hello, Dennis.'

He turned to her, smiling, but his eyes were sad. The whisky glass in his hand was almost empty.

'Val, you came.' He seemed to remember. His breath was fuelled with Scotch.

'Of course...'

Dennis waved to the barman. 'Please, George, whatever the lady wants.'

Val spoke to the young man in the white shirt. 'Just a tomato juice, please.' She turned back to Dennis and was hit by a sudden whiff of tangy aftershave. 'It was kind of you to invite me.'

'Annual business do – we go in for lunch at half one.' Dennis slurred his words. 'I was alone at this event last year. I used to bring my wife before that. She loved coming here. She was always the life and soul...'

'Oh?' Val wasn't sure how to respond.

He drained his glass. 'She was the love of my life, my Nicci. That's why I like Connie – she listens to me. She understands how I feel.'

'I'm sorry.' Val wondered if she should mention Ray and the fiasco of that last Christmas dinner, and quickly decided against it.

'Have a few drinks with me, Val. You're not married, are you?'

'Divorced,' Val replied grimly.

'Ah, I'm separated. But I still love Nicci. I live in hope. Not a week goes by I don't beg her to come back.' He swayed towards Val.

'I have an idea. Let's get totally drunk. I can tell you about the past, about what happened, and we can drown our sorrows.'

'Remember, you promised me you wouldn't drink too much...' Val said. 'Let's just have lunch.'

'A drink or two helps though...' Dennis sighed. 'I might not make lunch. I might just stay here at the bar.' He waved his glass towards the barman. 'Stay with me, Val. We can be our own lonely-hearts club.' He placed a heavy hand on her shoulder. 'You're a nice woman. You have a kind face. Let me get you a double gin and tonic—'

'I'll just pop to the ladies, if that's okay...' Val left the tomato juice on the bar and moved away.

She pushed through the crowds of drinkers, mostly couples and groups, wondering what she should do for the best. Then she saw Mr January standing by a window, holding a glass of white wine. Her heart flipped in a way that was becoming too familiar. He was elegant in a grey suit, a red tie, his beard neatly clipped. Val thought that this might be an opportunity to be grasped: Connie would be so thrilled to hear about it afterwards and Val was determined to have something exciting to report. Besides, she was out of practice at talking to men she hardly knew, so she took a deep breath and walked over, already smiling. Timothy Keita was peering out of the window. He didn't notice her as she approached so she murmured, 'Hello there,' in her best sultry voice.

He turned, no recognition in his eyes, so she cooed, 'I'm Val. You're the writer, aren't you?'

He inclined his head, a slight smile hovering around his mouth. 'Tim Keita.'

Val's grin was glued to her face as she met his lustrous brown eyes. She was suddenly nervous, stammering. 'Yes. I just... I mean, I think I've read one of your books, the... latest one.' She wondered at the wisdom of her words as soon as she said them.

She was improvising, which was unwise, but somehow her mouth was moving and she couldn't stop the words. 'It was totally wonderful.'

'Really?' Tim was pleased. 'You've read *The Mystery of Baily's Beads*?'

'Yes – it was one of the best books I've ever read.'

'Oh, I'm so glad.' Tim was suddenly delighted.

Val couldn't stop herself – she suddenly launched into the conversation with enthusiasm. 'Absolutely. I adore mysteries. I loved the character of Baily... and his beads... they were really...' she realised she was out of her comfort zone now, obviously winging it, so she finished her sentence quickly '... really fascinating...'

'You liked Baily?' Tim was confused.

'Oh, yes, I adored him,' Val gushed, then she wondered if he was a criminal or a psycho killer, so she added, 'I mean, he was really well written.'

Tim shook his head. 'Baily's Beads is the intensely bright photosphere of the sun shining through valleys at the edge of the moon, and the end of totality in a solar eclipse.'

'Ah,' Val said. 'That Baily... those beads...' There was an awkward silence, so Val said, 'You write books about astronomy?'

'That's correct.'

'I'm so sorry, I must have got your book confused with something else...' Val put a hand to her face; her cheeks were warm.

'You must have.'

Val was determined to have one last try. 'Oh, wait, I know where I've seen you – walking on the beach with your dog. A gorgeous Chow Chow.'

'Goliath.'

'Yes, Goliath,' Val said enthusiastically. 'He's so lovely.'

Tim opened his mouth and Val wondered for a split second if he was going to tell her that his handsome dog had an incurable disease and had just been put down. Then he asked, 'Have I seen you on the beach?'

Val was about to reply that she'd seen him lots of times but she wondered if she should play harder to get, so she said, 'I think so, yes, possibly.'

Tim seemed to be trying to work out a difficult problem, then his face lit up. 'Oh, I remember. You were singing Bob Dylan songs.'

Val was flushed with success. 'Yes, that was me.' She hoped they had found a mutual topic of interest. 'Do you like Bob Dylan?'

'I totally love all American music of that time. That's my era.' Tim beamed and Val was momentarily stunned by the captivating smile. 'I always listen to The Beach Boys, Jefferson Airplane and Jimi Hendrix while I'm writing.'

'Oh, so do I,' Val babbled. 'I sang "Wild Thing" in a karaoke performance once.'

'How cool.' Tim was impressed. 'I can't sing very well, but I love dancing. Do you dance?'

'Oh, yes, most definitely, all the time, non-stop—'

Val was about to do a little jig to prove that she danced all the time, but a sudden buzzing came from Tim's top pocket. He whisked out his mobile phone and said, 'Oh, I'm so sorry – I must take this; it's my publisher – do excuse me...'

Val watched him move away from the window, murmuring, 'Hester, yes, of course it's not inconvenient...' Then he moved to a quiet corner, turning his back. She exhaled slowly; Tim Keita was handsome and intelligent, and they'd started a conversation. Val wondered whether to wait until he'd finished his call. He seemed preoccupied, deep in conversation, so she wandered away. They could talk again over lunch.

She gazed towards the bar. Dennis hadn't moved, except to flop further forwards towards the bartender who was pouring him another whisky. She noticed a clock on the wall above the bar; it was twenty minutes past one.

'Hello. Are you here by yourself?'

Val gazed into the blue eyes of a friendly face, a man around her own age, standing a few feet away. He was slim in a grey suit, a little taller than she was, with neat white hair and metal-framed glasses.

She smiled politely. 'No, I...' Val decided that the truth was the way forward. 'I'm supposed to be Dennis Cargill's plus-one but I think he's had a few whiskies.'

'Oh dear,' the man said, but he was smiling. 'That's Dennis for you nowadays, I'm afraid.'

'You know him?'

'He's my accountant,' the man replied, his eyes twinkling.

Val wasn't surprised. 'He seems to be everyone's accountant, but I don't know when he finds the time to do any accounting.' She gazed back at Dennis, who was staring into a glass. He seemed to have forgotten about her.

'He's very unhappy,' the man said. 'And he has a sober team who look after everything.' The man put out a hand. 'I'm Freddie.'

'I'm Val,' Val replied, shaking his warm hand.

'Might I get you a drink?' Freddie asked.

Val met his eyes. He was good-looking, friendly. For a moment, she wondered if she should stay: he'd certainly be a pleasant lunch companion. But she was Dennis's guest and he was still at the bar; he probably wouldn't make it as far as the dining table. She had met Mr January and she'd intended to stun him with her wit but it would be difficult now. Dennis was her lunch date; it didn't seem fair to turn her back on him to talk to Tim and Freddie. Val imagined Dennis watching her as she sat between gorgeous Tim and charming Freddie, scintillatingly chattering her way through lunch while Dennis stood lonely and rejected at the bar. It might be wiser and kinder to make a stealthy exit.

'Thanks,' Val said. 'It's lovely to meet you, Freddie, but I think I'll pass on a drink. I agreed to have lunch with Dennis as a favour but I don't think I'll stay now.'

'That's a shame.' Freddie's face showed his disappointment. 'Perhaps some other time?'

'Perhaps.' Val smiled warmly. 'Please can you pass on my apology to Dennis? It was nice meeting you.'

Val fixed her eyes on the double doors of the exit and wriggled her way through the throng of couples drinking and chattering. She wondered if she should have offered Freddie one of the favour boxes in her handbag but it was too late. She could have given one to Tim Keita too; he was probably still in the corner chatting on his phone to his publisher about black holes and quasars, but at least she'd had some success.

Val sashayed to the exit and out towards the stairs, letting the doors swing behind her. Leaving The Unicorn Hotel was certainly the best option. She rushed down the steps, her heels clacking on stone. She was filled with a new feeling of determination, a fresh confidence: Freddie had been a pleasant man and he'd clearly liked her. Tim, too, was starting to respond to her charms. Despite not wanting to find a Mr December, she wondered if she had made up her mind too quickly. It might be worth one more try. Perhaps now, even after Ray's rejection, she could still turn heads.

Val's step was light as she walked away from the hotel. The next time she met Mr January on the beach, he'd remember who she was. She'd certainly made an impression. So she'd talk to him, make light of their conversation about Baily and his beads, discuss West Coast music and their shared passion for dancing, let him know how keen she was on astronomy and big fluffy dogs. After all, he was devastatingly handsome. It couldn't do any harm, could it?

MR MAY

Val was hunched at the table in Connie's cosy kitchen, the Rayburn blasting out dry heat. Outside the rain was thrumming against the window, dripping from gutters in a steady stream. Her hair was plastered to her face: her clothes had been soaked during the short run between their houses. Val was glad to hold a hot drink between cold palms. A scented candle breathed the sweet aroma of cinnamon. Several photos were grouped on the dresser: a young Connie, fresh faced and stunning, hugging a handsome man with a lean jaw and a wide smile; the man again, a little older, a close-up of his face, eyes shining, clearly in love with the person behind the lens; Connie and the man again and a blond teenage son, their arms wrapped around each other.

Connie sat opposite, her mug of fruit tea untouched. 'So, is Mr January still a contender?'

Val nodded. 'Maybe.'

'You did so well. You know the name of his book. You know the name of his dog.' She was delighted. 'He knows your name.'

Val smiled, remembering. 'I left quite an impression.'

Connie said, 'He'd be great in a wedding photo.'

'I know I'd decided no more dates... but he's very nice, so I could make an exception.'

Connie's china-blue eyes were intense. 'Please, Val – just one more try.'

Val was reluctant. 'Okay, just one.'

'So, Mr February doesn't count. Mr March is Ollie. Mr April is Dennis, and it was sad that he couldn't make lunch, but at least you made good progress with Mr January.' Connie smiled triumphantly.

Val was unsure. 'So what do you suggest next?'

'We'll keep Tim Keita in the mix for Mr December,' Connie said.

'All right.' Val imagined him in the photo. She grinned – the dog was in the wedding photo too, although she knew he'd have to leave it behind. She found herself wondering if he knew someone who'd look after it while they were in Montréal.

Connie interrupted her thoughts. 'I wonder if Dougie and Boo are having any more parties?'

'Oh no – Nigel might be there.'

'Good point.'

Val sipped tea. 'Let's just concentrate on ourselves and see what happens.'

'Right,' Connie said. 'We should go on a fun outing – The Eden Project, The Lost Gardens of Heligan.'

Val agreed. 'I'd love the chance to explore Cornwall a bit this summer: beaches, parties, events. Who knows what will happen?' She smiled brightly. 'After all, you know the story about men being like buses – there's nothing for ages, then two turn up.'

'You don't need two men,' Connie countered.

'I don't need one. But we could find Mr May anywhere. We could even bump into him at the town hall – we're meeting Loveday at three.'

'Oh, I almost forgot,' Connie said.

'We're due at Henry Scott's office. Loveday made an appointment.'

'Do you think she'll be a bit cross with him, Val?'

'She's an eco-warrior, so passionate about everything, and that's something I really admire,' Val replied. 'Alice is coming too. It'll take all our wits to charm Henry – she'll certainly speak her mind.'

'Maybe Henry Scott has a handsome dad.'

Val laughed. 'Come on, Connie, let's have some soup and then we'll set off into Lowenstowe. We can't afford to be late, not with Loveday after Henry's blood.'

* * *

The rain had stopped but the skies were heavy with the threat of another downpour. The pavements were spattered with puddles; water dribbled towards gurgling drains. Loveday was already outside the town hall, a white building with arched windows and stone steps leading up to a red door. She was carrying a huge hand-made placard that proclaimed *'Don't be a punk – recycle your junk'*. She was swathed in a huge coat, a black beret over pale hair, waving furiously to Val, Alice and Connie.

'Three o'clock, that's what I said to the secretary on the phone. I want to make sure Henry knows about the emmets dropping litter everywhere, buying second homes, pricing locals out of the housing market. I don't mean all of them, most of them are good as gold, they just want to enjoy Cornwall as much as the rest of us do. But Henry needs to know that there's a problem here with housing families and young people.'

'That's a good point,' Connie said brightly.

'Shall we go in?' Alice asked. 'Only Kev's looking after Dolly and I can't be too late.'

'Well, he'd better be there.' Loveday grunted.

'Why wouldn't he be?' Val put a gentle hand on her arm.

'I told the secretary what I have to say is important and he should stop what he's doing and talk to me. She told me he couldn't see me as he has a meeting until four.'

'So, we don't have an appointment with him?' Val said soothingly.

'Not exactly, no.' Loveday's eyes blazed. 'Have you ever heard of the Bastille?'

'Of course,' Connie replied. 'On 14 July 1789, the angry working people in the French revolution stormed...' Her voice trailed off.

Loveday put her hands on her hips. 'Exactly.' She took a deep breath. 'Are you ready, girls? What was the revolutionaries' cry? *Liberté! Egalité! Fraternité!*'

Val covered a smile. 'If we don't have an appointment, should we just go in and talk to Henry's secretary?'

'She was a nightmare on the phone.' Loveday folded her arms. 'All she could say was "Mr Scott is a very busy man" and "Mr Scott shares your concerns but..." Waste of time. I told her I don't want the bleddy monkey, I want the organ grinder.'

'I bet she was pleased,' Alice said.

'No, she was proper shirty with me,' Loveday grumbled. 'But he *will* see me and he *will* listen, you mark my words.' She took a breath. 'Anyway, let's see what he's got to say for himself.'

Loveday turned, leading the way as she marched up the town hall steps and through the entrance. She stood in a large foyer and gazed around. Her voice echoed. 'Henry's office is on the third floor.'

'Shall we take the lift?' Alice asked.

'Lift?' Loveday's eyes flashed. 'I'm eighty-two years old and I'll walk up every step. It's how I keep myself in peak condition.'

Loveday charged ahead, the placard clutched in her hand, followed by Val, Connie and a hesitant Alice. By the third short flight of steps, she was panting. Alice, who was the youngest by at least fifteen years, slumped against the wall and closed her eyes. 'I'm puffed out.'

'Let's catch our breath... we'll need it.' Loveday bent forward, inhaling sharply for several seconds, then she stood upright. 'Right, my luvvers, let's go and tell Mr Scott that he needs to be an ambassador for the people of Lowenstowe.'

Loveday pushed open a set of double doors and walked briskly over to a small reception desk. She handed the placard to an unsuspecting Alice, who shifted awkwardly behind Val and Connie, and placed both hands meaningfully on the counter. 'Good afternoon. I want to speak to—'

The receptionist didn't look up. She was examining the pages of a book with her index finger. 'One moment.'

Loveday huffed audibly. The receptionist glanced up, offering a professional smile. Loveday showed an unimpressed face and said, 'I want to speak to Henry—'

'And you are...?'

'I'm here on behalf of the people of Lowenstowe to discuss housing and recycling. I'm here on behalf of the planet, where too much rubbish is deposited in the sea and I have to go down there three times a week to collect it all up. I'm here to get some action.'

'You must be Mrs Moon,' the receptionist said.

'I certainly am.' Loveday folded her arms. 'Can you tell Henry I'm here?'

'Mr Scott is busy.'

'Then tell him to finish.'

'I'm afraid I can't do that.'

'I wonder...' Val tried a calm and concerned voice. 'Could we have a very brief word with him? To register our concerns?'

Loveday frowned. 'He knows my concerns. I've registered them with him ten bleddy times. I want some action. He needs to get his backside in gear and do something.' Loveday puffed out her cheeks. 'We can't do it all by ourselves.'

'Mr Scott is in a meeting.'

'Tell him to come out.'

'That's not possible, Mrs Moon.'

Loveday retorted, 'Oh, yes, it is. He just puts down his cup of tea and biscuit and says to his friends, "Excuse me for a minute," and then he comes out here and talks to me.'

'He's busy, I'm afraid.' The receptionist went back to her notebook.

'Then we'll wait,' Loveday announced.

'He'll be unavailable for another hour, after which he has another appointment.'

'I'll need to get back for Kev,' Alice said anxiously.

Connie moved over to a seat. 'We could hang on for a while longer.'

'I won't wait for any man,' Loveday gazed around and fixed her eyes on a door marked 'private'. 'Is he in there?'

'You can't go in, Mrs Moon.'

The receptionist's words propelled Loveday forwards. 'He *is* in there, then. Good. I'll just have a word.' She marched towards the door.

The receptionist met Val's eyes. 'I'll have to call Security.'

Val rushed towards Loveday, who had flung the door wide, followed by Connie. Two men were sitting on armchairs inside the room, laughing, sharing a cup of tea. A plate of biscuits was on the table between them. Loveday waved an arm. 'Henry? You and I need to talk.'

Both men turned to face her. Henry, wearing a crisp white shirt and blue tie, stood up. 'Mrs Moon...' He came towards the door, an expansive smile on his face. 'I can give you a moment. You're doing wonderful things on behalf of Lowenstowe.'

He left the door ajar as he walked over to Loveday. Val peered into the room, Connie gazing over her shoulder. The other man lifted his cup to his lips. Val stared. She had seen the same movement before, when she'd had dinner with him in Plymouth before going to the opera. It was Nigel Carrow, Mr February.

Henry placed a hand on Loveday's arm. 'I know you pick up detritus on the beach. That's wonderful. But, of course, the council are responsible for litter clearance—'

'Then how come you can't sort it out properly?'

Val peered into the office again and Nigel turned in the direction of the voices. He saw Val and his face filled with recognition. She waved and he replied with a weak smirk, twisting away quickly. Connie nudged Val gently, raising her eyebrows. Val closed the door with a crisp snap. She was puzzled: she'd seen Nigel twice recently and both times he had ignored her.

Henry was deep in conversation with Loveday. 'So, is this just about litter on the beaches?'

'*Just* litter on the beaches? What about the need for more food banks, social housing? Next, I'm talking to the newspapers and writing to the MP about the environment, overfishing, the lot.' Loveday faced him, her fists clenched.

'You are a great pillar of the community.' Henry's expression was unreadable. 'Audrey, will you make an appointment for me to see Mrs Moon at my earliest convenience?' He swept his gaze over Loveday, smiling at Val and Connie. 'I think we have more in common than Mrs Moon might think. I can squeeze half an hour in, perhaps next month. So, if you'll excuse me, I was in the middle of an important meeting.'

He moved back to the door marked 'private', closing it behind himself with a click.

The receptionist glanced at the notebook, then gazed at Loveday nervously. 'Friday, 10 June at nine thirty?'

'Nothing before then?' Loveday was fuming. 'What does he do all day but drink tea and eat biscuits? What about next week?'

'I'm sorry, Mrs Moon, but Friday the tenth...'

'Oh, all right, Friday the tenth it is. But mark my words, if we can't get some changes in place by then, I'll be depositing all the trash I pick up from the sea on his doorstep.'

The receptionist froze. 'That would be illegal, Mrs—'

'Just a figure of speech.' Val wrapped an arm round Loveday, guiding her towards the door. 'Come on, ladies. How about coffee somewhere? I'm buying.'

'I have to get home to Dolly,' Alice said as they rushed down the stairs, her expression registering disappointment.

'So much for the French revolution.' Loveday made a grunting sound. 'My John's in need of some company. I'm going home to put the kettle on and I'll tell him all about being fobbed off with a load of ridiculous excuses. Then I'll write a list of demands for June the tenth.'

'You're right about what needs to change.' Val offered Loveday a reassuring smile. 'But why don't we try the softly-softly approach this time?'

Loveday was sad. 'I'm eighty-two. How much time do I have to take things softly-softly?' She met Val's eyes, her face concerned. 'I need things done. I'm just desperate to do my best for the place where I was born, the place I love...'

'I know. And we will,' Val promised. 'We'll do it together.'

They stood in the street. 'I'll come for a coffee. We have some things to discuss.' Connie moved her mouth close to Val's ear and whispered, her voice full of concern. 'What was Mr February doing in the meeting room? I thought it was awful, the way he just blanked you. Do you think he's upset because you wouldn't date him again?'

'Perhaps,' Val replied, but she doubted it.

'So, what about Mr May?' Connie began.

Loveday faced them, her hands on her hips, her face reddening with passion. 'There's more pressing matters than bleddy romance to discuss here. It's May already. The emmets are arriving from all over the country – they love Cornwall, and I'm not surprised, it's the most beautiful place in the world. But there will be even more litter on the beach, the oceans will be full of even more rubbish.'

'We'll definitely help. We'll be a smart, organised team from now on. You're not on your own,' Val promised, pressing Loveday's arm. 'We understand how important it is.'

Loveday huffed. 'It certainly is. The situation is urgent. This year is passing us by and we haven't achieved anything yet.'

Connie raised an eyebrow meaningfully. 'You're right, we haven't...'

'We need to get moving, throw ourselves into some action, start getting some results.' Loveday folded her arms.

'Definitely, we do,' Connie agreed.

'Time is a major factor – we need to get a move on,' Loveday said desperately, looking up and down the road. 'Who knows what the wind will blow in during the summer?'

'Who knows, indeed?' Connie met Val's eyes with a complicit smile. Val knew she wasn't just thinking about pollution.

17

Val was sitting by the till in the charity shop, serving customers who came and went, watching Loveday at work in the stockroom with the door wide open, sorting through and pricing new objects. Loveday's face was set in concentration as she selected items, placed them in a neat pile, writing each one down in her small notepad. She was sourcing clothes and toys for a family who lived nearby, the Penroses, a woman with growing children who barely had enough money. Loveday paid for the items herself, often finding something special for Jenna, the mum, who Loveday said was harassed and tired and shouldn't have shacked up with the 'gate bleddy tuss, who chased everything in a skirt from day one and left her with five mouths to feed'.

Loveday emerged a few minutes later with two cups of tea and planted one on the counter next to Val. 'Guess what I found out back?' She waved her cup triumphantly. 'Someone has donated a box of French perfume. Proper posh stuff, it is. I'm going to put a fiver in the till and give it to Jenna. That'll cheer her up.'

'You're just so thoughtful, Loveday.' Val picked up a mug of tea.

'So...' Loveday began, 'Ollie tells me your search for a bloke isn't going too well.'

'It's because I'm not trying very hard.'

'Your friend Connie thinks you need to meet someone nice.'

'I think she's a romantic,' Val suggested.

'I think she's lonely,' Loveday said bluntly.

Val sighed. 'You're very lucky to have your John.'

'I am.'

'I'd love to meet him.' Val was thoughtful. 'Is he like you, outgoing and energetic, or is he quiet, you know, the strong, silent type?'

'Ah, Valerie.' Loveday closed her eyes for a moment. 'Once, he could give me a run for my money. Full of energy, my John was, full of jokes. He'd chase me round the house, up the stairs, you know what I mean...' She winked and gave a soft laugh. 'And he loved a drop of proper cider. He was the life and soul.' She nodded sadly. 'Now he's not so strong. It's me who does everything nowadays...'

Val's expression was sympathetic. 'I hope he gets better soon.'

'In sickness and in health, for richer and poorer, until death...' Loveday paused. 'Of course, you've dumped your husband so that doesn't apply.'

'I suppose it doesn't,' Val said.

Loveday slurped from her cup. 'Do you know, John and I have only been outside Cornwall twice. Once was to London; we went just to see the capital city for a weekend. It was a funny place, too big for me, too noisy. The other time was a trip to Füssen in Germany. John wanted to go; a friend of his in the police force had a house there and we stayed for a week. We were emmets, I suppose. But do you know, it was the cleanest, tidiest place I've been to? The air was so sharp, everything neat, not a scrap of litter anywhere. I remember thinking, why can't we keep our own place this nice?'

Val hugged her. 'You're remarkable, Loveday. Cornwall's best.'

'I do what I can. These things matter to me. They should matter to everyone.' Loveday pointed to the doorway where a man was selecting an item from the bric-a-brac shelves. 'Oh, look over there. There's a customer. I'm off back to the stockroom. I've got clothes to find for the Penrose kiddies: the oldest one, Pawly, is growing out of everything so quickly. I can't be nattering all afternoon.'

A broad-shouldered man in a sheepskin jacket was approaching, carrying something carefully in both hands. Loveday grunted. 'I want to find some toys for Jenna's youngest too; little Tegen is three next week.' She scuttled away. Val watched the man place four pale wine goblets on the counter. He spoke in smooth tones. 'I think these are onyx. Four onyx goblets for ten pounds. Things of beauty. A bargain.' And then he said, 'Oh, goodness – it's Val, isn't it?'

Val stared at him, remembering the cultured tone, the swept-back hair, the roman nose, and how they had danced The Gay Gordons, The Dashing White Sergeant and Strip the Willow. He smiled and his face was suddenly handsome.

'Hello, Dougie,' she said.

'How are you?' Dougie Fraser flourished a ten-pound note. 'I didn't expect to see you here.'

'I volunteer once a week.' Val took the money. 'How's Boo?'

'Ah, Boo. Yes, indeed, Boo.' Dougie seemed sad. 'She's busy, as ever, with her passions, as I call them. It was antiques for a long time. We shared it together, it was our hobby, but now she's on a fitness kick.'

'Fitness? That's good, isn't it?' Val said.

'I suppose so. I'd go with her – it might be good for me too but...' He indicated his rounded stomach. 'She has this women's group, you know the sort of thing, yoga on Monday, weight training on Tuesday, Pilates on Wednesday, swimming on Thursdays, then they all meet for drinks on Friday.'

'Sounds exhausting.' Val put his money into the till. 'I'll wrap them in a recycled bag.'

Dougie shook his head. 'No need for that. I'll just pop them in my pockets.' He stuffed each of the goblets into his sheepskin jacket and turned to go. Then he paused. 'Val, I don't suppose you'd have lunch with me tomorrow?'

'I don't think so,' Val replied. 'You're a married man.'

'Oh, no, I didn't mean...' Dougie's shoulders slumped forward. 'I was due to have lunch with Boo – it's my birthday. And she's just cancelled – she can't break the engagement with the fitness girls. On Fridays they compare notes and set targets.' His face was sad. 'I'm seventy-four tomorrow and I'll be all on my own. It's so pathetic. I don't suppose you would join me – as a friend?' He gazed at her with puppy-dog eyes and even lifted a paw. 'Of course, I'd tell Boo – she'd be glad to have me out of her hair. It would mean so much. Just as acquaintances...?'

Val breathed out slowly. 'Lunch?'

'I'll book a table somewhere – a nice restaurant. My treat.'

'I'm not sure...'

'Val, Val, I can't spend my birthday alone. I rang a couple of friends this morning but they can't make it at short notice.'

Val agreed that it would be a shame, Dougie eating alone on his special day. 'Just lunch? A one-off meal? And you're sure Boo won't mind?'

'Mind? She'd be thrilled. And I'd be eternally grateful, you know, someone to share a bottle of claret across the table...'

'Do you want me to drive?'

Dougie was delighted. 'That's sweet of you. No, I'm going to push the boat out and hire a taxi.' He beamed. 'Where shall I pick you up?'

'Outside the shop, here – that makes things easy.'

'Splendid. Twelve thirty. Wonderful. I'm so grateful.'

Val immediately felt sorry for him. He had a hangdog expression, the physiognomy of a man disappointed. Val offered an optimistic smile. 'Tomorrow then, Dougie. And happy birthday.'

'Oh, it will be now.' He turned to go, the pockets of his sheepskin coat bulging with the goblets. In seconds Loveday was next to Val's side. She'd overheard.

'Big date tomorrow, then? He's a bit posh for you. Or do you like these well-to-do types?'

'No, it's just a favour,' Val said.

'He bought those onyx goblets, though.' Loveday grasped Val's arm. 'There's a little matching decanter that goes with them. I tell you what, Valerie, give me a tenner for the till and you can take it on as a birthday present. After all...' she shrugged '... if he's buying you lunch, you ought to get him a nice present in return.'

* * *

Connie stood at Val's front door the next day, disappointed. 'I wish you were meeting Mr January instead.'

'So do I, but it's not a proper date,' Val said. 'I still need to practise the art of conversation. I haven't dated in fifty years, if you discount Nigel.'

'You're right,' Connie agreed. 'Let's organise some fun days this summer. Cornwall comes alive when the tourists arrive. There's St Neot in July, the sea shanty festival in August, and the pub will be full of new people, holidaymakers...'

'All right – but for now I need you to help me decide what to wear.'

'Oh, you mean for lunch with Dougie?'

'Of course. Will jeans be okay?'

'Whatever you feel comfortable with.' Connie gave Val a hug.

'It's almost summer, the weather's lovely. And we all know what happens in summer, don't we, Val?'

'Sunshine?' Val shook her head. 'Cornish rain?'

'Romance.' Connie had perked up. 'I can't wait.'

Val felt light-hearted. She didn't care about romance, but sunny days in Cornwall's most picturesque locations were just what she needed. She was determined that it would be as good as having her own long, luxurious, sun-drenched summer holiday. She set off to meet Dougie humming a happy little tune.

18

Val sat in the back of the taxi, staring out of the window at the scenery. She and Dougie were in Merrynporth and, although she hadn't visited her old home town since she moved, the streets and houses were sharply familiar, as was the sinking feeling of rejection and sadness. Everything she saw through the glass reminded her of life with Ray: the park they'd walked through each week, the shops and cafés they'd visited, the little church. She looked away.

Dougie was handsome in a suit and a crimson dicky-bow tie, but Val was leaning away because of the overpowering scent of his aftershave, which made her think of a skunk in a barber's shop. Val was breathing as lightly as she could. She pressed a button to open a window then closed it quickly as cold air rushed in, blowing her hair across her face. She noticed the taxi driver, a young man with a thick beard, watching her through the driver's mirror. She spoke to Dougie, trying not to inhale. 'So, which restaurant have you booked?'

Dougie didn't answer. He examined his fingernails for a moment and when he met her eyes, Val thought he seemed a little awkward. 'Ah, well...' He said quickly. 'The one I was going to choose was, ah, fully booked... Fridays are popular so... I managed to find us a lovely little inn. We're nearly there.'

'Right.' Val rummaged in her capacious bag. Her fingers touched several small boxes at the bottom – the five remaining favour boxes. She kept forgetting all about them. Her fingers connected with a hard object wrapped in tissue. She found the neat onyx decanter and handed it to Dougie. 'Happy birthday.'

Dougie pulled the present from the tissue paper. 'Well, how clever of you. I didn't expect this.' He placed it on the seat next to him and leaned over, planting a damp kiss on her cheek. 'Thank you, Val.'

Val wheezed as his aftershave stuck in her throat. She nodded energetically, implying that she was glad he liked the gift. Then Dougie gazed through the window and said, 'Good – here we are.'

The taxi turned a corner and pulled up a small hill into a car park. Val recognised the place; she had been here several times, and the last time she'd visited she'd driven home alone. She exhaled. 'Oh – this is The Sprat.'

'Indeed.' Dougie patted his breast pocket, checking for his phone or wallet. 'Have you been here before?'

'Once... or twice.' Val was determined not to give anything away.

Dougie suddenly seemed nervous. 'Well, our table's booked for one o'clock, so we should be getting a move on.' He waved some money towards the taxi driver. 'Can you come back in a couple of hours, Wayne?'

The taxi driver took his payment and grunted affirmation as Dougie pushed open the door, wriggling out. 'Come on, then. Let's have a spot of lunch, shall we?'

The inside of The Sprat was exactly as Val remembered from Christmas Day eighteen months ago. Groups of men were leaning on the bar, drinking and talking. There was no one Val recognised and, thankfully, Ray wasn't there. A waiter showed them to a table in a huge wooden conservatory at the back of the pub. There were a few other guests, couples eating quietly, and a group of six women who Val thought must have been there for some time. They were shrieking and laughing amid empty bottles and glasses. Dougie was watching them from the vantage point of their table. Val twisted round; the women had finished their meal but they were having a raucously good time. She stared at them with a sinking feeling. One of the women seemed familiar. It was Monica. Val turned back to Dougie, hoping that Monica wouldn't recognise her.

Dougie said very little as he gulped soup. He peered at the group of women enjoying themselves then, as he wolfed down his whitebait in silence, his eyes strayed to the opposite table.

'Are you enjoying lunch?' Val asked tentatively.

'Ah? Oh, yes, delightful,' Dougie said, his gaze drifting back to the women.

Val was puzzled. She'd been hoping to practise conversation, but Dougie was fixated on the nearby table. While he was tucking into sticky toffee pudding, his eyes flickered again to the women, who were snorting at a joke. Val decided to ask the question uppermost in her mind.

'Do you know those women, Dougie?'

'What? Ah, no, I... ha, ha, they are a little loud. It seems they are having fun...'

'It's just that you've been watching them...'

'Ah, no, yes, no.' Dougie filled up his glass with wine, ignoring the fact that Val's glass was almost empty. 'It's...' He leaned forward confidentially. 'I think this is the pub where Boo meets her friends on a Friday. I think that might even be the fitness club over there, those ladies.'

A cacophony of screeches came from the table. Val smiled. 'They don't take their fitness too seriously...'

He was suddenly anxious. 'But she's not here. Boo's not with them.'

'Perhaps it's not the same group?'

'I don't know... I assumed she'd be with them. That was the whole point of coming here, to be honest, to check,' Dougie hissed. 'Val, I wonder – would you go across and ask?'

'Me?' Val shook her head. She had no intention of talking to Monica.

'Please? I have to know...' He made a pained face. 'Go and ask.'

Val sighed. 'What do you want me to say?'

'Ask them if they are The Sprat Ladies' Fitness Group. Ask them... if they know Boo...'

There was no way out of it. Val dabbed her mouth with a napkin and stood up slowly. She approached the women's table cautiously and made eye contact with the woman directly opposite Monica, a tall dark-haired woman in spectacles. 'Er... excuse me?'

The woman clearly thought she was about to be asked to be quieter. She frowned. 'Yes?'

Val smiled to ease the tension. 'Are you The Sprat Fitness Group?'

One of the women hooted. 'We're fit for nothing now.'

The dark-haired woman in glasses leaned forward. 'It's our day off. On Fridays we come here and put all the calories back on that we've lost in the week.'

Val heard Monica chortle as she sipped beer enthusiastically; Val watched her from the corner of her eye and hoped she didn't recognise her.

'Why? Do you want to join up?' the dark-haired woman said.

Another woman joked, 'We're better at drinking than we are at Pilates.' Someone else found the comment hilarious.

'No, it's just – Boo Fraser told me she'd joined a local group...' Val took a breath. 'I wondered if it was this one.'

'Boo Hoo?' One woman began to cackle.

'Oh, I know who you mean.' Monica's face showed no recognition. 'A tall slim woman. She came once, a few weeks ago. She was much better than all of us put together.'

'Oh, you mean the posh woman who spoke non-stop about antiques – yes, I remember.' The dark-haired woman met Val's eyes. 'She doesn't come any more.'

'Oh, thanks...' Val was backing away. 'Sorry to disturb your lunch.'

'No problem,' someone called loudly. Val sat down and met Dougie's eyes. His face was distraught; he had heard every word.

Val said, 'Maybe she goes to a different club?'

Dougie shook his head sadly. 'No, she definitely said The Sprat. That's why we came here, Val... I had to find out for sure.' He rubbed a hand across his face. 'And my suspicions were right – she's been lying to me.'

Val exhaled. 'There's probably a good explanation.'

'I can only think of one.' Dougie was almost tearful now. 'We've been married for twenty years but she's years younger than me and still so very attractive. I can't bear to think of where she might be... and with whom...'

'Try not to worry.' Val patted his hand sympathetically. 'Go home, have a rest, concentrate on enjoying your birthday, and then ask her. She's probably plotting something nice – you know, a portrait of herself that she secretly commissioned, that she'll give you for your birthday...'

Dougie brightened. 'Do you think so?'

'I hope so,' Val said. 'There are all sorts of possible innocent explanations.'

'Thanks, Val.' He breathed out a long huff of relief. 'Right. I'll just go to the bar and settle up. You've been great company.'

Val was about to protest that she'd been no company at all but

Dougie hadn't wanted company, he'd wanted to check if Boo was in The Sprat. Val felt sorry for him; she hoped Boo would be waiting for him at home with a card and a present, and everything would fall into place. She offered him an optimistic smile. 'Okay, I'll pop to the loo and meet you outside at the taxi.'

Val knew her way to the ladies' toilets, a pink porcelain room with green wall tiles and bright ceiling lights. Mercifully, she was the only one there; she was glad not to be sharing the mirror with The Sprat Fitness Group.

She walked through the bar and out to the fresh air, glancing around for the taxi, a black Mercedes. She spotted it in the car park; she could see the driver at the wheel, his head to one side, probably asleep. Then a voice murmured. 'Val...'

She turned to gaze into a pair of familiar blue twinkling eyes, a rugged face, still handsome, white curls under a cap, and caught her breath.

'Ray.'

'I didn't expect to see you here.' His expression was sombre. 'You're looking well.'

Val was suddenly awkward. She took in his jacket and jeans, the way they skimmed loosely over his body. He had lost weight. She saw something of the young man he had been when they'd first met: hopeful, good-natured, sometimes unsure of himself. She wondered sadly where that Ray had gone, reminding herself that she didn't really know this version of him. But he wasn't hers to know now.

He said simply, 'I've come to collect Monica... to drive her home.'

'I saw her,' Val replied. 'She's in the pub.'

He was still staring at her. 'I thought you were marvellous... in the karaoke.'

'Oh...' Val glanced away.

'I never knew you could perform so well.'

Val was tempted to tell Ray there was a lot he didn't know about her despite their forty-seven years together but she said nothing. Meeting him had brought old emotions flooding back. Then he said, 'You're going to Tom's wedding in December. We're going too. It will be nice to get together.'

'Yes.' Val couldn't think what else to say.

'Tom says you're taking a plus-one to Canada.'

'Yes.'

'So...' Ray was about to ask something but Dougie was by Val's side.

He said, 'There you are, Val. I wondered where you'd taken off to. Are you ready to go now, my dear? The taxi's waiting.'

Val could see Ray scrutinising Dougie, waiting to be introduced. She offered a breezy smile, hoping he'd assume she was with someone else. 'It was nice to see you, Ray.'

'Val...' he called after her but she and Dougie were strolling towards the Mercedes.

'Who was that?' Dougie asked.

Val wasn't sure if Ray could still hear her. She held her head high, determined not to look back. 'Just someone I know.'

'So, shall we go back to Lowenstowe? I won't come in for coffee – I want to get straight back home and see if Boo's there. I'm rather hoping that you're right, that she has a secret birthday surprise for me. Who knows? Thank you for accompanying me to lunch, Val, and for cheering me up. I've had a splendid time.'

They were inside the taxi, but Val hardly heard a word Dougie was saying. She was still reeling. She hadn't spoken to Ray for such a long time, not since the divorce, and then it had been routine, exchanging information. But bumping into him outside The Sprat had taken her by surprise. He had been so close, just a few feet away, and the old feelings of familiarity, warmth and affection had returned, tumbling back on a tidal wave of emotion. Val had wanted Ray to believe that she had moved on but now her hands were shaking, her heart bumping fast. She clearly wasn't over him at all. She sat in the taxi, lost in her own thoughts. As Dougie chatted she tried hard to listen, to reply with a chirpy comment, but she felt numb, stunned and confused.

MR JUNE

19

Val was attempting to cut her side of the hedge that she shared with Crab Claw Cottage. It had become unruly and too high, so she was reaching up on her toes, wobbling as she balanced on one foot, waving the clippers above her head. She wasn't doing a very good job of it.

She was still thinking about her meeting with Ray in the car park of The Sprat, although it was two weeks ago. He filled her thoughts when she least expected it: the moments before she fell asleep, when she was washing dishes, and now, while trimming the hedge. She pushed the image of him away and listened to the rhythm of the clippers. The summer sun was meltingly warm; new blooms were opening in the small front garden, long tongues of lupins, pale peonies. The last two weeks had flown by: Val had been busy decorating the smallest of the three bedrooms, stripping off the My Little Pony wallpaper and rendering the walls a clean sail-white colour. She'd found prints of some of her favourite abstract paintings, a Kandinsky, a Pollock, framed them and attached them to the wall, putting up white curtains, letting fresh air stream through the open widows. She was imagining Tom and Lottie visiting the following summer. She would decorate the middle room next with them in mind: the current purple and pink wallpaper with skulls, hearts and the black calligraphed print Love Kills wasn't really appropriate for a newly married couple.

Then yesterday, when she'd been in the charity shop putting price labels on teacups, Dougie had arrived to donate two sacks of previously loved clothes. He'd told Val that he'd enjoyed his birthday lunch with her immensely and, upon his arrival home, Boo had been waiting for him with a gift, a beautifully engraved antique pocket watch. Then she had taken him out for supper. Furthermore, Dougie proclaimed that he had been a silly duffer: he'd completely misunderstood his wife's exercise regime. She had tried The Sprat Fitness Group but found that the women didn't take it seriously enough, so she'd joined a hotel gym in Lowenstowe. And, Dougie had to admit, she was looking better for it: her face shone, her eyes sparkled and she was even more confident. Dougie was so impressed, he'd considered signing himself up. He'd thanked Val again and presented her with two black plastic sacks. Loveday had taken over at that point, sorted through the bag of women's clothes and found a pair of designer jeans that she believed Jenna Penrose would give her eye teeth to own.

Val stopped clipping. The hedge was uneven and she'd hacked some parts of it too low. More to the point, the hard work had given her backache. She decided to go over to Connie's for a cup of mint tea and popped inside for her handbag and door keys.

Val had just closed her front door when she heard a chirpy voice behind her. She turned to see Kevin with Dolly on a lead.

'Ah, Val. Gardening, eh? Nice day for it.' He surveyed her handiwork. 'That hedge looks like it could do with a good tidy.'

'It does,' Val decided not to tell him that she'd just finished. She gazed down at the dog. 'How's Dolly?'

Kevin's face settled itself into an anxious frown. 'Not good. She's been scratching herself and I think her skin has become a bit infected. I'm a bit worried. I've got her an appointment at the vet's.'

'Oh, poor thing. When's she going?'

'In half an hour. I just wondered if... I mean, I was going to ask you for a favour. Unless you're too busy...'

'Oh, I'm not busy at all.' Val surveyed the hedge. She'd be glad to leave the mess she'd made.

'I've just had a call from a woman in Merrynporth, a good customer who phoned to tell me that she has a leaky tap in the bathroom.'

'Oh, dear.'

'I ought to go round. I rang Alice but she's stuck in the charity shop – there's no one else there at the moment. And I need to take Dolly to the vet.'

'Do you want me to take her?' Val offered.

Kevin laughed. 'It's either that or you could go to Mrs Cowan and fix her leak...'

Val gazed at the dog who was panting excitedly. 'I don't have a dog seat in my car though.'

Dolly gazed up at Val, her almond eyes appealing. Kevin said, 'The vet is only a short walk into town... if you wouldn't mind?' He gazed upwards. 'It's a nice day for it and she loves a stroll with you.'

'No problem.' Val took the lead Kevin was holding out. 'Which vet?'

'Seymour and Oldbury. It's in the new-build block, just round the corner from The Unicorn Hotel.'

'Oh, I know where that is,' Val said, remembering.

'The appointment is at half two with Matt Seymour.' Kevin rolled his eyes. 'Alice will be sorry she's missed the opportunity. Matt's a bit of a charmer.'

'Oh?' Val raised an eyebrow.

'He's youngish, in his forties. He looks like Ryan Reynolds. I don't suppose you know who that is?'

'He was in *Deadpool*.' Val recalled seeing the film with Ray at home. Ray had loved it. (He was invading her thoughts again.)

'Alice likes his films – we've seen them all,' Kevin said. 'I bet you prefer the ones with the classic actors, you know... Sean Connery, Clint Eastwood? The ones that used to be big in the sixties.'

'The older ones, you mean?' Val teased, enjoying the horrified look on Kevin's face as he held his hands up in protest.

'Oh, no, Val, I didn't mean—'

'Steve McQueen was my heart-throb, but music was my big thing. I was a huge Cat Stevens fan as a teenager and I adored The Beatles.' She was enjoying pulling his leg. 'I don't suppose you've heard of the Fab Four?'

'I listen to them in the van.' Kevin grinned, an expression of relief. 'But my favourite is Dolly Parton. I adore her music.'

'Come on, then, Dolly, let's take you for your appointment and check out this drop-dead-gorgeous vet.' She winked at Kevin. She was fond of him and Alice. They both had hearts of gold. 'What time will you be back?'

'Ah, well, Alice should be back just after four if I'm late. I don't suppose you could hang on to Dolly until then?'

'We'll walk on the beach,' Val replied with a grin. The beach always held the possibility of a chance encounter.

'Thanks, Val. I owe you big time.'

Val was about to suggest he might have a go at levelling her massacred hedge, but he'd launched himself towards his Transit van, on his way. Val checked her pockets for the door keys, swung her handbag onto her shoulder and tugged Dolly's lead lightly. 'Come on, then, let's get you to your appointment. You'll be a good girl at the vet's, won't you, Dolly?'

The Staffy was already off at a fast pace. Val realised she'd left the hedge-cutting shears on the grass in the garden. She hoped no one would steal them, but it was too late now: Dolly was unstoppable.

* * *

Upstairs in Crab Claw cottage a weather-beaten hand let the curtain fall. Ben had been watching Val's efforts at cutting the hedge. He'd observed her talking to Kevin, walking away with the dog on the end of the lead, and he scratched his head thoughtfully. He had been busy all morning painting the landing ceiling; he'd intended to introduce himself to Val once he'd finished, but now she had gone. It didn't matter – he was in no hurry. She certainly kept herself busy. He glanced at the hedge again, thinking she'd made a pig's ear of cutting her side. But she was a good neighbour and Ben was about to do some gardening of his own. It wouldn't be any trouble at all...

* * *

Val stood in the newly built vet's surgery at the smart reception desk. There was a cat in a basket on a seat in the corner meowing loudly and an anxious owner making tutting noses to calm it, repeating, 'Be quiet now, Jennifurr.' Val glanced down at Dolly, meeting her eyes, willing her to behave. The receptionist, who couldn't have been twenty years old, cooed, 'Who have we here?'

'Val Maxwell,' Val offered.

The receptionist swept a hand through her short dark hair, fingered a small earring and gazed at her appointments on the laptop. 'Val...?'

'I'm here for Kevin—'

'Oh, no – I need the dog's name, please,' the receptionist trilled. 'Is this Dolly Holmes?'

'Yes.' Val gazed around but there was no one in the surgery apart from Jennifurr and her anxious owner.

'Right, take a seat. I'm afraid Mr Seymour's not in currently but we have another vet in his place.'

Val led Dolly away gently, finding a seat in the opposite corner to the cat in the basket. The cat meowed again and the owner whispered, 'There's my little love, Jennifurr.'

Val sat down and patted the Staffy. 'Good girl, Dolly – the vet will be here soon.' She smiled – even she was at it now, having a conversation with the pet. Val gazed at the wall, at posters about pet obesity and diabetes. She glanced at the rotund dog and hoped Dolly wasn't going to get a telling-off.

Then a male voice called, 'Jennifurr Jones?'

The woman with the cat basket leaped up and said, 'Yes, that's me,' and disappeared into the surgery. Val and Dolly were alone in the waiting room.

Her thoughts slipped back to her meeting with Ray in the car park of The Sprat. Something about him, the sparkle in his eyes, had taken her back to happier times, to when they were younger. She tried again to examine her feelings: regret that their marriage had failed; dismay that he had chosen Monica. But there was something else, deep beneath, that wouldn't shift. Val knew what it was in an instant. She had loved him absolutely, and it was difficult to stop those feelings. She'd heard stories of people who had lost a limb and yet felt the sensation of it being there. That was how she felt about Ray. She recalled the happy times, the affection, the golden memories, but, like a severed limb, their relationship wouldn't ever grow back. It had been a shock seeing Ray; she hadn't been prepared, but now her feet were steady and back on the ground. She'd try to find herself again.

A door opened and a voice called, 'Dolly Holmes, please.'

'It's us now,' Val whispered and the Staffy padded towards the door. The surgery was a small box room equipped with a tall table, a basin, a desk and a computer. A man in his seventies, slim in a white lab coat, a little taller than Val, with neat white hair and metal-framed glasses greeted her. 'Hello. This must be Dolly. What seems to be the problem?'

Val realised Dolly was probably too heavy for her to lift onto the examining table. She gazed at the dog then at the table and finally at the vet. 'I'm here for my neighbour, Kevin. He says Dolly has been scratching herself and it looks infected.'

'Right.' The vet met Val's eyes. 'Your neighbour's dog?' He paused. 'Haven't we met before?'

Val was trying to remember. The vet was definitely familiar. Then it became clear. 'Were you at the lunch in The Unicorn Hotel?'

'Of course.' He held out a hand. 'I'm Freddie Seymour. Val, isn't it? You were with Dennis Cargill.'

Val recalled the large warm grasp. 'It was The Unicorn, yes.'

'I remember you made your escape early.' Freddie's face shone with recognition. 'I wish you'd stayed. As I recall, lunch was quite dull after you'd left.'

Val noticed the blue eyes twinkling behind the glasses. She watched as he heaved a complacent Dolly onto the table, who sat placidly and gazed at them both roundly. 'So, you're the vet?' she said, immediately feeling silly for stating the obvious.

'My son Matthew's the vet here now, but he was called away – a problem on a farm.'

'Ryan Reynolds?' Val suddenly felt sillier.

'Pardon?'

'So you're retired?'

'Yes...' Freddie examined Dolly, who was gazing serenely up at the vet. 'I'm just helping out today...' He was checking Dolly's belly. 'I see the problem... She has a bit of atopic dermatitis... It's an allergic skin disease... common in bull terriers, and it can cause quite a nasty itch, which I can see has been bothering her. I can give her some Apoquel. It's not a severe case, it should disappear in a week or two. If it persists or she keeps itching, we can give her an injection, but I think the Apoquel should sort it out.' He wandered over to the computer and typed something. 'Megan will give it to you at Reception.'

'Oh, that's good.' Val was watching the vet, taking in his easy manner, his gentle hands and his warm smile. Dolly was watching him steadily too, breathing loudly. Freddie glanced at Val. 'So, you're Dolly's neighbour?'

'Kevin and Alice's neighbour,' Val said. 'I moved in last Christmas.'

'They must be pleased to live next door to someone so accommodating – it was kind of you to bring Dolly here on their behalf.'

'Oh.' Val waved a hand. 'I wasn't busy – only cutting the hedge. Making a hash of it, in fact.'

'You're not a lover of gardening, then?'

'It's only a small patch.' Val shrugged. 'But no.'

'My wife used to love growing flowers.' Freddie sighed. 'I can't be bothered with them myself, not now she's gone...'

'Oh,' Val replied. 'I'm sorry...'

'Dementia, such a cruel illness,' Freddie said sadly. 'I'm glad to get the chance to come into the surgery nowadays – gives me something to do instead of being in an empty house by myself. It's tough after so many years. Are you on your own, Val?'

'I am,' Val heard herself say. 'Well, thanks for sorting Dolly's skin problem.'

'Also... one more thing...' Freddie added, and Val wondered if he was going to ask her for a date. Instead, he said, 'Dolly's carrying a few extra pounds. You might ask Kevin to keep an eye on her waistline…'

'I'll tell him to hold back on the snacks,' she said without thinking. Dolly wrinkled her nose, unconvinced. A thought popped into Val's head. 'I have something for you, to say thanks.'

'Indeed?'

Val delved into her huge handbag and pulled out a favour box. 'So, thanks for helping Dolly. I painted the pebble myself.'

Dolly was squatting on the table, her stomach folded between her hind legs, watching them. Freddie picked up the little tartan box.

'Thank you, Val. That's so kind.'

'Not at all – thank you.' Val was gazing into his eyes. Freddie was staring back.

Dolly snorted, frowning into the distance. Clearly, she was unimpressed by the stupidity of human behaviour. She furrowed her nose as if to imply that the love life of animals was far superior: they didn't waste time with small talk and favour boxes. Then she sniffed again and showed her disgust, a trickle of urine flowing in a steady stream across the vet's table and dripping persistently into a puddle on the tiled floor.

20

Val sauntered through town, the handbag on her shoulder containing the Apoquel and one less favour box. She realised that she was smiling. Dolly was trotting along next to her, cheerful and carefree, despite having disgraced herself at the vet's. Val had been so apologetic but Freddie had been charming, reaching smoothly for an industrial-sized kitchen roll, explaining that it was often a sign that dogs were relaxed, which was always a good thing.

Val knew that Connie would be thrilled that she'd found a contender for Mr June. Freddie was friendly and attractive. She had to admit, a date with him might be nice. Again, it was therapy, building her confidence: she hadn't thought about Ray since she'd entered the surgery. And although she was no longer looking, Freddie was definitely wedding-guest material.

Val was deep in thought, wondering if Freddie might ask her out. Something told her he would, especially when he found her email address inside the box. It had been a stroke of genius.

'Val. Wait up for me. Hang on.'

She heard a familiar voice behind her and paused as Ollie caught up with her. Despite the warm weather, he was still wearing the green anorak. 'It's Dolly.' He bent down and stroked her fur from the top of her head to her tail, then stroked her again. 'She's so nice.'

'The vet didn't think so,' Val joked. 'She just peed on his table.'

'Oh, no.' Ollie was momentarily alarmed. 'I'd like to paint her picture though – but without the pee. She's got a very noble face and I love the shape of her head. Her fur's so smooth.'

'The vet was very nice about it,' Val said, still thinking about Freddie. Ollie clutched her arm.

'Val, I wanted to ask you about a film I saw on the television yesterday with my mum. It was about a boy with blond hair who is in a gang, but he's very romantic and he meets this girl at a party and she's dressed as an angel and he falls in love with her, but everyone says he's not allowed to because she's from a posh family and he's only a gang member.'

'*Romeo and Juliet*?' Val was on the ball. Ollie's face shone with admiration.

'How did you know that?'

Val winked. 'I know all the romantic ones.'

'But they die at the end of the film. And it was the same actor in *Titanic*. He died too and my mum sobbed into a tissue. I want to watch something that has a sensible ending, not unrequited love.'

'Some films are sad but not all of them,' Val said. 'At the end of *Notting Hill* the happy couple stay together and have a baby.'

'Really?' Ollie was thrilled. 'I want to watch *Notting Hill* with my mum. It would be nice for her to see an uplifting film where the man and the woman are compatible and happy ever after. I think it's important to focus on positives and not watch too many sad films that make people cry.'

'I can lend you the DVD,' Val offered.

'That's great,' Ollie said. 'When can we have lunch again?'

'What about next Tuesday, twelve o'clock at Pizza Palace? My treat.'

'I've never been there. I love pizza.'

'Me too. And I'm seeing Loveday on Friday.'

'For a pizza?'

'No...' Val recalled Loveday's first meeting with Henry Scott. 'It's a meeting about our plans for improving community life in Lowenstowe. But we'll catch up on Tuesday, shall we?'

'Great.' Ollie rubbed his hands together. 'And will you bring the DVD?'

'Of course, I'll see what I can find.'

'That's brilliant.' Ollie pushed his hands into his pockets. 'Tuesday at twelve for pizza. My favourite's Hawaiian, but I don't like anything with olives on. It's not to my taste – olives smell funny. I'll see you, Val.'

He turned to step off the kerb and a black car whizzed too fast around the corner, almost touching the sleeve of his anorak. Ollie flung himself backwards with a yelp. 'Did you see that, Val?'

Val put a hand on his arm. 'The driver wasn't paying attention.'

'Idiot,' Ollie shouted before bending down to stroke Dolly protectively. 'It's a good job Dolly didn't walk into the road. She might have been run over.'

Val was still staring after the car, a sleek black Audi. She had recognised one of the occupants, the driver, sitting next to a red-haired woman in sunglasses, talking, his eyes not on the road. She had only glimpsed him fleetingly, but she knew exactly who he was. Nigel Carrow had been paying more attention to his companion than to road safety.

* * *

As Val approached the little row of cottages, Dolly trotting beside her, she was humming a song in her tuneless way. If Alice was back, she'd deposit the dog and the prescription, then she'd call into Connie's house for a cup of tea and tell her all about Freddie. Connie would be delighted with Val's new conquest, and impressed by her quick thinking with the favour box. Then she arrived at Teasel Cottage and her mouth dropped open in surprise. The hedge had been neatly clipped, the top levelled perfectly straight, and the hedge clippers had been deposited on her doorstep. Next to them was a bunch of sweet peas tied with string. Val picked them up and wafted them beneath her nose; they smelled heavenly and she closed her eyes and sighed.

Next door, Ben lifted the upstairs curtains and leaned forward, a smile on his face. He was about to put a second coat on the landing ceiling. He'd introduce himself soon, but for now he was delighted to be able to do something kind for his good neighbour.

On Monday morning, Val and Connie were sitting in the lounge of Val's cottage, sipping tea. Val frowned; she was perplexed and a little disappointed.

'Freddie's had the whole weekend to contact me. I was sure that he would.'

'Perhaps he's been busy standing in at the vet's?'

'All weekend?' Val lifted her cup to her lips without drinking. 'I've been checking my emails regularly – nothing! I was sure there was a spark between us.'

Connie was sure. 'He'll email.'

Val sighed. 'I woke up this morning and my heels ached.'

'Oh, poor you,' Connie said sympathetically.

'It means I'm getting old,' Val wailed. 'So, it follows that no one will be interested in me any more. I'm falling apart. I'm better off by myself. Do I really want to go out with Freddie just for the sake of a wedding photo?'

Connie met her eyes. 'No, I think you really like him. We're not all meant to be on our own.'

'I'm not sure I can be bothered, not now... I keep changing my mind but, in all honesty...'

'I'm the one who isn't bothered.' Connie smiled sadly. 'I was never in love until I met Mike, then we were everything to each other. He was my world, and I lost him.' She shuddered. 'I'd rather be lonely than with someone I can't love. But you can still meet someone.'

'Connie, I never really explained how awful I felt when Ray left me.'

Connie took her hand. 'It must have been a terrible experience. But you're so strong.'

'Sometimes I'm not sure...'

'Not sure you're over him?' Connie said. 'Of course, you and he split up relatively recently and I'm still going on about Mike, all those years ago. How insensitive...'

'You don't think you could ever move on?'

'Mike has stayed in my heart. I've never thought about letting go. But everything you do, meeting these new people, going on dates, gives me hope for the future. I hope that I can start to live a bit, that I can perhaps turn a fresh page of my life, as you're doing.'

'That's so good to know.' Val smiled. 'The truth is, I still feel a bit vulnerable. I don't want to be hurt again. But Freddie is a nice man, and I shouldn't assume he'd do what Ray did to me.'

'I can see you're attracted to him – your face lights up.'

'But he hasn't contacted me so it's a non-starter.' Val sipped her tea gratefully. 'Connie, I'm so glad you're my friend. It's so good to have someone to share these things with.'

'Likewise.' Connie was thoughtful. 'Sometimes having a good friend is best, someone who understands...'

Val agreed. 'And you won't find yourself dumped.' She thought of Ray again, then hauled her thoughts away. 'How's Will?'

'I spoke to him last night on the phone. I'm trying to persuade him to come here next spring but he says I should go to New Zealand – one person flying would be cheaper than a whole family.'

'That makes sense. I've been chatting to Tom about the wedding.' Val took a breath. 'It's only six months away.'

'Time's rushing by.' Connie gazed into her teacup as if trying to work out the future. 'We need to find you someone.'

'Maybe, maybe not. I'll be happy whatever happens.' Val closed her eyes, imagining her son and new daughter-in-law at the reception. Then Ray appeared in the space of her imagination, awkward but handsome in a new suit, Monica tucking her arm possessively through his.

'Right.' Val stood up and picked up the empty cups. 'Let's go for a stroll before lunch. It's beautiful outside. It's a sunglasses and T-shirt day.'

'Maybe we'll see Mr January,' Connie said hopefully. 'We haven't spotted him for a while.'

'He's probably knee-deep editing comets and meteors...'

'I bet he's gorgeous in shorts though,' Connie suggested, and Val thought how he and Connie would make a lovely couple. Then she had an idea. 'Oh, I must make a cake for the sailor man next door.'

'Ben Berry? Have you seen him?'

'No, but I wanted to thank him. I told you he sorted out the hedge and gave me some lovely sweet peas. I peeked at his back garden through the bedroom window and he's made it really nice – vegetables, flowers. I've never seen him working out there though. Do you think he does the gardening at night?'

Connie said, 'I haven't seen him for a week or so. I usually bump into him when he's off to his boat. I know he's always out fishing at this time of year. Dave says he's in the pub sometimes.'

'What does he look like?'

'Tall, slim, quite handsome. No, I did see him last week – he was going fishing early in the morning and I was in pyjamas talking to the postman. He's quite shy.'

'The postman?'

'No, Ben. Well, maybe not shy... private.'

Val agreed. 'He's so private I haven't met him yet.'

There was a soft knock on the front door. Val raised an eyebrow. 'Perhaps that's him now, come to introduce himself at last?'

Connie stood up and stretched out her arms. 'No, he'll be out at sea in this weather. What a lovely life he has, the ocean, the freedom.'

The soft knock came again. Val gazed at the empty teacups in her hand. 'Would you just get that, Connie? I'll wash these, then we can go out.'

'Of course.' Connie was on her way to the door. Val hurried into the kitchen and turned on the tap, swishing the cups, inverting them on the draining board. She heard soft voices, Connie's and a deeper tone. She took a quick breath; it was a voice she recognised, and she remembered when she had last heard it. She rushed into the lounge: Connie was standing with a tall man wearing metal-framed glasses. She was smiling. 'I think you two know each other...'

'I should have emailed but I thought I'd pop round...' Freddie Seymour was all apologies. 'I have Dolly's address on file, so it wasn't hard to work out where you live. Hello, Val.'

'Hello, Freddie.' Val wasn't sure what else to say.

'So...' Freddie was awkward too. 'This is where you live – and I've just introduced myself to Connie here...'

Suddenly, an idea came to Val. 'Connie and I were just off for a walk. Would you like to come with us, Freddie?'

Connie was horrified. 'Oh, no, I should go back home, really – I just need to—'

Val gave her a meaningful stare. 'We should all go. It would be lovely. What do you think, Freddie?'

Freddie gazed from Val to Connie and back to Val, then a smile spread like sunshine across his face. 'Do you know,' he said, 'I can't think of anything I'd enjoy more.'

21

Val whispered in Connie's ear that she'd prefer company: she was not ready to be with Freddie alone. And now Connie was smiling with delight as the three of them headed for the beach. Freddie was such fun, recounting anecdotes that had happened to him as a vet, including the story of an old colleague who'd advertised his cat-neutering service as Fifty Shades of Spey. Val was the life and soul, telling stories about her time as a primary school teacher, how she'd once asked a class to paint a picture of great legends and a nine-year-old had drawn Elvis.

The sun warmed their skin as they strolled along, the tide rolling in making a low whispering sound. Seagulls swooped overhead; people basked in deck chairs and children built tall sandcastles. The tourists had started to arrive in large numbers now: toddlers rushed into waves, jumping and screaming; single adults stretched on colourful towels. A man kicked a ball gently towards a tousle-haired child who tried to tap it back with a pudgy foot.

Freddie paused to check his watch. 'This walking is thirsty work. Is there a nice pub nearby where we might call in for some refreshment? I could buy lunch – it's past one.'

'The Boat House,' Val said enthusiastically. 'We could sit outside – it's such a lovely day.'

Half an hour later, they were seated in the beer garden bathed in glowing sunshine, drinking wine. Dave was delighted to see them, boasting that the fish dish of the day was delicious and they wouldn't regret sampling it. During lunch, Val glanced from Freddie to Connie, chattering easily, and she felt a warm glow: this was how she wanted life to be, sharing the companionship of kind, genial people. What mattered most was the feeling of belonging, being wanted and cherished. Val was filled with a contentment that felt special. She sipped wine and held the taste in her mouth, savouring a moment filled with sweetness. Her eyes met Freddie's: he was having similar thoughts. Things were going very well.

Then Connie said, 'I'm just popping to the ladies.'

Val and Freddie watched her disappear into the pub, then Freddie turned his attention to Val. 'She's very pleasant, your friend. She's a widow, isn't she? I heard her mention it during our walk.'

'Connie's lovely,' Val agreed. 'Yes, she lost her husband years ago.'

'That's sad. But it's important to move on.' Freddie's face was suddenly serious. 'Andrea and I were together for fifty years; she was a wonderful woman but...' He managed a smile. 'I've enjoyed myself today more than I thought possible. Thank you, Val.'

Val said, 'I enjoyed it too.'

'I wonder if...' Freddie pushed his plate away. 'Could I take you out to dinner? Somewhere up the coast a little way, somewhere nice...'

'I'd like that.' Val smiled. 'Yes, that would be great.' She made a joke. 'Is that just me for dinner, or me and Connie?'

'I like Connie but it's you I'd like to take to dinner.' Freddie's expression was open, honest. 'I think we have so much in common. I'd like us to get to know each other.'

Val agreed. Freddie was very nice indeed: he was pleasant, intelligent, generous, witty, warm. She thought about asking him what his plans were for Christmas and if he'd like to go to Canada. But a different question had been buzzing like a bee, whirling around her mind, and she needed to ask it now. She took a breath. 'Freddie, when did your wife die?'

'Andrea?'

Val nodded. 'It must have been so difficult for you.'

'It's tragic...' Freddie looked around him, his shoulders hunched awkwardly. 'The thing is, she's still... I mean, she's very, very ill, so unwell, she's being looked after.'

Val closed her eyes for a moment; she knew something had been bothering her. She put it into words. 'So, Andrea is alive.'

'She's in a nursing home. She doesn't recognise me any more. It's as if she's gone already.' Freddie rubbed a hand over his face and when it came away, his eyes were misty.

'I thought you were a widower,' Val said.

'I never said so.'

'You didn't, you're right. That's what made me wonder.' Val sat back in her seat. 'But I thought you were free to...'

'To start again?' Freddie exhaled. 'I'm sorry. I didn't mean to deceive you, Val. I thought we might be together as friends, and later, we'd perhaps become more than that.'

'Yes, I understand...' Val shook her head slowly; she had been developing feelings for him. It was taking her time to adjust, to process new thoughts.

He took her hand, pressing it gently. 'Don't blame me, please. It's so difficult, what with Andrea being the way she is now, and being in the house by myself. I'm... lonely.'

'Oh, Freddie.' Val's hand was still in his. 'It must be so hard for you. I'm really sorry.'

He bent forwards, deflated. 'It is...'

'I think it's probably best if we don't see each other.' She lifted her head up to look at him. 'Not right now.'

'Can I call round to see you sometime?'

'I don't think so.'

'Maybe we could just have a drink together, as friends?'

'I'm not sure that would be a good idea.' Val swallowed hard. She had made a mistake; she'd believed he was single. It was not anyone's fault but something between them had shifted. 'I'm sorry.'

'But perhaps we could—'

Val took a breath and spoke her thoughts aloud, 'I can't see you. It doesn't feel right. Not at the moment.'

'Oh.' Freddie stared at her, full of sadness. 'I see.'

'I'd feel better if we didn't meet – out of respect for your wife.'

Freddie nodded slowly. 'I understand. The last thing I want anyone to think is that I'm being disrespectful to Andrea. I still love her deeply.' He breathed, then stood up tall and smoothed his clothes. 'Thanks for giving me hope though, Val. Well, I'll be on my way. Perhaps you'll ring me one day... It would be nice to spend time with you.'

'Perhaps one day. But not now. I'm sorry, Freddie.'

'No, I should apologise. You're absolutely right, it's too early.' Freddie shook his head. 'Goodbye, Val. I wish you the best of luck.'

Val watched him walk away and disappear around the corner. She wiped a tear lodged in the corner of her eye. She felt sorry for all three of them.

Then Connie was behind her, sitting down eagerly, smiling. 'It's taken me ages to get out of the pub – I was chatting to Dave, then I bumped into Dennis. He wanted to tell me he'd seen his ex out with someone else,' she said, a little breathless. 'So, where's Freddie? Where's Mr June?'

Val met her eyes. 'He's gone, Connie. We both agreed, it's for the best.'

* * *

The next day Val was sitting in Pizza Palace with Ollie. Val was gazing at the brightly painted walls, the crimson tablecloths and the scarlet chairs, waiting for the waitress to bring their food. Ollie was gazing at the young waitress. He whispered loudly to Val. 'Her badge says she's called Jasmine.'

Val reached into her handbag. 'I brought you these.' She put a pile of DVDs on the table and Ollie inspected them: *Notting Hill*, *Dirty Dancing*, *Chocolat* and *Pride and Prejudice*. She wasn't sure they were exactly what Ollie wanted but it was all she could find. Ollie flicked through each one, a smile on his face, then he gazed at the cover of *Dirty Dancing*, his eyes gleaming. 'My mum will love this one. They look nice, the man and woman together. I wish I could dance like that.'

Val agreed, 'Don't we all?'

Ollie turned his head to the side, examining her, suddenly thoughtful. 'Have you got a boyfriend now, Val?'

Val leaned forward confidentially. 'I thought I had but now I haven't.'

Ollie frowned. 'What happened? Was he incompatible?'

'Yes, he was.' Val knew she'd done the right thing to put space between herself and Freddie before her feelings became stronger. She thought how lonely he must be, how his wife and he must both be suffering, and she wondered if, in time, she'd give him a call and they could become friends again. But at the moment she needed to keep her distance: it would be easy to fall in love with him and, with his wife so ill, it wasn't fair all round.

The waitress arrived, her bright red hair tied in a ponytail, her uniform crisp. She deposited two hot thin pizzas on the table. Ollie gazed up at her. 'You have lovely hair, Jasmine.'

Jasmine marched away without saying anything. Ollie gazed down at his fingers. 'She doesn't like me.'

'There are plenty more fish.' Val was tucking into her pizza.

Ollie ripped his pizza in half, the yellow cheese stretching into a ragged elastic line and eventually breaking. 'The problem is, Val, I don't want a fish.'

'There are plenty of nice girls in the world, Ollie, who'd just love to be your girlfriend.'

'Yes, but...' Ollie pushed a torn piece of Hawaiian pizza into his mouth '... none of them have met me yet.'

* * *

Early on Friday morning, the sky overcast, Loveday was waiting on the steps outside the town hall when Val arrived, Connie and Alice in tow. Loveday glanced at her wrist. 'The appointment's at half past nine.' She was staring at bare skin; she had no watch. 'I've been here since nine and I haven't seen hide nor hair of Henry Scott.' She was wearing aviator sunglasses and a Greenpeace T-shirt with a picture of a boat in rainbow colours. She frowned furiously, raising a fist as if she meant business.

'Perhaps he arrived early?' Val suggested.

'I wanted to stop him and explain a few things,' Loveday said.

'We have made a list.' Connie indicated the folder she had tucked under her arm.

Alice nodded in agreement. 'I'm sure he'll meet us halfway.'

'Halfway's no bleddy good. Come on. Let's go and see what he has to say for himself,' Loveday announced, pushing through the red door. 'It's twenty-five past at least, by my reckoning.'

Upstairs, at the reception desk, there was an older woman in glasses, her shoulders rounded as she examined a diary. She glanced up, her face composed. 'May I help you?'

Loveday pushed to the front. 'You may. I have an appointment with Henry Scott.'

'Ah, Mrs Moon.' The receptionist singled out Loveday. She had clearly been forewarned. 'I'm sorry, but you can't see Mr Scott today.'

'I have an appointment.'

'I'm afraid he's been indisposed.'

'What does that mean?' Loveday asked. 'Does he have a cold? Or is he just having a nice jaunt up country somewhere and he couldn't be bothered to come and see me?'

The receptionist waved her fingers as if she were momentarily bothered by a buzzing fly. 'I can make you an alternative appointment.'

'I want to see him now.'

'I'm afraid that's not possible.'

Val rested a hand on Loveday's shoulder, hoping it might calm her. 'When's the next available slot, please?'

'He has several meetings booked, and then he's on holiday...' The receptionist paused. 'He has various commitments, but I could offer you... half past two on Wednesday September the fourteenth.'

Loveday was outraged. 'Bleddy September?' She huffed. 'Can't you get him in here tomorrow?'

'Book us in for the fourteenth, please, at half two.' Val made her voice syrup smooth. 'But please let him know that, in the interim, we're going to be very busy. Also, please tell him to keep a close eye on the media – because we're going to talk to the newspapers and the television. They are all giving us their backing on this issue.'

Val heard Loveday gasp in surprise behind her. The receptionist raised an eyebrow. 'The press and the TV?'

'Of course,' Val said. 'The wildlife on our beaches is at risk. The seagulls feed on garbage. And it's summertime, which means tourists and more litter. We won't stand by. And the more people who know about it through the media, the better support we'll have.'

'There will be petitions,' Connie called over Val's shoulder.

'And protest marches,' Alice added hopefully.

'In fact, everybody in Lowenstowe will be on board,' Val explained. 'So do tell Henry that we expect him to be very busy on our behalf when he returns.'

'Oh, right, yes. Of course. I'll make sure I pass that on...' the receptionist said, but Val and Loveday were already marching downstairs, Connie and Alice trailing behind.

Outside, Loveday flopped back against the white brick wall of the town hall and closed her eyes behind the sunglasses. She was exhausted. 'I thought the woman on the desk was going to get the better of us.' She exhaled. 'Thanks, Valerie. You told her what's what. But how are we going to get the media on our side?'

'I'm all over it,' Val replied, her eyes flashing. 'We're taking our protest to the next level. Right, come round mine and let's have a cuppa. We'll contact the newspapers and the TV this afternoon and get things moving.'

'Great,' Connie said. 'I like it when Val's in this mood. Things get done.'

They began the walk back. Val surged ahead, she and Alice chatting about how Dolly's course of Apoquel had cured the raw skin problem; the vet had worked wonders. Two steps behind them, Loveday pushed her arm through Connie's and muttered, 'She's on a roll today, our Valerie. I don't think I've seen her quite so fired up.'

Connie shrugged. 'That's how you mend a broken heart, by being busy.'

'Ah, she's been disappointed again, has she? A local chap?' Loveday was suddenly interested.

'Yes, he was lovely,' Connie said. 'But then she found out he wasn't free.'

Loveday's brow clouded and she clenched a fist, fiercely loyal. 'I'd give him a piece of my mind.'

'It's sad. I thought he might be Mr December.'

'So, we need to find our Valerie a proper gentleman. I don't suppose you need any help with that, do you?'

Connie smiled. 'Well, I was going to take her out for a day somewhere, to cheer her up.'

'I'll come along with you.' Loveday grinned. 'And then we'll find a perfect bloke for her son's wedding photo. She deserves some happiness and I still know how to chat up a man. You leave it all to me.'

22

Val, Connie and Loveday drove across Cornwall on the B3273 towards Mevagissey along the rugged coast past an old tin mine, a conical stone-chimneyed structure that stood abandoned on the moorland high above the frothing turquoise ocean. The sun streamed relentlessly through the windscreen, warming Val's face as she followed the signs to St Austell. Connie sat next to her wearing shorts and dark sunglasses, repeating that the weather was glorious and they'd have the loveliest day, it would cheer Val up. Val protested that she didn't need cheering up, she was fine, while Loveday muttered that she'd packed sandwiches because the prices in these tourist places was bleddy ridiculous.

They parked in one of the bays outside The Lost Gardens of Heligan and traipsed towards the entrance. Loveday frowned as Connie bought tickets.

'*How* much?' she asked the young woman who took the payment. 'We don't want to buy shares in the place.' She gazed up at the sky. 'Weather's going to change.'

'I don't think so,' Connie said, enjoying the warm sunlight that illuminated the grass leading to the woodlands, giving it the texture of velvet. 'Well, here we are, The Lost Gardens. We can explore the estate, the sculptures, the jungle.'

'I won't be able to walk around all of it on these legs,' Loveday complained. 'I might just sit on a bench and eat my sandwiches and let you two young ones run amok in the jungle area.'

'Come on, Loveday,' Val wrapped an arm around her shoulder. 'This is Cornwall in all its natural beauty.'

'Lowenstowe is Cornwall in its beauty too,' Loveday insisted. 'Once the emmets have gone in September – the careless ones, that is.'

Val hugged her affectionately: she was used to Loveday's complaints. Her pessimism hid a fear of disappointment, and she clung to it like a safety blanket.

Loveday offered a grim smile. 'All right, I'll do my best to have some fun, Valerie.'

'Let's go and see the sculptures.' Connie clapped her hands. 'I just love them.'

The three friends made their way towards Woodland Walk, strolling through trees where light filtered through leaves, stippling the ground below. There were so many different plants: tall ones that opened wide leaves, bending like palms; filigree ferns, pale shivering leaves, dense foliage, spiky branches, crimson rhododendrons. Then Connie pointed. 'Oh, look.'

At first, it appeared that a young woman was lying on the ground, asleep. Her face was mottled with moss, her clothes clustered ivy. She rested on a slender arm, fingers outstretched, a figure of peacefulness.

Loveday grinned excitedly. 'Oh, that's proper clever.' She turned to Val. 'How do they do that?'

'She's a sculpture, made of straw, cement, and clay,' Val said.

'She's the Mud Maid. She changes with the seasons,' Connie added. 'In the summer as the plants develop, she grows long hair.'

'Can we see some more sculptures?'

Connie met Loveday's gleaming eyes. 'Yes, there are lots of them around the woodlands.'

Loveday was off, chuntering happily. As Val and Connie followed, they heard her exclaim, 'Will you look at this chap? Oh, I do wish my John could see this. There's a monster buried in the ground, with just his head sticking out.'

Val and Connie stood at Loveday's shoulder and gazed at the top of the rounded head of a green-skinned man. His nose touched the grass, the rest of his face seemingly hidden below, bright blue eyes staring upwards towards his leafy hair. Loveday clapped her hands. 'It's the Giant's Head.'

'And the hair is made from crocosmia— it's a type of weed-like plant that flowers orange in July,' Connie added.

Loveday frowned. 'How on earth do you know that?'

Connie smiled and waved a brochure. 'It's all in here.'

'He's proper handsum. Where do we go next?' Loveday was thoroughly enjoying herself.

They visited the 'jungle', an area of tall, luxuriant foliage and exotic plants where Val coaxed Loveday across the hundred-feet-long rope bridge. Loveday clutched Val's hand. 'I can't look down there, Valerie. It's a long way to the bottom.'

'Look up,' Val said. Above them, a yellow canopy of leaves draped from a tall tree. The air smelled fresh and earthy, the scent of rich soil mixed with sweet pollen.

'This is a Burmese Rope Bridge,' Connie said, reading the brochure and Loveday rolled her eyes. They passed a glass-smooth pond, a bamboo tunnel, and Connie pointed out giant rhubarb and banana plantations as they strolled through avenues of palms. Loveday's eyes were round with excitement. Then she said, 'Can we find somewhere to sit and have our lunch?'

Loveday plonked herself down on her jacket, grumbling that

she didn't want the damp grass to give her piles and tucked into her sandwiches from reusable beeswax wrap. Connie and Val sat beside her and Val offered Connie something from a sandwich box. A pheasant emerged from the bushes, its long speckled tail swishing behind it, brushing the ground, its inquisitive beady eye surrounded by yellow and red feathers. It ruffled amber plumage, approaching Loveday, its blue head nodding.

'What do you want? Go away,' Loveday screeched. 'You're not having my cheese roll.' She turned to Val, the widest smile on her face. 'I'd have loved to have brought John here, Morwenna too, when she was young. Oh, there's so much I wish I'd done. Thank you both for such a nice day. It's been handsum.'

Then a fat drop of rain plopped on Loveday's face, and another. Val gazed up and felt a wet spattering on her forehead. Connie looked aghast at her legs in shorts, and muttered, 'It's raining.'

Loveday struggled into the raincoat she had stuffed in a tote bag. 'Cornish weather, what do you expect?' She smiled. 'Come prepared, I always say. Well, it's been a long day, Valerie, but we should be getting back to the car.'

The rain began to tumble, splashing on leaves overhead, a soft drumming. The air was newly scented with freshness as the drops soaked into damp earth and dry clothes. Val and Connie linked arms with Loveday as they hurried back towards the car park.

'I love this smell,' Val said.

'Isn't it called petrichor?' Connie asked.

'How do you know that?' Loveday grunted. 'Was it in the bleddy brochure?'

Connie grinned; she and Val increased their speed as much as they were able with Loveday lagging behind. As they reached the car, Loveday shuffled into the back seat and shrugged off her damp coat. 'Well, I have to say, I enjoyed today more than I thought I would,' she announced. 'We must go on another one.'

'Me too.' Connie closed her eyes. 'Do you know, it's probably the first day in twenty years where I haven't spent a single second feeling sorry for myself.' She smiled. 'No, today was about me, my time. I really enjoyed myself. Thank you.'

'So, when are we going on another day trip? I like being an emmet.' Loveday gave a wicked laugh. 'It's more fun than getting let down by a man. What do you say, Valerie?'

Val started the car, a smile on her face, and replied, 'It certainly is.'

* * *

That night, the hot weather brought in a clattering storm, thunder rolling and rain battering the cottages. The following morning, a Sunday, the warm sunshine had returned, along with a fresh breeze. When Connie knocked at the door, Val was sitting at the table writing notes in a well-used notepad. She leaped up to let Connie in.

'Great to see you. I was about to stop for a cuppa. I've been trying to arrange a meeting for everyone for next week.' They brought mugs of tea to the table and Val pushed her notepad away. 'I think we have Caden Curnow on board, and that should be really useful. He's a reporter who works for the local newspaper. We've emailed each other several times. He's keen to feature some articles in *The North Cornwall Gazette* about our summer campaign to clean up the beaches. I'm meeting him next week.'

'Oh, that sounds really good,' Connie replied. 'Loveday will be delighted.' Then Val's phone buzzed loudly. Val grabbed it, frowning as she listened.

'Alice? Whereabouts are you? Who? Ah, right. No, Connie's here... I'll make a quick call then we'll be down... Yes, in a few minutes.'

Connie's brow furrowed. 'What's happened?'

'It was Alice. She and Kev and Dolly are down on the beach. So's Loveday. There's a bit of a commotion going on. A creature has washed up on the tide, a turtle, Alice thinks. Loveday's telling everyone the poor thing has been poisoned.'

'Oh, no. We should get down there now.'

'I'm just thinking...' Val clutched her phone in her hand. 'I'll give Caden Curnow from *The Gazette* a ring – I'm sure he'll be up for a story, even on a Sunday.'

Half an hour later, Val and Connie were pushing their way through a crowd of some two-dozen people. Loveday was standing at the front wearing her aviator glasses, jeans rolled up to the knees and a white T-shirt proclaiming the slogan 'Find the Fish' with a cartoon graphic of plastic bottles masking one solitary fish. At her feet was a huge turtle, some six feet long, a beige shell blotched with dark patches, its stiff limbs sticking out. It wasn't moving.

Loveday was shouting for the whole crowd to hear. 'It will have swallowed plastic, that's for sure. The poor creature has no chance out there with all the waste that's thrown into the oceans, bottles and bags and such like. Its stomach is probably like a bleddy land-fill site.'

A woman's voice came from the crowd. 'I've seen jellyfish on the beach before but never a turtle.'

A child asked, 'Is it dead?'

Another replied, 'Well, it's not moving, is it?'

Val touched Loveday's arm. 'I've invited someone from the press to come down. He should be here any moment. Has anyone called the RSPCA?' She gazed down at the turtle. 'Poor thing. What happened to it?'

Loveday placed her hands on her hips. 'Pollution, that's what happened.'

Connie gazed around. 'It's drawn quite a crowd.'

Alice came to join them, her expression anxious. 'Kev's taken Dolly off for a stroll – she wanted to sniff the poor turtle, so he thought it'd be best to keep her at a distance.'

Val said, 'Good move – well done, Kevin.'

Then a slim young man with perfectly styled blond hair pushed through the crowd, calling, 'Hello. Is Val Maxwell here?'

'I'm Val.' Val thrust out a hand. 'Hello. Are you Caden Curnow?'

'I am.' He hiked up the sleeves of his jacket. 'I'll take photos and comments on my phone and get photos and some bystander statements.' His eyes gleamed.

Val took in the youthful appearance, the earnest face, the flowery shirt beneath the light jacket, the Bermuda shorts. 'Thanks for coming down so quickly, Caden. This is Loveday Moon.'

Loveday was by her side, squinting at Caden through the aviator glasses. 'Are you the reporter?' She wrinkled her nose. 'You can't be more than twenty-two.'

'Oh, I won't see twenty-two again, that passed me by years ago,' Caden said, pushing a hand through his hair. 'Pleased to meet you, Loveday – I've heard about you.' He tugged out his phone. 'I'll get some photos.' He turned to the crowd. 'Could you all move back, please? I'm from the press. I need to get some shots of the turtle with the waves coming in.'

Most people shuffled back, but Loveday stood her ground, posing next to the turtle, her hands on her hips. She said, 'I'm the spokesperson. You'll want to interview me about the work we do locally – and the lack of help we get from—'

'Does anyone know anything about the turtle?' Caden asked as he took more photos. 'I assume it's dead.'

'It's a leatherback.' A calm voice came from behind him. Val turned to see Freddie Seymour move forwards, kneeling next to the turtle. 'I've informed the RSPCA. Yes, it looks very dead to me.' He avoided her eyes. 'I'd be pretty sure the turtle will have plastic in its stomach. It's a known fact, most turtles do.'

Caden stood back, taking photos, then he held out his phone to record the comments. 'So, do you think it was plastic waste that killed the turtle?'

'Of course, it did.' Loveday put her mouth close to the phone, her brow clouded. 'What else would have happened? The poor thing's been poisoned.'

'I suspect the turtle's been out at sea for a while and was washed in with last night's storm,' Freddie said softly. 'It's quite decomposed already. And these deep cuts across its shell are probably propellor wounds – it's clearly been caught by a boat.'

'Are you an expert?' Caden turned his attention and the phone to Freddie.

'I'm a vet. I heard about the turtle and came straight down.'

'So, some background, please – why do turtles ingest plastic, Mr...?' Caden asked.

'Freddie Seymour. It's because they mistake it for jellyfish, which is their usual prey. I can't say for certain, but I would imagine its stomach will contain some plastic. It's fairly normal.'

Loveday was livid. 'Make sure you put that in your paper.'

'I will,' Caden said emphatically. He spoke to Freddie again. 'Where do leatherback turtles come from?'

'It's possible that it's come from as far away as the Caribbean.' Freddie stood up. 'I'll phone a colleague of mine who's a researcher at a university. I can ask her to come over and collect the turtle and do a post-mortem, if you like. Then we'd have more information.'

'That would be good.' Caden held out a business card. 'Contact me at *The Gazette*.'

'Hello, Val.' Freddie turned round hopefully. 'It's good to see you.'

'Hello, Freddie,' Val acknowledged him awkwardly, inclining her head.

'You look well.' He shuffled his feet.

'Thanks.' Val met his eyes. She wanted to add that he looked well too but his expression was sad. Their eyes locked for a moment then she said, 'Thanks for coming to look at the turtle.'

'I'm always glad to help.' Freddie bent forward to gaze at his shoes for a moment; they were damp with sand. Then he stared into the crowd that had stayed behind to listen.

Caden broke the silence. 'Right. I'd like to buy you ladies a drink in the local hostelry and have a long discussion about the good work you're doing. I'm volunteering my services as from today...' He met Loveday's eyes, his own twinkling. 'I want to be a member of your group, Mrs Moon.'

'That's a bleddy handsum idea. Let's go and get ourselves around a drink.' Loveday grunted.

Connie, Alice, Loveday and Caden led Val in the direction of The Boat House, Caden asking excitedly about what the group would be called. Alone on the beach, Freddie stood next to the turtle gazing at the broken, immobile creature. As the tide rolled in and soaked his shoes, he put his hands to his head and sighed.

MR JULY

23

Caden brought a tray of drinks, four balloon glasses of gin and tonic and an orange juice, placing them on the table in the beer garden.

'What's this?' Loveday reached for a large glass.

'I bought you all a G and T.'

'I don't think I like gin,' Loveday announced and took a swig, smacking her lips. 'Ah, but this is handsum.'

'Mine's the orange juice,' Caden explained. 'I'll have to zoom back home and send in my pic and the story by three.'

'Don't you drink?' Alice asked.

'Like a fish,' Caden admitted. 'We'll save that for another time. I want to hear all about your group. But first, oh, Val...' He puffed out his cheeks. 'Did I notice something going on between you and the vet on the beach? I mean – do you two have history?'

'Not really,' Val said sadly. 'But he's a nice man. We were friends for a while.'

Caden agreed. 'I could tell by his face – you must have broken his heart. Are you all right?'

'I'm fine – it wasn't even a June fling.' Val sighed.

Connie was disappointed. 'We'll find someone better for July.'

Val wrinkled her nose. 'Oh, no, I don't really think...'

'Really?' Caden was amazed. 'Are you doing a different lover every month, Val?' He raised his eyebrows. 'That would be a great story for the paper.'

'What?' Val was aghast.

Loveday grunted. 'You're a sharp one – you don't miss much.'

'Oh, don't mind me.' Caden waved a hand. 'I sympathise totally. I'm the king of break-ups. I've been dumped more times than Cornwall refuse.' He beamed. 'Believe me, there's bound to be someone out there.'

'I'm not sure I want anyone.' Val swigged from the glass. 'I think I'm better off without.'

'I'm definitely better off without,' Connie said.

'I've got Kev but sometimes I think he loves Dolly more than me.' Alice lifted her glass. 'I sit next to him while he watches TV and tells her how gorgeous she is while he ignores me completely. What does that say about my marriage?' She sighed. 'And I love him to bits.'

'I'm the luckiest of all of you,' Loveday announced. 'I've got my John. I couldn't have a better man in the world. We married when I was twenty years old and we didn't have a penny. We've been together through thick and thin and now I'm eighty-two.' She folded her arms. 'You see, it's about loyalty. John and I stick together like chewing gum to a shoe. Nothing will separate us, not ever.' She gazed around the table, four faces staring back, and she continued. 'You kids nowadays have no stickability. That's your problem. Marriage is for life – it's forever, it's not something to be treated like the tide, in one minute and out the next.'

There was silence, then Caden said, 'My partner's just the best. We've been together for almost a year. Mind you, he finds it hard to put up with all my annoying habits. He's always telling me

I never clean the bath; I forget to flush the – well, you can imagine.'

'Right, time for some action,' Loveday announced. 'We need to plan what we're going to do. Have you got a good story about this turtle, Caden, or are you just a load of hot air?'

'I can be both, at the same time,' Caden told her. 'You just wait until *The Gazette* is out tomorrow. You'll be so impressed. I have some great photos of you, Loveday, next to the turtle, and with you wearing the fish T-shirt, it'll be perfect. So...' Caden stood up. 'I'm going to the bar to buy you all another drink, then I'll have to rush home to finish my article.'

'I've time for just one more, then I have to get home to my John,' Loveday said.

'And I'd better be back for Kev – he'll wonder where I am.'

Val was disappointed. 'I was going to invite you all back for supper.'

'I'll come.' Connie patted her hand. 'We'll have a glass of something and put the world to rights.'

'Right, that's decided,' Caden said, rubbing his hands together. 'We can set a time and place for our next meeting and get some serious planning done. Let's meet here, shall we?'

'Here is good,' Loveday agreed.

'There will be festivals and all sorts of exciting things happening here over the summer. Lots of new faces, tourists, holidaymakers. It's a perfect opportunity to whip up interest about our campaign,' Caden enthused. Then he set off for the bar.

Alice leaned over and spoke in a loud whisper. 'He's a live wire.'

'He's very keen,' Connie admitted.

'I think he's just what we need,' Val said.

* * *

The following Thursday, Val leaped out of bed at eight o'clock, fully energised and ready to face the day. She'd do her stint at the charity shop then she'd visit Connie. Val was nibbling a piece of toast when she heard a sharp rap at the front door. Assuming it was the postman, she hurried, toast in hand and tugged the door open to see Caden waving a newspaper.

'Have you seen this piece of brilliant journalism?'

Val smiled. 'Hi, Caden. Yes, I read it. Fantastic.'

'Four articles – one each day. There's so much interest in the campaign since poor Amy died. That's what I'm calling the turtle, after the woman in *Crossroads* years ago – lots of our readers are old enough to remember Amy Turtle and it's all local interest and emotion-twanging stuff, so they've taken the poor thing's dilemma to heart. I'm going to ask you to do a weekly update.'

'Surely it ought to be Loveday?'

'Oh, it will be – it will come out next week, every Thursday, a column about what we're doing with our group. Loveday wants to call us the Lowenstowe Buccaneers – she likes the association with pirates. And her column is going to be Loveday's Plastic Rapping.' His face shone with confidence. 'Only she's nominated you to write it for her.'

'Ah... all right.'

'So, I'm on my way to work in the office. Loveday said you're volunteering in the charity shop today, so I thought I'd give you a lift. Oh, and – I found these on your doorstep. I think the tin's empty.' Caden flourished a cake tin and a healthy plant in a terracotta pot.

'That's from Ben, my neighbour,' Val said. 'I made him a Victoria sponge a while ago and he's given me a tomato plant. I must see him at some point and say thanks.'

'You can make me a sponge cake any time.' Caden licked his lips. 'I love all sorts of cake. Oscar, my partner, tells me I'm getting porky and I should go on a diet...' He patted his perfectly flat stomach beneath the crisp shirt. 'Come on then, let's get you into town and you can tell me about your recently broken heart and I can tell you how we're going to fix it.'

'My heart hasn't been broken...' Val grabbed her bag and followed Caden towards an untidy black VW Golf, which looked as if it had suffered years of abuse. He held a creaking door open for Val and she struggled inside, finding herself surrounded by empty Coke tins, crisp packets and sandwich wrappers.

Caden laughed. 'I know – it doesn't look great for an eco-warrior who believes in saving the planet. I'm such a slob.'

'I could have walked, Caden – it's only fifteen minutes,' Val protested.

A figure caught her eye as Caden started the car. A lean man in a yellow oilskin jacket was closing the front door to Crab Claw Cottage, walking down the path. He waved a hand to Val in greeting and she waved back. It was Ben Berry.

'So Val, who's going to be your Mr July?' Caden started the engine and manoeuvred the car into the street.

Val was momentarily amazed; Caden hardly knew her and suddenly he was showing interest in her love life. She shook her head sadly. 'Freddie was a nice man but the timing was wrong.'

'So, who's next?'

'What do you mean?'

'Loveday filled me in when I gave her a lift home after the pub. We have to find you a candidate for each month so you can pick the right type for your son's wedding in December.'

'We?'

'Oh, I think it's great fun. I love matchmaking.'

Val was horrified. 'I'm not interested and you're making me sound desperate.'

'Not at all.' Caden guided the car around a bend. 'I have a plan.'

'Really?'

'Oh, yes.' Caden pressed her arm confidentially. 'I'll be your Mr July for you. We can hang out with the group, have fun and definitely not mope any more.'

Val said, 'Who's moping?'

Caden continued, full of enthusiasm. 'Tomorrow's the first – that's a fresh start. There will be all sorts of events – St Neot feast at the end of July and the big sea shanty festival in August. So, in the spirit of Val not needing a man, which is certainly the impression I'm getting, we'll go out, have fun, talk about Lowenstowe Buccaneers and concentrate on partying and enjoying the sunshine with all the emmets.'

'I'm sure I don't need help,' Val protested.

Caden wasn't listening. 'Drinks in beer gardens, fresh local food, parties on the beach, oh, I'm the man for that. Then, by the end of the month, you'll move on.'

'I *have* moved on—'

'There will be loads of nice older men around this summer, enjoying the festivities. That's how we'll find you a Mr December.' Caden tapped his nose with his index finger. 'Believe me, Val, I've had my share of heartaches. Oscar and I have been together for almost a year. He's a good influence on me, the sensible one – he keeps me in line. Before that, I was like a fish at sea, a grouper tossed on the flotsam and jetsam of love.'

'Oh, I'm not like that—'

'My dad was always there for me: I'd be sobbing on my pillow and he'd say, "Come on, Caden, we're going down the pub. A glass of wine and a live band, that'll cheer you up." Then I'd meet someone new, fall for them, get dumped, and the carousel would start all over again.'

'Your dad's good to you.'

'He is. He's my guardian angel. My mum left when I was sixteen and my sister Heidi was eleven. He's been both mum and dad to the pair of us for years. It was tough for him, of course. But I turned out all right.'

'And your sister?' Val asked.

'Oh, she's a rebel. She's still living at home with my dad at twenty-two. She paints pictures and sells them. Weird abstract squiggly things. Let's just say Heidi is Heidi and leave it at that.'

'Don't you get on?'

'We get on great,' Caden said. 'Especially if we don't see each other.' He gave a single laugh. 'She's not like me. I've always been fussy about my appearance – she's a goth. And if you think Loveday is passionate about the environment, you should meet Heidi. She's like a whirlwind.' He turned a corner. 'Ah, here we are. The PDSA. I bet Loveday's already busy. She asked me for any old computer games so that she could give some of them to a neighbour and sell the rest in the shop.'

'That'll be for Jenna Penrose's children – Loveday's always bringing them things.' Val reached for her bag. 'Thanks for the lift, Caden.'

He handed her the newspaper. 'Here – read all about Amy Turtle again. The deadline for Loveday's Plastic Rapping is on Sundays please.' He leaned forward. 'And we're meeting at The Boat House this Sunday evening at six for a meeting. You can email me the draft for the column by then.'

'Okay,' Val said resignedly and attempted to close the passenger door several times. The catch wouldn't work so Caden leaned over.

'You have to whack it.' He slammed the door and roared away, a puff of smoke belching from the exhaust. Val muttered something about carbon monoxide and hurried into the shop.

24

The first meetings of The Lowenstowe Buccaneers were held in the beer garden of The Boat House. Loveday was delighted with her column in *The Gazette*, which readers were already hailing as articulate and informative. Many local people had written in spurred by the plight of Amy Turtle, demanding that single-use plastic should be reduced. Two letters from locals had been particularly well received. Mrs Diane King, manager of Finest Choice, wrote that her supermarket offered locally sourced loose fruit and vegetables, free from packaging. A local vet, Mr F. J. Seymour, furthered the interest in the Amy story in a lengthy epistle about a post-mortem carried out by Exeter University, explaining that a great deal of plastic had been found in Amy's stomach. He also applauded the work of the local people and pledged his support, should they need any help.

Then on Sunday the twenty-fourth, with a week to go to the feast, the wild rains came in from the sea so the team huddled inside the pub. Dave was busy at the bar where thirsty customers thronged. Val led the way into the snug and they sat by the fireplace, which had been filled with logs and a display of teasels in a vase for the summer. There were six of them at the meeting: Val was snuggled in an armchair next to Connie; Caden was making notes; Loveday was telling everyone what was going to happen; Alice and Kevin sat together, Dolly perched on his knee as he fed her salt and vinegar crisps.

Loveday took charge. 'Right, in my column this week, I suggested that the people of Lowenstowe should get more involved, didn't I, Val? I mentioned the need for more contributions for the food banks and I wrote about walking to the shops rather than driving. So – what shall we do now?'

Caden winked at Val. 'Well, we have Finest Choice on board with their latest push for selling locally-produced food, and the letters are still coming in about Amy Turtle.'

'But it's the summer. Have you seen the state of the beach?' Loveday swigged the gin Caden had bought for her; she'd taken quite a liking to it. 'I was down there yesterday picking up rubbish. It's all empty drinks bottles and takeaway food wrappers.' She glared at Kevin as he emptied the last of the crisps into his palm, fed them to Dolly, then deposited the packaging on the table.

Connie spoke up. 'The beaches are always a mess in the summer. People leave bottles and cans everywhere.'

'I know.' Loveday's eyes widened. 'Last summer I told Henry Scott to put more litter bins out but he only added two more, one at either end of Breakstone beach.'

'It's a good job you pick up the mess, Loveday,' Alice said. 'But I think we should all help. Otherwise, by the end of the summer our beach will look like a landfill site.'

Kevin burst open another bag of crisps. 'People will always keep chucking litter down though.' Dolly licked his face. 'The tourists are the worst because they don't live here.'

'Most of the emmets are all right – and they bring revenue and employment to the town.' Loveday folded her arms. 'Some of the locals are bad enough – and we're the ones who should take responsibility for Lowenstowe.'

'Why don't we invite the local people to do a big litter pick?' Val's eyes met Loveday's. 'You could put it in your column.'

'Brilliant.' Loveday punched the table and Kevin's beer slopped over the top of the glass. 'Can you write that for me?'

'Of course,' Val agreed.

'I'll ask my editor if I can do a big feature,' Caden said. 'You know, summer's over in September and the beaches are littered with rubbish and we the local people can have a special day. We could make it fun by going out on the beach in fancy dress while we pick all the rubbish up. It could even be a competition.'

'I could dress up as a Teletubby,' Alice suggested. 'The yellow one... Laa Laa.' She beamed at a frowning Kevin. 'You could be Tinky-Winky.'

'Why do we need to dress up?' Loveday frowned.

'Publicity – great photos – it will attract lots of people.' Caden's eyes gleamed.

Connie leaned forward. 'We could organise it for September. The first Saturday, the end of the holiday season.'

'Great,' Val said. 'Or... why not arrange it for the week after we meet Henry Scott? Then we can insist he comes along too?'

'I agree.' Loveday folded her arms. 'We're meeting him on the fourteenth. We can do the litter pick on the following Saturday.'

'That's the seventeenth – let's make it the twenty-fourth and give him plenty of notice, so he can't get out of it.' Caden grinned. 'We have a couple of months to do the big build-up – Lowenstowe's Big Beach Litter Pick. I'll get local businesses to sponsor it, prizes for the best fancy dress and the most litter collected, and get the school kids involved.'

'I'm writing it all down in the minutes.' Connie's fingers were busy tapping on the keyboard.

'Excellent.' Caden sat back in his chair. 'Shall I get us another round to celebrate?'

'It must be my turn...' Connie said, reaching for her handbag.

'We'll get the drinks together, Connie,' Val offered, wriggling from her chair.

Caden stood up. 'I'll come to the bar with you.'

Kevin piped up, 'And some crisps, please – she likes salt and vinegar best.'

Alice gave a long-suffering sigh. 'That's Dolly he's talking about. I'm strictly a ready-salted girl.'

'Okay, we'll bring back some nibbles, crisps... and nuts,' Caden promised.

'Not those roasted bleddy peanuts that get stuck in your teeth,' Loveday grumbled. 'Proper pork scratchings, that's what I'll have.'

Val, Caden and Connie managed to wriggle through the throng of drinkers, finally leaning against the woodwork. Dennis Cargill was hunched over a glass of Scotch. Dave winked. 'I'll be with you in a minute, Val.'

Caden wrapped an arm around Val and Connie. He was pleased with himself. 'I think we're really getting somewhere with our campaign, don't you?'

'I love the idea of us all clearing up the beach,' Connie said. 'It could be a really fun day.'

'And Loveday's happy with her column in *The Gazette*,' Val added.

'I'm not surprised – my editor loves it.' Caden beamed. 'He says it's informative, amusing and fun. You're making Loveday a local heroine.'

'It's no more than she deserves,' Val replied.

Dave smiled from across the bar. 'I just wanted to check, Val, Connie, you're still good for a few dishes of food for the St Neot next week? Jackie's still under the weather.'

'Of course,' Connie agreed.

'We won't let you down,' Val promised. 'Quiches, salads, bread, cakes. We're on it. Oh, and could we have the same again and some nibbles, when you're ready, Dave?'

Dave wiped perspiration from his brow. 'Thanks, girls. Give me five minutes.'

A voice from the end of the bar crooned, 'It's Connie.' Dennis raised his glass.

Caden asked, 'Who's the man in the suit? He looks plastered already.'

'Hello, Dennis. How are you?' Val called out.

Dennis called again. 'How about a drink? Come and talk to me.'

'Oh, I'm sorry, Dennis...' Connie said.

Caden couldn't help it; his eyes twinkled as he leaned across the bar. 'Well, it's a kind offer Mr Hunky Buns, but I'm not sure I'm your type.'

Dennis turned back to talk to a companion at the bar. Caden whispered, 'That poor man looks like he's been through the wringer. I thought I'd cheer him up. Do you think I should go over?'

Connie shook her head. 'He drinks so much...' On cue, Dennis stumbled, knocking over a row of glasses as his drinking buddies gave a loud whoop. He was more drunk than ever. Dave arrived with a tray, rushed back to clear up the spilled drinks and broken glass and the three friends hurried back to the snug.

Almost half an hour later, the meeting was over and Alice and Kevin were ready to leave: Dolly was tired out apparently from having eaten too many crisps. As they waved goodbye, Loveday stared at her bare wrist. 'It's late – my John's missing me. He's not used to evenings on his own.'

Alice and Kevin exchanged meaningful looks. Alice clearly thought John was a figment of her imagination. Caden dug his hands into his jacket pockets. 'I'll give you a lift. It's past nine.' He turned to Val. 'Do you and Connie want a lift? I'm going past the cottages.'

'It's only a short walk, thanks.' Val indicated her drink, half full.

Connie wrapped her fingers around the stem of her glass, which had been almost untouched. 'Val and I need to discuss Mr August.'

'Do we?' Val asked.

Caden placed a friendly arm around Loveday and ushered her towards the door. Over his shoulder he called, 'I just know Mr August will be *the* one. I can feel it.'

Val waved his remark away with a gentle flutter of her fingers as the others disappeared into the night air. She stretched her legs. 'Well, this is nice. I have to say, I'm looking forward to the summer.'

'Me too.' Connie watched Val as she sipped from her glass. 'Do you know, Val, until you came to live here, the seasons seemed to all merge into one. I suppose I've just been ticking over...'

Val squeezed Connie's hand. 'I can't imagine how difficult it's been.'

'It has.' Connie's eyes filled again. 'I built my future around Mike. And now one year becomes another and then another and suddenly I'm in my seventies and alone. I ought to have tried harder to move forward...'

'Perhaps counselling might help?'

Connie nodded. 'I've let grief take hold. Then when Will moved to New Zealand I grieved for him too.' She stared into the distance. 'I should have gone with him but staying in Cornwall felt like staying close to Mike.'

'I can understand that,' Val said.

'And what about your ex, in Merrynporth? Do you ever see him?'

Val shook the memory away. 'Once or twice. I don't really want to see him, to be honest.'

'Are you fully over him?'

'I'm not sure.'

'Do you think meeting someone else might help?'

'I thought it might. But then I'm worried I might get hurt again.' Val was thoughtful, then a grin filled her face. 'I still haven't ruled out Mr January, though.'

Connie agreed. 'He's quite special.'

'Getting over Ray is a different type of grieving,' Val said. 'It all takes time to feel stronger.'

'It does,' Connie replied sympathetically. Then she smiled. 'But since you've been here, I feel much more positive. Life's better and I think I'm improving.'

'Me too. I'm so glad we met.' Val wrapped an arm around Connie. 'Shall we go?'

Connie pushed her glass away and reached for her jacket. 'Do you think it's still raining outside?'

Val picked up her handbag. 'Hopefully it's blown over.'

Outside, the rain had stopped, but the air was damp. Connie tucked her arm through Val's as they walked away from The Boat House, leaving the glare of the pub lights against the wet pavement behind them. They passed the holiday house with the desolate garden. There was a light on inside, the flickering of a television screen. Val gazed up; the moon disappeared behind a few straggling clouds that dissolved to nothing. The sound of their feet on the tarmac made a dull thump, then a soft squelch as their shoes met water. Connie huddled closer to Val. 'It's cold for July.'

'It'll be August soon.'

Connie said, 'You know, Caden is a really nice young man. There aren't many youngsters who'd spend time with older people, and what he wants to do to raise awareness in Lowenstowe through his newspaper articles is wonderful.'

'He makes me smile,' Val replied. 'He drives that old banger full of empty bottles and cartons. His heart is in the right place though.'

She was thoughtful. 'I hope we can meet his partner soon. Caden says he's desperate to bring him along to our meetings but Oscar is always busy. Apparently, he dabbles in investments. Perhaps Caden will bring him to St Neot. It would be nice to meet him.'

'It would. He seems really loved up.' Connie frowned. 'So, what are your plans for the summer, Val?'

'I intend to have the best time. We should do another day trip together. We had a great day at The Lost Gardens of Heligan. Loveday had a blast too.' She sighed. 'It's a shame she can't bring John.'

'I don't think he's very mobile. But it was special, the three of us together,' Connie said. 'We'll all go somewhere soon. And now the tourists are here, the town's buzzing...' Connie froze. 'What was that?'

They were almost home. The group of cottages was in half-shadow, lit by the fuzzy yellow smudge of a dim street light.

Val lowered her voice. 'What?'

'I saw something move.'

'It'll be a fox, Connie – a cat, maybe.'

Connie shook her head. 'It was large. It was human. It might have darted into Ben's garden. No look – someone's there.'

'It's probably Kevin, taking Dolly for a pee.' Val hugged Connie's arm tightly as they approached Crab Claw Cottage. Then they saw a figure concealed in the shadows, just inside the gateway. Val heard a low drawl. 'Evening, ladies.'

Connie gasped. 'Oh, Ben. You gave me a scare.'

The man walked forwards two paces into the light. 'Nothing to worry about, it's only me.'

'Pleased to meet you, Ben.' Val stared at the lean man in a dark jacket and beanie. 'We've been to The Boat House. You should join us sometime.'

'Ah, maybe I will. I like a nice pint of Bodger's from time to time.' They heard a soft chuckle, then Ben murmured, 'You're safely back home. That's good. Then I'll say goodnight.'

Val and Connie watched as he waved an arm, then he slipped like a shadow along the path and disappeared inside the house.

'Well,' Connie said. 'That was Ben Berry. You've finally met him.'

MR AUGUST

25

The Boat House was decked in colourful flags and bunting proclaiming the annual St Neot festival. The beach was basted in an intense golden heat all day, cooling down in the late afternoon. Tables were laid outside in the pub garden, filled with dishes of food. A makeshift bar had been rigged up holding casks of cider, beer and soft drinks. Pop music jangled through speakers and, by five thirty in the afternoon, sun-bronzed holidaymakers began to turn up in droves. Families with children arrived, ushering their toddlers into the huge space in the centre of the beer garden designated for dancing, decorated with fairy lights where they could jump about to the music. Val, Connie and Alice were arranging dishes, slicing portions; Loveday was putting up posters urging everyone to save the planet and Kevin was helping Dave to bring extra beer, wine and soft drinks up from the cellar. Jackie, Dave's wife, prepared bowls of fruit punch, one alcoholic and the other alcohol-free, before taking herself off to bed complaining of stomach ache.

Dave watched her go. 'I'm properly worried about her. She has stomach cramps all the time. She's only tiny, my Jackie, but her belly's as tight as a drum, swollen as if she was in the family way.' He frowned. 'She's poorly every other day now.'

'Has she seen a doctor?' Alice asked.

'She's afraid to go. I've said I'll go with her, but she's fretful.'

'If she needs a friend, I don't mind going,' Connie said kindly.

Val placed a reassuring hand on Dave's shoulder. 'You must be worried – shall we have a quiet word and persuade her that it might be worth talking to someone at the surgery?'

'Oh, would you?' Dave was relieved. 'Maybe the doc can give her some pills.'

Loveday arrived at the makeshift bar, her aviator sunglasses in place, wearing a loose shirt that proclaimed 'Global Warming is Global Warning'. She leaned over to inspect the disposable beer glasses. 'Not very environmentally friendly, these, David.' She huffed crossly. 'The Boat House is a flagship for Lowenstowe Buccaneers. You'll have to get something else.'

Dave frowned. 'I can't have real glass – it'd be smashed up everywhere by the end of the night, mostly stuck in the punters' feet. All those kiddies dancing around with no shoes on... I can't bear to think of it.'

'You can get biodegradable plastic glasses, paper cups.' Loveday folded her arms. 'We all have to do our bit. Connie and Valerie have covered food stuff in wax wrap; the dinner will be served on wheat pulp plates; all the tea is made in pots with proper tea leaves now, no teabags. We're all doing what we can.'

Dave agreed. 'All right, Loveday. I'll make sure my next order of disposable glasses is, whatever you call it, environ-mental.'

Loveday strolled over to the food tables and reached for a sandwich. Crowds of people had started to arrive and were greeting each other, thronging around the tables. It was five minutes to six and food was already being piled onto plates and glasses filled to the brim.

Then as the sun dipped lower behind the ocean, the noise level increased, people talking loudly over booming music. Val glanced around. 'Dennis isn't here tonight.'

Connie met her eyes. 'Do you think he's dating a Ms August – a holidaymaker, perhaps?'

'I hope so. He was really the worse for wear last time we saw him.' Val remembered him stumbling at the bar, his friends' whoops of laughter. 'Shall I get us some more of Jackie's delicious punch?'

At the makeshift bar, Alice was at Val's elbow, her brow creased. 'Kev's taken Dolly for a walk. I wanted him to dance with me. He always says the same thing when I ask now – he doesn't like dancing – but when we first met, we used to smooch all the time.' Her face was sad. 'I miss those times.'

'We'll dance with you,' Val said. 'We can have a drink later.'

Alice tugged Val and Connie to the floor area beneath the twinkling fairy lights. T. Rex were singing 'Get It On', and Alice, Val and Connie wiggled their shoulders. T. Rex faded into David Bowie's 'The Jean Genie' and the friends danced on. Then Val felt someone tugging at her wrist and she whirled round to see Loveday, aviators still on despite the darkening skies overhead. She bellowed over the music. 'Can you come over here and talk to me, please, Valerie? I can't hear myself think over all this bleddy noise.'

Loveday led her away from the dancers to the edge of the beer garden that overlooked the pub car park, towards the sea wall. She huffed. 'Now will you just look at that?'

Val stared. 'What am I looking at?'

'There's a van in the car park, over by the sea wall.' Loveday folded her arms. 'There's a light on in the back – that's very suspicious.'

'Why?' Val was puzzled. 'It's just a van.'

Loveday took her sunglasses off and put them back on. 'There's

someone in there, I reckon, and they are camping. I saw a light on –
there, now.'

'I can see...'

'It's a wild camper, come here to doss down in his van by the
sea. It's not allowed. I know what those wild campers are like. They
light fires and dump bottles all over the beach, leave their trash
everywhere. He'll have to go.'

Val glanced at Loveday, the determined set of her jaw, the way
she had folded her arms tightly and thrust out a hip. She smiled.
'Do you want me to find out?'

'If you don't, I bleddy will, and I'll certainly tell him where to get
off.'

'It might be a family; perhaps the van's broken down and they
need help.'

Loveday shook her head. 'It's a man, on his own. A surfer type,
probably – we get a lot of them here.' Loveday was on the warpath.

Val had an idea. 'All right – leave it with me.'

She returned to the table and filled a plate with rice, salad,
quiches, bread. She was about to select sausages but she thought
again; the van owner might be vegetarian. But, she decided, he'd be
more likely to leave if she was polite and if she offered him supper
first. She noticed Loveday watching her in amazement as she
walked across the beer garden carrying a piled plate, setting off at a
brisk pace towards the car park.

She approached the van. It was a Transit with two huge top
boxes clamped to roof bars; the sides were painted black, but a
green tree with yellow roots had been stencilled on the side. She
could hear music playing quietly inside, gentle reggae, a lilting
rhythm. She wandered round to the back. The double doors were
open and she peered in, staring at a tiny home. At the far end,
behind the driver and passenger seats was an elevated bed with a
grey striped duvet beneath a wooden ceiling with a skylight and

glowing lamps. To the left was a sitting area with bright zebra-striped cushions and on the right, a kitchen sink and a thick wooden draining board, a small fridge and a cooker. Beneath the bed were drawers and cupboards and on top of a striped rug was a box containing a mallet, chisels and pieces of wood cut in a variety of sizes. Val stared: there was a framed picture on the wall, an ancient map showing the west coast of England.

She heard a footfall and a quiet voice behind her. 'Hello?'

Val spun round to see a man watching her. He wore faded jeans, a thick jumper and a trilby hat. His face was composed. 'Can I help you?'

Val thrust out the plate of food. 'I brought you this – we're having a feast over at the pub.'

'St Neot,' the man said as he took the food. 'That's very kind of you.' He lifted the plate high, examining the underside carefully. 'Wheat pulp plates. I'm impressed.'

Val wasn't sure what to say next. She watched his easy manner, his calm movements as he leaned against the camper van and broke off a portion of quiche, pushing it into his mouth. 'Mmm, this is good.'

He was about her age, Val thought; his hair was visible beneath the trilby, a dark grey colour and his face was deeply tanned, lines around his mouth. But what caught her attention were his eyes; in the darkness they seemed strange, at odds with his complexion, a light colour, a distant gleam. He turned the disconcerting gaze on Val. 'I could hear the celebrations going on. It's nice to hear people enjoying themselves.' He was eating with his fingers as if he had done it all his life. 'I'll be turning in when I've finished this. It's been a long journey.'

Val was about to ask him where he had come from, if he was local, but she remembered why Loveday had sent her. At this very moment, Loveday would be observing her through aviator glasses from the beer garden. She gave a little cough.

'Are you thinking of... staying here overnight?'

The man didn't blink. 'Yes. I can hear the sea from here. I like that.' Val was about to speak, but the man beat her to it. 'If you're worried that I might be breaking rules, I rang the landlord a few days ago. Dave said I was welcome to stay in the car park. In return I'll pop in for a beer or a meal every so often. That's the deal.'

'Oh, that's good.' Val was still staring.

The man handed her the empty plate. 'Here. Perhaps you'd be kind enough to recycle that for me.' Val wondered if he was being sarcastic, then he added, 'It was nice food, very thoughtful. Thank you.'

Val stood, the plate in her hand, still gazing at the man. She wasn't sure whether to introduce herself or to ask how long he intended to stay. Instead, she said, 'Well, it was nice meeting you. Goodnight.'

The man inclined his head. 'Goodnight.' Then he closed the back doors of the Transit and disappeared towards the front. Val began the walk back to the beer garden. She felt suddenly cold. She glanced up at the sky, crammed with tiny stars, and shivered.

It was around midnight when Val and Connie walked towards home, a few paces behind Kevin and Alice, arm in arm, and a frantic Dolly, who was rushing towards home on the end of a lead. Connie was chattering softly. 'It was a shame Caden couldn't come. I've grown fond of his company. But he had to go to a dinner party with his partner and, of course, he'd naturally want to be with people his own age.' Val was deep in thought and Connie took her arm. 'Val?'

'Mmm?'

'Did you hear what I was saying?'

'Mmm...' Val shook her head. 'Sorry, Connie.'

'Caden and Oscar had to go to a dinner party. He said he'd rather come here but his partner was insistent. I thought he seemed a bit upset.'

'Yes,' Val said. 'We'll catch up with him at the pub next week, I suppose.'

They walked on in silence, then Connie said, 'You were somewhere else.'

'Oh, sorry,' They were almost home. 'Yes, I suppose I'm a bit tired. All the dancing.'

'It was fun, wasn't it?' Connie agreed. She dug deep into her bag and pulled out her door keys, then she gave Val a quick hug.

Val waved her fingers, calling 'Goodnight' to Alice and Kevin, who already had their front door open. She listened to their voices, one deep, one high, calling back.

Then she stepped into the darkness of her home and flicked on a light. She wouldn't go to bed yet. She'd have a warm drink; there were some things on her mind, the usual things, Tom's wedding, what she needed to plan for next week's article for Loveday. But something else was in the way, crowding her thoughts, pushing everything else to one side. She didn't know why but an image of the man in the Transit van wearing the trilby hat filled the space behind her eyes. She wasn't sure what it was about him, his calm expression, the intensity of his stare beneath the brim of his hat, but he was fixed in her thoughts. And, Val mused as she filled the kettle, she must be able to think of some good reason to walk down to the seafront tomorrow, to check that he was still there, to say hello again, just once more.

26

The next day Val woke early, showered and breakfasted, then sat at the table watching the second hand of the kitchen clock tick. She gazed at the conté portrait Ollie had sketched of her, attached to the fridge with magnets. She had to admit, he had caught her expression perfectly: her thoughtful eyes, the twitch of humour around the mouth. Outside the window, sunshine illuminated the little back garden, tingeing everything dazzling gold. In the kitchen gloom, the clock hands twitched slowly. Val made a second cup of tea. She imagined strolling towards the beach in the afternoon glow of the sun, pausing as she passed the back of the Transit van where the interesting newcomer would be sitting drinking water from a metal bottle, watching the world go by. Of course, he'd recognise her, call across, thank her for the food she'd brought him last night and invite her to The Boat House for a drink.

Val replayed the scene in her head: what if he didn't recognise her? She'd call, 'Hello again – how are you?' He'd have to talk to her then. But what if the van wasn't there? Or what if he had a companion with him this time, a woman whom Val didn't meet last night?

Val shrugged – she was behaving ridiculously. She didn't know the man at all: why was she making so much fuss? She wouldn't sit in her kitchen waiting for another three hours, she'd go now – it would be better than being hunched over a cup of tea overthinking and behaving foolishly. Val jumped up, grabbed a light jacket, checked her reflection in the mirror, sprayed on perfume. She wasn't bothered if she met the man or not, she told herself as she set off from the house with a light step, shutting the door behind her with a snap, humming a little tune. She hurried along the street past Honeysuckle House; as much as she adored Connie, she didn't want to take a friend with her today. Perhaps she'd visit later, if she had anything interesting to report.

She saw the van from the distance outside the pub, the large boxes attached to the roof rack. There were two figures standing beside it, deep in conversation. She could see him, the perfect stranger, lean and interesting, wearing a trilby hat. Next to him, waving her hands, was a woman wearing aviator sunglasses. The two figures appeared to be exchanging words. Val quickened her pace, wondering what Loveday was saying. She feared the worst.

As she approached, Val could hear Loveday's voice soaring on the air, '... he has no idea at all. I try to explain but it's like he's living in the Dark Ages – you'd think he'd be doing more for Lowenstowe, but...' She spotted Val. 'Oh, here's my sidekick. Valerie, come and meet my new friend.'

Val walked towards the van, smiling in Loveday's direction, then her eyes flicked to the lean man in the trilby hat. His eyes beneath the brim were serious as he held out a hand. 'We met last night. Thank you for the plate of food – it was very kind of you.'

Val took his hand briefly; it was a workman's hand, hard and dry. She turned her attention to Loveday, who was holding forth again.

'We were just talking about all the changes we need to make for the planet. I think we might have a new recruit to Lowenstowe Buccaneers here.'

The man spoke to Loveday. 'Cleaning up the beaches is a great place to start. I spent last week in Dorset; the beaches are beautiful there, spotless.'

'They'll be bleddy spotless here too when I've finished. How long are you staying in Lowenstowe, Mr...?'

'Just Carver.' The man spoke softly. He turned to Val and for the first time she realised why his gaze was so disconcerting. A stark contrast to his weathered face, his eyes were light blue, the colour of the sea. She couldn't pull her gaze away. 'I haven't been called anything but Carver for years.' He pointed to the van. 'I'm a wood-carver; that's why I'm here, to sell a few of my sculptures. I might stay for a few days, a week, more if I have enough customers.'

'Oh?' Val was interested. 'What sort of things do you make?'

'Whatever people want me to.' His hands were deep in his jeans pockets. 'Statues, masks, figures, animals are very popular – owls, hedgehogs, horses. Apparently, meerkats are the latest thing.' He shrugged casually. 'A customer ordered a six-foot deer earlier this year.'

Loveday raised an eyebrow. 'I bet that was dear, the deer, I mean. All that wood must cost a pretty penny.'

Carver smiled. 'It paid for my summer travelling round the coastline in the van. I thought I'd spend August in Cornwall. It's beautiful here.'

'Well, I'm glad you've offered to give us a hand with the campaign,' Loveday said. Her eyes were small and thoughtful behind the sunglasses. She studied Val, then her intense gaze shifted back to the man in the trilby. 'I'd like to tell you more about our work, Carver, but I have things to do, I'm a busy woman. But Valerie here, I don't suppose she's doing much...' Her expression was suddenly sly. 'Valerie, why don't you both take a walk down to the beach? You can show Carver around and tell him about the turtle.'

Val was uncomfortable. 'Oh, well, I don't know if—'

'That would be lovely.' Carver took off his trilby and pushed a hand through thick dark grey hair, replacing the hat. 'It would be good to be on the beach.' His eyes met Val's, the blue of the ocean, and she blinked at the brightness.

'Right...' Loveday made a satisfied sound. 'Well, I can't stay here yapping all bleddy day. I'll see you in the shop, Valerie. And Caden has organised a campaign meeting in the pub. We're going to plan the beach clean-up.' She turned to Carver. 'I hope you'll be there too, of course. We need all the help we can get. Well, that's it, I'll see you dreckly...'

She turned and ambled away, her shoulders hunched. Val thought she could hear Loveday's faint laughter. Then she was aware that Carver was looking at her, an appraising gaze. She tilted her chin. 'I was going to the beach – I go there all the time. You're welcome to walk with me.'

Carver fiddled with a key and the van flashed its lights, safely locked. He fell in step with her as they walked towards the sea wall. Val decided that she was not going to be intimidated by the newcomer or his disconcerting stare, so she began to chatter gaily. 'So, how come you're here in Lowenstowe, Carver? Is it just to sell your carvings or are you on holiday?'

'Both,' he said. 'Life is a holiday.'

'It is,' Val agreed. 'I love living here. Whatever the season, it's the most beautiful place.' She gave him a sidelong look. 'Are you from Cornwall?'

They had reached the beach. The sea sparkled in the distance, the sky was cloudless, meeting in an indigo line on the horizon. A few tourists were already out in full force, stretched on towels in sunglasses, reading beneath sunshades and hats, screaming, playing in the sea. Carver shook his head. 'I'm from all over. I have the van and my woodcarvings and tools, and I travel around as I choose in the summer months.'

'And in the winter?'

Carver smiled and Val noticed the pleasant creases around his mouth. 'I have a crofter's cottage in Scotland. I live there when it's cold.' He walked easily next to Val, his stride matching hers. 'I love Scotland. It's a beautiful country – mountains, lochs, wildlife.'

'You don't sound Scottish.' Val could hear no trace of an accent.

'I was born in Buckinghamshire. My parents sent me to school in Scotland. I fell in love with the Highlands as a teenager. That was a lifetime ago.' He made a low sound. 'But not the school...'

'Didn't you like school?' Val was conscious that she was the interviewer, asking twenty questions.

'I was expelled at seventeen,' Carver said. 'I wasn't good at conforming. It was an expensive private school. My parents weren't pleased.'

'Ah...' Val wondered what to say next. 'Is that how you came to do carving for a living?'

'I love working with wood, carving, whittling, using a knife, a chisel, a gouge, feeling the wood change in my hands, watching it take shape.' He turned his attention to Val. 'And what about you, Valerie? What do you do, other than help clean up the environment?'

'Val,' Val replied. 'Valerie reminds me of the times I was told off in school. Loveday always calls me Valerie though. I think it's her way of being respectful.'

Carver raised an eyebrow. 'I bet you were a lot of fun at school.'

'Oh? What makes you say that?' Val was intrigued.

'You're a strong personality; I can't imagine you conforming unless you wanted to.'

Val wondered how he knew. It was probably a guess. Val

recalled a particular teacher of needlework, furious because she could no longer endure Val's shoddy work and her ridiculous attempt at humour, her bubbly way of amusing the rest of the class to prevent boredom setting in. Val, a lively fifteen-year-old, had been sent to stand outside the classroom and, long plaits swinging, she'd strutted to the door and slammed it after her. That had been the end of her sewing days.

She was aware that Carver was watching her. They had almost reached the sea, the sand now damp beneath their feet and, several steps away, the tide was tumbling in, a frothing of spreading foam almost touching their toes. Val felt the breeze in her face and she gazed around the beach. Children were playing ball, digging, building astonishingly detailed castles in the sand. A few deckchairs had been set out; people were stretched on mats, basking. In the distance, Val noticed a handsome muscular man in shorts walking beside a large brown bear-like dog. It was Tim Keita, Mr January, and his Chow Chow. She glanced at Carver. 'This is the spot where the turtle was found.'

He shook his head sadly. 'Do you know how it died?'

'I think it floated in on the back of a storm. Someone...' Val remembered Freddie, feeling a momentary pang of sadness. 'I think someone from Exeter University did a post-mortem. The poor thing had ingested plastic but it died from being caught in a propellor. Loveday was furious about it all.'

'She's quite a character, Loveday,' Carver said. 'I met her for the first time this morning. She just strolled up and told me not to leave my mess everywhere. I explained that I'd just got back from the municipal tip, where I'd deposited all the litter I collected first thing this morning. After that, we got on like a house on fire.' Then he paused; a thought had entered his mind. 'Val...'

Val offered him a cheerful expression. 'Carver?'

'You've been very kind, showing me round, bringing me food last night just after I arrived.'

Val's tone was breezy. 'A Cornish welcome is a very real thing. We're accommodating folk around here.'

'I thought I might reciprocate.'

'Oh?' Val imagined he'd offer her a small woodcarving, a meerkat to put on a shelf in her lounge.

'It's almost lunchtime.' Carver pushed his hands into his jeans pockets. 'And I haven't had breakfast. So...' He offered her a hopeful look. 'Would you let me buy you lunch?'

'Well...' Val thought about inviting him to Teasel Cottage. She could make soup; they could sit together across the table and share conversation. But it was August, too warm for soup; she could make a sandwich. Then another thought came to her: inviting a man she'd just met into her home might be unwise. She imagined Connie gazing through a window of Honeysuckle House, watching her and a stranger in a trilby hat saunter through her front door. Val realised she was still very much out of practice.

'If you're busy,' he said. 'If you have other arrangements...'

'Oh, no, not at all, nothing, no...' Val's voice was suddenly too high; she was too eager. She made her tone level. 'Lunch would be nice. Thank you.'

Carver's eyes twinkled, sunlight sparkling on the sea. 'Right, so I can either offer you beans on toast in my van or, if you can recommend somewhere a bit more exclusive...'

'I know lots of places,' Val said. 'There's The Tasty Plaice, or Pizza Palace, The Unicorn Hotel or The Boat House...' Then it came to her. 'Or there's a little crperie further down the beach that does pancakes and salads... It has the most ridiculous name.'

'Oh?'

'Planet of the Crêpes...'

Carver smiled. 'It sounds perfect. Can we walk there from here?'

'It's a stroll – twenty minutes.'

'Great.' Carver offered his arm. 'Shall we...?'

Val slid her wrist through the crook of his elbow and they began to walk along, Carver asking her all about her campaign to improve Lowenstowe, then about herself, her hobbies. Val chatted about her love of art, how she hadn't been to a gallery in ages, and about her awful singing at the Valentine's karaoke, missing out the part about Sonny and Cher. Carver described a bespoke stag-headed story-telling chair he had made for a primary school in Inverness, fashioned from oak and embellished with the line 'words are an everlasting source of magic'. Val began to reminisce about her days as a deputy head at the primary school, recalling the time she had to inform a young student teacher that her lessons were not good enough and that she needed to improve her classroom practice. Val had asked her gently, 'Where will you go from here?' meaning how might she improve, and the young woman had replied, 'Down the pub for a double vodka.'

Val watched Carver as he smiled at her joke. They walked along the beach together, arm in arm. The sun was shining, the skies were clear and her spirit soared; she was truly happy. She had been on the beach with Carver for no more than two hours; she hardly knew him. Yet for some reason she couldn't explain, it felt right, as if she had known him for years.

27

Every day had become hectic, the heartbeat of summer pounding faster. The following Tuesday and Wednesday Val and Carver travelled in the Transit, selling wood carvings on busy beaches and by roadsides. They prepared food together in the van, eating lunch outside on a rug during the warmest time of the day, watching the sun sink into the sea late in the evening before he drove her back home. After her work in the charity shop on Thursday, she and Carver walked on Breakstone beach; later they shared wine and a takeaway meal huddled in the van, talking until midnight and she gave him one of her favour boxes containing her email address. On Saturday they arrived early at a market near Bideford where Carver sold several expensive pieces, mostly oak sculptures of animals. Val enjoyed watching him. There were so many things she liked: the easy way he spoke to customers, the light in his eyes as he talked about his work, the deep indentation in his thumb where once a knife had slipped.

Then on Sunday evening, she was almost ready to leave home for the meeting at The Boat House when Connie arrived at the door, breathless. She hugged Val enthusiastically. 'I've missed you, Val – I haven't seen you all week.'

'I messaged you.' Val was pleased to see Connie. She knew her friend was about to ask a flurry of excited questions, so she said, 'I told you about Carver. I've been helping him with his business.'

Connie put her hands on her hips. 'You've hardly told me anything.' She clutched Val's arm. 'He's Mr August, isn't he?'

Val said, 'He might be...'

'Or he might just be *the* one?' Connie's face shone.

'It's early days.' Val changed the subject; in truth, she was a little nervous. He'd be at the meeting tonight; it was their first outing as a couple, if that was what they were. Val wasn't completely sure.

'I can't wait to meet him.' Connie threaded an arm through Val's as they began to walk towards the pub. 'Is he nice? Is he handsome? You hardly told me anything on the phone.'

'There's not a lot to tell. Yes, he's nice.'

'And?'

'He's sweet, Connie. It's...'

'I know, early days, but I can tell, you like him.'

Val didn't reply. She wasn't sure what to say.

Connie persisted. 'So, he's got a camper van?'

'A Transit.'

Connie wasted no time. 'Have you spent the night there yet?'

'Connie!' Val was surprised by Connie's blatant enthusiasm. 'No, I haven't. I've only known him for a week, less.'

'Oh, I didn't mean...' Connie's eyes were round with apology.

Val smiled. 'You'll meet him tonight.' She hugged her friend's arm. 'You'll have to let me know what you think.'

'I can't wait,' Connie said.

They walked along, Connie's face shining with anticipation, Val quiet, deep in thought. In truth, Val wasn't sure quite what to say to her friend. Yes, she liked Carver; the time they had spent together had been lovely. But there was a small problem: she wasn't exactly sure of their couple status. He hadn't kissed her yet, and she hadn't wanted to be the one to make the first move. It was stalemate. Val wondered whether Carver just saw her as a companion; after all, he was a visitor, on holiday. Val resolved to ask him, but maybe not this evening.

She knew he was sixty-nine years old, that he had lived with several partners and had never married. But she liked him instinctively, his warmth, his easy manner, the intense eyes that made her forget what she was saying. Val and Connie passed his Transit van as they entered The Boat House, but it appeared to be empty. Val's heart was beating faster than she wanted it to.

At the bar, Dave and Jackie were serving customers. Val's eyes flicked to the corner, where Dennis usually lounged against the woodwork, staring into a glass. 'I haven't seen Dennis for a while...'

Dave grunted. 'He's gone to stay with his sister – she lives up country.' He shook his head. 'She's taken him in hand. She drove down to visit and he was in here, worse for wear. She insisted he needed a break. She told me she'll take him under her wing for a bit.'

'I hope it works,' Connie said.

'He was jilted. That's women for you.' Dave winked. Jackie, Dave's wife, had arrived by his side. She was slim, with short red hair and a matter-of-fact expression. She pointed towards the snug. 'Your drinks are already on the table. Your newspaper friend bought them.'

'That's Caden...' Val didn't know Jackie well; she'd seen her in the bar a few times but mostly she'd been upstairs, indisposed. She offered a kindly expression. 'How are you feeling?'

Jackie rolled her eyes. 'The ongoing saga of the barmaid and the terrible stomach ache?' She pointed to Dave. 'Someone's got to help him out, bless him. No, I'm feeling a bit better today.'

'Perhaps you should pop in to see a doctor.' Connie was anxious.

'That's what Dave says,' Jackie replied. 'I usually just put my best face on and get back behind the bar. "Jackie," I say to myself, "you can't wallow in bed all the time, you have to pull some pints."' She sighed. 'Maybe it was just a long-term bug and I'm a bit better now.'

'I hope so,' Val said. Connie tugged at her sleeve, eager to move on to the snug. Val suspected she wasn't just in a rush to get to the meeting.

The snug was empty except for the five people seated around a table. Kevin was next to Alice, Dolly on his knee. Caden, dressed in a floral T-shirt, was sharing a joke with him; Loveday had pushed her aviator glasses onto the white plaits that crossed over her head and was laughing, patting the arm of Carver, who was next to her wearing the trilby hat. He glanced up as Val and Connie came in, then he stood up, indicating the empty seat next to him. 'Hello, Val.'

She sidled into the space, sitting down, as Carver extended a hand. 'You must be Connie. Pleased to meet you.'

Connie took his hand shyly and squeezed between Val and Alice. Caden indicated the tray of glasses. 'There's a gin and tonic with your name on.'

'Thanks, Caden.' Val reached for her glass and met Carver's ocean-blue eyes. He smiled. Then Loveday banged the table with her fist. 'So, where were we up to, before you came in?' She flashed a glance in Val's direction. 'We should recap for these latecomers.'

Caden gave a little cough. 'The Big Beach Litter Pick is scheduled for 24 September. We're not doing fancy dress as Loveday thinks it will detract from the focus...' Caden looked disappointed.

Alice was dismayed too. 'I wanted to be Laa Laa.'

Kevin smiled. 'I'm with Loveday on that one. No fancy dresses.'

Caden continued, 'Instead, we'll all wear green as we're promoting a green planet. It will look nice in the photos, at least.'

'Bleddy Laa Laa.' Loveday grunted. 'We want to look like we know what we're about, not prancing everywhere in costumes, and Carver here...' She tapped his hand with her fingers. 'He's kindly offered a prize for the most litter picked.'

'Oh, that's nice,' Connie said, her eyes shining.

'I have a fairly sizeable oak sculpture of a Green Man you can have,' Carver murmured. His hand touched Val's fingers beneath the table, squeezing them lightly. 'It's the tree face, a symbol of rebirth.'

'Oh, that's perfect,' Connie breathed. Val put a hand over her face to hide the smile; her friend was clearly quite taken with Carver.

'Great,' Caden added. 'And I've got an idea for fundraising and promoting the event.'

'You can promote it all in *The Gazette*,' Loveday said.

'Yes, but I thought, since it's summer—' Caden's face shone '—we'd attract the crowds by having some beach events first.'

'There's the sea shanty festival. We could put posters up in here?' Alice offered.

'I thought we could have a big sporting event on the beach. Cricket, I thought.'

Alice pulled a face. 'I don't like sport.'

'It could be fun,' Kevin agreed.

Caden rubbed his hands together and continued. 'So, I thought I'd advertise it in *The Gazette*. An event on the beach, spectators welcome, five pounds a head, children free, free ice creams, on behalf of our campaign.'

'Who's paying for all the ice creams?' Loveday asked.

'*The Gazette* will. I've already arranged it with the editor and Joe's Gelati in town. It's publicity for the paper too. My editor loves the idea because we look like an environmentally-supportive publication.' Caden put on his most posh voice. '*The North Cornwall Gazette*, a sponsor of the campaign to clean up Lowenstowe.'

'So when's this cricket match then?' Loveday folded her arms.

'Saturday the twentieth, the week before the sea shanty night here, which is 27 August. I'm going to organise it so that we have huge teams and everyone who turns up gets to bat and field. Basically, it will just be a fun event for everyone.'

'That sounds like a plan,' Kevin agreed.

'I'll see if I can get Oscar to come along,' Caden said, his eyes shining.

'Is he any good at cricket?' Val asked.

'Oh, he's good at everything,' Caden replied. 'Especially making money. He says I'm hopeless.'

Val leaned forward. 'I can't wait to meet him.'

Loveday tapped Carver's arm. 'You could set up a stall on the beach, sell your bits of wood.' She offered him a meaningful nod. 'I'm assuming you'll still be still hanging around in the pub car park by 20 August?'

'And for 24 September, for the litter pick?' Connie said, her eyes moving to Val's.

Carver pressed Val's fingers beneath the table. 'I hope so.'

'Right.' Loveday drained her glass and stood up. 'I declare this meeting over.'

'But...' Caden was puzzled. He lifted his glass of orange juice, which had hardly been touched. 'We've only had one drink.'

Loveday said, 'You can give me and Connie a lift home in your old banger. Alice and Kevin can walk, because they've got the dog. We'll all meet up for the cricket on the twentieth.'

'I don't understand... why are we going home so early?' Kevin rubbed Dolly's damp nose.

'Duhhh!' Loveday screwed an index finger into her temple and winked. 'Get with the plot. Valerie and her boyfriend need some time by themselves.' She folded her arms. 'They can have another drink in this lovely pub before they go on their way.' She breathed out impatiently. 'Besides, my John is on his own. Your dog can still stuff her face with crisps in front of your telly, Kevin.'

'Oh...' Kevin's face was filled with surprise. 'All right. Come on, Alice.'

'I'm ready.' Connie glanced across the table and Val felt her cheeks tingle.

'I certainly won't stand in the way of young love.' Caden drained his orange juice and laughed. 'Oscar will be glad to see me back home. He complains when I go out to meetings.'

'He should bleddy come along himself and help,' Loveday retorted.

'That's what I always say.' Caden jangled his car keys. 'Right, everyone. Your taxi awaits.' He leaned over and pecked Val's cheek affectionately. 'Have a lovely evening now, Val.' His mouth close to her ear, he whispered, 'I predicted Mr August, didn't I? The big summer romance...'

Val watched Caden saunter from the snug, followed by Connie and Loveday. Connie offered Val a little wave of her fingers, a smile of complicity. Alice grabbed Kevin's arm as he plodded away, Dolly scuttling behind. Val reached for her drink. Caden's words were still lodged in her ear: big summer romance. That meant temporary, short-lived. But Carver had suggested he'd still be in Lowenstowe for the litter pick, and that was over a month away. He clearly wanted to stay. Val had no idea what to think.

She noticed Carver's eyes on her face and she found herself drawn into the power of his gaze. Her fingers were still in his hand. 'They are nice people.'

'They are,' Val agreed. 'It was kind of you to come to the meeting, Carver.'

'I want to help,' Carver said. 'I like being here.'

Val couldn't help it. 'I like you being here too.'

'That's good.' Carver wrapped an arm around her, easing her closer. 'Everyone's happy.'

'I'm happy,' Val agreed.

Then his lips were against hers and she closed her eyes. As he kissed her, she briefly recalled the last time Ray had attempted a kiss. It had been passionless, a peck, an affectionate brushing of lips. It occurred to Val that she hadn't thought about Ray in several days. And her relationship with Carver was completely different. The powerful feeling expanding in her chest was satisfyingly warm, wonderful, completely right. She wrapped her arms around Carver and allowed him to pull her closer. Then she lost all sense of time and place; it was just her, him and the melting kiss.

28

'I think you're in love with him,' Connie said as they stood in Val's lounge trying on their best attempt at cricket whites. Connie's pale shorts and cream top would suffice but Val, in white jeans and an orange vest, felt nothing like a sportswoman. However, her face and arms were tanned; she'd spent the last two weeks on beaches or at markets with Carver, helping him sell sculptures, or in his arms on the top of a hill somewhere in North Cornwall watching the sun set.

'You are, aren't you, Val?' Connie touched her arm with light fingers.

Val pulled herself from her reverie. 'I like him, yes, but...'

'He'll look gorgeous in Tom's wedding photo. I can just imagine him in a suit, standing next to you.'

Val thought about the image for a moment, her feelings suddenly soft, then she joked, 'In the trilby hat?'

He would certainly look nothing like Ray, stiff in a jacket that would swamp him. Val imagined herself with Carver at Tom's wedding in December. It would be wonderful, standing outside the church as snow fell like confetti on their faces. Then she took a deep breath. 'We should be going, Connie. The match starts at twelve.'

Connie said, 'I'm so pleased for you, Val. When I met him, I thought he was perfect – so handsome, so calm and, oh, my goodness, those striking eyes...'

'I think you're a bit in love with him too, Connie.' Val smiled.

Connie's face fell. 'Oh, no, no, I couldn't.'

Val wrapped an arm around her. 'Come on, let's get down to the cricket match.'

They picked up bags filled with picnic food and cool drinks. Outside, the August weather was perfect with clear skies, a hint of breeze. As they reached Breakstone beach, the crowds had already started to gather. Joe's Gelati was doing great business; ice creams were being handed from a small pink cart with a huge cartoon picture of a blonde child enjoying an enormous creamy whipped cone. The waves whispered softly, shuffling in and out, the vast ocean glittering in the sunshine. Caden, in perfect cricket whites, was organising proceedings with Loveday waving her arms, her aviator glasses in place. Lots of families had gathered, sitting on beach towels, building sandcastles. Val noticed the sinewy man in shorts, a beanie on his head, jogging near the sea. She was looking for Carver. Then she spotted him seated on a rug wearing cut-off shorts and a vest top. She and Connie rushed forwards and he leaped up, hugging her, kissing her lips. He turned to Connie. 'Good to see you both.'

'We've brought lunch.' Connie lifted one of her bags.

Val pushed a hand through her hair as the sea breeze blew it back across her face. 'Have you sold many pieces?'

'I've just sold two this morning in the car park.' Carver's eyes gleamed. 'I'm really enjoying being in Cornwall.'

Val and Connie seated themselves on the rug and Connie poured cool drinks from a flask. Caden was organising everyone, shouting and waving his hands; then the cricket match was under way.

There were far more spectators than players, seated on rugs, eating and drinking. Caden was instructing two teams, calling one The Googly Gazetters, a group of men and women in proper cricket whites strutting around looking muscly and competitive, and the others the Howzat? team, a group of people in an assortment of ill-fitting clothes in shades of off-white, mooching around as if they had no clue whatsoever about what they were supposed to do. Caden waved his arms, in charge as umpire, and Loveday had appointed herself coach of the Howzat? team, which meant she shouted encouragement from the sidelines and criticised every decision. At first, no one was keeping score so Kevin found himself a chair, pulled on a sporty cap, sat Dolly on his knee and wrote down a list of runs for each team. Alice perched herself next to him, a half-hearted assistant.

Kevin called out, 'The Googly Gazetters are winning by a mile, give or take a few runs,' which pleased The Gazetters.

'Come on, my team,' Loveday bellowed in the direction of several young men who didn't seem to know which team they were on.

Val's innings lasted under a minute – she hit the ball once and was immediately caught out. Connie lasted longer – she was athletic and competitive, but when the bowler knocked over the stumps, she returned to the rug and handed the bat to Carver who immediately took up position.

'You're good at cricket,' Val said as she poured herself and Connie a cold drink.

'I was sporty at school.' Connie was thirsty, having exerted herself more than any other member of the team so far. 'Do you know, Val, I enjoyed myself out there, batting, running. It was just me pushing myself, moving forward. It was a nice feeling.' She was thoughtful for a moment. 'I'm really enjoying this summer.'

They watched as Carver walloped the ball expertly. It soared into the air as he started to run.

'He's been to public school,' Val said with a smile. 'He's played before.' Her words were drowned out by Loveday screeching and clapping as he scored another run.

Connie sipped lemonade. 'Loveday likes Carver.'

'It was Loveday who brought us together,' Val recalled. 'She sent us off for a walk on the beach. It wasn't subtle.' She laughed, remembering. 'Loveday has a heart of gold.'

'And she's so enthusiastic,' Connie agreed. She was watching Carver, lean in cut-off shorts, scoring runs. 'He has nice legs.'

'Everything about him is nice.'

'Do you think he will stay in Lowenstowe?' Connie looked hopeful. 'I mean, he said he'd be here for the sea shanty festival next week, then the litter pick in September then... perhaps he'll move in with you.'

Val shook her head. 'I haven't invited him round yet.'

'Why ever not?'

'The Transit van's his home,' Val said. 'Perhaps being in a house would constrain him.'

Connie squeezed Val's arm. 'Invite him round. Make him some of your lovely food.' She leaned forward. 'Show him what he's missing and then he'll stay.'

Val shook her head slowly. 'I'm taking each day as it comes. It's a summer romance, after all.'

'It doesn't have to be,' Connie insisted. 'You have to hold on to love with both hands.'

'We'll see.' There was a flurry of applause and Val turned her gaze back to Carver, who had thwacked the ball high again and was taking off on another run.

Connie leaned closer. 'So is he Mr December, the wedding plus-one?'

Val was still watching Carver; he was so self-assured, even the way he played cricket. 'I haven't ruled it out.'

'Val.' Connie's expression was earnest. 'Invite him back to yours. Cook something wonderful. Have wine, soft lights, music. Then maybe...'

Val stifled a smile. 'You're such a romantic, Connie.' She hugged her friend. 'We'll see.'

She was thoughtful, watching Carver, the concentration on his face, the lift of his arms, the movement of the muscles in his legs. Perhaps Connie was right. Perhaps it was time to invite him round to her house. Then a loud roaring sound erupted as someone caught a ball. It was the end of Carver's innings. He strolled back to the rug, a smile on his face, and flopped down next to Val, throwing an arm round her. 'We're ahead, apparently.'

Connie handed him a glass of lemonade. 'Here – you must be thirsty. And later, I suppose – you'll be hungry...' She threw Val a glance. 'Val's a great cook...'

'I'm sure—' Carver suddenly reached into the pocket of his cut-off jeans and pulled out his phone, staring at the screen. 'Oh, sorry – I have to take this call.' He moved away a few paces and Val watched him talking, a hand scratching his head beneath the trilby.

Val was still thinking about what to say to him when he returned, how to invite him to dinner, when something caught her eye. The sounds of cheering and clapping had faded to silence and a man was standing at a distance, shouting at Caden. She stared harder, listening. '... supposed to be going out.'

Caden had frozen, staring at a tall broad-chested man with dark hair. He was impeccably dressed for someone on the beach, in smart trousers and a light jacket. His hands were on his hips. 'So, what time do you expect to finish this little spree?'

Caden was flustered. 'I said I'd be home at three, Oscar. It's not two yet.'

The man bellowed, 'You didn't listen. I said we had to leave at one. We need to be in Bideford. This is an important afternoon for me.'

'Is it?'

'We're going to my father's – we're meeting him to discuss the loan he promised me.'

'I thought that was next week.'

'No, it's today, Caden. It took me hours to write the business plan.' The man was furious. 'And now we're late.'

Caden put pale hands to his paler face. 'Oh, Oscar, I'm so sorry.'

Loveday rushed into the space in between them and took over. 'What's all this bleddy shouting about?'

'This is Oscar.' Caden was suddenly awkward. 'Loveday, I have to go.'

Loveday turned her attention to the man in the dapper jacket. 'Caden can't leave now – he's our organiser. Without him we have no game.'

Oscar brushed loose grains of sand from his trousers, examining his beach-soiled shoes. 'You can please yourself. You get involved in these stupid ventures and when I need you, you don't come up with the goods.'

'Oh, Oscar…' Caden wailed.

Loveday was suddenly furious. 'Why, you pompous bleddy tuss.' She made her hand into a fist. 'What we're doing here is very important—'

'I don't really care, Caden.' Oscar turned to leave. 'If you stay here, you needn't bother coming home.'

'Oscar…'

'Sling your hook,' Loveday yelled.

Oscar's face was flushed with anger, his expression unpleasant.

'Why don't you mind your own business, you stupid old bag?'

Caden rushed to Loveday, flinging an arm around her shoulders. 'Don't talk like that to my friend.'

'I don't mind being called old or a bag,' Loveday scoffed. 'But I'm definitely not stupid.'

Oscar stood tall. 'I'm going to meet my father now.' He jabbed an angry finger towards Caden. 'You can come with me or you can pack your things and just go.' He started to walk away and then called over his shoulder, 'I really don't care any more.'

Oscar strode away at a brisk pace. Caden brought his knuckles to his lips. Loveday grasped his arm. 'Let him go, Caden. He's just rude.'

'I have to talk to him.' Caden was suddenly shaking, his eyes full of tears. 'I have to go after him.'

'That's just what he wants. Bleddy bully,' Loveday said. 'I know his type.'

Caden nodded. 'Yes, he has a temper on him – oh, but it's my fault. I've been so focused on our game today, I got the dates mixed up and now I've upset him.' He noticed the crowd for the first time, many pairs of eyes watching him. 'Oh, this is so embarrassing,' he blurted. 'And I'm so sorry, Loveday – it's all my fault – I'll make it up to you...'

Then Caden leaned over and grabbed his bag, hurling it over his shoulder, and took off at a pace, calling, 'Oscar – please wait.' His bag bobbed against his back as he ran, like a series of smacks.

Loveday put her hands on her hips and bellowed, 'Well, that's the end of the cricket game. We've got no umpire now so we're stumped.' She folded her arms. 'Well and truly.'

Val leaned towards Connie. 'Poor Caden.'

'So that was Oscar?' Connie observed drily. 'He didn't seem very supportive.'

'I'll ring Caden tonight. I'll check how he is.'

She turned her attention to Carver, who was standing a few feet away, pushing his phone into his pocket. She noticed he hadn't moved, so she clambered upright on the rug and wandered towards him, laying a hand on his arm. 'Carver, is everything all right?'

Carver took a few seconds to answer. 'No. No, not really.'

Val put her arms around his neck. 'What's happened?'

He sounded troubled. 'My sister just rang from Wales.'

Val's first thought was that she didn't know he had a sister. 'Is she all right?'

'Yes, Helen's fine, but her husband has just had a stroke. He's been rushed to hospital.'

'Oh...' Val wasn't sure what to say.

'I have to leave – I have to go to Swansea.'

'Now?' Val heard the foolishness of her words. 'Of course.'

Carver said, 'Come with me.'

Val blinked. 'You want me to go to Wales?'

He squeezed her fingers gently. 'Come with me. We can be together...'

Val's mind seemed to slow, a cog in a wheel that had ground down and stopped working. She didn't know what to say. Carver kissed her once, then he took a step backwards. 'I'm going to the van in the car park. Val, I'll pack up and leave in an hour.'

'Carver...'

He stepped forwards, kissed her again. 'I have to go. I'll wait until three o'clock. Go home, pack a bag, come with me.'

Val couldn't move. Indecision had pinned her to the spot. Carver was on his way. 'Three o'clock, Val. Please. I have to go but... be there.'

She watched him moving across the beach in the direction of The Boat House car park, his walk becoming a jog then a run. He became smaller, then he disappeared behind the sea wall and was gone. Val couldn't move. She had no idea what to do.

29

Val stood in her bedroom staring at the wall, an unzipped holdall on top of the bed. She had put underwear in it, pyjamas, and now she was thinking, her hands to her mouth, wondering what to do next.

Connie had rushed home with her, talking excitedly all the time. She insisted that Val should go with Carver; she had to be by his side now. He needed her; it would cement them as a couple. She could meet his sister, support them both during this worrying time. In a week, a month, she and Carver would come back to Lowenstowe, and then he would stay forever.

But a doubt had crept into Val's mind. She wasn't sure she wanted to go to Wales with a man she'd known for such a short time and leave her home behind, her friends, the charity shop, the campaign work. She had thought she might be falling in love with Carver but now, standing on the edge of a precipice that propelled her forward into uncertainty, she wasn't sure. But perhaps she ought to at least go with him, to see what might happen, to follow her heart, as Connie had put it.

She couldn't decide. She could pack a bag and go, take a chance.

But it might be for a month, longer: she would miss the sea shanty festival in The Boat House; she would miss the Big Beach Litter Pick; she would miss her home, her friends. Val caught her breath: she was being pulled two ways. Earlier, on the beach, she had thought about inviting him to visit her home. Now she wasn't sure there was enough space in her life for Carver.

She'd discuss it with him. She would rush over to The Boat House; he'd be in the car park, and they'd talk, face to face. She could be there in ten, fifteen minutes – there was still time. It would be a way to deal with her indecision. He might tell her his feelings for her were strong and beg her to accompany him to Wales. Val wondered if seeing Carver, hugging him, might be enough to persuade her to take the risk; Val might just choose to follow a path she couldn't predict over the one she could.

She left the holdall on the bed, feeling instinctively that her decision was almost made: no bag meant no journey. She hurried downstairs and into the street. As she passed Crab Claw Cottage, she noticed the front door was open; a figure was slipping inside the house. Val could make out a tall, sinewy man: any other time, she'd have loved to stop, to get to know Ben Berry better. But her mind and her feet moved forward towards Carver. She needed to talk things through. She needed to be sure of her decision; she owed him and herself that much.

Val increased her pace, passing several cottages and the holiday home. Range Rover was parked outside, the boot open. The front door had been flung wide and a woman and two chattering children were carrying luggage inside. Val urged herself forwards, her head buzzing with thoughts, planning conversations, working out how to phrase what she was going to say. 'I'd like to come with you, but...' 'Sorry, Carver, I'm not sure I'm ready to...'

Then she could see the car park in the distance. The Transit wasn't there. Several other cars parked outside The Boat House, but the space the Transit had occupied was empty. Val arrived, breathless, looking in all directions, hoping that Carver was waiting somewhere else.

In a nearby parking space was a red Peugeot; a family of four were sitting inside, munching sandwiches, drinking from a flask. The window was half open, so Val approached the driver, a man wearing sunglasses. 'Excuse me – I don't suppose you've seen a black Transit van parked here, with top boxes clamped to roof bars. There's a green tree painted on the side.'

The man leaned towards her, nodding, wiping his mouth. 'Man with a trilby hat, yeh. He must've left about, I don't know, when was it, Rose?'

The woman replied, 'It was about twenty minutes ago. Just after we arrived. We were going to watch a cricket match on the beach but they've all packed up and gone home.'

'Twenty minutes?' Val frowned. 'What time is it now?'

'Around three, maybe five minutes to...' The man took another bite of sandwich. Val noticed it was ham, the pink meat poking out between white slices. She muttered her thanks and turned away, taking the road back towards Teasel Cottage. So he had left early: Carver had not waited. He hadn't wanted to take her with him, or he had changed his mind.

Val felt breathless as if she had been punched in the stomach. She blundered forwards, not sure if she wanted to cry, if she was angry or if she needed to stop, think things through and, once she was past the immediate feelings of rejection and hurt, she'd agree that it was all for the best. She wouldn't have gone with him, she thought as she rushed towards home. He had come to the same decision. It had been good while it lasted, a summer romance, that was all.

Her cottage was in sight; Val wondered why a stifling ache surrounded her heart. Then she understood. Carver had rejected her and she felt saddened, but beneath the sensation of being unwanted, she was reminded again of the wound left by Ray, of seeing him in The Sprat with Monica. Carver had been another attempt to disguise the past, but the pain was still there. She'd probably never hear from him again.

Then she saw a black Golf parked outside her gate. A man sat on her doorstep hunched over, his arms around his knees and his head down, fair hair drooping forwards. Val called out, 'Caden?' He gazed up, his face miserable. He stood suddenly and handed her a box of tomatoes. 'Your neighbour just called and left these.'

'Connie?'

'A man with white hair.'

'Oh, you've seen Ben?' Val noticed Caden's eyes were brimming with tears. 'Let's get inside the house and you can tell me what's happened.' She pushed her keys in the door. 'Tea?'

'And sympathy, please, Val.' Caden sniffed.

They sat at the kitchen table and Caden inhaled the steam from a mug of tea. Val sat opposite, pushing her own thoughts away, and exhaled. 'So, what's this all about?'

'I've left Oscar.'

'I see.' Val nodded slowly. 'He seemed very upset when he came to the cricket match.'

'It was worse after we left.' Caden wiped a hand across his brow. 'I caught up with him and apologised and then we had a terrible row. Basically, he told me I had to choose between him and my friends.'

'He did seem a bit controlling...' Val said.

'Controlling? He's King Controller.' Caden was horrified. 'I couldn't believe what he said to Loveday at the cricket match. He called me immature, saying I was just playing games when he was trying to sort out a future for us and when I said that the environment was important, he just laughed in my face.' He took a breath.

'He humiliated me on the beach in front of everyone.' He put a hand across his mouth, his eyes wide.

Val reached across the table and patted his hand. 'So, what happened next?'

'I walked out.' Caden shrugged. 'Just like that. I drove here, with nothing but my keys, my phone, my wallet and the clothes I'm standing in. I've left him.'

Val made a sympathetic clucking noise. 'So, what will you do now?'

'I don't know.' Caden rubbed his hands together. 'Find a hotel, maybe. Go and collect my stuff later, when he's out.'

'Can you go back home, stay with your dad for a while?'

Caden made a face as if Val were crazy. 'And live with Heidi?' A shuddering sigh came from deep in his chest. 'Dad's great, but Heidi and I would be at each other's throats after about two seconds. Seriously.'

Val squeezed his hand. 'Why don't you stay to dinner, Caden? Give yourself time to think things out. If the worst comes to the worst, I have a spare room.'

Caden was confused. 'Aren't you seeing Carver tonight?'

'He's gone.' Val stared at her hands. 'It's a long story.'

Caden's eyes widened. 'Are you all right?'

Val reached for her mug of tea. 'Let's have dinner and we can cheer each other up. We'll open a bottle of wine and tell each other that we'll get over it in time.'

'There are other fish in the sea,' Caden said, his eyes misty.

'Or not,' Val replied grimly. 'I'm not playing this dating game again.'

'Nor me,' Caden agreed wholeheartedly. 'From now on, it's just me. I'm not getting my heart broken ever again, I can promise you that.'

Four hours later, Val and Caden were eating chilli and rice from small bowls. A second bottle of wine had been opened and Caden was refilling their glasses, taking hurried gulps as if it were life-saving oxygen. He pushed food into his mouth and murmured, 'Oscar can go to hell.'

'Be honest, Caden...' Val reached for her glass. 'Is it a tiff or is it really over?'

Caden exhaled. 'I love him, Val. But he's not good for me. He's my longest ever relationship and I worship him, but I've been lying to myself.' He pushed back his hair. 'He criticises me constantly, nothing I ever do is good enough and I've passed it off as my fault.' He lifted his glass. 'But after a few of these, I can see everything much more clearly.'

'Is that wine talking?'

'No, it's me – I'm totally lucid,' Caden protested. 'But what about you and the gorgeous Carver? Do you think he might contact you? You seemed really close.'

Val said, 'I thought so too but, in the end, I think we both decided it would be too difficult to keep going.'

'So...' Caden asked. 'Did you ever find out his real name?'

'Of course.' Val leaned forward confidentially. 'It was Simon Nicholson. He told me two days ago, when I asked.' She chewed thoughtfully. 'But I'll remember him as Carver. That's if I remember him at all.'

'Our hearts are on the mend already.'

'I think we'll live.'

'It's good food, friends and wine that matter, not lovers who let you down.'

'Agreed,' Val spoke into her glass.

'He cared for you, though,' Caden said sadly. 'It wouldn't surprise me at all if at some point in the future he comes knocking at your door one fine summer's day...'

'I don't think so,' Val replied. 'I've learned from Mr August: some things aren't meant to last.'

There was a rap at the front door, a persistent banging that demanded immediate attention. Caden was wide-eyed. 'Do you think that's Carver?'

'It'll be Connie,' Val replied matter-of-factly.

Caden was on his feet. 'I'll go, shall I? Just in case.'

'If you're sure...' Val was almost relieved that Caden was rushing towards the door in her place. She had no idea what she would say if Carver was standing there and she didn't particularly want to explain to Connie yet that he had left Lowenstowe without talking to her.

Val listened as Caden was talking outside. She could hear a low voice, a man's. Val wriggled from her seat and moved to the hallway. Caden was deep in conversation with an impeccably dressed man, his hands on his hips, his face flushed with anger.

'Come on, Caden – we're going home.'

'How did you know I was here?'

'You left a book on the table with notes about your campaign and some addresses in it. I called in on that wretched Loveday woman first, and then I came straight here.'

'Oh, Oscar, you didn't...'

'Come back home with me – you're forgiven. Just don't keep messing up.'

Val heard Caden take a deep breath. 'No.'

'What do you mean, no?'

'I'm not coming back with you.'

Oscar breathed out audibly. 'I just don't understand you, Caden. You've changed since you got yourself involved with this pointless campaign thing. And why you're hanging around with all those ridiculous old crones, I don't get it...'

Val thought about stepping into the doorway, helping Caden

out, giving Oscar a piece of her mind. But she'd drunk a lot of wine and decided it would be wiser to think before she spoke. She heard Caden say, 'How dare you?'

'Come on. I won't ask you again.'

'No.'

'Caden...'

'It's over. You're not the man I loved. You're nasty, bossy, and I don't want to see you again. I'll collect my stuff and then – that's it. We're done.'

'If that's how you want it...' Oscar's tone was an unpleasant sneer '... then you can pick your things up tomorrow. You've become high maintenance, if the truth's told.'

'If the truth is told,' Caden huffed, 'I should have knocked all this on the head ages ago, when you told me I was getting fat, when you complained about how I never flush the toilet – no, Oscar.' He inhaled deeply. 'You can just go to hell.'

Val listened as Caden slammed the door, then he turned to face her, breathing out in relief. His eyes shone with tears. 'It's over, Val. Shall we go back to our supper and our wine?'

'I think we should.' Val was watching him. 'Well done.'

He shrugged. 'We're both alone now. And I have no idea at all what I'm going to do with my life.'

Val patted his hand. 'Finish your meal, have another glass of wine. And until you've worked out what you want to do and where you want to go, you can stay here in the spare room.'

'Oh, thank you.' Caden threw his arms around Val and hugged her so tightly she found it hard to breathe. As she pulled away, her shoulder was damp and Caden was still sobbing, a smile of relief on his face.

MR SEPTEMBER

30

The rest of August passed quickly. Val threw herself into cooking
sumptuous suppers for Caden, hoping hearty meals would cheer
them both up. She took long walks on the beach with Connie,
protesting that she wasn't missing Carver at all and she certainly
wasn't in the market for a replacement. She hadn't messaged him
and he hadn't contacted her despite having her phone number and
her email address from the favour box. In truth, Val wasn't
surprised. It was for the best. And she had Caden for company, who
had moved into the spare room with the purple and pink wallpaper,
skulls, hearts and the black calligraphed print 'Love Kills'. He had
announced that the décor suited his mood perfectly.

The month ended with a lively sea shanty festival in The Boat
House. Val and Connie helped prepare the food. Jackie felt well
enough to help behind the bar – she complained that her stomach
was bloated and sore again. Several musicians dressed as sailors
and pirates arrived with concertinas, accordions, violins, penny
whistles, drums – there was even a man who played the bones,
which Loveday found hilarious after two gins. Everyone joined in
with the shanties, swaying together in their seats, their drinks held

high. Connie stood quietly and sang a plaintive solo about a wife waiting on the seashore for her drowned husband to return, which made tears spring to Val's eyes. She knew that every note, every word was for Mike and in the depths of her own heart, Val felt the stirring pang of loneliness. Caden sobbed on Loveday's shoulder, saying that love always ended badly one way or another, and Loveday folded her arms firmly, telling Caden that he was better off without 'that bleddy tuss Oscar' before loudly reminding Val that if she'd had any sense, she'd have hung on to that 'handsum' Carver, who Loveday had gone out of her way to find for her and who, in her opinion, had been 'the proper job'.

Then September came and with it, sweeping rainstorms. Val was sitting in Pizza Palace with Ollie, who was tucking into a Hawaiian while she played with her pepperoni. He met her eyes, his mouth full. 'Grannie Loveday says you and your boyfriend were all loved up.'

Val shrugged. 'I suppose we were, a bit.'

'So why did he go away?'

'Sometimes love doesn't last, Ollie.'

'I'd make it last.' He licked his lips. 'I'd work hard at it.'

'So, no one for you yet?'

Ollie's face was sad. 'No new girls at Finest Choice. Nobody compatible in my life.' He devoured another mouthful. 'Grannie Loveday says things come to patient people.'

'You'll find someone in time.'

'I will,' he agreed. 'I wrote down a list of all my attributes. Those are the things that would make me a good catch – not that I'm a fish. But I wrote down that I was cheerful and kind, good-looking and patient, I can draw and paint and do maths well, and I feel confident about myself. It's a long list and it made me concentrate on positives. You should do the same.'

'Should I?'

'Yes, you're friendly and funny and clever, you have a nice smile.' Ollie had cleared his plate and was looking with avaricious eyes at her pepperoni.

'I'm too old,' Val murmured, pushing her plate towards him. 'And too tired to bother any more.'

Ollie grabbed a slice of her pizza. 'No, you're not.' He munched happily. 'You might live for at least another five years and you don't want to be lonely all that time, do you?'

Val conceded that he had a point and took herself off to the counter to pay the bill.

* * *

Several days later, on Wednesday the fourteenth at exactly 2:30, Val arrived at the town hall where Loveday was already waiting, wearing a warm woollen hat and a raincoat against the downpour, the aviator sunglasses in place. Val was sure she was frowning behind the shades. 'Where's Connie?'

Val hugged her coat and lifted the umbrella over them both as a shield against the drumming rain. 'She's gone with Jackie to the doctor's. Jackie's feeling poorly again.'

'That Dave would give anyone gut ache,' Loveday admitted. 'I've tasted his fish pie.' She looked around. 'Well, there's no point us standing out here in the rain and getting wet, Valerie. We have an appointment with Henry bleddy Scott.'

Val took a breath. 'Remember what we agreed. We'll invite him to the litter pick on the twenty-fourth.'

Loveday huffed. 'He should be biting my hand off to pick up litter.'

There was a sloshing sound by the side of the road and Val eased Loveday away from the kerb as a black Audi slowed down, spraying puddle water over the pavement. Loveday called out, 'Hey, watch it!'

The door opened and Henry Scott sprang out, holding a laptop case over his head against the rain. He called back to the driver, 'I'll ring you.'

The car sped away, too fast, Val staring after it. Loveday had collared the councillor, grasping the arm of his jacket. 'You're late, Mr Scott.'

'Ah, Mrs Moon. Yes, we have a meeting. It'll have to be a short one though. I'm pressed for time.' Henry was already on his guard.

'And the community of Lowenstowe's a big priority.' Loveday puffed out her chest.

Val said smoothly, 'We can make our meeting very short. Shall we just stand inside for a moment?'

Loveday's eyebrows shot up above the aviators; her eyes asked Val what on earth she was doing. Val winked back as she led the way up the stone steps and paused in the foyer of the town hall, then she coughed, a sign that she meant business. 'So, we'd like you to be at the litter pick on the twenty-fourth.'

'Ah, yes, I did read about it in *The Gazette*,' he countered. 'Of course, I'd like to be there but I can't promise anything, with it being a Saturday and—'

Val said, 'Nigel was looking very tanned. Has he been on holiday?'

'Nigel?'

'Nigel Carrow, your driver, in the black Audi.'

'Ah, how do you know him?' Henry Scott was suddenly interested.

'Nigel and I go back a long way...' Val waved a careless hand. 'We've been out, dinner, the opera. We went to see *The Magic Flute* together.'

'Oh, so you know Uncle Nigel? He's just back from Italy.'

'Of course – we've known each other for ages.'

Henry was impressed. 'I'd no idea you two were acquaintances.'

'Oh yes...' Val was on a roll, watched by Loveday whose mouth was open. 'I'm sure he would want you to come to the litter pick. As a financial analyst, he's very keen on Cornish issues. Maybe he'll come along too. And it will all be in *The Gazette* – and on TV.'

'Ah, well...' Henry faltered. 'What time does the event start?'

Loveday was quick as a terrier. 'Ten sharp, and wear something green.'

Val offered a charming smile. 'It would look good if you were there too.'

'Mmm.' Henry was thoughtful. 'Well, I'll make sure I'm there for ten – I won't be able to stay all day... just long enough to pick up a piece of litter on camera.'

'Excellent,' Val said. 'Your uncle Nigel will be so impressed. I must catch up with him again soon.'

'He's a busy man nowadays,' Henry replied quickly, then added, 'And so am I. So, if you'll excuse me...'

'Just one more thing...' Val smiled, pushing a large brown envelope into Henry's hand. 'This is our list, in lieu of a longer meeting. It contains all our local concerns, from inadequate housing to raising awareness about coastal and marine wildlife, so essential to the local economy. Why don't you have a look at it, at your leisure, see what you can do to help, and then we'll set up another meeting to discuss the way forward?'

'Yes, yes, of course.' Henry clutched the envelope. 'I think I can do that.'

'Good. Meeting over,' Loveday hooted, looking very pleased. 'Well done, Valerie. That'll do.'

* * *

Later that afternoon, Connie and Val were sitting at the kitchen table in Teasel Cottage, cradling a hot cup of peppermint tea. Connie was attempting to persuade Val to talk about her favourite theme, romance.

'I don't suppose you've heard anything from...?'

'Carver? No,' Val said quickly. 'I don't expect I will. I'm all right with that.'

'There are only three-and-a-half months to Tom's wedding.'

Val exhaled. 'I'm quite happy going by myself. And I'm enjoying having Caden as a house guest.' She sipped from her cup. 'By the way, how did Jackie get on? I should have asked.'

'It went well. Poor Jackie was terrified that she had something really serious, but the doctor said it was probably irritable bowel syndrome, so she gave her a prescription and we went off to the chemist. Oh, and you'll never guess who was there...' Connie leaned forward. 'Nigel Carrow, looking very tanned.'

'He gets around,' Val said. 'Loveday and I saw him drop Henry off. He's his uncle.'

Connie lowered her voice, although no one was in the room. 'He was at the counter. He didn't see me.'

'Oh?'

'He had a strange expression on his face – Jackie said he looked like he was buying one of those medications for...' Connie lowered her voice '... men who are trying to improve performance in the bedroom...'

Val stifled a smile. 'Oh, well. Perhaps it's just as well he didn't see you. He'd have been mortified.'

'I wonder if he has a girlfriend?'

'Who knows?' Val thought briefly about the red-haired woman she'd glimpsed with Nigel twice. She rested a hand on Connie's arm. 'Stay to dinner tonight. I'll make something nice; we'll share a bottle of red and the three of us can put the world to rights.'

'I'd love to.' Connie was delighted. 'Caden is such good company. I'm glad he's staying here.'

'Only while he sorts his life out,' Val reminded her. 'That's what he and I agreed.'

Connie sat up straight. 'Was that someone at the front door?'

Val listened. There was a soft rapping sound. Her first thought was that it might be Carver or Freddie, then she smiled; her busy love life was catching up with her. She glanced at the clock. It wasn't five yet and Caden wouldn't be home, so it wasn't him at the door having forgotten his keys.

Val hiked up the strap of her dungarees and rushed to the front door, whisking it open. A man was standing in front of her holding a bunch of flowers in one hand and a plate with a pollock on it in the other. He gave a little bow. 'You must be Val, I presume?'

She made a face. 'Well, I've been offered some strange things before but never flowers and a dead fish.'

'Ah,' the man said. 'The flowers are mine but the fish just came from your neighbour. He pushed it in my hand and asked me to give it to you.'

Val gazed at the man, who seemed familiar. He was smooth-headed, a handsome face, a broad grin, an open orange anorak over floral shorts and muscled legs. He waved the fish. 'Well, can I come in?'

Val stared at him. The rain was falling fast, making his head and his face shine. He tried again. 'I'm Jago Curnow, Caden's father. This is the address he gave me. And I have to say, you're every bit as lovely as Caden said...'

Val pushed the door wide. 'Oh. Do come in. Let me make you some tea.'

'I wouldn't say no to a cup of coffee, lots of milk, no sugar – I'm sweet enough.'

Moments later, he stood in the kitchen, pushing the flowers and the fish into Val's hand, removing his damp anorak, standing in a thin T-shirt and shorts. 'Hello, my lovely,' he said to Connie. 'I'm Jago, Caden's dad. He gave me his new address and I just wanted to say thanks for putting him up.'

Val placed a mug of coffee on the table and he sat down. She noticed that his mannerisms were exactly like Caden's, as were the china-blue eyes, the easy smile. She pointed to the shorts. 'Aren't you cold?'

'I refuse to go back to long trousers until October,' Jago insisted. 'I get my legs out in March so's I can hang on to the summer as long as I can.'

Connie smiled. 'I'm sure it will be sunny for the litter drop.'

'I read all about the litter event in *The Gazette*.' Jago rubbed his hands together. 'I'm so proud of Caden. And I'm glad you've taken him under your roof.'

Val raised her hand to show that he was no trouble. 'He's lovely company.'

'To tell you the truth,' Jago confided, 'I'm relieved Caden's not with Oscar any more. I'd never have said anything, of course, but I always thought he was a bit mean.'

Connie said sympathetically. 'It's so hard being a parent.'

Jago leaned forward confidentially. 'My youngest, Heidi hated Oscar – she and Caden had words over it. She's like her mother, strong-willed and she speaks as she finds.' For a moment, Jago was thoughtful. 'I'm more like Caden: we like the quiet life.' He exhaled. 'My wife, Libby, left us years ago – so I'm on the market for a new lady.' He raised his eyebrows meaningfully. 'Especially good-looking ones...'

Val rolled her eyes as he wrapped his hands around the coffee mug and stretched out his legs beneath the table. 'It's nice here. I might move in too.' He winked at Val. 'I'm very self-sufficient – I brought my two youngsters up on my own.'

'That must have been so hard,' Connie said.

'Chalk and cheese, they are,' Jago agreed. 'And they fought like cat and dog when they were kids. But I think they'll get on a bit better now Caden's left Oscar.' He smiled at Val. 'Of course, I'm always open to new offers. I'm available: a good-looking chap, well mannered, clean habits, cheap to take out...'

Val suddenly had a thought. She found her handbag and plunged her hand in, pulling out a favour box. She handed it to Jago.

'What's this, then?'

Val felt Connie's eyes on her, excited by the prospect of romance. 'It's a small box with a painted pebble with my email address in. Now Caden's living here, you can contact me if you need to.'

'Well, that's very nice of you. Maybe I'll email you about the campaign you've got going on, give you a bit of a hand with it and we can all get to know each other a bit better, eh? Maybe I'll just email you for a chat. I can come over whenever you like, catch up with Caden, have a cuppa with my two new favourite ladies. I think we all have a lot in common...' He gestured in the direction of the pollock on the plate. 'Nice bit of fish you got there. I'm very partial to a tasty piece of pollock. Your neighbour must be a fisherman, then.'

'He is.' Val suddenly understood. 'Jago, I'm making fish pie tonight for me and Caden, and Connie's staying too. Why don't you join us?'

'I thought you'd never ask.' Jago looked from Val to Connie and back to Val, rubbing his hands together hungrily. 'Well, why ever not?' he agreed. 'Dinner with two good-looking women, nice bottle of wine, cosy cottage? My luck's in tonight. Thank you very much, Val, that would be proper handsum.'

31

On the day of the litter collection, Loveday was in the centre of the
bustle wearing thick-soled boots and aviator sunglasses, organising
proceedings, shouting instructions through a megaphone. The
beach was bathed in soft honey sunshine and the sea shone like a
gemstone. A breeze swirled the sand, whisking up grains, shifting
drinks cans and covering cigarette butts. Most of the tourists had
disappeared; local people dressed in green swarmed across the
sand, gathering in excited groups. Many carried their own
containers to pick up refuse. Caden and helpers from *The Gazette*
had put up a huge banner announcing The Big Beach Litter Pick
Lowenstowe; Caden was currently talking to a woman holding out a
microphone, surrounded by several other people with cameras and
wires, shouting to each other about 'fisher booms', 'wind muffs' and
'dead cats', much to Loveday's confusion. Caden was in his element,
waving his hands, explaining to the woman with the microphone
how he represented *The Gazette* but she really should talk to Loveday, the organiser, and Henry Scott, who was due to arrive at any
moment.

Down by the shoreline, two seagulls squabbled over a stray

carton, their sharp beaks pulling in a tug o' war. Val, Connie and Alice, dressed in green jumpers, rushed around, handing out recyclable bags to anyone who asked for them. Kevin sloped off with Dolly to do her business down by the sea, carrying a folded newspaper under his arm. Mrs King from Finest Choice had set up a little stall promoting Lowenstowe's most environmental supermarket, handing out discount leaflets to prospective shoppers. Dave and Jackie from The Boat House had organised a small beer tent, offering drinks and refreshments. Jackie, her eyes sparkling, proclaimed the new medication was working a treat.

Val gazed around the beach. There were several people she recognised. Ollie had turned up in his huge green anorak and was energetically scooping up waste paper from the sand into a sack. Then Val noticed a handsome man in a brown coat with a handsome brown dog walking along the beach and she rushed over to him, greeting him with a grin.

'Tim, how nice to see you.' For a moment he was puzzled. She helped him out. 'I'm Val, remember? We talked at The Unicorn about your book? The one about Baily's beads...'

'Oh, Val, yes.' He offered her a tentative smile. 'We talked about music too. You sang "Wild Thing".'

'I certainly did,' Val said as she thrust a recyclable bag into his hand. 'I'm assuming you and Goliath have come to help with the litter pick?'

'Er, well, in fact we were just out for a—'

Val smiled. '*This* planet should be your immediate concern.'

'You're so right.' His expression was earnest. 'It certainly should be. Thank you.' His smile broadened. 'Oh, I remember we talked about dancing. And you said you've read my books. I must tell you about my latest one. It's good to see you again.'

'Likewise,' Val agreed. 'I'm off to pick up litter now but I'll see you afterwards.' She rushed back to Connie, who was standing with her mouth open.

'That was Mr January,' she whispered. 'He's still top of my list for you.'

'Yes, he's totally gorgeous and we're on first-name terms, which bodes well. But right now he's helping us clean up the beach,' Val replied, feeling calm and pleased with herself. Her heart was beating at its normal rate; there was no excitable racing of her pulse. She was in control now. She noticed that Henry Scott had arrived with his wife and two children, all wearing perfect green clothes. His family stood next to him smiling appropriately as he spoke to the reporter, cameras trained on his face. Val watched as Loveday strode over to greet him, shuffling closer in order to hear what was being said.

Henry's voice was thick as dripping treacle as he enunciated clearly into the microphone. 'As local councillor, I am absolutely behind this initiative to make Lowenstowe Cornwall's most environmentally friendly town. My family and I are very keen on environmental issues at home: we have a meatless meal once a week and I am going to swap my car for a hybrid...'

Loveday was at his shoulder. She hollered, 'Last year, I told you we needed more litter bins here but you only added two more...'

Henry's smile broadened. 'Ah, might I introduce my associate, Mrs Moon, who has been quite proactive in helping to organise this event?'

'Rubbish,' Loveday shouted at the camera. 'That's what I pick up on this beach every week. You wouldn't believe the bottles and cans and dog dirt I collect, especially this time of year after the emmets have left...'

Caden threw his arms around her and Henry in one smooth move. 'The wonderful thing about life in Lowenstowe is that we all work together for the environment.' He breathed positivity. 'Loveday's leadership is incredible and she sets such a wonderful example to us all, and our councillor, Mr Scott, is completely on board, making sure that important innovations will happen in the future.'

'Of course, absolutely,' Henry added quickly. 'I have received a list from Mrs Moon, all hugely significant issues for the local community, and I will be working closely with her group to begin to address each and every one of the concerns by the end of this year. Today's litter pick is just the beginning of a great partnership between the council and the community.'

Val turned, walking straight into a tall man with swept-back hair and broad shoulders. Inside his dark coat he seemed slimmer. He smiled and suddenly his face became handsome. Val said, 'Hello, Dougie.'

Dougie Fraser was pleased to see her. 'I read about this event in *The Gazette*. I came across to help. You're doing a wonderful job, Val.'

'Oh, I do my best.' Val smiled. 'So how are you? How's Boo?'

'Tremendous. Couldn't be better,' he enthused. 'I've started going to a gym – Boo suggested it – and I've lost ten pounds. I'm much trimmer and I feel better for it.'

'That's wonderful. So, where's Boo now?'

'Oh, she's at her languages class. That's her latest thing, learning foreign languages. She's trying Italian at the moment. She's just back from Rome.'

'Oh, you went to Rome? I'd love to go there – the art, the history.'

'No, I didn't go – just Boo,' Dougie explained. 'She went with the girls from her language class. And she looks so well. She brought me back a lovely food hamper.' He tapped his stomach with thick fingers. 'Of course, I'll save it for a special occasion when she and I can share it together.'

'Well, it's nice to see you, Dougie.' Val handed him a bin bag.

'And you too, Val.' Dougie squinted into the distance. 'Is that Connie over there? I must pop over and say hello.'

'One minute.' Something about Dougie's excessively positive expression made Val reach into her handbag. She pulled out a favour box. 'I never gave you one of these.'

'Whatever is it?'

'A favour box from Burns Night. It has a painted stone and my email address...'

'Excellent – I enjoyed the Scottish tablet you gave us immensely. I'll talk to Boo, and you and Connie must come round. It's hard to pin her down these days – she so enjoys gadding about.'

Val watched him walk away; she was thoughtful for a moment as she saw him greet Connie with the same jovial enthusiasm. She gazed around; the litter picking was well under way, hundreds of people in green scurrying around with bags, Loveday barking orders through the megaphone. She spotted Alice, Kevin and Dolly at the refreshments tent next to Dave and she waved. Beyond them, close to the sea, she saw a familiar lean jogger in a beanie. Then Connie arrived, her eyes twinkled. 'Do you think Jago will be here soon?'

'He said he'd be here around eleven.'

'It must be that now,' Connie said. 'He's nice, isn't he?'

Val was a step ahead. 'He's Caden's dad, Connie.'

'But he's handsome – and such a flirt.'

'He's a pleasant man.'

'Val, he could be Mr September.'

'I think that I should avoid flirtatious men.'

'You gave him a favour box.'

Val exhaled. 'I've got several left over from Burns Night. Anyway, I had to give him my email address – after all, Caden is living in my home.'

'Invite him round to dinner again.'

'Connie...'

'You'd make a lovely couple.'

'Connie...'

'Don't you think he's attractive, Val? And he's single.'

A male voice was too loud in Val's ear. 'Hello, are you talking about me again?' Val turned to see Ollie, wearing the green anorak. 'I'm here to help save the planet. I've picked up a ton of rubbish already today for Grannie Loveday. Well, not a real ton, but three full sacks.'

'Well done,' Val said. 'We'll have to go for a pizza soon.'

'I fancy something different next time,' Ollie suggested. 'Something a refined artist might eat.'

'Leave that with me.' Val winked.

'Well,' Ollie sighed as if hard work had made him weary, 'I'd better get back to picking up rubbish. I don't want to make Grannie Loveday cross with me.'

'Absolutely,' Connie agreed. 'Val, you and I had better pick up some litter too.'

'Just one more bag, Ollie,' Val called as he trotted away. 'Then meet me at the beer tent and I'll buy you a drink.'

Ollie shouted back, 'I don't like beer but you can get me a cola.'

'You're on,' Val yelled as she and Connie began to scan the beach for anything to collect. The beach was almost spotless. Caden and Loveday had their heads together, talking to someone else from the television crew. There was no sign of Henry; he had gone home. Val picked up a crisp wrapper, an empty drink can, a bottle top and then she caught Connie's eye. 'Time for refreshments?'

They headed to the beer tent, a trestle table beneath a bright green canopy, where a smiling Jackie, full of energy, rushed over with two disposable cups filled with pink liquid and chunks of fruit.

'It's a Buccaneers' Special punch,' she announced. 'Lemonade, fruit juice and segments of raspberries, apples and pears.'

'Delicious,' Connie said.

'And refreshing,' Val added.

'You'd better let me have two more,' a deeper voice came from behind them. 'Hello, lovely ladies – sorry we're a bit late.'

'Jago,' Connie exclaimed, delighted to see him. He was with a young woman dressed in a long lace gown with a handkerchief hemline, her blue-black hair standing out around her face like a daisy. Her skin was pale except for dark lipstick. Jago wrapped an arm around her. 'This is my daughter, Heidi.'

Heidi seemed bored. 'Do they have anything to drink other than weak punch? Gin, maybe?' Her expression was unreadable. 'Vodka?'

Val held out a hand. 'Pleased to meet you, Heidi. I've heard so much about you.'

Heidi's fingers were limp, her handshake as indifferent as her voice. 'Not from Caden, I hope? He talks complete shit.' She took the disposable cup her father held out and put it to her lips. 'This stuff tastes minging.'

Jackie raised an eyebrow and moved off to serve someone else. Jago broke the silence. 'The litter pick is going well, all you lovely ladies in green.'

'Henry Scott came along,' Connie said. 'I thought Loveday was going to argue with him. Caden was wonderful – he smoothed everything out.'

Heidi rolled her eyes. Jago seemed delighted. 'I'm so proud of Caden. He's organised everything so well.'

'Good job one of us turned out all right then,' Heidi replied, her tone deliberately sweet. 'It's a shame I'm the disappointing one of the family, Dad.'

Val had already decided she liked Heidi. She was plucky, yet vulnerable beneath the veneer. She met her eyes. 'I've heard you paint, Heidi?'

'You wouldn't like my pictures.'

'Oh?'

Heidi sighed, bored. 'They are abstract.'

'She's really good,' Jago said proudly.

Val was thoughtful. 'Do you mean Kandinsky abstract or more in the style of Mondrian, or maybe Pollock?'

Heidi's eyes widened. 'I totally worship Kandinsky.'

'My favourite of his is *Swinging*,' Val said. 'I just love the shapes.'

'I think it's a great picture – but my favourite is *Composition VIII* – oh, those colours.' Heidi actually smiled. 'Thank God my dad has a decent friend at last, someone who knows something about culture.'

'It's years since I've been to a gallery.' Val spied Ollie from the corner of her eye, marching towards them, his face full of enthusiasm. He rushed forward, then smiled shyly at Heidi, looking away briefly, then down at his fingers. 'Hello. I'm Val's friend, Ollie.'

Heidi held out a hand. 'Cool. I'm Heidi.'

Val said, 'Heidi's a painter. She does abstracts, Ollie.'

'That's nice.' Ollie's glance flickered towards her, away again, and his smile widened. 'I like sketching people most.'

'Ollie did a great sketch of me – it's on my fridge,' Val said.

'I saw that one – it's really gorgeous, the image of you,' Jago added.

Heidi scowled. 'I'm rubbish at portraits.' She had a sudden idea. 'Could you draw me? I'd love a proper portrait, the real me, as only a true artist sees me...'

'Of course, I could.' Ollie's face flushed with excitement. He linked long fingers, then brought one to his mouth, chewing a nail.

'Oh, yes, please.' Heidi actually smiled.

Val wondered if he'd pull a sketch pad out of his pocket and start drawing straight away. He said, 'I like your hair. It's very pretty.'

'Thanks,' Heidi replied. 'I like yours.'

Ollie didn't miss a beat. 'I love pictures with lots of colour best. Do you know what Paul Gaugin said? He said, "Colour! What a deep and mysterious language, the language of dreams."'

Heidi clapped her hands. 'Oh, I love that! Gauguin's so right.'

Ollie's face was serious. 'But I like Kandinsky's view of it most of all. He said, "Colour provokes a psychic vibration. Colour hides a power still unknown but real, which acts on every part of the human body."'

'It does, I completely agree.' Heidi met his eyes. 'I understand that, the psychic vibration of colour.'

'That must be because you're a good artist,' Ollie said.

'We're both artists having a meeting of minds,' Heidi added. 'We are completely in tune.'

'We are,' Ollie agreed wholeheartedly.

Val took a breath. 'I'm starving. Would anyone like to go for lunch?'

'I would.' Ollie glanced at Heidi.

'Count me in.' Heidi's eyes shone. 'But not anything minging like greasy chips.'

'I'm off chips too,' Ollie spoke to Heidi. 'I want to go to a place where they serve healthy food.'

'I'm so with you, Ollie,' Heidi said.

Val winked at Jago. 'How about Planet of the Crêpes? It's just down the beach, twenty minutes away.'

'Oh, I absolutely love crêpes,' Connie smiled.

'So do I.' Jago rubbed his hands together. 'Especially in the company of lovely ladies.'

Heidi pulled a face. 'Right, so now going for pancakes with all the old people in the world's a thing.' She linked her arm through Ollie's. 'Thank God you're here.'

32

It was the last day of September; the chilly breath of autumn blew in from the sea and cooled the evening air. Connie and Val rushed up the path towards Crab Claw Cottage, Val clutching an apple pie wrapped in wax paper. The garden was tidy, the damp grass cut short. She placed the pie on the step, not bothering to rap at the door, and turned to Connie.

'I hope he likes apple pie.'

'He'll love it,' Connie said. 'You make the crumbliest pastry.'

Val glanced at the upstairs bedroom. Behind a curtain, a shadow moved. 'He's up there,' Val said in a low voice, then she lifted a hand and waved. Connie copied, wriggling fingers. Ben was visible through the window for a while, as he raised a flat hand in reply. Val saw a shimmer of white hair, then he stepped back and was gone.

They dashed to The Boat House for seven o'clock, as arranged. Caden had left earlier; he was taxi driver for the evening, collecting Loveday and Ollie. The sky was already darkening, indigo tinged with pink as the sun sank behind the sea. In the snug, seven people were sitting around a table; two chairs were empty, two glasses of gin already waiting. Loveday waved a commanding hand. 'Sit down, then – you're late. I declare this meeting open. Caden, do you have an update?'

'I do, indeed.' Caden grinned as Jago, seated on the other side of him, clapped him on the shoulder proudly. Next to Jago, Heidi and Ollie were oblivious, sharing a sketch pad, pencils in their hands. Alice was drinking a pint of lager; Kevin was attempting to do the same, holding the glass away from Dolly, whose tongue flicked towards his beer. 'So, the litter pick went really well. We were on local TV. *The Gazette* had a front-page picture of the family who won the green man, the wood sculpture donated by Carver...'

Loveday shot Val a meaningful look. 'It's a good job I got that one from him before he cleared off.'

'The Loveday's Plastic Rapping column is getting rave reviews,' Caden added as Loveday breathed on her fingernails and polished them on her jumper. 'In fact, we've been contacted by Cornish Beach Guardians, and they'd like us to join them, so I think we should do a fundraiser on their behalf.'

'Good idea,' Loveday boomed.

'And Henry Scott has written an open letter to *The Gazette*, commending the wonderful work we're doing, promising that he's the ambassador that Lowenstowe has always needed.'

'I should think so,' Loveday said.

'That's good news though,' Caden insisted. 'He's pledging money to improve recycling facilities. Plus, he's talking about how the council can build more sustainable, affordable homes in the area.'

Loveday lifted both thumbs cheerfully. 'Well, things are on the up.'

'Didn't we all do well?' Alice said smugly.

Jago raised his glass. 'Well done, lovely ladies.'

'We're not finished yet.' Loveday threw him a savage look. 'We need to take things further. We're being noticed – now we need action.'

'Fundraising for the Beach Guardians will raise our profile – develop what we're doing further afield,' Connie suggested.

Loveday's eyes were small with concentration. 'How do you suggest we raise money, Connie?'

Connie looked worried. 'I'm not sure...'

'Heidi and I have an idea,' Ollie said.

Heidi slipped her hand in his. 'We were talking just last night – a Christmas card competition for the kids would be popular. We could ask them to design something with an environmental theme.'

'Great idea.' Jago beamed. He and Caden both rubbed their hands.

'And who's going to organise that?'

'Heidi and I will, Grannie. We'll design posters and Caden can put them in *The Gazette*.'

'Then the winner will get their pictures made into Christmas cards, and we can sell them on a Christmas stall in town or through the paper,' Heidi said matter-of-factly. 'I can make up batches of cards. Just leave it to Ollie and me.'

Loveday folded her arms. 'Right, that's sorted. Any other ideas?'

Val lifted a finger. 'What about something here in the pub, an evening celebration, such as a bonfire night party?'

'A celebration's good.' Jago nodded towards Val.

'Not bonfire night, though...' Kevin hugged Dolly on his knee.

'Dolly hates fireworks,' Alice explained.

'The dog can stay at home,' Loveday said.

'I know...' Heidi leaned forward. 'Why don't we talk to Dave and Jackie and see if we can do a big Thanksgiving night here?'

'What's a Thanksgiving night when it's at home?' Loveday grunted.

'Like they have in the USA, Grannie, but not a family dinner, a celebration for the whole of Lowenstowe.' Ollie's expression was one of affectionate tolerance. 'Being thankful for food, family...' He glanced at Heidi. 'For people we love.'

'Oh, what a brilliant idea,' Caden exclaimed. 'We can have a themed Thanksgiving night here and sell tickets: there could be stars and stripes, flags and costumes, then we could sell pumpkin pie and American beer, get a band in and have lots of great songs.' He clapped his hands. 'I met some interesting people at the litter pick from the television, Louise and Martin, and they said they'd be keen to help. We could maybe have the event mentioned on TV.'

Loveday was thoughtful. 'I like the idea of a themed night. I'll talk to Dave. Maybe get the TV cameras in for publicity, Caden. But we don't want the pub inundated with hooligans from outside Lowenstowe.'

'Right.' Jago rubbed his hands together. 'Time for another drink, lovely ladies?'

'I'll get them,' Val offered.

'Me too,' Connie added.

Caden stood up. 'I'll give you a hand.' He wrapped an arm round Val. 'Anything for my favourite housemate.'

As they gathered round the bar, Jackie approached them, her manner efficient and brisk. 'Same again?' she asked with a smile.

'You look well,' Val said.

'Oh, it's unbelievable,' Jackie enthused. 'The IBS meds have changed my life.' She spoke pointedly to Connie as she put her hands around the pump to pull a pint of lager. 'I'm so glad you made me go to see the doctor.' Then she spluttered a laugh. 'I wonder how that man is doing, the one we saw in the chemist who we thought might be buying love potion pills...'

Connie leaned towards Val. 'She means Nigel Carrow.' Val nodded; it was none of her business.

'Oh, Jackie – are you and Dave up for a themed night for

Thanksgiving at the end of November?' Caden asked as she placed an orange juice in front of him.

'If it helps us and it helps you, absolutely.' She picked up a glass and sashayed over to an optic, measuring gin. 'It might be fun to make food, you know, maple-glazed turkey rolls, pumpkin pie, cranberry punch.'

'Fabulous,' Caden breathed. 'So, we have lots to look forward to.'

'The Thanksgiving event in November?' Val smiled. 'It'll be great.'

'I was thinking about the event I'm organising for this weekend.' Caden grinned. 'The Lowenstowe Buccaneers' first annual outing. We're off on a trip.'

'Are we?' Val asked. 'Where are we going?'

'There will be two cars full. I'm taking Ollie and Heidi and my dad; you're taking Connie and Loveday. I've organised tickets already.' Caden waved his fingers in a flourish of triumph. 'We're all going to The Eden Project.'

* * *

The following Saturday, Val drove down the A30 behind Caden, smoke spluttering from his exhaust with every gear change.

Loveday was in a good mood. 'I've always wanted to go to The Eden Project. There's so much to learn.'

Val glanced in the mirror. 'I've never been.'

'Nor have I,' Connie admitted.

'It's a dramatic global garden housed in tropical biomes that nestle in a crater the size of thirty football pitches.' Loveday rubbed her hands together and grinned. 'I read that in the brochure.'

'It's a perfect day.' Val glanced up at the November sky, vast and bright, the deep blue blotched with a few shreds of clouds. 'Well at least it won't rain.'

Loveday barked a laugh. 'This is Cornwall, Valerie. Don't you be so sure.'

'But it's our Cornwall.' Connie smiled.

'And we're looking after it.' Loveday cheered. 'So, let's go and see this feat of biological engineering and see if we can't learn something new.'

An hour later, overlooking St Austell Bay, seven members of the Lowenstowe Buccaneers were wandering around beneath a giant greenhouse dome, supported by a steel frame. They became six when Jago started talking to a woman in sunglasses who was by herself, speaking loudly in a soft Texan accent, claiming not to know which way to go. Suddenly Jago was the personification of helpfulness and had appointed himself her guide for the afternoon.

Then Heidi and Ollie took off by themselves with their sketch pads to draw the Infinity Blue sculpture. Val, Connie, Caden and Loveday stood inside a vast conservatory housing a majestic rainforest.

'It's like being inside a transparent beehive.' Loveday's mouth hung open. 'It's just incredible.'

They wandered down the canopy walkway following Caden, who brandished a pamphlet, claiming to know where he was going. Loveday pointed. 'Look up there – bananas. And are those cacao trees? Oh, this is just the best place.'

Connie felt the thrum of wings above her head a feathered ball flung itself upwards. 'They have all sorts of unusual birds in here.'

'Listen.' Val stood still, listening to the sound of rushing water crashing in the distance. 'There's a waterfall too.'

'Can we go and see it?' Loveday's eyes were wide with excitement.

'All in good time.' Caden marched on. 'Here we are. The cloud bridge.'

They climbed onto a rickety structure made of slats of wood, high above the ground level. Connie grabbed Val's arm. 'What do we do now?'

'It's just like a real rainforest.' Loveday strode ahead. In front of her, jets of warm steam pushed out huge clouds that hung heavily on the air like shifting ghosts. She strutted into the swirling mist and yelled, 'I feel like Thor, the god with the big hammer. I could just shout a command and there would be a thunderstorm.'

Val followed Loveday into the clouds. The air was warm and moist against her face. She felt the rising humidity of the rainforest below, a clammy heat. She whooped a loud cry of joy. Then Caden, Connie and Loveday joined her, their arms tightly entwined, and they leaped up and down hooting and laughing, faces red and stretched with smiles.

Connie called out, 'This is what life is all about. Friends, fun, and your head in the clouds.' Then they broke apart, falling forwards, catching their breaths, eyes brimming with happy tears.

Caden marched out of the cloud mass, his hands stuck out in front like Frankenstein's monster. 'Anyone fancy a monster cup of tea in the café?'

'Tea?' Loveday placed her hands on her hips. 'I've got all this learning to do. I want to find out as much as I can about atmosphere and climate change. I'm certainly not going to waste my precious time in here drinking bleddy tea.'

Loveday was still full of her adventure as they drove back four hours later, chattering about how rainforests reflected sunlight, absorbed carbon dioxide and helped cool the planet, and what she was going to say to her John when she got home. Then, rocked by the sway of the car and the dull thrum of the engine, she fell asleep.

Connie leaned over to Val and smiled. 'It's been a great day.'

'It's been wonderful.'

'So... what shall we do about Mr October?'

Val said, 'I don't think there will be one, to be honest. I just want to go to the wedding by myself.'

'You're right,' Connie conceded. 'It was a nice idea, but it's run its course. After all, who needs men, even photogenic ones, when we've got happiness, health and good friends?'

Val grinned in agreement as she turned the car onto the A39 and headed for home. 'Not us, Connie – we're perfectly all right as we are.'

She thought of Ray and Monica at the wedding together holding hands and she waited for the twinge of pain, the sensation of sadness and loss that she always experienced when she thought of them together. But she felt nothing. She was strong, happy – she was looking forward to being there, on her own, holding her head high, and she'd be positive, cheerful, able to greet Ray and Monica with a new, genuine warmth. Val squeezed Connie's arm. 'I'm ready for Tom's wedding now. I'm the mother of the groom and I don't need anyone else in my photos. Just me, my son and his new bride.'

MR OCTOBER

33

October was a cold month, the sea breeze blowing an icy chill from the east. Val decided she'd take brisk walks among the elements during the day, then hunker down in the evening, lay a fire in the lounge and enjoy the impulse to hibernate. She had picked blackberries and made lots of jam, leaving a pot on Ben Berry's doorstep. She took a batch of scones round the following day, hoping he'd enjoy them Cornish-style, spread first with jam then cream. In return for her trouble, she discovered another fish wrapped in foil on her doorstep that evening.

Val threw herself into baking; her home was her refuge now. She and Caden sat by the fire, talking into the evenings, although he was out every weekend: he was becoming friendly with several people from the TV crew he'd met on the litter pick. Connie came round for lunch and Val invited Jago, Heidi and Ollie for Sunday lunch. She'd also invited Loveday, who'd apologised, saying that she was 'too bleddy busy'. She was almost always in the charity shop, sorting out warm clothes and items that might make Christmas gifts for Jenna Penrose and her family before rushing home to her John. She'd told Val during her last Thursday shift that

Jenna rarely had enough left over for herself. Loveday had written to her MP and planned to visit Henry Scott to ask for his support.

Val had knocked on Ben Berry's door twice; she wondered if he'd like to share supper with her and Connie one night. Ben, however, didn't answer; no lights were on inside, so Val assumed he'd gone fishing.

On 22 October, a Saturday, as Val walked on the beach, she became enveloped in a dense mist that blew in from the sea. It was as if her eyes were blurred: the sand was a pale-yellow haze like knitted yarn, the ocean a smear of blue chiffon. Then the mist thickened into a tight fog, bulky cliffs looming in the distance like ghostly battleships. Val turned round, cold vapour in her nostrils, and wandered back towards the shelter of Teasel Cottage.

After a warming cup of tea, she felt a surge of energy and decided to clean the house. Caden was out; he'd gone shopping in Penzance with Lou and Martin, his new pals from the television crew. They were meeting at a trendy wine bar; he'd probably be home late. Val decided she'd vacuum downstairs, then clean upstairs, omitting Caden's room, which she'd never peeked in, but she hoped it was tidier than his car. She knotted her hair in a ponytail, turned up the smart speaker and started to make the house sparkle. She laid a fire in the grate and cleaned the lounge, lifting the nozzle of the vacuum cleaner high to reach the cobwebs that lurked in corners and crevices. Then she turned her attention to polishing, paying particular attention to the photos on the mantelpiece. She dusted the one of Tom in Canada, skiing, wearing a red woollen hat, a broad smile on his face. She gazed tenderly at her son; she missed him every day. She breathed in sharply, reminding herself that she'd be going to his wedding. She ought to buy her plane ticket and a new outfit. It occurred to her fleetingly that Connie might enjoy helping her find something to wear; it would be easier to find a dress than a photogenic man.

Val picked up a cloth and attacked the wooden coffee table, polishing energetically. From the smart speaker, Wham! sang 'Wake Me Up Before You Go-Go' and Val joined in, her tuneless voice loud and joyful. She stood back and surveyed her handiwork. The lounge was looking cosy but clean and fresh. Val lit a candle, inhaling the sweet scent of strawberries. She plumped cushions, picked up the vacuum cleaner and was about to lug it into the kitchen when a melodic tune began. George Michael's plaintive voice began to croon 'Last Christmas'. Val paused, thinking: this coming Christmas would be such fun. She would be in Canada, celebrating with Tom. She imagined visiting a huge house, powdery snow banked high as flakes tumbled in thick crumbs. Inside, a fire would roar in a huge hearth and she'd sit in a soft armchair, drinking mulled wine, talking sleepily with Lottie's family in front of a log fire. She wondered if she should buy a new wardrobe to accommodate the Canadian winter and she was still immersed in images of herself in chunky sweaters when she heard a soft knock at the door.

Val guessed it would be Connie. It wasn't yet lunchtime and it would be typical of her to turn up with freshly baked rolls or a pan of soup. Val hiked up the straps of her dungarees, shook her hair loose from the scrunchie and rushed to the door. As she tugged it open, an eager smile already on her face, she felt the air sucked from her lungs as she stared into familiar blue eyes, a rugged face, still handsome, white curls under a cap. It took her a few moments to speak. All she could think of was that she had just been visualising Tom's wedding, and yet Tom's father hadn't entered her thoughts at all.

'Ray.'

He was even slimmer than when she'd last seen him; his dark overcoat hung loose. His face was sombre as he murmured, 'Val – can I come in?'

Val glanced over his head to see if anyone had noticed his arrival, if Alice was outside on the street with Dolly, or Connie was peering from an upstairs room. Then she nodded. 'Yes – all right.'

He walked in, inhaling the fragrance of cinnamon, staring around at the comfortable sofa, the polished coffee table, the fire laid in the grate. 'This is a nice place. You've got it cosy here, Val.' He was standing awkwardly and Val realised she had no idea what to say.

She took a breath. 'Coffee?'

'Please.' He smiled weakly. 'Milk, one sugar, in case you've forgotten.'

Val made no comment. She rushed into the kitchen and realised that her hands were shaking. She frowned; she had been married to Ray for forty-seven years and now her fingers trembled as she filled the kettle. Something else was bothering her: Ray's smell, something in his aftershave that was too cloying, a blast of cedar and shower cleaner. She poured the coffee and hesitated, flummoxed, by the biscuit tin. It would be natural to offer him something with his coffee, but she didn't want to invite him to stay long. Fear and panic were fists clutching Val's heart; she had no idea why he'd called or what he wanted. She scuttled back into the lounge gripping the steaming mug and stopped in her tracks; Ray had taken off the coat, laid it over the back of the sofa and was lounging against the cushions, his legs stretched out comfortably. Val placed the coffee cup on the table and stepped back, as if Ray were a firework that might suddenly start to fizz and explode and she'd need to be at a safe distance.

Ray was watching her. 'You've let your hair grow. It looks nice.' She nodded. He picked up the coffee and took a sip. 'This is very pleasant.'

Val exhaled, feeling sad. 'What can I do for you, Ray?'

'I called in to see you.'

'Ah.'

'It's been a long time, Val.'

Val moved her shoulders uncomfortably. She had no idea what to say. Then Ray closed his eyes. When he opened them, he said, 'Monica and I have split up.'

'Oh.'

'Last week. She's gone back to her ex.'

Val wasn't sure how to respond so she repeated, 'Oh.'

Ray put his face in his hands. 'I've been such a fool.'

Val wondered if he was crying. She was tempted to rush across to the sofa, to sit beside him, but she stood her ground.

Ray met Val's gaze directly. 'I wanted to come and see you, to apologise for everything.'

Val waved his words away with a flip of her hand. 'I'm fine.'

'I can see that.' Ray seemed sad. 'You're looking well.'

'I am well.'

'I've been thinking. I messed things up but...' Ray swallowed, thinking how to express what he had to say. 'Val, I want us to try again.'

Val opened her mouth but no words came out. Ray stood up and walked over to her, putting his hands on her shoulders. 'I was stupid. Monica was a mistake.'

Val shook her head, bewildered. 'A mistake?'

'I was taken in – she seemed so much fun. She promised me a new lease of life, something new, a change from the old...' His words dried up and Val took over, suddenly finding her voice, her tone hushed.

'A change from the old wife, Ray?'

His hands fell from her shoulders and he looked miserable. 'I didn't treat you well. I didn't give you the attention, the respect, the love you deserved. Oh, Val, if I had the chance again...'

Val inhaled the intense scent of aftershave and pressed her lips together. For now, she was saying nothing; she'd let him continue to dig the deep hole of apology that he was about to clamber into. She felt sad for them both.

'I always loved you, Val. Even when I was with Monica, I was always comparing the two of you in my head. I knew what I'd lost. Monica blinded me at first, but I was just a fool who wasn't thinking straight. Then you saw us in The Sprat on Christmas Day...'

'I did,' Val said.

'You locked me outside in the cold during Christmas dinner.'

'I did,' Val agreed.

'Oh, Val.' He grasped her hands, his face taking on a pleading expression. 'Are you happy here, by yourself? All alone?'

'I love it,' Val admitted. 'It's who I am.'

'But wouldn't you rather...? We could be together again. We could try... pick up where we left off...' He looked hopeful, then he played his trump card. 'We could go together – to Tom's wedding, as his parents, as a couple.'

'Ray...' Val said. 'I'm happy by myself now.'

His expression clouded, his eyes widening as if she had slapped him. Then there were tears on his face. 'I've been so stupid... what a mess.'

Val felt sorry for him. She *had* loved him; she still felt the ache of familiarity. Again, she was reminded of the amputated limb; she knew something had been there, that he had been a part of her life, and now the skin had grown over, she had healed. But she felt sympathy for him, shrunken, his head down, tears dripping. She put a hand on his shoulder. 'Ray, I'm sorry. It's too late now.'

She stopped speaking. She sounded like a woman in the middle of her own soap opera and it was no use: there was no remedy; she did not love Ray enough now, and she could not rediscover those feelings. More than ever, she knew she had moved on. He was the man she had loved, married, but she was happier alone now. There was nothing she could do to console Ray.

She spoke from her heart. 'I'm really so sorry.'

He walked backwards, one, two steps and sniffed, lifting his chin, looking directly at her. He took a breath. 'What's left for us, then? What do we do now?'

Val forced a smile. 'We enjoy ourselves. We have our different lives.' She gave him a look that was kind, even affectionate. 'We're Tom's parents. But we're separate people now. Ray, just find out who you are, enjoy what life brings to your doorstep and then give me a call.'

'Do you think there's any chance for us?'

'No – but we can become better friends. We can learn to like each other again.'

He made a snuffling sound. 'I don't like myself very much.'

'You will, in time, I promise,' Val told him warmly. 'That's the way forward for us, to be strong apart and friends together. You'll meet someone and fall in love again...' Val wondered if she sounded like Connie, if her friend's focus on romance had rubbed off. But Ray seemed pleased.

'I'd like to, Val. I'm lonely. I need someone.' He was puzzled. 'Don't you?'

'Not really, to be honest. I have my life, my friends, my independence. I mean, I can't predict my future, but I'm happy now, and that means that I'm likely to be happy in the future.' She smiled warmly. 'We can make peace, you and I... I wish you all the happiness, Ray, I really do.'

Ray sighed, a deep shudder of accumulated sorrow. 'Can I see you again?'

'Perhaps...' She gave a light shrug. 'But take some time – sort out your life first. Then we'll meet at Tom's wedding.'

Val put out a hand. 'We'll be all right. I know we will.'

He touched her fingers and Val felt the familiar dry warmth. He sighed. 'You're a good woman. I know what I've lost. But you're right – we can't go back.'

'And you're a good man. Find someone who will make you happy. I'm here – I'm glad to be your friend.'

He reached for his coat, struggling into it. It swamped him. 'It was good to see you, Val. As I said, you're looking well.'

'Take care, Ray,' Val said, her voice full of affection.

They moved to the front door and Val held it open. Ray was hunched over as he shuffled down the step. He turned back with a smile. 'Bye, Val.'

Val smiled back and closed the door with a clunk. She exhaled and put her hands to her head. She'd go to the kitchen, make herself a cup of tea, then she'd cry a few final tears. But now, more than ever, she knew she'd be all right.

MR NOVEMBER

34

Val closed the front door behind her, crunching brittle golden leaves that had accumulated on the step underfoot. She had just returned from a walk with Connie, Alice and Dolly. Despite the pale sun high in the sky, it had been chilly on the beach and Alice had complained constantly that she hated winter. Val wished she'd worn gloves: her fingers were red and tingling. She tugged off her coat, reminding herself to wear an extra layer of woollies the next day, and rushed into the kitchen, filling the kettle, selecting tea leaves for the little metal infuser. She glanced up at the wall clock; it was past three. Caden would be back from work around six o'clock and she'd have a meal ready. Val smiled; she was becoming quite used to having Caden around. The evenings were seldom quiet. They chattered constantly, although he liked to watch TV more than she did.

Val took a steaming cup of tea into the lounge and sat on the sofa. She studied a new email on her phone. It was a brief message from Dougie Fraser: the colourful rainbow-painted stone in the favour box was delightful, he'd use it as a paperweight, and would she and Connie like to come round to dinner with him and Boo on

24 November, a Thursday? Val was about to find her diary and check the dates when the phone buzzed with an incoming call. It was Tom. Val pushed the phone to her ear so that his voice would fill it.

'Hi, Tom – how's it all going?'

'Great – have you bought your plane ticket yet, Mum?'

'No – I'll sort it out this week. What time is it in Montréal now?'

'Just after ten. I'm at work but I wanted to call and ask a couple of questions. I heard from Dad...'

'Oh?'

'He's not bringing Monica now.'

'I know,' Val said.

'So, what about you? Who's your plus one? Only I need to confirm accommodation...'

'I think I'll be coming by myself. But I'll just find a hotel.'

'Lottie's family are going to put you up. I wanted to check. You and Dad – do you want to be in the same place?'

Val took a breath. 'It might be better if we weren't.'

'Okay.' Tom's voice was light. 'Lottie has a big family so we'll sort out accommodation for you in different places. How long can you stay?'

'Well, if you're not going on your honeymoon until the new year, it would be nice to stay over Christmas.'

'Lottie and I thought so too. A family Christmas dinner would be lovely. Her parents are great – they'll arrange for you to see all sorts of sights, the old town, the national parks, even Mont Tremblant. You could go skiing.'

Val laughed. 'I'm just coming to your wedding – I hadn't thought about staying for a holiday.'

'Of course,' Tom agreed. 'But the day after the wedding is Christmas Day, which will be a big family get-together, and it would be a shame not to stay, and then you might as well turn it into a fortnight.'

'Well, I'd hoped to be there for at least a few days.'

'Stay until the new year, longer,' Tom coaxed. 'We can spend time.'

'If you're sure – I'd love to see you. But you'll be newly married, Tom.'

'Lottie and I have the rest of our lives, Mum – and I want you to get to know her. You'll love her. And her parents, Frances and Kit, are so looking forward to meeting you.'

'Okay, that would be wonderful.'

'Dad suggested I leave his plus one place open – even though he's not bringing Monica. So, would you like me to leave yours open too – in case you want to bring someone to keep you company?'

Val wondered for a moment if she should ask Connie to go with her. It seemed like a sensible solution, and a much better idea than taking a man she didn't know simply to balance the wedding photos. Monica's absence meant that the photos would be perfectly symmetrical now. But Val thought proudly, she didn't care about any of that. 'All right, Tom – I suppose I could always ask a friend.'

She knew that Tom was smiling. 'I'm really looking forward to seeing you, Mum. It's been too long. And you'll love Lottie. Oh, I can't wait.'

'It will be the most beautiful wedding…'

'So, buy that ticket, Mum – come on the twenty-second and stay until the new year, longer if you like. It will be so nice to catch up.'

'It will.' Val was surprised that tears had sprung into her eyes. 'It's next month. I'll have to start buying warm clothes.'

'That would be a good idea. We're due some snow this week, and it gets pretty cold in December, minus six sometimes. You'll need a warm hat and coat.'

'And gloves.' Val recalled her cold tingling fingers on the beach.

She felt her heart leap. 'Oh, I can't wait.'

'Get that ticket booked, then,' Tom said warmly. 'I'll ring you in a week or so with all the arrangements. Lottie says they're all fighting over who gets you – they all want to take you skiing and skating.'

'Oh, I'm not sure I'm up to skiing.' Val smiled. 'But I can't wait for the treks in the snow.'

'I'll get back to you soon.' Tom spoke quickly. 'I have work to do. It's been great talking to you though, Mum.'

'You too, Tom.' Val's voice cracked with emotion as the call ended. She flopped back in her seat, staring at her phone. She'd book the ticket straight away. It all felt so real now: Tom's wedding, Canada, the prospect of snow, a different country and new people. Val was looking forward to it. It didn't matter that Ray would be there, or that Val would be on her own in the photos. She would see Tom, meet Lottie and have the time of her life. She sat in front of her laptop and began to hum a happy tune.

Val was still humming three hours later when Caden came in. She'd cooked a Thai green curry and the kitchen was filled with the sweet heady fragrance of lemongrass, garlic, ginger and cumin. Caden collapsed onto a chair.

'Something smells heavenly, Val. Oh, you've no idea how much I need this today.'

'Tough day at the office?'

'Not at all.' Caden waved a hand. 'The editor's really pleased with me; apparently, the paper is up for an award because of our stance on the environment. I was even told I should be looking for promotion – get this – "beyond the confines of Cornwall", the editor said.'

'Confines?' Val laughed, ladling food onto plates. 'So why the long face? It's not Oscar?'

'Oscar who?' Caden gave a single bark of laughter. 'No, it's the

Thanksgiving event on the twenty-fourth. It's in just over a week's time and it's turning out to be such a headache.'

Val sat down opposite Caden and she lifted a fork. 'How can I help?'

Caden blew air from his cheeks, frustrated. 'Well, the event is advertised in *The Gazette* and in various shops around town, Finest Choice, and in the town hall; the food's organised – the band is booked. Would you believe they are calling themselves Pumpkin Pie and Pasties just for the night? Unreal.'

'It sounds perfect. So, what is there to worry about?'

Caden spoke between mouthfuls. 'The tickets. Hardly any have been sold.' He rolled his eyes. 'It seems that the people of Lowenstowe don't want to go out on a cold November night to celebrate Thanksgiving.'

'Maybe people will buy tickets at the door?'

'But what if they don't?' Caden's eyes widened. 'I'll have egg on my face, just me and seven other people, a band singing "American Pie", surrounded by lots of turkey rolls and Loveday calling me a silly tuss.'

Val smiled. 'We can sort this. Don't worry.'

'How?'

'There's me, you, Connie, Ollie, Alice, Kevin – and Jago. If we each contact everyone we know and we each invite five people, that's over thirty people. And if they each bring a plus one, that's sixty. Success... tickets all gone.'

'I suppose so...'

'We'll just pass the word on.' Val poured water into two glasses. 'Henry can bring his family – the band can bring friends – maybe Loveday can bring her John. It'll be fine if we all pull together.'

Caden closed his eyes and sipped water. 'Thanks, Val. I'm feeling much better now.' He forked the steaming curry and rice. 'And this is delicious. What would I do without you?'

* * *

True to her word, Val set about mobilising the troops; despite having lived in Lowenstowe for less than a year, she had several ideas about who might buy tickets. She made a list, then crossed off several names: she wouldn't contact Freddie and she wouldn't ask Ray. But there were plenty of other people.

Several days later, she and the other members of the Lowenstowe Buccaneers grouped around glasses of gin and tonic, apart from Caden, who was drinking orange juice as he was chauffeur again. Loveday initiated proceedings, throwing out her hands dramatically.

'The tickets don't seem to be selling like hot cakes, do they? I invited my neighbours but they are too busy. Jenna Penrose couldn't afford six tickets, although I'm sure they could all do with a big plate of food, so that's a big fat zero from me.'

Caden's shoulders slumped visibly. 'Lots of people from *The Gazette* said they might come, and Lou and Martin from the TV crew promised to buy a ticket each, but so far no one has put their money where their mouth is.'

'I spoke to my sister, Sarah, in Bideford and tried to persuade her to buy two tickets, but she's like me, she prefers the fireside in winter,' Alice added sadly.

'So that's another zero. It's not going well.' Loveday folded her arms.

'Well, as it happens...' Jago rubbed his hands together optimistically. 'I rang a couple of mates and they might bring their wives, and my neighbour likes a knees-up, so that's five possibles from me.'

'Five possibles?' Loveday lifted one hand to emphasise the paltry number. 'Five's not many, and possible is nothing at all.'

'I could ask a plumber friend or two...' Kevin suggested.

'Two more who just *might* come?' Loveday said. 'That's still zero.'

'I have sold tickets to six of my friends and four more to their parents,' Heidi added.

'I sold ten to people from Finest Choice.' Ollie was pleased with himself.

Everyone turned to Val, who produced a piece of paper. 'Right. I went to see Henry Scott at the town hall and he bought several tickets; his receptionist bought two more. I have sold tickets to Dougie and Boo. They asked me and Connie to dinner on that day so I just invited them to the Thanksgiving evening instead. Then I was walking on the beach this morning and I bumped into Tim Keita, out with his dog. He bought one straight away. I went into Finest Choice and Diane King bought two tickets and she mentioned it to people she knew, and they bought another twelve, so that's twenty-four. Oh, and I took a few tickets into the PDSA last Thursday and got rid of another six so, in total, that's thirty tickets.'

Caden gave a long sigh. 'Val, you're a miracle worker.'

'And Dave has sold twelve behind the bar, so there are – how many did he say? – about a dozen left. They will easily sell on the door or over the next week...'

Loveday clapped her hands. 'Valerie, you are wonderful.'

Caden agreed. 'I think this calls for another round.'

* * *

An hour later, Val walked home arm in arm with Connie; Alice and Kevin were next to them, Dolly trotting alongside on the lead. Alice appeared a little downhearted. She and Kevin were discussing the Thanksgiving event. 'I was really looking forward to us going together.'

'I was only saying that Dolly doesn't like staying at home by herself.' He shrugged expansively. 'I just thought maybe you'd like to go with Val and Connie, you know – you all like dancing. Dolly and I could stay home, watch the sport on TV, have a beer.' His face was hopeful. 'Wouldn't you enjoy that more?'

'We need to spend more time together, Kev.'

Kevin sighed. 'I love spending time with you, Alice, but dancing? It's not me, love.'

'It used to be,' Alice said sadly. 'You've changed.'

'I've got older. I like my home. I'm tired after work.' Kevin tried again. 'It's only one evening...'

Alice sighed, a deep, drawn-out sound of despair. 'Do what you want, Kev. I don't really care.' Then she increased her pace, walking briskly ahead, and called back without turning round. 'I'll see you at home. I'm cold.'

'Now what have I done?' Kevin was astonished.

Connie, ever practical, asked, 'Does she have keys?'

'Yeh, she can let herself in.' Kevin scratched his head beneath the woollen hat he was wearing. 'How come she's so upset with me?'

Val offered him a warm smile. 'Talk to her when you get in. Ask her.' She pressed her lips together. 'I suppose she was just looking forward to a nice evening out with you.'

Connie agreed. 'Alice is quite a romantic at heart.' She gave Val a meaningful look. 'Most women are.'

Val laughed. 'Not me. By the way, I was thinking of calling round to Crab Claw Cottage to sell Ben a ticket. He might enjoy Thanksgiving down The Boat House.'

'I saw him yesterday leaving really early in the morning. He fishes all day long, even in this cold weather,' Connie said.

'Oh, my goodness me!' Kevin exclaimed. 'That's it – when you said romantic, Connie. Oh, no, that's done it now.' Dolly gazed up at him anxiously, her paws tapping on the ground.

'What did I say?' Connie was bemused.

'You said romantic. November the twenty-fourth. It's only our wedding anniversary, isn't it?' Kevin put a hand to his head.

'How many years?' Val asked, interested.

'I've no idea.' Kevin was distraught. 'Our kids are twenty-five and twenty-seven so it must be at least that many...' He wiped his brow. 'Now I'm really in trouble.'

'Poor Alice,' Connie said. 'Can you buy her something nice?'

'I could but...' Kevin turned desperate eyes towards Val. 'I've no idea whatsoever about what she likes.'

'Not even after twenty-something years?' Connie asked, covering a smile.

'Not a clue.' Kevin groaned. 'Dolly's easy – a bag of crisps and a hug and she's fine but Alice – I love her to bits but she's... a complicated woman, and I'm just so rubbish at these things.' He shook his head. 'Val, Connie, can you help? I mean...' He waved a hand. 'She's upset and I've no idea how to sort it out.'

They had reached the cottages. Ahead of them, Alice opened the door and slammed it crisply behind her, not looking back.

'See?' Kevin said. 'I've really messed up now.'

'Go after her,' Connie suggested. 'Tell her you love her.'

'That won't be anything like enough. I know Alice – I've upset her...'

Val patted Kevin's arm. 'Connie and I will see what we can come up with. Connie's an expert at romance.' She winked at her friend. 'I'm sure between us we can help sort out something that will make Alice's anniversary special.'

'I hope so – I'm desperate – I need to get her something special, whatever it costs...' Kevin looked down at his Staffy, who was tugging at the lead. 'Otherwise, that's both of us in the doghouse, Dolly.'

35

Val, Connie, Loveday and Caden had finished decorating The Boat House function room and were slumped against the bar, already exhausted. Dave gazed affectionately towards where his wife was busy arranging the spread. 'My Jackie's done a wonderful job.' At the far end, a long table had been placed, covered in red, white and blue paper, laden with plates of food. Dave winked at Jackie, his face delighted. 'She's done more tasty things with turkey than I've seen in my life – crunchy turkey, plant-based ones, turkey in sauce, bagels... and so many salads and pumpkin dishes. She's excelled herself.'

Jackie was talking to the band, five men in waistcoats and jeans who, despite being in their sixties, still sported long hair of various styles: the drummer had a curly perm and the singer wore his hair to his shoulders, although much of it at the front had disappeared. The guitarist with a long mop of grey hair and round glasses was playing chords, turning up the volume, competing with the drummer who would crash a cymbal every so often. Jackie returned to the bar, pleased.

'I've been through their playlist. It's all popular American songs people can dance to. We'll have an interval for food at about eight thirty and then they'll play from half nine until half ten. You've done so well with the décor.'

'It's bleddy handsum.' Loveday pointed to the walls, where a huge decoration of flags, all stars and stripes, had been arranged. There were hearts and pumpkins and smiling turkeys in bright colours and strings of twinkling lights. Ollie and Heidi were putting the finishing touches to a huge picture of the Statue of Liberty, their faces focused in concentration. Jago was standing on a ladder, smelling of sharp aftershave, wearing a checked shirt and freshly ironed jeans, attempting to fix more fairy lights to the ceiling.

Val glanced at the clock. 'It's almost seven. People should be arriving soon.'

'I wish we'd all worn fancy dress.' Caden indicated his cowboy hat, the leather trousers and boots. 'I thought everyone was going to dress up.'

'I'm wearing a denim skirt...' Connie said kindly.

Loveday folded her arms. 'I thought it was daft to wear costume. Americans are the same as us, cousins across the pond...'

'Ooh, look, they're here.' Caden turned excitedly towards a young man and woman who had just arrived carrying bags of cameras and equipment. 'Lou, Martin – glad you could make it. Can we fit in an interview before the hordes arrive?'

'It's going to be a great evening.' Val winked at Connie. 'Apparently, the Cornish Beach Guardians rang Caden; they want us to join their campaign across the county.'

'It makes sense,' Loveday agreed, her face glowing with pride. 'We're just little people in Lowenstowe, but together we can change the world.'

Kevin and Alice arrived, both dressed in their best. Kevin was uncomfortable in a stiff suit and Alice looked sophisticated, her hair pinned up, wearing a long ball gown under a huge coat. Connie clapped her hands. 'You both look incredible.'

'I'm celebrating something special tonight.' Alice made a little pirouette.

Kevin pulled a glum face. 'Alice said it was either this suit or she'd hire a turkey costume complete with snood and wattle and make me wear it.' He sidled over to Val and whispered, 'She thinks I've forgotten our anniversary – it's our thirtieth, too.' His expression was desperate. 'Have you got the surprise ready, like we agreed?'

'Trust me.' Val gave him the thumbs-up sign discreetly; Connie turned from listening to Alice complain about how Kevin had tucked Dolly up on the sofa and left the TV on for her, and winked towards Kevin. His face was perspiring above his tie. 'I hope this goes according to plan.'

'It will, don't worry.' Val squeezed his arm.

Caden was talking into a camera, gushing about the success of the campaign against waste, then Loveday joined him. Val heard her say, '... and even our councillor Mr Scott is supporting our work. He'll be here with his family tonight.'

'We're all one big happy family here,' Caden agreed. 'And this is a real celebration, giving thanks for friendship and for those we love because, after all, we want to make the world cleaner and better for those we care about.'

Val wanted to cheer: Caden was a real trooper. He and Loveday wrapped their arms around each other, speaking over each other, words bubbling enthusiastically. Val closed her eyes, thinking. She had been in Lowenstowe for almost a year and she had made real friends, such lovely people. She felt blessed; her life was blossoming. As she opened her eyes, people had filled the room, their excited chatter and laughter fizzing. The band struck loud chords then began to play Bruce Springsteen's 'Born in the USA'; Dave was serving the heckling crowds waiting at the bar and Alice and Connie had started to dance. The band launched into CCR's 'Proud Mary' and suddenly Heidi and Ollie were leaping around, waving their arms. Soon the dance space filled and everyone was reeling with wild abandon.

Then Connie was by her side, squeezing her arm. 'Look who's here – Mr January. Oh, Val, he's gorgeous.'

'I sold him a ticket,' Val said matter-of-factly. But Connie did have a point; standing at the bar in a dark jacket and white shirt, he looked very attractive, Val thought, even without his Chow Chow.

'Go and talk to him.'

'I will, later,' Val promised. 'Look – Dougie and Boo are here.'

'Connie!' Boo had already seen them. She rushed over, smart in a black dress, her red tresses swept in a coil. Dougie arrived behind her; he was even slimmer and dapper in a dark blazer. 'And Val too.' She air-kissed them both. 'Lovely to see you again or, as they say in Italy, *bellissimo rivederti.*'

Dougie's face shone with pride. 'Boo's an incredible linguist. A polyglot.'

Boo's voice rang out. 'So nice of you to invite us here. What a great idea, celebrating Thanksgiving.' She gazed around. 'This is wonderful.'

Dougie agreed. 'And it's nice to have Boo to myself for once. She's very busy. Do you know, she's taken up the salsa on Saturday mornings?'

Boo waved her hand, pushing his comments aside. 'I'm a woman of many facets.'

The band began to play 'Sweet Home Alabama' and Dougie whisked Boo into his arms to dance. Val stared at them, recalling the foyer of The Unicorn where she had last seen a tall redhead, her hair in a similar style; her thoughts were interrupted by Connie, pressing her arm.

'Boo looks well. Dougie too. Something is clearly agreeing with them.'

'Indeed,' Val said. 'Shall we get a drink?'

They moved through the crowds to the bar passing Jago, who was dancing cheek to cheek with a woman Val had never seen before. Loveday was already at the buffet table, sampling the turkey dishes, despite food not being offered until eight thirty. Caden was standing by the door talking to his two TV friends. Dave greeted Val and Connie, placing two glasses of wine on the bar. 'Here – for you. You've worked hard helping us organise this evening. These are on the house.'

'Thanks.' Val lifted her glass. 'It's going well.'

'We're doing good business behind the bar – and having the pub on TV is great publicity.' Dave was pleased. 'In fact, everything tonight has been champion.'

Val and Connie were about to move away. More people had arrived; the function room was becoming crowded. Then Val felt a gentle pressure against her elbow. 'Hello, Val. What a fantastic event this is.'

Val looked into the luminous brown eyes of Tim Keita. 'Hello,' she greeted him warmly. 'This is my friend, Connie.'

'Hello.' Tim glanced at Connie and then turned back to Val. 'I was wondering...'

Both women leaned forward at the same time, equally interested.

'I was wondering,' Tim said again, 'since you enjoyed *Baily's Beads* so much, if you'd like to hear about my next book, *Procyon and the F-Spectral Class*.'

'It sounds like a Greek drama,' Connie was impressed.

'Or one of James Bond's super-turbo cars,' Val mused.

'Oh, no.' Tim didn't notice Val's smile. 'They are all stars with a

6,000 – 7,500K effective temperature; they're a white-yellow colour...'

'Fascinating,' Val agreed.

'So my next book...' Tim looked hopeful '... is all about the supergiant Canopus and the main sequence star, Orionis.'

'No astronomy.' Val shook her head. 'We're strictly dancing tonight.' She indicated Tim's glass of lemonade. 'When you've finished that, come and join us.'

'Oh, right, I will.' Tim was suddenly enthusiastic. 'This is my kind of music, American West Coast. I used to be disco champion at uni in the seventies. Do you know, I haven't let my hair down in ages.'

'Then come on, let's hit the dance floor.' Val grinned.

Tim raised his glass and drained the contents. 'I'm right behind you.'

Val and Connie threaded their way back to the dancers, followed by Tim. The three of them threw themselves into lively moves, Tim smiling broadly, turning to each woman in turn, wiggling and gyrating. Connie threw him a look of pure rapture and admiration; he was easily the best dancer in the room with his sharp footwork and the hypnotic rhythm of his hips. The band was playing 'Ramblin' Man'; Ollie and Heidi had their arms around each other, swaying. Alice was attempting to persuade Kevin to dance. He looked around wildly for help and Val moved over to the band, making a gesture to the bass guitarist, then she nodded once towards Kevin. Alice was oblivious, her arms around Kevin's neck.

Then Val noticed a broad-shouldered man in a smart suit dancing slowly, a blonde woman in his embrace. She stopped and stared: it was Dennis Cargill smooching, his eyes closed, his face set in an expression of pure love. He looked slimmer, sober and much happier. Val gaped at the woman in his arms, her head resting on his shoulder. She leaned towards Connie and said, 'Look – it's Dennis.'

Connie put her mouth close to her ear. 'I heard he was back with his wife – Dave said something about it. He stayed at his sister's and came back feeling much more positive – he asked his ex to come back, and she did.'

'He's with Monica.' Val hardly believed her eyes.

'That's right,' Connie replied. 'Apparently, she left the man she was living with, and fell straight back into Dennis's arms.' Connie inhaled sharply: the penny had dropped. 'Oh, Monica, his Nicci.' She clutched Val's arm. 'I hadn't realised. Are you all right?'

'I'm fine – I knew she'd left Ray. I'm glad Dennis has got her back.' Val shook her head, a little stunned. Then she felt a light touch on her shoulder. Tim Keita was urging her to dance again. She whirled towards him, Connie following, and the three of them thrashed and wriggled to the beat.

The song ended and the bass guitarist stepped up to the microphone, his voice low. 'There used to be a song called "Living Next Door to Alice", but we're not going to do that one...' There was cheering from the crowd. 'Because she's here with us tonight. Everybody, please welcome on stage – Alice Holmes.'

Alice looked terrified, a rabbit-in-the-headlights stare, as Kevin guided her towards the stage. The bassist helped her up and Alice whimpered, 'Please don't ask me to sing.'

'No, you're not singing, Alice...' The bassist smiled for the crowd. 'But it is your wedding anniversary today so we thought we'd make it a special one for you. Do you know a man called Kevin?'

Alice mouthed, 'What?' and gazed around, stunned. The crowd of dancers whooped as Kevin clambered up, positioning himself next to the microphone, bashful in his stiff suit. He was holding an orange in one hand and a set of keys in the other, items Val had quickly found in her bag and thrust into his sweating palms.

'So, Kevin...?' The bassist with the ponytail gave him a gentle nudge. 'What do you have to say to Alice?'

'Er, Alice.' Kevin looked at his shoes and back to his wife. He thrust out the items, his arms straight. 'Happy thirtieth anniversary.'

Alice stared at the orange and the rusty keys. 'I don't get it.'

'Ah, for our anniversary... ah, because I... ah... I love you, I just want to say, ah...' His words were drowned out by clapping and whooping. Kevin's shoulders hunched in embarrassment but Alice's face was flushed with happiness.

'Go on, Kevin,' the bass player prompted.

'An orange? A set of keys?' Alice's eyes were only for her husband. 'What does this mean, Kev?'

'Oranges come from Florida – and – and I'm taking you to Florida Keys after Christmas... It's all booked... a second honeymoon... because I know you don't like the cold weather.'

Kevin's cheeks perspired as the audience applauded and roared. Alice could hardly catch her breath.

'Florida?' she gasped. 'What about Dolly? Is she coming too?'

'Your sister, Sarah, said she can stay there... I want us to spend time together.' Kevin's hands were in his pockets and he was staring at his toes again as Alice flung herself at his neck and kissed him energetically. The bassist took over on the mic.

'And now we're going to play "Somebody to Love" by Jefferson Airplane, just for Kevin and Alice.'

The singer shook his mane, belted out the first line, then throbbing bass and guitar music shuddered through amplifiers as Kevin and Alice fell into each other's arms. Over Alice's shoulder, Kevin met Val's smile and mouthed a relieved, 'Thank you.'

Val and Connie threw themselves into dancing with Tim again, aware of the pulsating throng closing in around them swaying and waving arms. Val was enjoying herself: Tim was the most handsome man in the room, the niftiest mover, the best dance partner, but he no longer made her heart beat too fast. She had healed, moved on: she was at peace with herself. Jago was draped over the woman he'd been dancing with earlier; Dougie was not far away, struggling to keep up with Boo's energetic moves, and Caden and his friends were twirling alongside a smooching Heidi and Ollie. Loveday hovered at the buffet table, still tucking in. Tim whirled round, his arms in the air, fluid and flexible, and several people stopped to applaud his footwork.

Connie surged forward, her eyes shining. 'So, could Mr January be Mr December?'

'He's an amazing dance partner,' Val said. 'But no – I'm fine as I am.'

Connie nodded. 'I know what you mean. It's so empowering, isn't it, dancing just for yourself?'

They threw themselves back, linking arms, twirling one way and then the other. The band was playing 'Yankee Rose'. Val saw Henry Scott not far away, dancing with his wife, both of them in each other's arms, attempting to do the cha-cha-cha to rock music. Tim caught Val's eye and she smiled back; everyone was having such fun and it was all raising funds for the environment. The evening was going so well. Then she heard a voice to her right, clear and precise, saying loudly, 'I wonder – may I cut in?'

Val recognised the cultured tone, the smart clothes, the slightly soft chin. At first, she thought Nigel Carrow was talking to her, but then she noticed Dougie and Boo, as they stopped dancing and stared at Nigel, who stood nearby looking smug.

Boo snapped, 'Nigel – what are you doing here?'

'I came with my nephew and his wife and some friends – you know Henry, our councillor. But I wasn't expecting to see you here.'

'Quite.' Boo stared from Dougie to Nigel and back again.

'Dance with me,' Nigel's expression was suave.

'Not now.' Boo seemed irritated.

'If not now, when, darling?' Nigel said smoothly.

Boo put her hands on her hips and gave him a warning look. 'Nigel.'

'Boo, it's time it was all out in the open.'

'Nigel, no.'

'It's about time he knew, my love.'

Then Dougie stepped forward, moving Boo behind him. He said simply, 'I've known since May, Nigel,' then he positioned his feet, lifted a fist and punched him square on the jaw.

36

'I need to go home now, Caden.' Loveday was leaning against the door jamb, her hands on her hips, watching everyone scuttle around helping Dave and Jackie to rearrange the function room.

Dave glanced at the clock; it was well past eleven thirty. 'You all go on – you've done enough,' he said good-naturedly. 'Jackie and I will finish off tomorrow.'

Ollie and Heidi were talking quietly in the corner of the room. Val, Caden and Connie joined Loveday who was ready, wearing her hat and coat, her arms tightly folded. 'I want to get back. My John will be waiting.'

'We'd better get a move on, then. I'd love to meet John. I'll pop in and say a quick hello, shall I?' Caden was full of energy, despite it being almost midnight.

'Oh, no, no, he's not up to visitors.' Loveday shook her head.

'Everyone had such a good time tonight,' Val said.

'Except for your friend punching your other friend on the jaw,' Loveday observed. 'I suppose it helped his wife to make her mind up.'

Val replied, 'But what a fantastic evening. Thanksgiving was brilliant. I feel ready for Christmas now.'

Connie agreed. 'And it was so nice to meet Mr January at last. Tim asked when the next event was, he's enjoyed it so much.'

'He's the perfect dancing partner,' Val said. 'I think I'll ask him to join the Buccaneers too. He'd be really useful.'

'He's good fun,' Connie added. 'I think we've made a friend.'

Loveday was delighted. 'We've made a pile of money for charity too. And your dad seems to have found another lady friend, Caden.'

Caden waved a hand, exasperated. 'My dad must have half of the women in Cornwall on the go.'

Connie's face shone. 'I loved seeing Alice and Kevin so happy. They'll have a wonderful holiday together in Florida.' She gazed around. 'Oh, they must have left early. I expect they wanted to get home to Dolly.'

'Perhaps.' Loveday winked at Val.

Then Heidi and Ollie arrived, hand in hand. Heidi gave Caden a friendly dig in the ribs. 'Right, Mr Taxi Driver. Are we ready to go? I'm knackered.'

'Yes, let's hit the road,' Caden said. 'Put the kettle on, Val – I won't be long.'

Val heard Dave's voice at the bar shout, 'Hey, my man, come and have a drink – you deserve one.' Dave poured cider into a glass and handed it to a tall, sinewy man wearing a blue beanie, then he waved to Val and Connie. 'Come and join us – have one for the road.'

Val and Connie walked over to the bar. Ben Berry, his fingers around a cider bottle, smiled in their direction, his eyes twinkling. Dave grinned and placed two glasses of orange juice on coasters. 'Ben deserves some refreshment after all the work he's done tonight – I don't know how I'd have managed without him.'

Val was perplexed. 'I didn't see you here this evening.'

Ben smiled shyly. His voice was soft, gravelly. 'I'm not really one for dancing. I was helping out in the wings.'

Dave poured a cider for himself and took a deep draught. 'How do you think we managed to change the barrels, bring extra bottles up from the cellar? How do you think the band packed their equipment away in the van? Ben offered to help and I couldn't say no.'

'I wanted to give you some support, Val, Connie,' Ben said simply. 'And make sure you got home safely afterwards.'

Outside, the air cold against their faces, Val and Connie began the short stroll home, their arms linked for warmth. Ben walked next to them, his hands in his pockets. Val felt tired as she walked; she must have overdone the dancing, but it had been great fun.

Connie sighed. 'It was lovely to see Alice and Kevin so happy. You're so clever, Val, helping him organise the trip to Florida.' She was thoughtful. 'You're off to Canada; Alice and Kevin will be in the sunshine. I'll be here...'

'You could come to the wedding with me as my plus-one. We'd have a great time.'

Connie shook her head. 'I'm not sure I'd want to be in all the photos.'

Val laughed. 'You wouldn't have to be.'

'You'll be with your son,' Connie said. 'I ought to be with mine.'

Val squeezed her arm. 'You should visit Will in New Zealand. Stay there for a while.'

Connie sighed. 'I will. I'm ready for that now.'

'Are you going to Canada?' Ben asked.

'Just for my son's wedding,' Val explained. 'Until the new year.'

Ben glanced at Connie. 'So, what will you be doing over the festive season?'

Connie seemed momentarily thoughtful. 'I'll be on my own, but that's okay. Last Christmas was so nice, meeting Val. It seems such a long time ago now, so much has happened. I'm stronger now. I'll be fine.' Val, Connie and Ben walked in rhythm, their feet soft against tarmac. 'I'll put my energies into arranging New Zealand.'

They had reached the empty house; the garden had been cut back neatly, though there was no sign of any inhabitants. Overhead, the moon slipped behind a cloud.

Ben's voice was quiet. 'It's been a strange old year for me.'

Connie gazed at him. 'How strange, Ben?'

He smiled. 'Well, a very kind lady came to live next door and gave me fudge and cakes and jam, and I've given some fish in return...'

'And cut my hedge.' Val grinned.

'But the year has disappeared in a flash.' Ben scratched his head beneath the woollen hat. 'It's November already and all I seem to have done is work, fishing all day, gardening, keeping the house nice, a bit of jogging. It's all been routine. Yet you seem to have achieved so much, Val.'

'Oh, she has,' Connie said. 'She's certainly changed everything for me. I hardly went out before she came, and this year we've got involved in cleaning up Lowenstowe. And we searched for Mr December.'

Val laughed. 'I've learned so much about myself, meeting all those people.'

'We didn't find a wedding guest, but we found out a lot about who we really are.' Connie grinned. 'I certainly have.'

Val noticed Ben's perplexed expression. 'It was a bit of a joke, really. We were looking for a partner for me to take to Tom's wedding, but I've realised I don't need anyone.'

Ben took a deep breath. 'Perhaps *need* isn't the right word. Perhaps *want* is better – we might be independent and *need* no one, but we might *want* a someone to care about.' Ben shook his head. 'Love is something we shouldn't take for granted.'

Connie looked at him, surprised. 'What do you mean?'

'Ah.' Ben breathed out slowly. 'That's the reason I live like I do, always busy, always the same routine. This way, I don't stop to think. The world keeps turning, I live in the present and try not to remember the past. I don't *need* anyone, but some nights I sit by myself by the fire and I think about what might have been.'

Connie touched his arm. 'You loved someone once, Ben?'

'My wife died young.' He was silent for a moment. 'No, you can't take love for granted. Where there's no love at home, there's just loneliness sitting opposite in an empty chair.'

'That's sad,' Connie agreed. 'But I know exactly what you mean.'

'Yet life goes on, and where there's life there's hope, as they say.'

'You're so right, Ben,' Connie said.

'The world is full of beauty.' His voice was low. 'Each new dawn is a lovely thing to behold. I see the sun rise from my boat most mornings and I'm filled with gratitude.' Ben gave an easy grin. 'I was glad to help Dave out this evening, and do my bit for the community. I must do more of it in future.'

They had reached the little row of cottages, the dim street light glimmering overhead. Val had an idea. 'Ben – would you like to come in for a nightcap? Connie, will you come too?'

Ben seemed unsure. Val assumed he spent little time in social groups.

'I'd love to,' Connie replied quickly, then she glanced towards Ben. 'Please say you'll join us.'

'Please, Ben.' Val smiled. 'We have a whole year of conversation to catch up on.'

* * *

An hour later, Val, Ben and Connie were still sitting at the table in the kitchen of Teasel Cottage, cups of tea in their hands, empty glasses, a bottle of brandy uncorked on the table. Caden had joined them. He leaned over and grasped the neck of the brandy bottle, filling each glass. 'I've promised myself that next year will be my year,' he announced. 'This time a year ago, I was all loved up and blind. Oscar was a mistake. Now I'm going to move forward.'

'Are you applying for the job in London?' Val sipped brandy slowly.

'Definitely. I'm ready for a new challenge,' Caden said. 'London would do me the world of good. Yes, that's going to be my new year's resolution, to put myself first for a change, to make a new start.'

'I'm all for new starts,' Val agreed. 'Coming here was a fresh beginning for me. I started the year with so much determination. I intended to learn to put myself first. It took me a while to realise that forty-seven years of marriage wasn't something I could get over quickly, but I've made my peace with Ray now. We can both move on.'

'To putting ourselves first.' Caden knocked back his brandy and clinked his glass against Val's.

Connie frowned. 'I'm not so sure I want to put myself first, not any more.'

'But you live by yourself; you can do as you please,' Caden insisted.

'That's the problem...' Connie said. 'Living alone made me introspective. I was looking backwards. I became antisocial. It would be so nice to think of others now. Both Val and Loveday have shown me that. We have to get out there, learn to live a little.' She glanced at Ben. 'Like you said, we have to hope.'

Ben nodded. 'I've got used to living alone. But your gifts of jam and cake meant so much, Val. We do have to live for others – it makes us better people.'

'I agree.' Connie placed her small hand over Ben's large knotty fist. 'It's so important to reach out.'

Val gazed from Ben to Connie and then she smiled. 'What time do you come back from fishing tomorrow, Ben?'

He lifted broad shoulders in a shrug. 'I'll be back for two o'clock, probably.'

'Then come round for a late lunch. You too, Connie. Let's make an afternoon of it. I'll make something hearty, to keep the cold out.'

'Fish pie?' Ben raised his eyebrows. 'I'll see if I can't get us a nice piece of monkfish.'

'And I'll bring a bottle of something,' Connie offered. Her eyes shone as she glanced at Ben. 'That will be wonderful.'

'I'll be out – but I'm sure you'll manage without me,' Caden quipped.

'Well.' Val stretched her arms. 'I'm ready for my bed. It's been a nice evening.'

'It has, and a successful one,' Caden agreed. 'But I need my beauty sleep now.'

Ben stood up. 'I'll walk you to your front door, Connie.'

'Thank you, Ben.' Connie was beside him. 'That's really kind of you.'

'Oh, it's a pleasure.' Ben pushed his chair beneath the table. 'Thanks for the tea and the brandy, Val. And I look forward to seeing you for lunch tomorrow.'

Val watched as Ben shepherded Connie towards the door, stepping out into the night air, closing it with a clunk. She folded her arms and smiled.

Caden was watching her. 'What are you grinning about?' He shook his head. 'Are you hatching something?'

'I don't think I need to.' Val met his gaze. 'I think something may be hatching by itself.'

MR DECEMBER

37

December brought the cold rains from the north, whipping up the sea and battering against windows. Everyone was rushing around planning Christmas. By the fourth, every available space on the outside wall of Cloud Cottage had been crammed with fairy lights, twinkling brightly. A glittering Santa held up his thumb and winked as he clambered towards the roof on a ladder that flashed red and gold.

Val booked an air ticket to Montréal and threw herself into buying a new wardrobe that would be perfect for frolicking in the snow, although she had really no idea what sort of activities she'd be involved in. She had been shopping in Bideford all afternoon and arrived home in the twilight carrying bags of clothes. She was folding her new purchases, including a pale blue dress with matching hat and shoes that she thought would be perfect for the wedding when she heard a soft knock at the front door and rushed to let in Connie, who was breathless with excitement.

'Let's see the dress, then. Oh, Val, I should have come shopping with you.'

'You should have.' Val held up the dress. '*Ta-da.* What do you think?'

'Oh, it's so beautiful.' Connie touched the soft blue material. 'You will look ravishing. Some lovely man in Canada is bound to want to—'

'Stop right there, Connie.' Val laughed, tugging her friend by the wrist into the kitchen. 'Come on, we'll have a cuppa and set the world to rights.' She filled the kettle with water. 'So, out with it.'

'Out with what?' Connie tried to look innocent, but her face was flushed. Val noticed she was wearing a pretty blouse under a new jacket, and her hair had been freshly cut.

'The reason you couldn't come shopping with me?'

'Ah.' Connie folded her hands neatly. 'I was busy. I'm having a dinner guest tonight.'

'Oh?' Val arched an eyebrow. 'And what's on the menu?' She offered a playful smile.

Connie's face was serious. 'Ben's coming over – we've started spending time together.' A smile rushed to her lips. 'I like being with him, Val.'

'I'm glad. He's sweet and loyal and I can tell he's already devoted to you.'

'He makes me feel happy... no, it's more than happy, Val, it's... special.' Her voice trailed off and Val said nothing. She knew that her friend was thinking about her husband, Mike, and how Connie was coming to terms with her developing feelings for Ben. She squeezed her hand.

'I'm delighted. Ben is lovely. Just take it day by day, Connie, see how it goes.'

Connie frowned. 'I'm not a day-by-day person. I'm already imagining how it would be if he came to New Zealand with me next year, which is ridiculous.' Her eyes widened. 'Do you think I'm crazy?'

'No, I think you're perfect.' Val poured hot water onto leaves in the teapot. 'And, since I haven't seen you for days, we'd better catch up on the gossip.'

'Oh, I've been too busy for gossip...'

'I have loads,' Val said. 'Loveday's overdoing it, committed as ever. I was walking on the beach on Sunday and I saw her collecting rubbish. It was cold as hell, a north wind blowing in, and I offered to help but she told me that she was too busy to stop and natter. Oh, and Caden has a job interview.'

'Oh?' Connie leaned forward.

'In London, on a radio station – his TV friends told him about it. It's presenting a weekly show about the environment, starting in January. The interview's on Friday the sixteenth. He's so nervous. I hope he gets it – it would be a great life for him, living in London.'

'That's so exciting,' Connie said.

'And I had an email from Dougie and Boo, reminding us that their Burns Night is in January and could we go, and could I make several pounds of Scottish tablet...' Val laughed as she poured tea. 'I can't, of course. Do you know, I still have a favour box in my handbag that I never gave away?'

Connie closed her eyes. 'It's been an incredible year.'

'So, what are you doing tomorrow morning, Connie?'

She shrugged. 'Ben is going fishing early so...' She shook her head. 'What did you have in mind?'

'I help Loveday in the PDSA on Thursdays. I was going to go in and make the whole place look Christmassy – put up some decorations, add some sparkle and glitter. Do you fancy giving me a hand?'

'Why not? And maybe you can come to my house and help me put up a tree and some garlands?' Connie closed her eyes dreamily. 'Ben's promised he'll spend Christmas with me this year, so neither of us will be on our own and we can share lunch. It will be so lovely.'

Val cupped her palms around her mug. 'And I'll be in Canada with Tom. He'll be married and I'll be with him and Lottie and the in-laws. It seems to me that this year is turning out very well indeed for us both.'

* * *

The following day, Val and Connie were driving into Lowenstowe. Val had piled boxes of Christmas decorations in the back of the car; the radio was on, blaring out Christmas songs. Slade were heralding the season of goodwill as Connie rubbed her eyes.

'You look tired, Connie,' Val said.

'I didn't sleep well.'

Val arched an eyebrow. 'Oh?'

'It's not what you're thinking.' Connie sighed.

'So, how did the meal go?'

'Oh, it was lovely. Ben and I talked until late. He told me all about his wife who died in her forties. He's been quite reclusive since he lost her. He fishes, runs on the beach, keeps himself busy.' She breathed out slowly. 'We have so much in common, he and I. We talked and talked then, around two, he went back to his cottage.'

Val reached across and patted Connie's knee. 'What's worrying you?'

'It sounds silly but... Val, I like Ben and I want to spend time with him...'

'Then you should.'

'But what about Mike?'

'Mike was the love of your life, Connie. Nothing will change that. But you and Ben, it's not the same relationship. Being with Ben is about company and affection, two like-minded people who care for each other. There are so many different types of love. I'm sure Mike would be glad that someone is making you happy.'

'Do you think so?'

'I'm sure of it.' Val brought the car to a stop and switched off the engine. 'Spend time with Ben. You'll know that it's right.'

'I think it is,' Connie said, tears glistening.

'So – let's go and make the PDSA festive and Christmassy – Loveday will be delighted.'

Fore Street was already bustling with shoppers although it was only just past nine. Strings of bright lights had been hung between buildings, a crimson Santa, a row of reindeer, bursting golden stars. As Val and Connie arrived at the PDSA, a short woman in a heavy coat was staring into the window. She buttonholed Val. 'Have you come to open up?'

Val shook her head. 'Loveday usually does it.'

'She wasn't here yesterday or the day before. Shop's been closed all week.'

'Oh?' Val turned to Connie, her face anxious. 'That's not like Loveday.'

'That's what I thought,' the woman replied. 'I need to start my Christmas shopping and everyone knows Loveday gets the best stuff in here.'

'We'd better go round to her house.' Val felt in her pocket for her car keys. 'We need to check she's okay.'

Val and Connie rushed back to the car. Val drove quickly to Pennywell Road, parking next to the dull grey cottage nestled between two smartly renovated ones. The two women stared at Loveday's house, the plaster crumbling, the wooden window frames rotten. Behind the downstairs window hung yellow net curtains, several old china ornaments clustered in a row. No lights were on inside. Val rapped at the door and waited, then she rapped again.

Val and Connie looked at each other as Val knocked a third

time. She moved to the window and gazed through. No one was inside.

'Do you think we should ask the neighbours if they've seen her?'

'Maybe she's slept in?'

Val shook her head. 'The woman outside the PDSA said she hadn't been there all week.' She knocked again.

Suddenly a light flicked on inside the house. They waited, then the door creaked open and a man stood in front of them, breathing heavily. He was tall, broad-shouldered and bony, the skin on his face paper thin, his hair sparse. He stared at them through thick glasses. 'Hello?'

Val wasn't sure what to say, so she blurted, 'Hello – are you John Moon?'

'I am.' His voice was weak.

'We're friends of Loveday. She wasn't at the charity shop. We were worried...'

'Oh, you'd better come in.' He wheezed as he led the way towards the living room. Each step was slow and laboured.

Val followed him to a small dark room. Then she saw Loveday hunched on the sofa. She was huddled inside a dressing gown, her feet bare, her hair dishevelled and her face covered in a film of sweat. She said, 'Don't come any closer. You don't want to catch this,' then she bent over, caught in the paroxysm of a hacking cough. She fumbled in her pocket, pulled out a handful of toilet paper and blew her nose.

Connie stated the obvious. 'Loveday, you're not well.'

Loveday was about to speak and began hacking again, her chest heaving. Val was concerned. 'You should be in bed.'

'I told her that.' John hovered, unsure. 'But you know Loveday – she does as she wants. You can't make her do anything.'

'I'm bleddy handsum,' she began and coughed again.

Val sat down, her arm around Loveday. 'Let's make you something to eat, get you tucked up...'

'There's no need to fuss...' Loveday wheezed, then she leaned back, exhausted. Val picked up a blanket from the sofa and swaddled her, leaving just her eyes peeping out, then glanced around. There was no heating, just a wood-burning stove, the doors open, overflowing with ash. The room was ice cold; there was a collection of ornaments on every surface, so many photos crowded together, mapping Loveday's life. Val's eyes fell on a black and white photo of a smiling young woman, small by the side of a giant of a man, both smartly dressed. It was Loveday and John's wedding day. She saw pictures of Ollie as a child with a determined-looking woman, presumably Loveday's daughter, Morwenna. Val gazed at Loveday, who was shivering beneath the wrap. 'Have you seen a doctor?'

Loveday closed her eyes. 'It's just a bleddy cold on my chest. I got it off the beach when I was there on Sunday. The wind was bitter...'

'I'll make you something to eat,' Val said. Loveday had opened her mouth, so she added, 'And no arguing.'

Connie seated herself next to Loveday and John sank down into an armchair as Val rushed into the little kitchen. Pots and pans hung from hooks. She filled an electric kettle; inside one of the cupboards she found a tin of soup, cream of chicken, and two bowls. The bread inside the bin was stale. Val opened the soup, heating it up on an electric cooker ring, then made tea in mugs embellished with the slogan 'I'd Rather Be in Cornwall' and arranged them on a tray. At the back of the cupboard, there were some crackers. Val placed those on the tray too and carried it back to the living room. She placed one mug of soup in John's hands and he stared at it, then he lifted a spoon and began to eat slowly.

Connie had arranged cushions around Loveday and wriggled

some large socks on her feet. Loveday sniffed the food and turned her nose up. 'I'm not hungry.'

'You must eat,' Connie coaxed.

Val patted Loveday's knee. 'I'll pop out to the chemist's and get you a few things – cough medicine, cold relief; maybe I can get something for your supper later?'

Loveday almost smiled. 'The place is a mess, I know. I haven't cleaned up in days. Poor John can't do it. His chest is bad.'

'My heart's not good either.' John clanked his bowl with his spoon. He was halfway through the soup. 'I'm on medication. She's so good, Loveday. She does everything.'

Loveday guffawed, then coughed. 'I'd like to be able to, my handsum. But I've let things go these last few days. I just haven't felt up to it. I've been in bed – this is the first time I've got out of it in three days.'

John gazed at her, his eyes watery. 'She's one in a million, my Loveday. She always has been. I don't know how I'd manage without her.'

Loveday hacked into her hand again. 'Morwenna came round on Sunday afternoon and I've given the bug to her. She's been laid up with it. But I'll be on the mend soon.' Her eyes were on John again. 'Don't you worry, my luvver, I'll be back to normal soon.'

'Bless you, my darlin'.' John chuckled. 'Without Loveday the world wouldn't turn.'

'Ah, go on with you, John.' Her eyes were soft with love.

Val's voice was hushed. 'Can we get you into bed, make you warm and get you some shopping, ask if a doctor might pop round?'

'I'll get a fire going,' Connie offered.

Loveday heaved a huge sigh, as if she was conceding defeat. 'Well, I suppose you'd better. I need to get myself well again.' She paused, racked by coughing. 'After all...' she sat upright '... if we don't do something about all the issues in Lowenstowe, who will?

Jenna Penrose and her kids don't have a penny to their name. And I want to talk about better use of the bus service, and about all the extra cars that come down in the summer.'

Val shivered and glanced around, her eyes resting on the fire-lighters and logs, but Loveday was off again, waving a hand enthusiastically beneath her shawl. 'I've scheduled an interim review meeting with Mr Henry Scott for January – he's on our side – and I'm starting a conversation with our MP now. They'll all have to do more for Cornwall...' She turned fierce eyes on Val, her face glowing with perspiration. 'And I'll be damned if I don't sort it out. So, yes, Valerie – help me up to bed and get me some cough mixture, please. I'd be very grateful. I need to get myself well.' She twisted round to look at John. 'I've told you all about Valerie and Connie, haven't I, John? I told you they were good to me. They are all right, both of them.'

John took a deep breath. 'Thank you for that bit of soup. It was kind of you both to come round.' He breathed deeply as he held out the empty bowl towards Val. 'She's something, isn't she, my Love-day? She has always been special. That's why I married her. She does everything, looks after me and the people of Lowenstowe, saves the planet. I don't know what we would do without her.'

38

Connie, Ben, Alice and Kevin, with Dolly on a lead stood outside the little row of cottages to wave Val off on 21 December. It was a windy Wednesday, the sky bleached white. Val was a little nervous because the flight was so long, ten hours with just one stop, and she knew she'd be exhausted by the time she arrived in Montréal. Caden piled her luggage into his battered VW Golf as she tried to remember if she'd checked her tickets and passport again. Ben and Connie were holding hands outside Honeysuckle Cottage. Kevin's arm was looped around Alice's shoulders as Dolly strained on her lead, Christmas lights flashing behind them, as they wished her a wonderful time in Canada. Loveday had already sent her best wishes yesterday when Val had called in to the PDSA with a card and a present. She had been at the till, writing down numbers, promising to 'see her dreckly next year'.

Caden chattered non-stop as he drove, excited about his new job as a radio presenter in London and his ongoing search for accommodation, how Heidi and Ollie were going to visit and he'd take them to restaurants and galleries; how they were having Christmas dinner with Jago and his new lady friend. The car stopped at the station and Caden helped Val with her cases, tears in his eyes.

'I can't believe how kind you've been, Val.' She heard him sniff as they hugged, a sound like a hiccup. 'I'll leave my key with Connie when I go. Or Ben – it doesn't matter which – I think they're practically living together anyway.' He hugged her again. 'Come up and see me in London. Or I'll be at The Boat House one weekend, buying gin for everyone.'

'I'll see you very soon.' She squeezed him tightly and he carried her bags into the station. Then she was off. Trains led to Tube rides, which led to a long wait at the airport, a flight, another long wait, another flight, a novel, an inflight movie, a great deal of sparkling water from plastic bottles that would have made Loveday furious. There was excitement, boredom, restless sleep and aching legs. Then she was in Canada.

Val saw Tom first, tall above everyone else, his brown hair and straight nose, his dark coat. She thought he looked older, more serious. He waved and she tugged her luggage, rushing towards him, dropping it at his feet, and they were in each other's arms, the hug of a mother and son, all warmth and emotion, sadness of separation and happiness of reunion in one wonderful instant. His arm around her, he introduced her to Lottie, a slight woman with freckles and a nice smile. Val hugged her eagerly, then turned to the woman next to her who was clearly her mother, with the same slight build, paler hair. Val held a hand out. 'Pleased to meet you. I'm Val.'

The woman's hands were gloved. 'I'm Fran. It's so good to finally meet you.' She picked up one of Val's cases while Tom collected the others. 'You're staying with me, if that's all right with you. My house is on the edge of town.' They began to walk to the exit, Val so tired and happy, as if she were in a dream. 'You'll be really comfortable there. I expect you are exhausted after such a long flight.'

Val nodded. She was glad to be going back with Fran; in all honesty, she didn't care where the house was or how comfortable it was. She just wanted to hug her son, have a cup of tea, fall into bed and sleep.

The next two days were so busy as if life were on fast forward, with arrangements for the wedding, meeting people whose names Val hoped she'd remember, being whisked around the city and either trying to help or trying not to be in the way. Fran was delightful, kind-hearted and good company. She and her husband were divorced; she lived by herself in a pretty house, which was currently capped with snow. Val thought it looked like a fairy tale with the garden a crisp white blanket and snowflakes falling like feathers through the bedroom window, Christmas lights twinkling outside. However, in the busy whirlwind of two days of wedding preparations, there were two moments where time almost stood still.

The first time was at a family gathering on the twenty-third at Kit's house. Kit Walker lived ten minutes from Fran; his house was accessed by several steps, the gable roof painted black and white. The path was clear, snow banked to either side, and as Val arrived it was snowing again, fat flakes settling on her coat. Inside, jazz music played; a Christmas tree stood tall; a fire roared in the hearth and lights twinkled. Food and drink had been placed on a table and people stood talking, sharing laughter. Kit and Fran hugged each other; they appeared the best of friends. Kit was a tall man with a white mane of hair and the same easy smile that Lottie had. He was quietly spoken, thoughtful, and his movements were steady in comparison to Fran's speedy efficiency. Val liked the way his eyes gleamed when he spoke.

Val was holding a glass of wine, talking politely to someone who introduced himself as Lottie's uncle Cliff, when a familiar face caught her eye. It was Ray, speaking to Kit, their heads close together, then he noticed Val and waved a hand. She waved back and continued to listen to Uncle Cliff suggest that she should visit the Montréal Botanical Garden but as he left to refill his glass, Val met Ray's eyes. He smiled warmly and came over. 'How was the flight?'

'Long.' Val could still feel the stiffness in her legs from being in the same position for hours. She took a deep breath and concentrated on the conversation as time slowed: this moment marked her new relationship with Ray, her ex and now a friend. She was determined to emphasise their status from the beginning.

Ray's expression was enthusiastic. 'I came out early, on the twentieth. I'm staying with Kit. He's very nice.'

Val nodded. 'He seems very friendly.'

'We went walking in Mont-Saint-Bruno, an hour's drive from here. You should go. It's got lakes and mountains. We had a great hike. I told him all about you and we talked about the kids.'

Val thought that hiking sounded more fascinating than the botanical greenhouse, although she was sure that when she was not feeling so jet-lagged, it would all be much more interesting. She wondered if Ray had told Lottie's father about the Christmas where they split up, being discovered in the pub with Monica, the fiasco. She felt awkward and pushed the memory from her thoughts. Ray was about to tell her something.

'Ray?'

'I've met someone, Val.'

'Oh?' Her immediate thoughts were that he'd bumped into some famous Canadians, Jim Carrey or Michael Bublé in the middle of Montréal, but then her head cleared. 'Oh, that's nice.'

'I met her online. She's called Patsy. She's a widow from Barnstaple.'

'I'm glad you've found someone.'

'I'm lonely. I need another person in my life,' Ray said.

Val gazed over his shoulder. 'Is she here, Patsy? Can I meet her?'

'No, it's early days.' Ray's expression was a little awkward. 'I just wanted you to know.'

'Well, I'm pleased for you.' Val was genuinely happy. 'Can I get you another drink, Ray?'

'Oh, thanks.'

Val took his glass and moved towards the kitchen, where bottles of wine, beer and soft drinks had been laid out. She was contented: Ray could move forward with his life and they could become friends. She passed Fran, who patted her arm and asked if she was enjoying herself, and Kit, who offered her a warm smile, topped up her drinks and said he hoped she'd tell him all about Cornwall later. Then, on her way back to Ray, she bumped into Tom and Lottie.

'Mum, we were looking for you.'

Val suppressed the urge to hug him again; Tom's arm was around Lottie. She pressed a palm to his cheek instead. 'You must both be excited. The wedding's tomorrow.'

'That's why we wanted to talk to you. We wanted you to be the first to know... well, the second, we've already told Fran...'

Val waited, her mind racing, anticipating bad news: the wedding would be called off, someone was ill. Then she saw the soft sheen of Lottie's face and she knew instantly. 'Oh, Tom, Lottie, that's just fantastic.'

Tom was sheepish. 'Well, it's about time. I'm forty and Lottie's thirty-seven...'

Time stood still again. Then Val threw her arms around Lottie, being careful not to squeeze her too hard, then around Tom. She glanced surreptitiously at Lottie again; she was still very slim. 'When's the baby due?'

'The doctor thinks it's a girl. I'm fourteen weeks pregnant,' Lottie said.

Val counted quickly in her head. 'So, a June baby, perhaps?'

'You'll have to come over in the summer, Mum.'

Val pressed her son's arm. 'Try and stop me.' She closed her eyes. The room was whirling, the pace increasing, and Val felt wrapped in the centre, happy.

The next day, the twenty-fourth, was even more hectic. Lottie stayed overnight with Fran and Val, Tom having been banished to Kit's house, Kit and Ray being responsible for Tom's arrival at the church on time. Val was swept up in the frenzy of people arranging flowers, hairdressers arriving, veils and dresses being smoothed and, by the time it was ready to leave for the church, she was glad to share a small glass of sparkling elderflower with Lottie, Fran and the other women who had been clucking around the house all morning, helping with preparations.

Then it was 2 p.m., and they were in the vast church, which was surprisingly warm given the freezing temperature outside. Val, a handkerchief screwed in her fist, shed a few tears during the vows, her eyes straying to Ray, remembering their own wedding fleetingly, and then letting all thoughts of it go.

Outside, snow fell in flakes almost the size of a new baby's fist and Val glanced at Lottie in her fitted wedding dress and smiled at the thought of new beginnings. She and Ray stood with Kit and Fran for family photos as snow tumbled like confetti, and her mind wandered to Connie, who would be at home with Ben. Val beamed in the flash of the camera. She had never needed a partner for the photos: in her soft blue dress and hat, she looked poised and happy. She and Ray and Lottie's parents had gathered together to celebrate the wedding of their grown children, and there was a baby on the way. Val's smile widened as the camera clicked and clicked again.

* * *

On Christmas morning, the snow had stopped. Val wandered downstairs for breakfast at nine, bleary eyed, the taste of champagne still on her tongue, to be greeted by Fran, who was already bustling in the kitchen, wearing an apron.

'Hi, Val, I have things to do today – a Christmas meal to make for our children and ten other guests.'

'Then let me help.' Val was ready to roll up her sleeves. 'What can I do?'

'My sister will be round any time, and her daughter and son. We always make Christmas dinner together. It's a family tradition. I need you out of the way until two o'clock.'

'Oh?' Val wasn't sure how to reply.

'So, we've arranged an outing for you.' Fran peered out of the window. 'Put on your coat and take boots and a scarf. Kit has just arrived in his car – you're going for breakfast, then for a hike.'

'Oh?' Val said again and suddenly the thought appealed to her. Walking in the snow on a bright Christmas Day was a much better prospect than peeling potatoes.

39

Kit drove through slushy roads to Noam's Nosh Bar in town, where he and Val spent a pleasant hour in warm surroundings over poached eggs and coffee, then he took the road out of Montréal and crossed over the St Lawrence River as Val gazed through the car window. Houses and shops became fields, trees, rising hills glazed with snow. They stopped at a huge expanse of countryside, a winter wonderland of white trees, the river slicing through the centre. Val's eyes were wide. 'Imagine having all this on your doorstep. It's beautiful.'

'Are you okay to walk before lunch? I thought it might be nice to see the countryside outside town.' Kit held the door as she slid out, her handbag swinging from her shoulder, the icy air immediately making her catch her breath.

'Where are we, Kit?'

'Îles-de-Boucherville. It's a national park.' He offered an arm. 'Shall we take a hike?'

Val slipped an arm through his, partly because the snow was deep underfoot and partly because he was pleasant company.

Swathed in hats and huge warm coats, they walked along, snow cracking beneath their feet, below laden pine trees.

'So, tell me about this place.' Val was fascinated by the landscape, the still silver river, the snow-covered terrain tinged blue in the sunlight. 'It's really atmospheric, so beautiful.'

'The place goes way back to the First Nations people: I think The St Lawrence Iroquois used this site as a seasonal camp. You can see all sorts of creatures here, from muskrats to deer.'

Val gazed around at hills and open spaces; everywhere was white, brightly frosted tall trees, the path rising into the mountains, the pale sun high, making the snow gleam. 'It must be the best place in the world at Christmas.'

'So, tell me about where you live.'

'A little Cornish coastal town. I have the best neighbours. I go down to the beach to walk each day, whatever the season. I love it there.'

They strolled on; Kit's warm breath was moisture in the icy air. 'It sounds like a great place to live. I've never been to England, but it's always been on my to-visit list.'

'What makes you want to visit England?'

'I've seen pictures of London. There's so much there, galleries, museums, so much history. I've always wanted to go to the theatre and see a Shakespeare play. Then maybe I could visit the Lake District or Cornwall, the little seaside coves...'

Val smiled. 'But it's beautiful here.'

'Montréal's wonderful. But I'm at that stage of my life now, there's just me rattling around in a big house, Lottie's married, I have time on my hands, nothing much to occupy me – I need to get out there, do new things.'

'Definitely. When you're by yourself, you can do just as you please.' Val was thoughtful. 'You and Fran seem to get on really well.'

'We do, yeah.'

'Have you been apart long?'

'Fifteen years,' Kit replied. They were walking slowly, their feet sinking as they entered an awning of pine trees, their branches crusted with white. 'We married young, teenagers, and we didn't really know what we were in for. Fran's very driven and I'm too laid-back. We gave it a shot but we didn't make the long haul.' He gave a soft laugh. 'We get on much better now we're apart.'

Val sighed. 'I'm not at that stage with Ray yet, but we're working on it.' She stopped herself, surprised at her words. She hadn't intended to talk about Ray with Kit. They walked for a few minutes, her arm tucked through his.

'Ray and I took a hike yesterday – he's a nice guy,' Kit said. 'I have to say, Val, I feel I know you pretty well already.'

'Oh?' Val feared the worst, that Ray had spoken about their split, about Monica and the Christmas fiasco. But Kit's expression contained no judgement.

'Ray speaks highly of you. He told me about your time as a schoolteacher and how talented you are. Tom talks about you all the time; apparently, you belong to some kind of conservation group that cleans up the beach and campaigns for the environment, which is incredible.' His expression was full of admiration. 'I really couldn't wait to meet you.'

Val was surprised; Tom had said very little about Lottie's parents. It made her heart warm to think her son was proud of her achievements, that he had remembered the few nuggets of information she'd passed on over the phone and spoken to Kit and Fran about her with so much respect. She glanced up at Kit, a dark hat over his white hair, his face calm. She wanted to ask the next question and was surprised that it came from her lips easily. 'So, Kit, since you and Fran, has there been anyone else?'

'Not really, I never felt the need.' Kit gave an easy smile, the same warm grin as his daughter's. 'But I'm seventy-two now. Do you think I should be looking?'

Val met his eyes and saw the gleam of mischief there. 'No, I think going out to deliberately look for a partner is a really bad idea.' She recalled the search for a Mr December. 'I think these things will happen if they are going to, but you can't contrive or force it.'

Kit's expression was playful. 'Do you think that the right person arrives on your doorstep when you least expect it?'

'I think what will be will be. I have a great life, good friends, a nice place to live.' Val moved her gaze to the glistening snow, the hills beyond that pushed towards the blue sky. Then she smiled. 'But someone pleasant to spend time with is always a bonus.'

'I guess Ray used to be that person?'

'Ray and I never really had that much in common. You know, Kit...' Val was surprised to find herself confiding in him. 'Even when I first married Ray, I knew somewhere in the back of my mind that he was a nice man, good company. But we were never really soulmates.'

Kit was interested. 'Do you believe there's such a thing as a soulmate?'

'I'd like to,' she admitted. 'Yes, it's a wonderful thought that there's someone you click with as soon as you meet them, as if you've known them all your life.' She suddenly felt warmer, blood pulsing, making her cheeks glow.

'Someone who thinks as you do, feels as you do, at the same time?' Kit said. 'The one person you just know is right for you.'

Val felt his arm pressing against hers. They walked on and she realised she was smiling.

'Val...' An idea had occurred to Kit. 'How long are you staying in Montréal?'

'Until the new year.'

'I'd like it if...'

Val raised her eyebrows. 'If?'

'I'd like to spend time with you while you're here, get to know you, take you out to some local places.'

'Oh?'

'What I'm trying to say is...' The smile again, then a more serious face. 'I haven't done this in years, but... I'm asking you for a date... lots of dates.'

Val nodded slowly. Her arm in his, she felt comfortable; being with him was natural. 'I'd like that.' She delved deep into her handbag and her fingers found the final favour box. She placed it in his hand.

'What's this?'

'A painted stone. My email address is in there.' Val's eyes sparkled. 'Just for you.'

'Thanks.' Kit opened it carefully. Inside was a varnished pebble with a crimson heart. 'I'll treasure this.' Kit pushed the box deep into his pocket and smiled, pointing to a small hill in the distance. 'From up there you get a great view – the river, the whole park, you can even see Montréal. How about we clamber up there, take a few photos and then head off back for lunch?'

'That sounds like a great idea.'

Kit took her hand and they surged forward, their eyes on the blue sky at the top of the white-crusted hill. Their boots made a soft sound against the packed snow. Val was breathing hard with the effort, but they made their way upwards and finally they stood at the summit, breathing sharp clean air. Below, the river snaked away through rocks and widened; above, mountains leaned against the sky. Beyond the park, the city of Montréal was a collection of tiny buildings settled in snow, little decorations on an iced Christmas cake. Val exhaled, her breath a mist on the air. 'The view is stunning.'

'It is.' Kit's face was flushed with happiness. He wrapped an arm around Val's shoulders. 'Maybe we should be getting back? Fran will have dinner ready for two o'clock and I'd hate to be late, especially since she's put so much effort into preparing it.'

'Oh, yes, we must be on time for Christmas dinner.' Val smiled, remembering. 'Anything less might upset the cook.'

Kit hugged her closer as if he understood, then they began the trek downhill, back through the glistening snow beneath canopies of heavily laden pine trees.

ACKNOWLEDGMENTS

Thanks to my agent, Kiran Kataria, for her wisdom, professionalism and integrity.

Thanks to Amanda Ridout, Nia Beynon, Claire Fenby, Laura Kingston, Megan Townsend and the rest of the incredible team at Boldwood Books.

Huge thanks to Sarah Ritherdon for her insight and warmth.

So much appreciation to everyone who has worked hard to make this book happen. I'm so grateful to designers, editors, technicians, magicians, voice actors, bloggers – thanks to you all.

A special thanks to all the incredibly generous Boldwood writers and the wider community of authors and bloggers whose support is so valuable and valued.

Thanks to Solitary Writers, Julie Mullen and Martin Seager, Radio Dartington SoundArt, Radio Somerset, Planet Rock.

Much thanks to the talented Ivor Abiks at Deep Studios.

Thanks to so many supportive friends: Erika, Rich, Kay, Rog, Jan, Jan M, Bill, Ken, Trish, Lexy, Helen, Shaz, Frank, Ian, Susie, Chrissie, Kathy N, Nik R, Pete O', Sarah and Jim, Sarah E, Martin, Cath, Avril, Peter B, Slawka, Beau, Zach, Matt B, Casey B, Steve, Rose, Steve's Mum, Ruchi, Stephanie, Ingrid, Katie H, Jonno, Edward and Robin, Norman and Angela.

Thanks to my wonderful neighbours, Martin, Lindsay, Kitty, Ian, Nina, James and Jackie, and to Jenny, Sophie, Claire, Paul, Gary, Herman the chef, Joe and all at Books by the Blackdowns.

Special love to our Tony and Kim.

Love to my mum, who showed me the joy of reading, and to my dad, who proudly never read anything.

Love always to Liam, Maddie, Cait and Big G.

Warmest thanks to my readers, wherever you are. You help to make this journey incredible.

MORE FROM JUDY LEIGH

We hope you enjoyed reading *A Year of Mr Maybes*. If you did, please leave a review.

If you'd like to gift a copy, this book is also available as an ebook, digital audio download and audiobook CD.

Sign up to Judy Leigh's mailing list for news, competitions and updates on future books:

http://bit.ly/JudyLeighNewsletter

Explore more fun, uplifting reads from Judy Leigh:

ABOUT THE AUTHOR

Judy Leigh is the bestselling author of *A Grand Old Time* and *Five French Hens* and the doyenne of the 'it's never too late' genre of women's fiction. She has lived all over the UK from Liverpool to Cornwall, but currently resides in Somerset.

Visit Judy's website: https://judyleigh.com

Follow Judy on social media:

f facebook.com/judyleighuk

𝕏 twitter.com/judyleighwriter

◎ instagram.com/judyrleigh

BB bookbub.com/authors/judy-leigh

ABOUT BOLDWOOD BOOKS

Boldwood Books is a fiction publishing company seeking out the best stories from around the world.

Find out more at www.boldwoodbooks.com

Sign up to the Book and Tonic newsletter for news, offers and competitions from Boldwood Books!

http://www.bit.ly/bookandtonic

We'd love to hear from you, follow us on social media:

facebook.com/BookandTonic

twitter.com/BoldwoodBooks

instagram.com/BookandTonic

Lightning Source UK Ltd.
Milton Keynes UK
UKHW040702200322
400301UK00002B/238